BY JAMIE PACTON

*The Life and (Medieval) Times of Kit Sweetly*
*Lucky Girl*
*The Vermilion Emporium*
*The Absinthe Underground*

BY REBECCA PODOS

*The Mystery of Hollow Places*
*Like Water*
*The Wise and the Wicked*
*From Dust, a Flame*

BY JAMIE PACTON AND
REBECCA PODOS

*Furious*
*Homegrown Magic*

# HOME
# GROWN
# MAGIC

# HOME GROWN MAGIC

## Jamie Pacton
### &
## Rebecca Podos

DEL REY

NEW YORK

Published in the United States by Del Rey, an imprint of Random House, a division of Penguin Random House LLC, 1745 Broadway, New York, NY 10019.

DEL REY and the CIRCLE colophon are registered trademarks of Penguin Random House LLC.

ISBN 978-0-593-87365-6
Ebook ISBN 978-0-593-87366-3

Printed in the United States of America on acid-free paper

randomhousebooks.com
penguinrandomhouse.com

1st Printing

*Book design by Jo Anne Metsch*
*Map by Rebecca Podos*

The authorized representative in the EU for product safety and compliance is Penguin Random House Ireland, Morrison Chambers, 32 Nassau Street, Dublin D02 YH68, Ireland, https://eu-contact.penguin.ie.

For our "We Are All Bards" D&D group,
where Margot's and Yael's stories started.
Sort of.

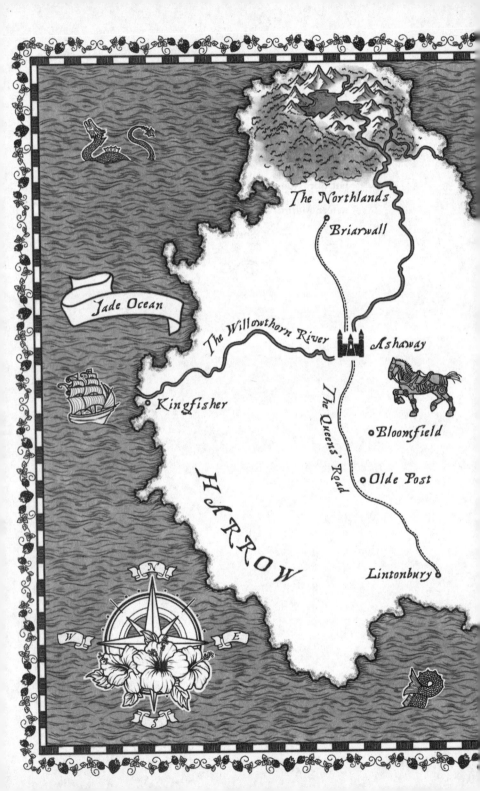

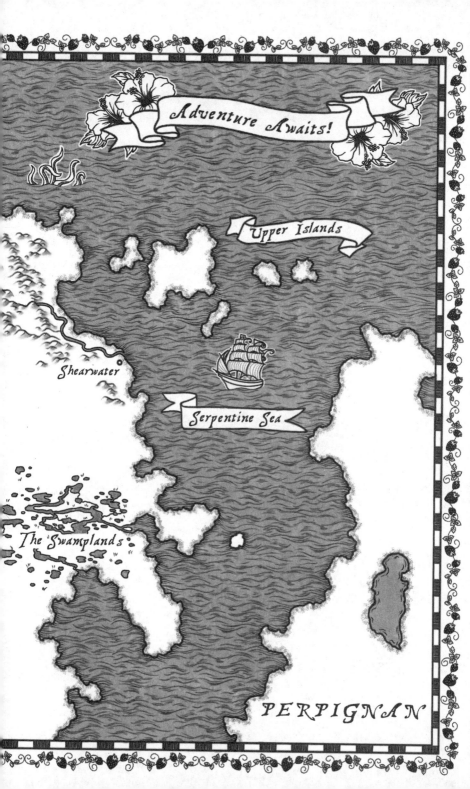

# HOME
# GROWN
# MAGIC

# 1

# YAEL

This party is supposed to be for Yael. So claimed the coveted invitations, heavy in their goatskin envelopes, thick paper addressed in malachite ink to the cream of society: *Mr. Baremon Clauneck and Mrs. Menorath Clauneck request the honor of your presence in celebration upon their child's graduation from Auximia Academy.* But it seems to Yael like any other company event. The jeweled suits and gowns. The deals being made around fountains of pale champagne and velvety red wine. The offering altar tucked inside a private chamber off the ballroom—one of half a dozen such altars scattered about Clauneck Manor, this one meant for guests to curry favor with the family's patron. It's nothing Yael hasn't seen at a thousand such dinner parties.

They weren't even consulted on the cake flavor. (*Hibiscus*, for fuck's sake!)

"Let me guess. Animal handling?"

They look up from sniffing the ten-tiered monstrosity of a cake on display and find Alviss Oreborn smirking at them over the lip of a massive silver tankard.

"Come again?"

"Your field of study at Auximia. Animal handling, wasn't it?"

Oreborn is teasing, clearly. He likes to pretend to be salt of the earth, the way he carries that tankard—albeit engraved with his own family crest—strapped to his belt like a short-sword and stomps around in mud-splattered boots even though there isn't an unpaved street in the capital. Not south of the Willowthorn, at least. But Oreborn is a major depositor with the Clauneck Company. His silver mines are used to mint half the coinage in the kingdom—mines he hasn't set foot inside for decades.

"Law," Yael corrects him, pausing to drain their third glass of champagne, "with a specialty in arcana and transmutation. Father's putting me in the currency exchange department at the company, apprenticed to Uncle Mikhil."

"Well now. There's a fancy job that'll take you to many foreign shores."

"I'm not sure it'll take me any farther than the Hall of Exchange or the Records Library." Yael grimaces, picturing the airless, echoing library in the bowels of the Clauneck office in the Copper Court.

If one were to gaze down upon Harrow from the back of a great eagle, the kingdom's capital city of Ashaway would be easy to spot by its black basalt walls, roughly hexagonal; by the deep silver slice of the Willowthorn River, which runs from the mountains of the Northlands down to the west coast, carving right through the capital on its way; and, perhaps most of all, by the triumvirate of shining courts at its very center. The Golden Court at the topmost point, where the queens' palace sits. The Ivory Court, home to the campus of Auximia, with its white stone towers. And the Copper Court, the main trading square in Ashaway—and thus, in the kingdom—named for its copper-tiled rooftops that blaze like bonfires in the sun. The

Clauneck Company office is the tallest of the court's fiery towers, but the library where records of every deposit, withdrawal, exchange, and investment are kept, accessible only by Clauneck blood, sits well below the earth. Its door is more thickly painted with security wards than the royal toilet.

"When you've seen one shore, you've seen them all, ey? Anyway, I expect you'll be occupied by the family business, as well as the business of family making." Oreborn claps Yael hard on the arm, and they almost fall sideways into the cake stand. "It's the same for my Denby. See him yonder? Grew up handsome, he did."

Yael looks across the ballroom at the towering Denby, shaped like a barrel with a beard. At twenty-three years of age, Yael has accepted the probability of staying five feet and a handbreadth tall forever . . . or mostly, they have. They've added a few inches this evening by fluffing up their finger-length black hair in defiance of gravity and the gods themselves. "Quite a specimen," Yael manages.

"Isn't he? I'll bring him around in a more, er, intimate setting and reacquaint you two from when you were small," Oreborn says with a wink. "Well, smaller." Then he claps Yael again, roaring with laughter as he swaggers off.

Massaging their arm through their dress coat—green silk so thickly embroidered with ferns, buds, and briars, it's stiff to move in, with a matching vest beneath—Yael watches Oreborn go. The man is a menace, and his son is a bully. They imagine having to talk to Denby, having to dance with Denby. It'd be like a squirrel waltzing with a big, mean tree.

Rather than consider it further, Yael makes their way to the bar counter to reacquaint themself with something stronger than champagne.

It's only a moment before one of the barkeeps hired for the night notices them and approaches the counter. "Something to drink, sir'ram?" She pulls a glass from thin air in a flourish of magic, without anything like the scent of ozone and iron that accompanies the Claunecks' own limited spellwork. A natural caster, then, of which there are none to be found in Yael's family. Truly, magic doesn't care whether you're born into a manor house or a hut in the Rookery.

Yael watches, mesmerized by the muscled forearms beneath her rolled shirtsleeves. "*Everything* to drink, if you please." They grin and prop their elbows on the counter, their chin on one fist. "Where do you suggest I start?"

"We've a fine Witchwood Absinthe. Folk say you can hear the voices of the dead if you drink enough. Or perhaps a Copperhead. Ever had one?"

Yael flicks their eyes to the barkeep's cinnamon-colored braids.

Flushing beneath matching freckles, she laughs. "It's an ale with a shot of whiskey and just a few drops of snake venom." She leans forward conspiratorially. "Most only feel a little numb in their fingers and toes. There's a slight chance of paralysis, but that wears off before the liquor does."

"Sounds like a quick ticket out of a boring party. I'll take it, if you promise to drag me behind the counter where no one can step on me should things go sideways."

"I think I can manage that." With a wink, she turns toward the back bar to collect the necessary bottles and vials.

How times have changed. When Yael and their friends were children, they would creep out of the manor house to beg the stable hands for a few sips of whatever they were drinking; even Yael couldn't have sweet-talked the barkeeps into serving eleven-year-olds in front of their rich and powerful parents. Though sometimes, Yael could distract one long enough for Margot Greenwillow—a natural caster herself—to send a spectral, shimmering hand floating beneath the bar's pass-through and steal them a bottle. But those days of running wild around the outskirts of parties are long gone. Their childhood pack has scattered. Some have left Ashaway as fortunes and alliances shifted. Some, Yael's lost track of altogether. Margot's family was omnipresent in high society before Yael left the city at thirteen for boarding school in Perpignan—Harrow's closest neighboring kingdom—and when they returned for college, the Greenwillows were simply gone, the best friend Yael ever had along with them. Impossibly, others are settling down and starting families of their own.

Oreborn was right about that much.

Yael's parents looked the other way during their teen years at boarding school and during their time at Auximia, spent stumbling between alehouses, drinking and dicing with the children of judges, archmages, and princes. Nights like those were half the point of the kingdom's premier school for noble and wealthy households. Even the months Yael's just spent abroad in Locronan after graduation, traveling with peers who couldn't bear to end the party yet, were begrudgingly permitted. But unlike many of their peers, Yael is no closer to marriage now than when they left for school. Baremon might have overlooked their mediocre grades and blatant disinterest in both law and the family business if they'd put as much effort into finding a suitable match as they had into spending their allowance and slipping beneath their peers' silken bedsheets. Alas, they had not.

While Yael waits for their drink, they glance out across the ballroom in its gleaming glory. Thick marble pillars rise from an ice-white floor so highly polished it reflects the gold stars inlaid in the midnight-black ceiling above. (If this were a dancing party and not a drinking party, it'd be a slippery death trap.) Thousands of candles in crystal holders have mirrors placed behind them to scatter the light, which ought to give the room a warm glow. But the flames burn cold purple, thanks to a spell many children can manage—even Yael, so long as they've beseeched their patron recently, which they have not. In the corner, a quartet of musicians play their violins and cornets as quietly as possible so as not to drown out the guests' wheeling and dealing.

Yael's uncle Mikhil seems to be engaged in said wheeling and dealing with another figure from the Copper Court—some high-placed peddler of rare items "discovered" by hiring adventuring parties to traipse across the kingdom, even across the seas into Perpignan and Locronan and beyond. Mikhil has his wife on one arm, husband on the other, and a pack of Yael's young cousins circling the trio like an obedient moat. Araphi, their oldest, stands among them, listening politely to what must be an excruciatingly boring conversation between businessmen. Their closest cousin in age, she'll be going back to Auximia for her fourth and final year this autumn. As a child, Araphi was beautiful and unserious. She's beautiful still, with dark eyes and a delightfully aquiline nose, shining in her silver-and-periwinkle gown cut high in the front, with matching, closely tailored trousers beneath. Whether Phi's outpaced Yael in seriousness, they're not sure.

It isn't a high bar to clear, they acknowledge.

When the barkeep sets a glass of a swirling, dark-gold drink on the counter in front of them, they take it gratefully. "To my health," Yael says, raising the glass.

It never makes it to their lips.

Snatching the drink from their hand, their father holds it just out of reach as he sniffs its contents and frowns. "In your haste to embarrass your family, I don't suppose you stopped to think about this lovely young barkeep, who—had she injured you, even if by accident—would've been dismissed from her job, then run out of Ashaway at swordpoint? You never *do* stop to think, Yael."

The barkeep's mouth trembles, her freckles the only color left in her chalk-white cheeks. She stutters an apology, dips her head, and slips away as soon as Baremon's turned his attention back to Yael.

They mumble, "I wasn't going to—"

"Tell me, Yael." Baremon holds the glass higher, as though inspecting the clarity of the poison. "Who is the heir to the kingdom?"

This is a bit much. Yael may not have been a model student, but they are at least aware of the royal family of Harrow, as is every child old enough to eat solid foods. "Princex Sonja," they answer dutifully.

"That's assuming the queens rule the kingdom."

Yael swallows a deep sigh. Clearly, their father has set them on the path to their own humiliation, and now they've no choice but to keep walking. "If not the queens, then who?" they ask blandly.

Baremon seems unbothered by their lack of curiosity. "Ask anybody in the Golden Court, and they'll claim that it's the seat of power in Harrow. Ask anybody else in the kingdom, and they'll tell you the Copper Court is where true power lies. And who is the king of the Copper Court?"

"You, I assume."

Baremon glares down at Yael. "Precisely. We Claunecks are the uncrowned monarchs of Harrow. Lenders to queens, cousins to the highest judges in the land, keepers of the keys to this country's economy. Nothing moves in the kingdom without flowing through us and the Copper Court, like blood through a heart." As he speaks, Baremon's eyes light as coldly purple as the candles throughout the ballroom, and the old, familiar smell of ozone and iron crackles around him.

Not natural magic, but Clauneck magic.

Just like fresh water or fertile soil, stone or sand or any other resource, magic exists in Harrow and the world beyond its borders in natural deposits. But instead of occurring in lakes and beneath fields, it occurs in living things, beasts and plants and people. In some of them, anyhow. While every life-form is, like a bottle made of cellular stuff, capable of containing magic, only some are born full up. Others, like the Claunecks, have the barest drop in the bottom of the bottle. It's been three generations since a natural caster—folk born brimming over with magic—married into the family. Such people are increasingly rare in a world that has largely moved on to silver and gold.

Still, like the metal at the bottom of Oreborn's deep-delving mines, magic can be found or borrowed or purchased for a price.

For folks who lack natural abilities but wish to cast anyhow, that means securing the favor of one of the deities or devils who exist in the planes beyond theirs, from which magic leaks into this plane. Those who work as healers may whisper a prayer to a god of health or medicine. A bard—a *true* bard, not just a common player in a tavern—may sing their prayers to a god or devil of revelry, hoping to please them in exchange for a bit of magic. Warlocks, on the other hand, make bargains. The Claunecks pay regular homage to their patron, fulfilling promises and performing tasks that increase his influence in the world, assuring his prosperity in exchange for magic they wouldn't have otherwise. This is the family way.

Generally, Yael's family prefers to speculate in stocks and bonds over spellwork, but they still rely upon their patron. And if the "offerings" their guests and customers leave on the altar happen to benefit the Claunecks financially? Well, their patron's fortune and glory will inevitably rise alongside their own.

"And you," Baremon continues his lecture, "are heir to the true power in this kingdom. You, Yael, are alas the only seed that I and your mother have sown."

"Uncle Mikhil has plenty of—"

"But you are *ours*," their father cuts in, voice sharpening to a dagger's edge. "And if you fail to produce, our efforts will have been for nothing. Can you understand that much, at least?"

"I . . . I understand."

"Then see that you remember it and behave accordingly." Finished with Yael, Baremon turns and strides to the center of the floor, where he booms out, "Friends, colleagues, I bid you welcome! Dinner will begin shortly, but first, a toast."

Every eye in the ballroom turns his way.

Baremon Clauneck is . . . well, everything that Yael is not. Tall—or taller, though the man is no Denby—and impossibly sharp in his pressed suit, stitched to resemble bronze and black dragon's scales. Somber. Square-faced. Sure of himself far beyond the film of false confidence that Yael wears at all times. And, as always, in total control. "To the future of the company," he says. "To the future of the family. To us." He hoists the Copperhead and drains it down, probably believing himself too important to be felled by paralytic venom. He's likely right. Wiping his lips, he says almost as an afterthought, "To Yael."

"To Yael," the vast ballroom full of clients and associates of the Clauneck Company echoes. None of them tear their eyes away from Baremon to find Yael in the crowd. A good thing, since nobody notices as they slip out through the towering purpleheart wood doors into the corridor and disappear.

Because the grand ballroom sits on the third of six stories, it takes a full quarter of an hour for Yael to make their way out of the suffocating manor house and into the chilled air of a late-winter twilight. The ornamental gardens and the aviary are likely occupied by guests pretending to care about cold-blooming flowers and winged things, so Yael heads for the stables. With the party well under way but far from over, they find it blessedly empty of people.

Instead, it's stuffed to the rafters with mounts from across the realm. Horses from the southeastern Swamplands, saddled with moss mats and bridled with vines. Sleighs from the civilized fringes of the Northlands, each pulled by half a dozen icy-eyed Laika. In one stall, a giant salamander—a dappled, poisonous-looking blue-and-gold beast—has its bloody snout buried in a ten-gallon bucket of mice.

The stable hands are probably sitting around a barrel fire out back right now, just as they used to, sharing their tips and a bottle among them. Yael would love to join them, hiding out until the dinner is over and the guests have departed.

But Yael has *responsibilities*. They have *obligations*. Their parents have been crystal-clear on that since the moment Yael returned from their travels.

Having floated through the academy on charm and the currency of their family name, Yael will now begin their meaningless job at their grand and meaningless desk in the Copper Court. Soon enough, there will be a meaningless political marriage with a partner approved by (or more likely, picked by) the Claunecks. Someone like gods-be-damned Denby. They will be expected to acquire children one way or another, and the children will be raised as Yael was: in a never-ending cycle of family duties and company parties, where they'll perform for guests as Yael once did, then be tossed off into the shadows until they're old enough for *obligations* of their own.

Suddenly, the air in the stable is too thick to breathe.

Yael tugs at the collar of their shirt, their vest, their dress coat, untucking and unbuttoning until they can gulp down the smell of sweating beasts and hay and blood. Which, in company with the wine and champagne, begins to feel like a mistake. Behind them is the manor and its ballroom, so they stumble toward the far end of the stable, bracing themself against support beams and stall doors as they go.

Until they grab for a door that swings open, sending them tumbling into the stall.

When they prop themself up, they're eye to pupil-less eye with a gleaming mechanical steed. The horse stands statue-still, as you might expect from a creature made of hardwood and iron, polished like starlight for the occasion. Its brass knee-cap is cool when Yael grabs its leg to hoist themself off the stable floor. The levers arranged in a mane-like crest down its metal spine have been switched off; with no need for food or water, the steed was powered down upon stabling. Probably it belongs to Oreborn, who keeps a small herd of them on his estate. He taught Yael how to ride years ago—or rather, taught them to canter around the paddock by themself while Oreborn discussed potential investments with Yael's parents. Mechanical steeds are remarkable inventions. Yael could ride this one all night and day without stopping if they wanted to.

They won't, of course.

They'll brush the hay from their coat and leave the stable. They'll pass the next few hours avoiding their parents when possible, laughing at jokes with cruel punch lines when they must. Tomorrow, they'll crawl out of bed to share a silent breakfast with their parents. After a compulsory stop to pray at their patron's altar—an act that more closely resembles checking in with one's coldly unpleasant boss for a performance evaluation than any kind of religious devotion—they'll head to the

office with their father. They will become who they were born
to be.

Then Yael will just . . . continue to float through.

This is the plan. This has always been the plan.

So Yael is shocked to find themself astride the mechanical
steed, having climbed up its body without meaning to. They
remain surprised even as they thumb the correct levers upward,
remembering their lessons. First lever raises the head. Fourth
lever starts its heart, driven by some combination of magic and
machinery. Sixth opens the valves for the heart to pump fluid
through its armored limbs. And so on. Running their fingers
over the steed's iron neck, they brush across the engraved name-
plate and bend forward to read it.

"Want to take a ride, Sweet Wind?" Yael hears themself slur
as if from afar.

They walk the beast out of its stall, steering clumsily at first
so that it weaves toward the stable doors. In their immaculately
tailored pants and dress coat, they ride out onto the garden
path, where they must admit that, planned or not, this is actually happening.

"We should go back," Yael tells Sweet Wind.

They flip the lever up from WALK to TROT.

When, moments later, they reach the private lane connecting the Clauneck estate to the Queens' Road, Yael promises
them both, "Just a quick ride, then we'll turn around."

If they head north toward the city's center, they'll pass a
dozen grand estates with sprawling grounds (though none so
much as the Claunecks') in an otherwise tightly packed capital,
where land comes at a higher price than almost anyone can pay.
Next, the ring of fine mansions without land to claim, then the
plazas containing the Ivory Court, the Copper Court, and the
Golden Court: the triumvirate at the heart of not just Ashaway
but Harrow itself, surrounded by fancy shops and luxurious

taverns and gilded offices, according to each plaza's specialty. Northward still are the factories and workshops bordering the Willowthorn River. On its far shore is what people call the Rookery—the mass of crowded neighborhoods that make up the top third of Ashaway, with small, sometimes tumbledown housing and taverns with leaking thatch roofs. That's where the service folk of the city live when they aren't laboring, the basalt city walls rising at their backs.

Yael could stop anywhere in between; the whole city is at their fingertips, the Clauneck name a key that opens every lock.

Instead, they turn south and switch the steed to CANTER.

Alviss Oreborn would be happy to have the Claunecks in his debt, though Yael's family can easily compensate him for the beast. But that won't be necessary. Even as they race along the Queens' Road toward the outskirts of the capital, where the estates give way to flat fields just inside the city's black walls; even as they approach the southern gate; even as they toss a few silver denaris from the belt purse they wore at the party to the watchmen, who are bewildered to see a lone young noble galloping into the sunset and the wild-smelling countryside, but have no orders to stop them; even then, they tell themself this is just a quick ride. One last chance to feel young again.

One last chance to feel as they did when they believed that growing up would mean a great adventure, and not the end of it.

# 2

# MARGOT

You'd think a plant witch with a degree from the Olde Post Community Magical School wouldn't have a weevil problem. Yes, Margot Greenwillow can mostly manage affordable, prepared-while-you-wait love potions out of dried lavender and a secret. And, yes, she's known in her small village of Bloomfield for coaxing night-blooming orchids to open up during the day. But weevils are another beast entirely.

"I'm begging you," Margot says, glaring down at the annoying little charcoal-colored bugs gnawing at the roots of her strawberry plants. There are just so damn many of them and only one of her. "Please save me a few strawberries."

Whether she's beseeching the weevils or whichever goddess of plant or animal magic is listening through the planes at the moment, Margot isn't sure. She just wants a reprieve from the nasty little bugs, especially since spring is right around the corner. The busiest season at the Greenwillow Greenhouses, it's when regulars from the village and folk from the surrounding areas visit the herb garden, the indoor perpetually blooming cherry trees that are in a constant cycle of flowers and fruit, the succulent grotto, the wild fern alcove, and the mushroom ring. It's nothing like busy seasons past, when Margot's grandmother's name had tourists flocking to the greenhouses from all over the realm, but Margot's strawberry jam is popular. Rumor in Bloomfield has it that a scoop can cure a broken heart, and Margot can barely keep it in stock.

Thanks to the weevils, it's looking like this year she'll barely have enough strawberries to make a few dozen jars. Well, people can fight over those at the Spring Fair, just two months away, and maybe Margot can charge enough to finally get out of the greenhouses for a while. Or find her parents medical care to the standard they'd approve of. Or restore the lost fortunes of their once powerful family . . .

Or not.

A few jars of strawberry jam aren't going to do all that. Not by a long shot.

How Margot has grown weary of strawberries. And weevils. And trying to single-handedly keep up the entire sprawling greenhouse complex, which was built decades ago by her grandmother Fern Greenwillow and mercifully not taken in the settlement that stripped Margot's family of their assets. (Of course, Margot knows it's not mercy but rather a keen interest in her alleged potential that's kept the greenhouses in her possession.)

Sighing, Margot takes off her cardigan, exposing some of her many tattoos—a teapot, a snail, some blossoms, two birds, and a few strawberries—and she whispers a small enchantment to charm the weevils into believing they'd rather be outside in the fields than feasting on her strawberry roots. They shouldn't even be here—growing strawberries indoors should keep most pests at bay—but Margot has been so overwhelmed with work, she didn't catch the invasion soon enough. There's a flash of shiny purple light as Margot's magic coats the stalks of the plants like maple syrup sticking to a fork. The weevils scatter for a moment, some of them hurrying away while others dig more deeply into the soil, determined.

Well, she tried.

Adding "find another weevil deterrent" to her endless mental list of tasks, Margot wipes dirt-covered fingers across her forehead, brushing aside a strand of her naturally purple hair. Her feet hurt; her back hurts. There's still so very much to do, and she's been going since before dawn already.

"Perhaps it's time for a cup of tea," Margot says out loud to Harvey, the munchkin cat who decided to move into her cottage this winter, not bothering to ask Margot her opinion about it. He's curled up around a bronze watering can like a tiny furry dragon guarding a hoard. Harvey gives a grumpy meow.

Temperamental old cuss.

Scritching Harvey behind the ears, Margot looks at the long rows of strawberry-plant-filled troughs in front of her, mind running through the day's chores. Suddenly, she wants nothing more than to go back to bed and sleep for a month. If only she had a potion for endless energy that actually worked. But she doesn't. Not yet, at least.

Margot shifts her shoulders as if making room for the many responsibilities she's carrying. "Right, yes. First tea, then onward."

After several cups of tea (all made with fortifying lemon balm and ginger) and a remarkable number of cookies, Margot resumes work. Her sensible green garden boots pick up bits of mud, mulch, flower petals, and other garden detritus as she tramps among the eight greenhouses, the front store and counter, and the outdoor shed where she keeps potting soil, large tools, and her favorite wheelbarrow.

"See you later today," Margot says to the wheelbarrow, patting it, because of course she's now talking to garden tools. It's not an improvement from the long chats with Harvey she has daily. She looks around the shed, more items piling onto her to-do list with each glance.

There's no way she's ever going to get it all done.

Certainly, she could ask some of the people in the village to help her, but they're so busy with their own projects and community activities, she hates to do that. Besides, admitting to them that she needs help means admitting to herself that she can't do it all. Which she refuses to acknowledge. Because she *has* to do it all.

Her stomach twists with guilt at the thought. The whole village is relying on her to be competent, to figure things out, to make it all work. Not that they know it. And if she told them? Well . . .

She shoves the thought aside along with a pile of empty seed bags. Telling them the truth of things is simply not an option. Exhaling sharply through the familiar wash of anxiety that always chases guilt when she thinks about the village and its future, she picks up a stack of pots and shifts them into the wheelbarrow. Spider silk coats her fingers as she does so, making them sticky. Margot swears, brushing the clinging threads off on her skirt.

Of course, if she did hire some help, she might get a day off. Or the chance to linger in bed past dawn or just have a few minutes to herself.

But there's no money to hire someone. And besides, how would she teach them everything they'd need to know? What if they overwatered the rowan saplings or forgot to prune the spider plants or flubbed a spell that Margot could perform easily, turning them into actual spiders intent on taking over the greenhouse?

Not worth the risk.

As Margot shifts around garden tools in the shed, looking for the spade she knows she left back here, her mind drifts to her plans for the evening. Her best friend, Sage Wilderstone, will be in town tonight. It's just a quick visit—Sage is passing through Bloomfield before she heads out on her next adventure—but the thought of talking to her best friend, not a wheelbarrow or a plant or a cat, is delicious. They're meeting for drinks in Clementine's Tavern at nine o'clock, which should give Margot enough time for a bath and change of clothes.

Pausing in her pursuit of the spade, Margot considers her soil-smeared strawberry-print dress. It's her least favorite, but since she didn't get to do laundry yesterday, it's also her second-to-last clean one. When she dressed in the dark this morning, she hadn't known she'd be meeting Sage tonight, and it's not like they're going somewhere fancy. There are no fancy places in Bloomfield. Still, she really should change into something less grimy and strawberry-forward.

Right, yes. She *will* make time to go home first.

Margot resumes her search for the spade, fingers scraping over empty clay pots and bags of mulch. How her parents would hate to see her now: dirt under her fingernails, garden boots on, looking so much like Granny Fern.

A pang of grief, sharp and sudden, sends Margot stumbling backward. She catches herself against the wheelbarrow, sitting heavily on the edge, letting the metal bite into the back of her thighs. How has it been more than four years already?

Granny Fern was a legendary plant witch—a natural caster too—whose remedies, magical plants, and many potions made the Greenwillow family a tremendous fortune. Over the years, even as her fame grew, Granny Fern stayed the same. Her home was the gardener's cottage she grew up in—the same one Margot lives in now—and she donated money and shared her land generously, including the fields, lake, and forests around her greenhouses. The community of Bloomfield had sprung up on that land, slowly growing from a few houses and families struggling together to carve out a life in the middle of the countryside into a thriving village of about two hundred people, built around the principle of mutual care for neighbors and the small joys of building and growing, books, tea, and a slow afternoon spent chatting with a friend.

None of which appealed to Margot's parents. They were cut from a different vine, and they hated how easily Granny Fern gave her money away. Unlike her own mother, Margot grew up in Ashaway among high society, and when Margot's parents could be bothered to visit Granny Fern, they insisted on staying in the enormous manor house they'd built near Granny Fern's cottage. Rare though they were, Margot loved those visits to Bloomfield. During summers and occasional long weekends in her childhood, Margot learned how to help green things grow over many cups of tea with Granny Fern. She even learned how to make a few simple potions, though she was nowhere near as good at them as Granny Fern.

But the summer Margot turned eighteen, Granny Fern got sick with something even her most famous remedies couldn't cure. She was gone before Margot could catch a coach to Bloomfield. Granny Fern's ashes were scattered under her favorite tree behind the gardener's cottage, and while Margot grieved by working in the greenhouses, Margot's parents giddily dug their hands deep in the family coffers. Which soon went spectacularly wrong . . .

Tears rise in Margot's eyes. *Feel your feelings, little Daisy, then get back to work,* Granny Fern always used to say.

Margot would love to, but who has time for feelings when

there's so much to do? The thought makes her reach into her dress pocket, as she's done so often over the last few years, her fingers brushing over the well-worn letter she has memorized by now. It's from the Claunecks, her parents' onetime friends and eventual creditors. Official Clauneck Company letterhead fills the top of the page: the distinctive outline of their towered offices in the Copper Court, with a *C* turned sideways atop its crenellated roof. When Margot first found the letter among her parents' things—almost a year after Granny Fern had died and soon after her parents had been moved to the Bloomfield Care Cottage—she nearly tore it up in rage. By now, the words are familiar, and they are the heaviest of weights. She reads them again:

Dear Iris and Welton,

Regarding your request, we feel it unwise to invest further in your ventures until we have fully recouped your considerable debts to the Clauneck Company, the sum of which the heretofore seized assets have not begun to erase. However, we are impressed by your generous estimations of your daughter's talents and intrigued by the Natural Caster Restoration Potion you claim she is close to perfecting. In remembrance of Fern— whose legacy looms large over Harrow and its economy still— we have seen fit to offer an extension on said debts. For a period of four years until that summer's end, we will delay the seizure of Bloomfield. We will allow you to occupy Fern's cottage on your former estate, and to continue to manage Greenwillow Greenhouses. It is our hope that Margot will inherit her grandmother's prodigious abilities and redeem the Greenwillow brand.

Following this four-year period, should your daughter's potential fail to bear out, then your remaining assets—the cottage, the greenhouses, and the land upon which Bloomfield sits—will be subject to immediate seizure, which we shall take no pleasure in. (Please know, it's nothing personal. It's just business.)

*We look forward to witnessing all that Margot will achieve during this grace period and remain cordially yours,*

Baremon and Menorath Clauneck

As she does every time she reads the letter, Margot wishes her parents hadn't desperately seized upon the one incomplete potion in Granny Fern's remedy book. It was an impossible potion, meant to give someone born with the shallowest pool of magic an infinite spring of power. Faced with utter financial ruin, they had wildly overpromised the Claunecks that Margot was capable of finishing the recipe, which was ridiculous. She's been trying for years to work it out—and now that it's mere weeks away from winter's end, with half a year out of the promised four remining, she's still no closer to completing it. She hasn't heard anything more from the Claunecks (it should be a relief, though sometimes she wonders about her childhood friend Yael, the Clauneck heir, who hasn't written to her in years), but that doesn't mean they've forgotten her.

*Please know, it's nothing personal. It's just business.*

Except it is personal. Extremely. Because if Margot can't figure out this recipe, then it's not just her home and greenhouses she stands to lose. It's the entire village of Bloomfield, though none of the villagers know it.

They still believe what Margot's parents told them—that despite losing the manor house to pay off their debts, nothing more would change after Fern's death. And Margot hasn't been able to bring herself to tell them that the village is also subject to seizure. How could she admit to her friends and community that Fern didn't leave a will, so if she'd meant for the land to go to anybody but Margot's parents, no one would ever know? It was so like Fern, who was a touch scatterbrained and more focused on plants and potions than lawyers and contracts. Or, in her words, as Margot found in one of Fern's journals, dated the day before her death, *I always thought I'd have more time.*

Now, after all these years of keeping her parents' secret, how can Margot tell the people of Bloomfield that their homes and businesses depend on her questionable potion-making abilities?

Margot shoves the letter back into her pocket, glaring around the shed. As if the bags of potting mix could fix all of her problems but refuse to.

"You still have nearly seven months," Margot whispers to herself. "That's more than enough time."

It will be. It has to be.

Tonight, despite her aching back and the need to go home and change clothes before meeting Sage, she'll squeeze some remedy making in after the day's work is done. The entire town is counting on her, even if they don't know it. Underlining "save the town by way of an impossible potion" on her mental to-do list, because it's always there at the very top, Margot moves a collection of empty plant pots aside and digs deeper in the shed for the spade. There it is, behind a sack of strawberry seeds. She grabs it and stomps back into the greenhouses.

As the day passes, Margot repots daylilies that shine golden with a bit of ensorcelled sunlight. She encourages the ivy plants to weave their long tresses, strong and true. She recites poetry to the annuals, a great riot of flowers filling an entire corner of the east greenhouse (they're blooming quite well now that Margot has discovered the power of iambic pentameter). This is growing magic, the kind that makes the power in her blood sing. It's different from remedy magic, at which Granny Fern was brilliant and Margot is barely passable. She feeds the koi in the small fishpond, keeps up with the few customers who come into the greenhouse, and chats with Ms. Estelle Willver, elderly owner of Bloomfield's bakery, who wants to preorder three jars of strawberry jam and purchase a simple love potion: a bottled spell that Estelle will take to help open herself up to love. The love potion is hope; the jars of heartbreak-healing jam, insurance against disaster.

Many hours and many cups of tea later, the day's work is done. But of course Margot has to do it all over again tomorrow. And she needs to work on the Natural Caster Potion a bit too. Because tomorrow morning, she'll be one day closer to the Claunecks' deadline.

With that thought heavier than the sacks of potting soil she carted into the greenhouse that afternoon, Margot locks the front door and slumps into the chair behind her workshop table.

The workshop is a small room with tall shelves lining the walls, each of them stuffed with glass bottles full of colored liquids, old books, stacks of silver bowls, dried herbs, strange-looking brass instruments, piles of notes bound in ribbon, a few vining plants that spill down the sides of the shelves, and dozens of teacups. A table sits in the middle of the room, covered in books, scrolls, dried leaves, and pencils. It's got an immense center drawer and dozens of smaller drawers in each leg, all of them filled with more ingredients, plant cuttings, and papers.

The workshop smells like mint leaves and burnt toast with the tiniest hint of cinnamon from the tea Granny Fern loved best. On the table, beside a tiny oval painted portrait of her and Granny Fern, Margot still keeps a few cinnamon sticks, so the room always smells like Granny Fern has just left it, cup of tea in hand. She pulls Granny Fern's spellbook toward her, flipping to the last entry.

THE NATURAL CASTER POTION is written across the

top of the page, and under that are a mere five lines of notes in Granny Fern's cramped handwriting, giving some thoughts on the potion and some ideas Fern had for creating it. She believed it could be made up of a few individual potions, perhaps ones representing the different affinities natural casters had for magical specialties such as enchantment, conjuration, divination, and elemental magic—which involved air, water, earth, or fire—and a dozen more. The end result, she thought, would be much greater than the sum of its parts. It was tricky and, according to one of the notes, gave Fern a lot of trouble, but she had high hopes for it.

Margot runs her finger along the short descriptions of each potion part. All of them note what it is and should do, but none include ingredients or instructions. Like the letter from the Claunecks, she's read this page hundreds of times, but she's no closer to figuring it out either. For years, she's been practicing by making the other remedies in Fern's book using her own magical education and experimentation, hoping those will at least improve her skills at remedy magic. According to the date at the top of the last page in the book, Fern had been working on this potion the week before she died, but there are pages torn out of the end of the spellbook. What had been written on them? Who tore them out? Margot has no idea, and there are so many questions she wants to ask her grandmother but never will.

A clock in the workshop chimes eight, and her stomach rumbles, reminding her she hasn't eaten since the cookies hours ago. But she's so tired. Perhaps that remedy she'd been working on last week—the one she'd brewed based on the description of the energy spell in Granny Fern's book—is ready. If Margot's calculations are correct, it should ease her aching muscles and grant her a burst of energy—enough to stay awake and alert for her evening ahead, so Sage and anyone else Margot runs into at the tavern don't suspect how run-down she actually is.

Margot pulls open a wooden table drawer, where the potion has been curing beside fifteen rose petals, two tears wrapped in spider's silk, and a tiny bag of red-and-white mushrooms. She holds the small bottle of liquid to the flickering flame of her candle. It sparkles emerald green, just like it's supposed to. There's a tint of purple at the edges that Granny Fern's notes didn't mention, but surely that's her own magic at work, which isn't exactly like her grandmother's (even as she wishes it was).

Margot uncorks the bottle, inhaling slowly as the smell of honey and lilac fills the air. She tips a few drops into her mouth. It's sweet on her tongue, a bit fizzy, and it fills her with something warm. She closes her eyes for a moment, feeling like a flower, stretching toward the golden energy of the sun . . .

She wakes minutes (hours? a whole day?) later. Swearing, Margot scrambles to her feet. So much for her glorious magical potential. She's drooled on the workshop table, and her neck has a crick in it from sleeping in a terrible position. Grabbing her tiny clock—the wooden one shaped like a snail that Granny Fern gave her for her twelfth birthday—she lets out a long sigh. It's only nine fifteen. She's not that late, though she doesn't have time to go home to bathe or change.

Strawberry dress and garden boots it is, then.

Throwing a hand-knitted purple cardigan over her dress and scowling at the disaster of an energy potion that put her to sleep, Margot runs out the door.

Margot met Sage Wilderstone—professional ranger and adventurer extraordinaire—three years ago, on her first day of college. Sage had been sprawled in a chair at a table near the back of their carnivorous plant management seminar, comfortable in her long-limbed body like no one else Margot had ever seen. There were no other open chairs in the room, and Margot was grateful for the chance to slide into the seat next to the stranger with short blond hair styled in a dangerous-looking undercut. She, at least, seemed like she knew what to do as the professor brought out three-foot-tall, snapping Venus flytraps.

"Ready for an adventure?" Sage said, her wide grin showing her remarkably straight teeth as the professor put a flytrap on their table and wished them luck.

Margot had nodded and smoothed out the next page in her notebook. As it turned out, she took no notes that day, and she and Sage failed miserably at the flytrap exercise, but they became fast friends.

Tonight, as Margot enters Clementine's Tavern—a two-story stone-and-timber building with several generously sized common rooms, an inviting hearth with a blazing fire, and tables full of townspeople—she sees Sage immediately. Long rows of candles dripping wax over their iron sconces cast a golden glow over the room, and Sage sits at the tavern bar, limned in their light. Her long legs are swathed in fitted trousers and knee-high boots, which she props on the chair in front of her. Her white linen shirt is open at the throat, showing her suntanned skin and collarbone, while her sword rests on the bar beside three empty flagons of ale. Her fingers tap along to the melody played by a traveling bard as she talks with Clementine, the curly-haired young woman who owns the tavern. Sage leans in closer across the bar counter, whispering something, and a blush rises on Clem's cheeks. Yep. They're most definitely flirting. Margot grins. Sage leaves a string of yearning hearts behind in every town she passes through, just as she did when she quit college months before their graduation, eager to set out on her next adventure. It looks like her brief time in Bloomfield will be no different. Margot is deeply grateful that one of her core rules is never to sleep with her friends; so much better to miss out on a one-night affair than to lose one of the few people she holds close.

As Margot strolls toward the bar, she waves to Mike, the enthusiastic collector of volumes for the town's library who also runs Honey and Wax, the town's bookshop. He's got a stack of stories on the table in front of him. Dara, the town's chicken witch, sits across from him with a pint of ale, her nose deep in a book as well. Beside her is her younger sister, Poppy, who runs a small workshop in town selling gadgets of her own invention.

"See you at the community dinner tomorrow!" calls Rosiee, the town's unofficial organizer, who's always got a cat or a funny story (or often both) on hand. Community dinner is a weekly Bloomfield custom—a time when everyone sets aside their work and chores and worries to spend a few hours with their neighbors. It's held in the courtyard at the town center when it isn't raining or snowing, and all of Bloomfield's residents settle around long trestle tables piled high with food brought by everyone, drink loads of ale and wine, and spend the evening catching up, laughing together, and making plans for the town. It's one of Margot's favorite community traditions and one more reason out of a million why she has to save Bloomfield. The thought of there being no more community dinners two seasons from now because Margot didn't figure out the Natural Caster Potion is unthinkable, and utterly not worth entertaining. Even if it's a very real possibility.

"I'm bringing roasted carrots and a fruit salad," Margot manages as more guilt twists her stomach. "Wouldn't miss it for anything."

Rosiee raises a tankard to that alongside Beryl, who runs the town's brewery, and Margot keeps walking toward the bar. She passes a few people clearly not from Bloomfield, who wear silk coats or dresses, and frowns in their direction. As much as she needs occasional tourists and passers-through to keep the greenhouse afloat—there are only so many heartbreaks to tend to in a small town—they can be a nuisance. They gawk at Bloomfield as though it's some quaint storybook place. As though the idea of a peaceful, supportive community is as adorable as it is unattainable.

"Margot Greenwillow!" booms Sage as Margot reaches the bar. Sage's delight dances through her words. "As I live and breathe, we'd almost given up on you."

Margot throws a sheepish smile in Sage's direction. "Sorry. I fell asleep."

Sage raises one eyebrow, the silvered whisper of a scar running through it. "Well, you're here now. That's all that counts!" She stands and pulls Margot into a tight hug and, despite their similar heights, lifts her slightly. A gasp of surprise escapes Margot's lips, and she hugs Sage back, then wriggles out of the embrace.

"I love the garden boots," Sage says, studying Margot's outfit.

Margot snorts. "I think they go well with this lovely, high-fashion frock."

"Which goes perfectly with the cardigan, so I'd say you're winning." Sage takes a full mug of ale off the counter and hands it to Margot. "You look like a woman who needs several of these. Sit, drink, tell me everything."

Relief tastes like frothy ale, sounds like Sage's laughter, and feels like settling onto one of the high barstools. The night unwinds in a cozy blur of music, friendship, and many drinks. Sage gives Margot a present: a pair of enchanted, mirrored compacts she picked up from a trader on the Queens' Road, which they can use to talk to each other across long distances; one of them need only scribble a short note on a slip of paper and close it up inside the compact, and the message will write itself across the mirror of the opposite one. Clementine keeps flirting with Sage, who tells them both about her next adventure, a mission to the Swamplands on the southeastern coast of the kingdom, where a network of marshes, mudflats, and ponds flood regularly with saltwater from the Serpentine Sea.

"I've always wanted to see the Swamplands," Margot says, her voice lighter from the ale and the thought of sleeping under the stars, the nearby sounds of the sea whispering into her dreams.

"Come with me!" Sage says, clapping Margot enthusiastically on the shoulder. "Our leader is still building the party—"

"Tell me this isn't going to be one of those shady adventure parties put together by a company out to exploit and destroy magical habitats?" Margot's parents had hired several of those after Granny Fern died, each of them promising wildly profitable discoveries, and each of them running away with her parents' money, never to be heard from again.

"You know me better than that. We're out to discover, not destroy or exploit. A trader in Ashaway told our client about a grove on the coast where no one has been able to venture more than twenty feet in on account of, well, probably monsters. But we're looking for a rare specimen of sea fern, and we could use a plant witch like you along for the journey."

"I would love to, but—"

"Think about it, it's perfect! We'll be back by midsummer, so you'll be home in plenty of time for community apple bobbing or whatever charming activities Bloomfield gets up to in autumn."

For a moment, with the ale making her brain fuzzy, Margot lets the fantasy wrap around her. She could wear an adventurer's outfit, like Sage's, instead of garden boots and muddy dresses. They'd pore over the map and then step outside it. Sage would pick through waist-deep mud and monstrous leeches to get to this rare fern, and Margot would study it, finding uses that she couldn't even imagine in her greenhouses. Maybe she could create the potion that snapped her parents out of—

Right, no. The thought of her parents is a pair of gardening shears chopping the buds of this fantasy to pieces.

"I can't, Sage." Margot takes another long swig of ale, finishing it. She slips a hand into her pocket, running her fingers over the letter from the Claunecks; she keeps it with her wherever she goes, partly to root herself in moments like these when she's tempted to drift into dreams of what could be. "I have to stay here. My parents need me. The greenhouses need me. I can't just run off."

She tries to keep the longing from her voice, but Sage shoots her a sympathetic look. "You're doing too much, love. You know that."

Margot just shrugs. Maybe she is. But lingering too long on the truth doesn't mark items off her to-do list. Or concoct magical Natural Caster Potions that will pay down her parents' massive debts and save Bloomfield.

The clock behind the bar chimes midnight. Sage finishes her drink and stands, buckling her short sword to her waist.

"Are you sure you don't want to stay the night?" Margot asks, suddenly desperate for her friend not to leave.

Clementine also looks eager for Sage to stay.

"I would love to, but I have to make up some time tonight." Sage shoots them both an apologetic half smile. "Need to get at least a few hours of riding in before I bunk up. There's an inn I can stay at about three hours from here."

Margot wants to say more, but there's no stopping Sage when her mind is made up. She's perfectly free to do what she wants, sleep where she wants, chase whatever adventure she wants.

What would such freedom feel like?

Margot can't even imagine.

"Take good care of yourself," Margot says, pulling Sage into a hug. "Please don't get eaten."

"I won't," Sage promises. "And you try to have a little fun, okay?"

Margot won't, but that isn't the point. Sage squeezes her fiercely and then says goodbye. As the tavern door closes behind her, a deep loneliness settles over Margot.

"All done, then?" Clementine wipes the bar in front of her.

Margot looks toward the door, considering her empty cottage, the work in store for her tomorrow, and all of the adventures Sage has in front of *her.*

"I think I'll have one more." Margot pushes her tankard toward Clementine, hoping to lose herself and her responsibilities for a few more minutes at the bottom of it.

# 3

## YAEL

Hard as it might seem to fall asleep on the back of a steed whose hoofbeats clang like anvil strikes, Yael manages. Though "falling asleep" feels a little more like passing out—especially when they wake dry-mouthed, shivering, and with a dire headache. Perhaps they should've eaten before downing several glasses of wine and flutes of champagne. They left the estate while the kitchen was still preparing its seven-course dinner, supposedly in Yael's honor. Now the sky has deepened considerably, dark as ink so far from the lantern lights of Ashaway, spattered with stars beyond counting. Yael is no ranger who can tell time by the constellations. But from the hollowness of their stomach—and the fact that they're sober as well as miserable—they guess it might be past midnight.

They should have waited to flee until after the mutton soup. Or the oysters. Or the cheese and mushroom pie. Or the baked giant toad . . .

Well, it's too late now. If the party went on without Yael, as it certainly would have, then the plates have long since been cleared. Besides, would Yael really slink home just for supper?

*Supper, and bedclothes, and a warm, safe place to sleep,* their patron's familiar voice (one that sounds very much like Baremon, but deeper, like measuring a lake against an ocean) rumbles inside their mind. *Or will you sleep in the weeds and die of the cold? You never do stop to think, Yael.*

Hearing that voice when they'd least like to is a consequence of the warlock's bargain, though thankfully, it's not a common occurrence. Yael's patron has only ever paid heed to them when they've disappointed him severely. Tonight's misadventure seems to have won Yael his attention—a most unwelcome prize. Perhaps Baremon or Uncle Mikhil or, who knows, even Araphi has an altogether different relationship with the family patron. Yael's certainly never asked. Rather, they've spent a lifetime trying to avoid their patron's notice as they avoid his offering altars, even if it means that the roadside weeds are capable of greater magic than Yael.

To prove the voice wrong, Yael flips the levers that bring the mechanical steed to a stop in the middle of the Queens' Road. This way, at least they can think without the frigid wind in their face and their head pounding in rhythm with Sweet Wind's gait.

The sensible thing *would* be to turn around and ride for the capital, as they'd always meant to when they set out. They might even make it back by breakfast. It'll be a miserable one after a mostly sleepless night, with their father and uncle glaring at them over party leftovers and tea—or, worse, laughing at them. Yael will drag their fork across their plate, trying not to vomit on their cold smoked fish. Probably, they'll beg to stop the carriage on the ride to the Copper Court to heave up into the gutter. Maybe they can sneak a midday nap in the Records Library, tucked behind a shelf with a pile of profitability analyses for a pillow . . .

Starting Sweet Wind up again, Yael clucks the steed onward

down the Queens' Road, no matter that it can't hear. If they're
not going back, they'll need to find a place to eat and sleep—
and soon. The sound of their chattering teeth is starting to rival
the steed's hoofbeats. But they've long since passed the first
ring of villages beyond Ashaway's walls, scattered amid farm-
land and riverland. Higley Brook, Poppler, and a mill town
hardly worth naming sit right beside the road but are too close
to the city to host an inn. Yael might've had to sleep in an
empty barnyard stall or rent a bed in some leathersmith's cottage, and that wouldn't have been a very comfortable start to an
adventure. They'd been sure they'd pass a crossroads eventually,
but they must've dozed through it. Honestly, it's lucky they
weren't found by bandits. They'd be lying in the weeds right
now without a steed, without the small purse they had on them
at the party to tip the hired servants, and probably with a dagger in their empty stomach.

So things could certainly be worse.

Maybe when they finally come across a town, they can barter
something. Yael's watched plenty of bards perform for supper
and lodgings in the alehouses, but Yael isn't what anybody
would call gifted. They can't even conjure a small flame for
warmth. Their ineptitude at spellwork without their patron's
favor was never a problem in the capital, nor even at Auximia.
But beyond the city and the reach of their family's credit, how
exactly are they going to survive?

They're on the brink of stopping again when, finally, they
see a crossroads ahead in the starlight. No inn, though. The
path that cuts across the Queens' Road—a highway several carriage breadths across and paved with six-sided capstones, which
runs from Briarwall, a military outpost positioned between the
forests and mountains of the dangerous Northlands and the rest
of settled Harrow, down to Lintonbury at its southern tip—is
little more than a dirt lane rutted by cart wheels and beast

tracks. There's a weathered signpost with one plank pointing ahead toward Olde Post, a sizable town Yael knows to be at least another day's ride south. A second plank points east, down the lane that winds off into the dark countryside.

BLOOMFIELD, it reads.

Yael is shocked to realize they know exactly where they are, after all.

※

"An entire day's travel just to visit a country estate? What were the Greenwillows thinking, and why the devils did we agree?" Baremon complained to his wife, not for the first or even fifth time since setting out.

They'd left Ashaway just after morning tea—Baremon, Menorath, and thirteen-year-old Yael, along with their coachman, a footman, and Menorath's maid—in order to reach their destination by evening. The party had stopped once along the Queens' Road for the coachman to feed and water the horses (not as impressive as the pair of griffins they'd left in the stable, but better suited for summer travel), and even then Yael had to sit in the stifling carriage with their parents. It had only grown hotter as the day grew longer.

"We agreed to visit as their major investor and as a personal favor to Iris," Menorath calmly reminded her husband. She had a knack for weathering Baremon's tempers; her own were much subtler, sometimes passing over Yael's head like a cloud, gone on the breeze before they looked up with no explanation for their accompanying chills. "Perhaps it won't be so bad. The estate was built with her mother's fortune after all, and I'm told it's comfortable, if . . . cozy." She made no effort to hide the distasteful twist of her sweating upper lip.

What with the heat, the faint tang of Clauneck magic in the carriage, and their proximity to their parents, Yael was more than ready to burst out the door by the time they passed through the high outer wall of Bloomfield, but there was still a ways to go. They jostled down the lane toward the turnoff to the manor—the first sign of human inhabitants in the village, and it was only an entrance gate to another path cutting farther into the woods. The open gate was flanked on either side by a pair of stone beasts, hooved and antlered, with beards of stone leaves. In the deep shade under trees taller than any they had in Ashaway, the statues seemed about to spring to life.

Little as Yael wanted to agree with their father, it *was* strange to see a fancy manor house way out in the woods, so many hours from anything important. The Claunecks had no real interest in being anywhere but the very heart of Ashaway, though they had estates in Lintonbury, the southernmost point on the Queens' Road where the royal summer palace stood, and on the shore of the Jade Sea in Kingfisher, with its vital trading ports. Proper cities. Yael had never even heard of Bloomfield before the invitation to dine with the Greenwillows arrived.

The house was very nice, though. Where Clauneck Manor was a solid, towering block of gray stone with its own ramparts, arrow-slit windows, and gable-roof towers tall enough to pierce the clouds, the Greenwillows' country estate was lower to the earth, three stories built of stone the same reddish brown as the surrounding tree trunks. Only one tower rose above the giant treetops, more like a fairy tale than a fortification.

On the grand front steps stood the Greenwillows, flanked by a small household staff and waiting to greet them; some enchantment on the gate must've alerted them to the Claunecks' arrival. Iris Greenwillow was high-cheekboned and beautifully plump, with violet hair plaited into a crown. Her hair color was a quirk she'd been born with, same as her mother, Fern's hair, and some said it was a sign of prodigious magical talents. Yael had heard their mother tittering with her landed friends over the fact that if such talent existed, it had yet to bloom in Iris. Her husband, Welton Sameshoe, stood about her height but stockier, beaming at them through a dark-brown beard. Their daughter, Margot—Yael's friend since they were old enough to be towed along to social functions like small pets or purses—was nowhere to be seen.

Perhaps Margot's absence had carved the worry lines between Iris's brows, even as she exclaimed, "Friends, welcome to our home! How pleasing it is to see you." As though the Claunecks' arrival was a most wonderful surprise and not an event the Greenwillows had doubtlessly been planning and scrambling over for weeks.

Menorath nodded graciously. "How pleasing it is to be here. We aren't given an excuse to leave the city often enough for my liking. And your estate—how quaint!"

Yael was attuned enough to the moods of grown-ups to guess that "quaint" was not the impression the Greenwillows wished to make. There was nothing quaint about their manner of dress. They were outfitted far more formally than the Claunecks in their traveling clothes. Of course, the Claunecks' traveling clothes were sewn of the finest silks and leathers, only giving the appearance of simplicity, while Iris's gown was encrusted with jewels. Vines of cut emeralds climbed her velvet skirt, blossoming into sunflowers with petals of lemon quartz and citrine. Welton wore a burgundy velvet suit to match, with a high ruffled collar. It seemed far too hot for such heavy finery, and in contrast with Yael's family, the pair looked . . . overdone.

If they noticed, neither Greenwillow let on. "Come, come," Welton cheered, "and make yourselves at home. What's ours is yours."

While their coachman and footman and maid were led away to the servants' quarters, the flock of waiting staff showed Yael and their parents through the arched main entrance and up a broad stonework staircase to their separate chambers. It was some time yet until dinner, and the Claunecks would be staying overnight. Yael had just finished unraveling the sweated-through linen bindings around their new and unwelcome chest to replace before dressing for dinner when a rapid knocking sounded at the door.

A voice called urgently through the keyhole, "Yael, let me in! Before Mama finds me and makes me wash!"

They grinned, hurrying to pin fresh bindings in place before tossing on a shirt. Not bothering with a vest or coat, they threw open the door, and Margot rushed inside. No wonder she was hiding out. She wore a plain brown dress that might've been long enough a growth spurt ago, a sweater that looked as if it had been knitted for someone Baremon's size instead of a skinny twelve-year-old girl, and garden boots splattered with drying mud.

"Won't you get in trouble if your parents can't find you?" Yael asked, plucking some kind of prickly twig from where it was stuck in Margot's hastily braided purple hair, the mirror of her mother's.

Margot blushed, then shrugged. "Only *after* they find me. So we'd better run away before they do. Granny Fern's packed me snacks for the road." She hoisted the checkered cloth sack looped over her shoulder for Yael's inspection. "Grab your riding boots, quickly, and we'll be halfway to the coast to board a ship for Locronan before they know we're gone!"

"Why Locronan?"

"Because they've still got dragons there," she whispered, her rain-cloud-colored eyes glittering.

"They haven't! There aren't any dragons anywhere." The great beasts that used to nest in mountain peaks and forests deep had been hunted down for the magical properties of their bones and scales ages ago, they'd learned at school.

"Well, how will we know if we never go?"

This was what Yael loved about Margot: She made everything feel like an adventure.

They slipped into their velvet dress shoes, perfectly impractical for running away from home. "Father would summon our patron himself to bring me back," they explained with a sigh. Not that he would try very hard, most likely. Yael heard their patron's voice about as often as they heard from their father's father, now retired to the seaside to clear the path for Baremon: on the occasional birthday, or when Yael's minor high jinks caused enough of a stir to merit a scolding from afar, usually delivered in a formal letter dictated to their grandfather's footman. Yael would never admit to Margot that they were afraid of the offering altars placed about the Clauneck estate, just as they were of those letters.

"Maybe just the tower, then," Margot conceded. "We'll come down in time for the dinner bell. Granny only packed us strawberry jam, anyway."

"Deal."

Yael grabbed their coat and slung their tie over their neck, and the two snuck past closed doors and empty rooms full of grand furniture, giggling all the while, until they reached the third floor. A winding stone staircase beyond a door at the end of the hall led them up. When they reached the round chamber at the top, a dozen paces across, the tower was miraculously cool in the summer heat. It must've been freezing in any other season without a warming stove up here, which explained why there was no furniture—only a steamer trunk with a strange collection of objects set on top. A little wooden clock carved like a snail. A brass spyglass. A few empty jam jars—still pink and sticky around the rims—containing handfuls of pebbles, and shells, and dried brown leaves.

Yael crossed to the tower window, and Margot swiped the spyglass from the trunk to toss it to them.

"Look down there," she instructed. "You can see Granny's cottage, with the chimney." Then she bent to set her bag on the floor, pulling out a jam jar and a silver spoon. She unwound the twine around the pink cloth lid to peel it back. "There's a grotto on the north side of the property with a little waterfall, but you can't really see it from here, with the trees in the way, except sometimes when the light catches the mist in the morning and makes rainbows above the treetops. Granny built it up with magic, and it's one of my favorite places anywhere. Maybe I can take you there the next time you visit."

"Next visit," Yael promised even as their heart sank like a pebble into a pond: Their parents would never bring them back here, they were fairly certain. Menorath and Baremon had sworn as much in the carriage. Besides, they were bound for boarding school in Perpignan at the end of summer and unlikely to be summoned home for holidays—something of a mixed blessing.

"Look a little south," Margot continued, "and you can see Bloomfield."

Yael pressed the glass to their eye. "That's the village, right?"

"Barely," she said, but fondly. "It's more of a . . . collection. Yes, a collection of people who moved there because of Granny. The walls you passed through used to be a military outpost, but it was abandoned years ago to rebuild closer to Olde Post. Granny bought the land when her business took off."

"Took off" was putting it mildly; Yael didn't know everything about their parents' peers, but they knew that much. They'd only met Granny Fern once, because the Greenwillow matriarch never seemed to come to Ashaway, let alone the Copper Court or the Clauneck offices. But nobles and royals and townsfolk alike would travel long distances for her remedies and potions. Fern was the whole reason Yael's parents were so eager to invest in Iris and Welton, and (no offense to Margot's parents) Fern alone. On the carriage ride to Bloomfield, they'd speculated as to whether Margot might equal her grandmother's talents someday—Fern's gifts had clearly skipped a generation. "We should keep an eye on the girl," Menorath had suggested, speaking over Yael's head.

Yael could've told them that Margot was already extraordinary, but when had their parents ever taken them seriously?

"So she's the landlord of Bloomfield?" they asked Margot.

She paused with the spoon in her mouth. "I suppose. But she doesn't collect taxes or make the laws or anything."

Yael frowned. "Who does, then?"

"Well, the community, I guess. Which is mostly people who came to live near a famous plant witch, or Granny's friends. Some from when she was our age. In fact, Granny used her own money to help build their houses and businesses."

"How did they pay her back?"

"They didn't. Granny does drink at the tavern for free, though. Shelby insists. But my parents won't let me go with her."

Yael had never heard of anything like that, and Baremon and Menorath probably thought Granny Fern was a bag of loose marbles. But Yael liked Margot, who clearly loved her grandmother. So they nodded as though they understood.

She took the spyglass from Yael, trading it for the spoon piled with bright-red strawberry jam.

"Is it magic jam?" Yael asked eagerly.

"People say so. They say it helps if you want to be in love. Or rather, if somebody doesn't love you back."

"Are *you* in love, Margot?" Yael teased. "I heard Sedgewick Wayanette asked you to dance at his birthday celebration. He's very . . . tall."

Margot blushed again. "I just like Granny's strawberries, okay?" she mumbled around her own spoonful.

It's been ten years since that night—the last time Yael visited the Greenwillows' country estate, as they knew it would be—and nearly that long since they last saw Margot. Yael had gone away to finish their secondary education at boarding school, as planned. It was tradition in their family, as it gave them a head start in mixing with their peers beyond the realm. A mutual friend had told Yael that Margot's family left the city in the spring before Yael came home to attend Auximia, and they'd expected her to return at the end of summer as well. She hadn't, though. Yael never saw her at the academy, or in the alehouses, or at parties. Never saw her parents, who used to be fixtures in the Copper Court. Eventually, they'd accepted that life must have led her elsewhere.

It would be so nice to see Margot again.

Yael turns Sweet Wind off the Queens' Road and down the rutted lane. The ride seems longer than they remember, even if it has been forever, and they've truly started to worry, when at last they see the stone walls of the old outpost, the abandoned watchtowers blotting out the stars behind them. The landscape that would've been cleared of scrub and trees in its military days is dotted with dormant berry bushes. No fires burn in the seemingly empty towers, and the heavy entrance gate stands open to travelers.

Baremon would scoff at the lack of fortification, as he did years ago. But Yael could hop off Sweet Wind and kiss the open gate with gratitude.

They ride through, and at last, after half a mile of forested road where they pass nobody, they see the manor. Or rather, the entrance gate. Two familiar statues stand at either side, moss grown up over their stone hooves, creeping vines twined around their legs and the bars of the shut gates. The starlight is thin through the trees above, but what looks like bird droppings spatter their antlers. Strange. Yael remembers Margot's parents being just as worried about appearances as Baremon and Menorath. Probably more so, since the Greenwillows could never quite rely on setting trends and dictating tastes the way the Claunecks always have. Near-infinite wealth and power will do that; were anyone to spot bird droppings upon the gates of the Clauneck estate, they'd be in fashion by the end of the week.

Yael peers through the thickly grown trees, attempting to see the house, but only the round tower pokes above the treetops, its little window dark. Obviously, the Greenwillows will be in bed at this late (or early?) hour. Yael could leave Sweet Wind at the gate, making their way to the house on foot, where they'll . . . what? Knock until they wake a maid? Charm them into popping down to the kitchen and putting some soup on the fire while they wait for Margot and her parents to rise for the day? They could throw pebbles at the window of Margot's old bedroom and hope for the best, but of course she might not even be in there. Maybe she's still away at school, wherever she ended up, or is managing an estate of her own. She could be married by now, settled down and all grown up like Yael is supposed to be.

The thought of their close childhood friend as a partner or parent suddenly fills them with longing. For what, they're not sure, but a Margot who no longer runs wild in the woods or sneaks up to secret towers to avoid dinner parties would be the world's loss.

Yael looks ahead up the lane. Margot mentioned a tavern in Bloomfield where Granny Fern drank for free. If it doesn't have rooms for rent, Yael can sleep on the bar counter, then ride back to the manor to bluster their way through that awkward conversation in daylight. They won't smell any better than they do now, but at least they won't be shivering and pathetic in the dark.

It's only another mile or so to the outskirts of the village, where they're relieved beyond belief to get their wish: a dark wood tavern with a thatch roof, the frames painted tomato red around windowpanes lit from within. No stable that they can see, and they hesitate to abandon Sweet Wind outside. The steed is all they have. But apart from the sounds of laughter and song inside, the rest of Bloomfield appears to be in bed.

Anyway, you'd have to know how to ride a mechanical steed to steal one. In a middle-of-the-countryside place like this, that seems unlikely.

After hours of riding on wood and iron, Yael can hardly feel their tingling thighs and buttocks as they climb down from the saddle (perhaps the inn has a healer on retainer who can lay on hands). Slowly and painfully, they make their bowlegged way to the red tavern door, where they push through and are greeted by a welcome blast of warmth. A hearth crackles in the corner, casting flickering shadows and dim light across a handful of patrons clustered at small, round, rough wood tables. Probably townsfolk rather than travelers; passers-through would keep their heads down in their drinks, but nearly the entire tavern looks up at Yael as they enter.

Self-conscious, Yael swipes their fingers through their wind-tangled hair to fluff it up and comes away with a palmful of road dust. "Evening," they say, aiming for charming as they wipe their hand on their hopelessly wrinkled trousers.

A teenage boy in a linen apron passes by with a tray of food, trailed by a sleek black weasel with a dustpan brush clamped in its jaws; a familiar, no doubt. Leaning in subtly to smell the brown bread and stew and golden ale held aloft, Yael feels their stomach nearly consume itself.

They hobble over to the bar counter, hoping for quicker service, and sink gratefully onto an empty stool. There's only one other customer at the counter, currently draining a large tankard with her head tipped toward the ceiling. From the corner of their eye, Yael sees a thick braid, dark in the shadows beyond the firelight, dangling halfway down her back. Her dress, roughly embroidered with strawberries, is streaked with soil. Another traveler? Garden boots and a cardigan seem like strange riding attire . . . but then, look at Yael in their dusty silk party suit.

"What'll you have, love?" a pretty young woman with an abundance of champagne-colored curls pulled back with a ribbon asks from behind the bar. "Kitchen's closing soon."

"The bread and stew, please." Yael flashes a smile despite their pounding head and sore backside, hoping for an extra ladleful. "And have you got a good wine here? I bet you've got a good wine." The purse at Yael's belt feels awfully light for good wine, but they decide that's tomorrow's problem. Especially if they can put off their hangover just a little longer.

She giggles. "We do, pressed from grapes grown in the village vineyard."

"Excellent. One for me, then, and one for my new friend . . ." They turn expectantly toward the customer in the muddy dress. No need to sleep at a tavern table if they can flirt their way into curling up in a fellow traveler's room, after all.

The woman sets her now empty tankard on the counter and looks their way, rosy mouth dropping open in shock. Yael nearly falls off their barstool at the one person they'd hoped to find in this town, but the last person they expected to see in a humble tavern after midnight, still wearing mud-caked gardening boots.

"*Margot?*"

# 4

# MARGOT

"Yael?" Margot chokes on the dregs of her ale, coughing. Some of it splatters the bar in front of her.

Smooth.

Almost as smooth as sitting across from her childhood friend and crush—whom she recognizes immediately, since they haven't changed all that much in the last ten years—in a stained strawberry-print dress and garden boots.

Margot swears inwardly and gestures for Clementine to refill her tankard. "Yael Clauneck?" Margot repeats, desperate to give herself time to think.

What is Yael gods-be-damned Clauneck doing in Bloomfield, of all places, wearing silver basilisk-skin slip-on shoes with jade buckles, looking like they've been quite literally dragged here? Are their horrible parents here too? Oh gods, what will Margot say to—

"In the flesh." Yael interrupts Margot's thoughts. They run a hand over their dusty-yet-expensive-looking green silk suit coat (how long has it been since Margot wore something that nice?) and then through their hair. Somehow they manage to floof it even higher as they peer up at Margot.

Self-consciously, Margot mirrors their movement, brushing an errant swath of hair off her forehead. She comes away with a strawberry leaf. Wincing, she shoves the leaf under the full mug of ale Clementine has just placed in front of her.

"What are you—" Margot starts to say.

At the same moment, Yael says, "Do you drink here often?" As if they're strangers in a gilded bar in Ashaway. As if it's perfectly normal that the golden child of the Claunecks, someone who probably sips champagne out of crystal goblets at breakfast, has just wandered into Clementine's Tavern.

"I . . . yes . . . of course . . ." Margot's words trip out of her. She takes a swig of frothy ale, swallowing hard as she tries to calm her racing heart. Her thoughts are already sluggish from the several drinks before this one, and now they churn around the same baffling truth over and again.

Yael Clauneck is *here*? Sitting next to *her*? Wearing that smug grin that always made Margot want to smack them, or kiss them, or something in between the two? Impossible. Utterly, entirely, ridiculously impossible.

Fighting against the urge to touch the letter from Yael's parents in her pocket, Margot sits up taller and wraps both hands around her tankard. "Yes. I come here almost every night. Well, that is, on the nights I can get away. Not that I drink every night; I just come here for company sometimes. Gods, that sounds pathetic. I mean I just come to chat or check in about an order at the greenhouse. Of course, sometimes I just head straight home. Or I fall asleep in the greenhouses, which is what happened tonight, which is why I'm still in my work clothes . . ."

*Stop talking. Please, Margot. Just breathe.*

Across the counter, Clementine's eyebrows are nearly in her hair as she looks between Margot and Yael.

"Friend of yours?" Clementine mouths.

Margot clamps her teeth down over her words. She isn't twelve years old, showing Yael Clauneck her tower hideaway, the two of them licking jam off the same silver spoon with Margot hoping madly that Yael shared her feelings—or at least that the jam would ease her heartache if they didn't. And she isn't seventeen, hoping to invite Yael to the Greenwillows' masquerade ball, though the two of them were barely friends by then, and she wasn't sure they could come all the way from their boarding school if she did write to invite them, but still, the thought of Yael in a mask and three-piece suit had made Margot's teenage insides twist . . .

No. She is twenty-two. Responsible. The owner of Greenwillow Greenhouses and a credentialed plant witch. Yael is just an old childhood friend somehow passing through Bloomfield. Surely they aren't here to check up on her?

It seems unlikely given how pleased Yael is looking with themself for running into Margot.

Clementine pulls a bottle of wine and two glasses from below the bar and sets them in front of Yael. "On the house for a friend of Margot's. Stew'll be right up, darlin'," she says with a wink.

Yael replies with some combo of banter and charm that draws a loud, delighted laugh from Clementine.

Margot frowns and looks away to clock how many Bloomfield residents are watching them. Exactly none, which makes her breathe a little easier. If the townspeople don't know who Yael is, then surely they won't put together who Yael's parents are or why that would matter to Bloomfield at all. Margot can't help herself this time, and her hand flies to her pocket and the Claunecks' letter.

"This girl's a good one," Clementine is saying to Yael while she swats at Margot with her bar rag, dragging Margot back to the moment at hand. "You're lucky you sat next to her."

Yael grins. "I assure you, I count myself the luckiest person in all of Harrow to be sitting beside her now." They turn the power of their charm on Margot, and her cheeks heat.

She finds herself returning their grin.

Ridiculous.

Clementine throws Margot another meaningful look and mouths, "Cute!" as she walks away. Margot rolls her eyes, not missing how Yael's gaze lingers on Clementine's retreating form. Not that it matters. Not even a little bit. Yael can look at whomever they want, however they want.

Probably they weren't ever friends, whatever Margot had hoped. After all, wouldn't a friend have sent a note after Granny Fern died? Or perhaps a "thinking of you" bouquet after Margot's parents decimated the Greenwillow fortune and the Claunecks finished the job? Wouldn't a friend have wondered where Margot was in all those long years after she left Ashaway?

She glances over at Yael, who's deftly opening the wine bottle with Clementine's pocketknife, oblivious to Margot's internal stewing. Clementine was right: Yael *is* cute. Margot remembers the way their eyebrows come together when they're concentrating, as they're doing now, and the way they chew on their lower lip.

Not that it matters. Margot is absolutely *not* thinking about nibbling on their lush lower lip.

That's just the ale talking.

Steadying herself, Margot glugs half her tankard in three gulps.

Yael pours the dark-maroon wine into two glasses. "Cheers," they say, sliding a full-to-the-brim glass toward Margot. "To old friends and to getting lucky."

Margot can't help the snort that escapes her. Yael is bold as always and charming enough to pull it off, unfortunately. Good thing they're not friends.

And since they're not friends, maybe that means Margot wouldn't be breaking her own rule, if . . .

No.

Not thinking about that.

Still, it has been so incredibly long since she's gotten lucky.

"To luck," she grinds out, raising her glass.

They both drink. A lot. Margot nearly empties her wineglass as a long, meaningful silence stretches between them.

"So, Bloomfield is . . ." Yael begins after a few excruciating moments. They look around the tavern. "Quaint."

In that one word, Margot hears her parents' disdain for the town Granny Fern loved. She remembers Yael's parents talking about how *quaint* Bloomfield was; they'd said it like the worst of slurs during their visit to Greenwillow Manor. She hears the way her classmates in primary school sneered when she'd read an essay on her summer vacation. She'd written all about Granny Fern and the wonderful summer they'd spent together far away from the city. Meanwhile, her classmates had spent the summer on the coast, or traveling across the Serpentine Sea to Perpignan, or the Jade Sea to Locronan. Only Yael hadn't laughed at Margot as she'd stumbled through four paragraphs about berry picking and jam making.

Not that Yael's kindness mattered. Not then, not after they left Margot behind in Ashaway—and especially not now, since they aren't friends.

"Bloomfield is a wonderful place," Margot says, the words coming out fierce and protective, if slightly slurred.

"Sure it is, especially if you wish to escape reality." Yael sounds surprisingly cheerful about the idea.

"This is reality."

"A better version of it, maybe, miles away from the Copper Court." Yael fills their wineglass again.

What is that supposed to mean? Margot fixes them with a long look, really taking in the dust caked onto Yael's expensive shoes. The rip in their perfectly tailored trousers. The way their hands shake, ever so slightly, as they drain their wine.

"What exactly are you doing here, Yael?"

Here it is, the moment of truth. The moment she'll know whether they have, in fact, been sent to check up on her and her progress on the Natural Caster Potion, or if it's just a wild coincidence that they're sitting across from her now, candlelight snagged by the flecks of gold in their brown eyes.

Yael refills Margot's glass, once again to the brim. "Well, I was passing through. And I remembered your family lived in Bloomfield, and I longed to see you again. Whatever happened to you? Last I knew, I left for boarding school the summer after our visit to Bloomfield, and when I came back to Ashaway for university, you were gone. None of us at Auximia ever heard from you again!"

Margot takes another long sip of her wine, swirling it around her mouth, savoring the dark berry sweetness and the tart notes. The grapes in Bloomfield's vineyard are of the non-enchanted variety, but they are delicious. She lets the taste linger as she considers her answer.

Maybe Yael really hasn't heard about the Greenwillows' fall, but how could they not know? Suddenly, Margot looks at Yael with new eyes, wariness settling over her. Yael—with their easy, wine-stained smile—doesn't appear to be a financial mastermind intent on ruining Margot's life further. In fact, as they take off their silk jacket and roll up their sleeves, they look as they always did. Carefree, confident, the life of every party.

And ridiculously hot, if Margot is being honest. Which shows just how off her judgment is after all the drinking. She really should go home now. Or soon, after a few more minutes with Yael.

"Can I tell you a secret?" Yael says, leaning toward Margot, forearms resting on the bar. Their casual posture is disarming, and Margot can't help but lean in just a little closer.

"What's your secret, Yael?" Her voice comes out huskier than intended. If they're only passing through, what's the harm in flirting a little bit?

"I'm on the run."

Margot fakes a dramatic gasp. "You're a fugitive!"

"I am indeed! I've stolen a horse, in fact." Yael's face lights up—eager, conspiratorial, stunning.

Giddiness rolls through Margot. Maybe it's the ale, or the wine, or the way Yael's eyes have strayed to the strawberry-embroidered neckline of Margot's dress. She shifts in her chair so her knees brush against Yael's calf. "Yael Clauneck, you rogue. I never thought you had it in you."

Yael shifts on their barstool, spreading their legs slightly farther apart, the gesture both intimate and playful. An invitation. A dare. "Then you never really knew me."

Margot's heart trips in her chest.

*Good thing we aren't friends.*

"Of course I know you. You're easier to read than that sign over the bar."

Yael glances up at the hand-chalked sign that spells out the tavern's weekly dishes and ales. "There's all manner of things you'd never guess about me, Margot Greenwillow."

"Like what? What depths are you hiding beneath this absurd waistcoat—" Here, Margot leans closer so her right knee is caged between Yael's thighs. She runs a hand along one of Yael's lapels, not missing how they shiver beneath her touch.

Hunger flares low in her belly. She's absolutely starving for things she shouldn't want.

"'Absurd waistcoat'!" Yael smirks, collecting themself—with effort, it seems. "I'll have you know this coat is bespoke and made by Rastanaya herself."

"Ooooh, so fancy," Margot says, laughing. "Any other secrets to reveal?" She shifts on her stool, the heat of Yael's thighs warming her leg. Now they're so close, Margot glimpses the tiniest of freckles nearly hidden under Yael's lower lip. How had she forgotten about that freckle?

"That I'm a proficient kisser," Yael says matter-of-factly as they lean a little closer.

Margot goes very still. Are they really talking about how good a kisser Yael is? Like two teenagers? Ridiculous.

Yael's hand rests lightly, ever so very lightly, on Margot's knee. She nearly faints.

Reaching out, she grabs for her wineglass. "I might have heard rumors of your talents," she says, wishing she would've just gone home the minute she recognized Yael Clauneck. "But then, I've also heard you once were caught with Sedgewick Wayanette on the boarding school lawn beside a fountain you'd dared him to turn from water to mead."

A laugh bursts out of Yael at that. "All lies, I assure you. Except the kissing part. That's entirely true."

Margot wouldn't doubt it. Yael's, ahem, *reputation* had followed them from the time they were almost teenagers all the way through school. Rumors even floated across the narrow strait from Perpignan to Harrow while they were away.

Before Margot can say more, Clementine appears with Yael's stew, and Margot immediately untangles herself from Yael. The stew is a gloopy brown mix of meat and vegetables, delicious but humbler than they must be used to in Ashaway. Still, Yael cheers as Clementine sets it down.

"I brought you one too," she says, setting a bowl in front of Margot. "Because I'm sure you forgot dinner again, yes?"

Gratefully, Margot accepts the stew, and she and Yael eat in silence for a few moments. When Yael's done, they turn back to Margot, eyes once again full of candlelight and danger.

"Well, now that I'm fed, do you know anywhere I can stay the night?" Yael asks.

The question is laced with so many unspoken ones that Margot has to let out a slow, steadying breath.

It's not that she's given no thought to her love life, or even her sex life, in the last few years, but something about concocting a potion that sends your parents into comas shortly after they've gambled away the entire family fortune on bad investments, combined with the pressure of needing to come up with a potion that saves the village and her greenhouses, does put a damper on things. That, and living full-time in Bloomfield, where the average age of the residents hovers above fifty, give or take a few people who took over their homes and businesses from their parents—like Clementine, whom Margot has known since she was a toddler.

There were a few nights of fun in college, of course—just casual encounters from when Margot and Sage would go to the alehouses in Olde Post. And there was the long-distance thing with Zella, Margot's on-and-mostly-off-again girlfriend during the last year of college, whom she communicated with via sending stones once they graduated. But that hadn't lasted after Zella took a job in Perpignan. There'd also been a tinkerer who came through Bloomfield at the start of last autumn, his wagon full of wares and soft furs. That was a fun evening, but it had been nearly six months since then.

Gods. Six months. Actually, six months and thirteen days exactly, but who was counting?

How has it been six months since Margot touched another person beyond hugging Sage or handing someone a plant?

She looks again at Yael.

*Do you know anywhere I can stay the night?*

She does indeed.

Good thing they aren't friends. Such a wonderful, delightful, deliciously good thing, because tonight, Margot's loneliness is an abyss.

"I have a place in mind," she says, finishing up both her wine and the ale, for courage's sake.

# 5

## YAEL

It's not that Yael's lived a hard life. Quite the opposite. They've spent twenty-three years stumbling through doorways that magically opened for the Clauneck heir. In most cases, magic wasn't even necessary. Wealth and power were a sufficient key, no matter that none of it actually belonged to Yael. But even for them, this is a wild bit of luck. Finding Bloomfield, then finding Margot, and now finding a much better place to sleep than a barstool or a pile of hay in a stable?

Maybe Yael has some secret store of magic in them, after all.

Trotting Sweet Wind back up the lane toward the Greenwillow estate with Margot's arms wrapped around their waist from behind, they feel on top of the world. The stew was excellent. The warm blur of wine has successfully pushed off what promises to be a vicious hangover tomorrow and eased the painful climb back onto a wooden saddle. Between that and Margot leaning closer to speak into their ear, pressing her curves flush against Yael's back, the night no longer seems cold.

"Turn off before the main gate," she tells them. "There's a service gate on the east side of the property that leads right to the cottage."

"Are we visiting Granny Fern first, then?" Yael laughs.

"It's, um, it's where I live now. Just me."

Their stomach sinks. Though they never really knew the woman, they remember Margot's love for her well enough. "Oh. Margot, I'm sorry—"

"Don't," she interrupts, arms clenching tighter around their middle—and probably not with desire. "Let's just . . . let's not talk about real things, all right?"

Maybe Yael should feel insulted. But Margot's just given them permission *not* to admit that they've run away from home on a total whim, with no plans or possessions. So they're happy to spend the rest of the night pretending that ten years haven't passed since they last saw each other, and that nothing bad has happened to either of them.

Margot points out the pathway into the dense trees beyond a simple, mossy wooden gate, propped open unlike the main gate, and Yael steers Sweet Wind through. They arrive at a rough wood picket fence, where they leave the steed, and a garden full of moonlit wildflowers up to Yael's elbows. Even in the dark, Yael can guess why Margot loved this place as a child. Built of the same reddish-brown stone as the manor, the cottage is just one story underneath a steeply pitched thatch roof with a little dormer window—a loft, mayhap. Flowering vines crawl across its façade, smelling better than any expensive perfume bottle on Menorath's boudoir table. Wind chimes jangle in the still-wintry breeze through the trees.

"This is like a fairy tale," Yael marvels as they enter the garden, then trip over what turns out to be a stone birdbath.

Margot catches them, hauling them up by the back of their coat. "Careful. There aren't many healers in Bloomfield. One was in the tavern when we left, if you noticed; that was Astrid by the fire."

"The one who nodded off and dropped her pipe in her lap?"

"Her wife is on a pilgrimage to re-swear her oath to a fish god. Astrid doesn't drink, but lately, she's fallen asleep in the tavern more often than her home. Probably feels too empty."

Yael could ask whether Margot's cottage feels empty, and why on earth she lives here instead of her family's fine manor house, but that would be something *real.* Instead, they spin and stand on tiptoe to face Margot, who still has a hand fisted in their coat. Which makes it easier to draw her in and find her lips in the moonlight, tasting of wine and ale—and, well, stew, as Yael's must also. And if Yael wavers a little in their efforts to stand straight, drunk as they seem to have gotten, Margot's very capable of holding them in place while they kiss. It ought to be surprising; they've never kissed Margot Greenwillow before tonight.

In truth, though, it's only surprising that they never imagined doing so.

"Show me what's inside?" Yael asks when they pull apart, their voice loose and low.

Margot accepts their challenge.

Pushing through the slightly crooked front door, unlocked like the gate, she lights a lamp.

Yael's seen the crowded little timber homes of the poorer districts in Ashaway. For a while, it was fashionable for Auximia students to visit one particular alehouse with sawdusted floors, gaming tables too sticky to make use of, and a retired tin soldier for a barkeep. But Granny Fern's cottage is nothing like what they'd pictured inside those homes. The walls are sturdy, the wood plank ceiling low, the furnishings in the front room clean and cozy. A squashed-looking love seat holds an equally squashed-looking orange cat asleep on the cushion. A stout table is still set with abandoned breakfast dishes, several emptied teacups included. Above the fireplace, with its little pile of wood, there's a woven clothesline with a few shirts and dresses and (gods) underthings pinned to it. The one doorway they can see leads to a tiny kitchen, where herbs and cooking utensils hang on plaster walls hand-painted with tiny blossoms in every color. "This is—"

"Quaint?" Margot finishes for them, no bitterness in her voice, just amusement. She turns away, stopping by the fireplace to pull a log from the small bin beside the hearth. From a tinderbox on the mantel, she pinches out scraps of black cloth and sprinkles them inside the fireplace. She strikes a flint against a curved piece of steel, holds it over the cloth to let the sparks catch, then slowly piles wood on top.

Yael watches, fascinated. They can't recall lighting a fireplace in their entire life.

"My, um . . . the bedroom is up there," Margot says as she works, jerking her chin toward a ladder in the corner of the L-shaped living area.

"Hmm. Bit of a toss-up, whether I'll make it to the top in this state," Yael admits.

"Would you like a ride, then?" Margot asks, apparently back in the spirit of things.

Good.

Yael laughs and shucks off their dress coat. Embarrassingly, it falls to the floorboards in a billow of dust the silk has picked up since Ashaway. They wave a hand through the cloud, grateful that Margot's back is turned to them, and for more than one reason: The generous curves of her silhouette in the low light are truly miraculous. "Is there a washroom I might use first?" Yael asks, kicking their filthy coat behind a chair cobbled out of a barrel.

If they'd paid proper due to their patron, they might've cleaned it with a few muttered words and a flick of the wrist—

a simple enough spell that even Yael can manage, with preparation. But of course they'd prepared nothing before galloping off into the sunset.

"There's an outhouse," Margot answers, "and a well. There's only a pitcher and bowl up in the loft."

Between the late hour and the number of drinks they've consumed, Yael doesn't trust their ability to find the well without falling into it. "Up it is!"

Hand over foot, they drag themself into the loft. Their head is swimming by the time they press their belly over the ledge, so they settle for crawling around a thick feather mattress on a low, wooden bedstead that nearly takes up the whole floor. Short as they are, they probably couldn't stand in here anyway, considering the steeply pitched ceiling. They find a porcelain bowl on a wooden crate in the corner with a matching pitcher beside it. It seems like too much work to do anything but fill the bowl (cold water sloshes out onto the planks, but that's fine) and then stick their whole head into it.

Face and hair still dripping, they crawl back over to the mattress and sprawl onto their back. They'll just rest for a moment while Margot finishes up downstairs, doing whatever people who own cottages must do before bed. There's a knitted blanket that matches her sweater thrown across the sheets—did she make this herself? Can Margot knit blankets *and* light fires?

Yael pulls the blanket over themself, lying back. The last thing they realize before plunging into a dead sleep is this: Whatever the state of her life right now, Margot Greenwillow has grown up, while Yael feels no less a child than they were in that tower nearly ten years ago.

# 6

# MARGOT

Despite her late night, Margot still wakes early. A sparrow chirps from the eaves of the cottage, and wind whispers through Granny Fern's many chimes in the yard with a gentle tinkling that's simply the sound of home. Margot hoists herself onto her elbows, peering out the round loft window as she does every morning. The morning sky is shot through with pink and orange, and the oak leaves from the enormous tree behind the cottage rustle.

She yawns and stretches, shifting on her feather mattress, digging her bare feet into her nest of silk sheets—the one luxury item she managed to steal from Greenwillow Manor before everything was seized and sold off by the bank. Gods, she's tired. A dull pounding fills her head, and her back aches. Surely, she can stay in bed just ten more minutes? Half an hour? An hour even?

Her ankle brushes up against an unfamiliar object. Margot flexes her foot, curling her toes around a lump of blankets or perhaps a lost sock. But no. It's solid and warm. Clearly, another human foot.

Yael's foot.

Margot yanks her own foot away as last night comes back in flashes. The tavern. Sage heading off on her adventure. Ordering one last ale. A stranger sitting beside her, striking up a conversation. That stranger being Yael Clauneck, somehow. And then they had . . . what? Come back to the cottage and . . .

Margot's memory is a little fuzzy after that point. She closes her eyes, feeling Yael's arms wrapped around her waist in the garden, their lips pushed against hers. (The rumors were true: Yael Clauneck is an excellent kisser.) Margot fumbling to open the cottage door. Yael stumbling up to the loft to get cleaned up. Margot slipping out of her garden boots and strawberry dress, hopeful, nervous . . . and then climbing the loft ladder to find Yael deep in the blankets, snoring. Margot tried to sleep in one of the chairs by the fire, but she'd given up after an hour or so of tossing and turning and snuck into the loft, curling up on her own side of the mattress while making sure there was as much distance as possible between her and Yael.

Yael is still snoring softly, the noise nearly lost beneath the birdsong and wind chimes. They're hidden somewhere under Margot's many pillows and quilts, a lump of a human tucked into the back corner of the large mattress, which is how Margot missed them. How could she have forgotten she'd brought Yael Clauneck home last night?

Or, better question: Now that she's remembered, what's she meant to do with them?

She was supposed to have one night of fun. Something quick, easy, and uncomplicated. Margot was supposed to break her incredibly long dry spell, but that hadn't worked out.

*Six months and fourteen days now.*

Should she wake Yael? Tell them to leave? Try to pick up where the two of them left off last night? That would be nice, to kiss passionately as the sun rises. Or to cuddle, or to just be held.

Margot stretches again, reaching for the shape of Yael. She pauses, though, halfway through.

Last night was all about putting off reality, but today there would be questions—*real* things that needed to be asked and answered—and far less liquor to soften it all. Better to get up and leave before Yael wakes. Shifting carefully, Margot swings her bare feet over the loft ladder. With practiced steps, she moves down into the main room of the cottage. She searches through her laundry baskets—*really, she must do laundry today*—and plucks her last clean dress from the clothesline that stretches across the living room. This one is dark green, so it hides the stains of her work, and is embroidered with flowers. Then, sliding the letter from the Claunecks into her pocket—she certainly can't leave it around for Yael to find—she puts on shoes, places a meowing, hungry Harvey into a basket, and slips out of the cottage, having managed not to wake Yael.

Hopefully they'll be gone by the time she comes back for lunch.

🌾

Hours later, Margot returns to the cottage, Harvey at her heels. She pushes the front door open, making dust motes spin in buttery slants of light. The door creaks, but beyond that, quiet fills the small house. Nothing has moved since this morning. Her piled-high dirty-laundry basket is still next to the front door, embers of a fire smolder in the grate, and yesterday morning's teacup rests on the kitchen table.

"Yael?" Margot whispers, her voice loud in the stillness. She closes the cottage door and steps into the living room.

There's no reply. Surely Yael's left by now. There's no sign of their mechanical steed, but then, she wouldn't hear or smell the thing, and in the blur of last night, she can't quite remember where they left it, or if they set it loose to roam. Margot isn't going to check the surrounding woods; that seems wildly un-necessary. It's almost one o'clock, and what grown-ups sleep past seven? Or nine at the latest? Certainly not Margot or any-one in Bloomfield. Most of the village's residents, including Clementine, who works late, are get-up-early souls who gather every morning in the town square, no matter the weather, for coffee and morning gossip or, occasionally, heated debate.

Margot yawns and slips off her boots. She's up the loft ladder in a few seconds, her tired body already dreaming of the mid-day nap she's going to take before returning to work. But she pauses at the top, swearing silently.

There, sitting up and framed by the light coming in through the round window, is Yael. They smile at Margot, looking ador-able and well rested.

"Morning to you," Yael says, giving a huge yawn.

"Hardly morning." Margot can't keep a waspish note from her voice. "It's nearly one."

"Oh! Not surprising at all, given how hungry I am." Yael peers out the window and nods, as if satisfied that the sun is exactly where it needs to be. "I suppose we worked up quite an appetite last night?"

Margot opens and closes her mouth, not quite sure what to say to that. Yael isn't meant to be here. They're meant to be gone, just a strange dream, with no impact on Margot's real life. "You don't remember?" she finally gets out.

"I remember kissing you." A wicked grin curls Yael's lips. "And I remember riding to your house, climbing the lad-der . . ." They run a hand over their face and look up through their long, dark eyelashes, sheepishly. "And then, um, it's a bit of a blur."

"That's because you fell asleep."

"I didn't."

"You were snoring. Loudly."

Yael groans, falling back among the bedding. "I swear, that's just like me."

"So much for your reputation." Margot can't keep a teasing tone out of her voice.

Yael flings a pillow at her, which Margot dodges. It goes sailing out of the loft, landing with a thump in the living room below.

"Let me buy you breakfast or lunch or whatever meal you want," they say, sitting up again, "to restore at least some part of my legend."

"I've already eaten," Margot says, "twice. But I'll make you a cup of tea."

"Or we could skip tea and drink more wine?" Yael's voice is hopeful. "Isn't that the best cure for a hangover? Drinking again? It worked last night."

Margot rolls her eyes and heads down the ladder.

When Yael joins her in the kitchen a few minutes later, she puts a steaming mug of tea in front of them. "Drink this."

"This isn't wine."

"Clearly."

"That was fast." Yael sits down. Their shirt collar (the same shirt from last night) is wet, their hair partially slicked back, as if they attempted to wash but gave up halfway through. Yael is probably used to a heated bath daily. "Though what do I know," they amend. "I've never made tea in my life."

Never made a cup of tea in their life? How Granny Fern would've cackled at that. She had always insisted that Margot learn to perform necessary skills—from making tea to doing laundry, weeding the garden beds, and grinding up dried plants for remedies—despite the protests of Margot's parents. "You might have servants now," Granny Fern would say, "but there's

no guarantee in the future. Best you learn to do for yourself."
And so Margot had. With a little magical help here and there,
of course.

"It does take time for water to boil, but I use spellwork to
make tea," Margot explains.

Yael's eyebrows shoot up in surprise. "Aren't you a plant
witch?"

"Tea is plant-adjacent, and it's a magic kettle."

"Meaning?"

"Meaning water boils the minute I fill it and recite the spell.
Something I picked up years ago. Want to try it?" Margot holds
up a green-and-blue ceramic teapot covered in runes.

Yael looks vaguely terrified at the thought. "I'm not . . .
great . . . with magic."

"Don't you have a fancy degree in something?"

"Animal handling," Yael mutters.

"What? Really?" Margot can't keep the shock from her
voice. Yael has made a point of scooting away from Harvey,
who's roughly the size of a loaf of bread. How in the world do
they manage griffins or manticores?

"No, it was a joke. A terrible one. Which I blame on the
tavern's excellent local wine and my crushing hangover." Yael
blows steam off their tea. "My degree is in law. Arcana and
transmutation law, specifically."

"Of course it is." Margot can't keep the bitterness from her
voice. "Going to work for your parents?" Margot stirs honey
into her own cup of tea and offers Yael the jar.

They take it, not meeting her eye. "That was the plan. Join
the family business, start a family of my own, you know the
drill. What kind of tea is this? It smells delightful."

"Ginger and hibiscus."

Yael groans. "Hibiscus?"

"It's good for hangovers, trust me. Just drink it."

"You're the plant witch." Yael spoons honey into their tea and takes a sip. A small, satisfied noise escapes their lips.

Margot sips her own tea, settling into the chair across from Yael. "So . . ."

"So . . ."

If last night had included a few awkward silences, they're nothing compared with this afternoon. What is she supposed to say to Yael now that they're not flirting and Margot's not recklessly thinking about kissing them again?

She is definitely not thinking about kissing them again.

Yael looks around the cottage, and Margot follows their gaze, her eyes moving over the rough river-stone fireplace, the painting of Granny Fern done by one of her friends that hangs above it, the mismatched armchairs with their stuffing poking out, and Margot's mountain of laundry. Suddenly, it doesn't look humble, charming, beloved. It's dirty, down-at-the-heels, the type of place where rich folk like the Claunecks probably wouldn't let their horses sleep.

"What's your plan, Yael?" Margot asks, setting down her cup of tea more aggressively than she intends. "Why are you really in Bloomfield?"

They exhale slowly. "Well, what I told you last night is true. I did run away—"

"You told me you're a fugitive."

"I *did* steal a mechanical horse. Though I'm certain my parents will pay off the owner, if they haven't already, so it's hardly a real crime."

"I'm sure the owner of the horse might feel otherwise."

Yael shrugs. "Also, I did flee my parents' house with no possessions or plans."

Of course they did. It's the ultimate act of a spoiled child who thinks the world is going to conform to their whims. And they're probably right.

"Can't you just go back?" Margot blows out a long breath, exhaustion and exasperation warring in her.

"I mean, yes, I'm sure I'm expected to, and I intended to when I started out, but now . . . I don't want to." They set their tea down on the table. "What I want is . . . Well, I don't know, except that I want some time to figure it out. What I *need* is a place to stay in the meantime, and a way to pay for it." They look around the cottage.

Oh gods, they can't stay here. But maybe . . .

"I suppose I could just keep going," Yael continues. "Move on to the next town, find a position there. Perhaps somebody out here needs an expert in law."

Maybe . . .

Slowly, the seeds of a plan begin to sprout in Margot's mind.

Somehow, impossibly, Yael Clauneck is drinking tea at Margot's kitchen table, like a gift from the universe. The scion of the very family who snatched up and divided the Greenwillow assets with a brusque efficiency that still takes Margot's breath away. It seems impossible that Yael doesn't know that their parents now own Greenwillow Manor—or at least the Clauneck Company does, which is the same thing—and have been letting it sit empty for the last few years.

The idea in Margot's mind grows tall, bearing fruit.

She looks down at her dirt-stained hands, gripping her mug of tea. Her lower back gives another twinge. She *is* drowning in work at the greenhouses, though realistically, someone like Yael (who doesn't even know how to make tea) would be of little help. Still, that hardly matters, because Yael won't stay in a place like Bloomfield for long no matter what they claim. They'll return to Ashaway in due time—to the social circles they move in and to the people who once dined at her parents' table. People who were perfectly happy to make money investing in her family's company when Granny Fern was in charge.

But if Margot can keep Yael close in the meantime, perhaps they can be helpful in more ways than one. Yael is a direct line back to their parents and would surely be willing to speak for the childhood friend who helped *them*. Perhaps they can convince their parents that Margot is living up to her promised potential and can crack the Natural Caster Potion with just a little more time.

If she's smart about it, perhaps Margot *can* crack the potion, save Bloomfield, and take back everything her parents lost. What other choice does she have?

Certainly, it would be easier done with a Clauneck on her side.

Besides, an extra pair of hands to help haul dirt and pots around won't hurt, nor will having somebody to talk to who isn't a wheelbarrow. "Are you serious about wanting a job?" Margot asks.

Yael nods.

"Then finish your tea. You're coming with me. We'll stop by the bakery on the way."

Yael looks as though this is the best idea they've heard yet, and they flash Margot a grateful grin. Margot returns the smile, ignoring the familiar twist of guilt in her belly. They could both use the help, after all.

Granny Fern taught her how to do everything herself, and that's just what Margot's going to do. Even if it means tricking Yael Clauneck into believing she's so much more than she actually is.

# 7

# YAEL

"This is exquisite," the tailor says, running Yael's coat through his careful, callused fingers. He traces the embellishments along the left cuff: a wispy branch of velvet oak leaves and acorns with caps of actual spun copper. Thank the gods that, on top of everything else, Margot offered to soak the coat for them overnight. Otherwise, the tailor would have the grime of the Queens' Road gathering in his fingerprints right now, and the smell of spilled ale in his nostrils.

"It's a Rastanaya," Yael offers.

The tailor—Arnav, they scramble to remember—looks up at them, his bearded brown face alight with wonder.

It should feel good. The whole point of owning a Rastanaya is to be able to tell people, *It's a Rastanaya,* and watch their opinion of you rise accordingly. Their mother explained this to them when they were still a child while filling their wardrobe with coats and dress shoes, trousers and even stockings. More than Yael could possibly wear to the parties of the season, all made by the designer whose own career the Clauneck Company had invested in decades earlier.

But Arnav's adulation for a piece that Yael might've drunkenly left in the tavern and never missed makes them feel . . . not very good.

"I wouldn't ask much for it," Yael hurries to add.

Arnav's brow wrinkles as he sets the garment gently on the counter, smoothing out the silk. "I'll tell you up front, I couldn't afford its fair price with a year's worth of my shop's profits. We deal in an odd mix of bartered goods, shared village funds, and coinage from folk traveling through."

Yael can work with that. "If you've anything lying around the shop that's a bit more appropriate for a greenhouse than a manor house, I'd be happy to trade."

"Are you sure? There's spellwork in these stitches like I've never seen, a boon to the charms of its wearer, and the sheer artistry—"

"I'm positive."

"Well then, come into my workroom and pick out whatever you like. It's worth that and more for me to be able to study Rastanaya's work. And after that, I have a granddaughter, the light of my life, who'll swoon when I send this to her. That's her portrait on the wall over there. She'll be twelve this summer."

"May she wear it for years to come."

"Mayhap not, but it'll fit her until her birthday, at least. What a party outfit that'll be!"

Yael wrestles a smile into place. "Children do grow so fast."

They leave the tailor's shop with a sack full of sensible clothing. Long-sleeved linen shirts and cuffed cotton trousers; sleeveless work tunics with slitted sides for ease of movement, tied with cloth at the throat; a pair of ankle-high leather boots; a waxed wool coat for rainy days. They choose one nicer outfit—a deep-violet shirt with matching dyed wooden buttons, and a fawn-colored vest and pants—just in case there's somebody they need to impress in this village, or the next. Arnav gives them all of it gladly in exchange for the dress coat, though parting with it hardly bothers Yael at all.

*Of course it doesn't. Not when you have a vast wardrobe at the manor waiting to replace it,* the not-quite-Baremon voice drones, like a wasp that's made its home inside Yael's head.

It seems Yael's patron has *not* forgotten about them as they'd hoped—probably foolishly—that he would.

"It doesn't matter," they insist, standing on the unpaved street outside the tailor's shop, "because I'm not going back to the manor. My parents can give every stitch of my clothing away to whichever twelve-year-olds they like for all I care." Remembering themself and the minor irritation they are to their very powerful patron, they begrudgingly add, "Sir."

The voice doesn't answer.

Maybe that's worse, as though Yael isn't worth arguing with.

❧

When they make it back to the tavern, the breakfast crowd is still in full swing. Yael takes this as a sign of their personal growth. Only two days in Bloomfield, and they're already rising with the working folk. Of which they are now one!

On Yael's first day in the village, Margot brought them back to the tavern to speak with Clementine—a figure they somewhat remembered from the night prior as a halo of pale-blond curls floating above mug after mug of ale. It was Margot who bartered with her for Yael's room and board. Apparently, Clementine had been trying to refuse payment from Margot for years in honor of Granny Fern and Fern's long friendship with Clementine's own grandmother Shelby, the tavern's original owner.

A deal was quickly struck. Margot would give Clementine the first pick of her mushroom crops and would visit the vineyard where grapes for the tavern's good wine were grown; a late-winter frost damaged a number of vines just as they were about to bud, and they required a plant witch's touch. From Clementine's knowing smile, Yael suspected she would've done as much anyway, but perhaps a bargain was easier for Margot Greenwillow to accept than a favor.

Now they wave to Clementine and with a deep bow accept the saucer-sized sweet bun she tosses to them from behind the counter. Her laughter rings in their ears as they climb the staircase to the corridor of rooms above, tearing off a mouthful of cinnamon and candied nuts with their teeth. The bun is already gone and they're licking their fingertips by the time they reach their door. There isn't much waiting for them inside. The bed is little more than a pallet with a mattress and a clean, soft quilt. There's a chest, which their new clothes fit into easily once they've folded them all (or rather, dumped the sack directly into the trunk and smashed it all as flat as possible).

Highly pleased with themself, they cross to the basin and pitcher. A small pile of toiletries sits on the washstand, including a bar of rosemary mint soap from the apothecary that looks and smells like a petit four and would probably sell like a drug in Ashaway. Margot spent the rest of yesterday taking them around Bloomfield to acquire things, bartering and bargaining as they went.

Yael washes the last traces of breakfast from their hands, cleans their teeth, then scrubs their wet fingers through their hair in the little round, speckled mirror hung on the wall. Bracing their palms against the wall planks on either side of the mirror, they give their reflection a rallying pep talk. "If you can steal a mechanical steed and sell your last worldly possession, then you can learn to use gardening shears without stabbing yourself in the leg. You *will* be of use to another person today, Yael."

They might be lying to themself.

Still, the line between believing one's own lies and believing in oneself seems pretty thin, so Yael will take what they can get.

Before they parted ways, Margot gave them directions from the tavern to the greenhouse along the lines of, "Walk out of the tavern and into the town, not toward the trees. Stop before you walk off into the trees on the other side."

It's more than enough. Encircled by the forest that's regrown inside the walls since the outpost was abandoned, the whole village is barely a dozen acres across. There's one main road, which runs from the tavern past the shops and to Granny Fern's greenhouses. Little dirt paths branch off from the road like the roots of a plant, leading to clusters of cottages, the community gardens, the small pastures farther off, and, in the distance, a lake that serves as a water supply and fishing grounds. Everything in Bloomfield seems to have been cobbled from materials available in the moment: native trees with their red-hued wood, bricks that were probably pried out of former military barracks, and stones ripped up from an old parade ground to make way for fields. Some shops are painted with murals to reflect their wares. On the apothecary's façade, a mortar and pestle. On the wall of the weaver's shop, a green field dotted with sheep and a pair of tusked mammoths. (Yael doubts that a shop in Bloomfield can actually claim mammoth wool, but they're not going to be an ass about it.)

Seems strange that Granny Fern built her own greenhouses as far from the gardener's cottage as possible, on opposite ends of the village. But maybe she wanted to walk the whole length of the village every day. Maybe she liked talking to the towns-folk, now greeting and gossiping with one another over mugs of steaming tea. They pause on the road, watching Yael pass.

Yael adjusts their tunic, pulling at the ties of their collar. *Blend,* they command themself. "Lovely morning!" they call out to the baker and the butcher—identifiable by the stains on their respective aprons—as if they belong here too.

It's impossible to mistake the greenhouses when they reach them. Margot described them as "my whole life and a never-ending fuckload of work," and Yael can see why. They'd imag-ined a neat set of cylindrical greenhouses, like the ones packed into Ashaway that nurture exotic plants for ornamental gar-dens, for potions, and for other industrial purposes. Of course, anybody wealthy enough for ornamental gardens has a grounds-keeper to attend them, so Yael has never set foot inside.

Greenwillow Greenhouses, by contrast, are a block of glass-roof buildings of differing structures and shapes, some round or square or octagonal, all interconnected like a crystal beehive.

They find Margot in the entrance to the strange complex, which looks to be the shop proper. She stands at the counter peering into the pot of a large jade plant, its trunk as thick as Yael's wrist.

"Abyssal gnats in the soil," she grumbles as a greeting. "Every spring, it seems we get them overnight, and they've ar-rived ahead of schedule this year."

"Why don't you magic them away? Cast an expulsion spell on them or something?"

She looks at Yael from beneath knitted brows. "Can *you* cast an expulsion spell?"

"Well . . . no." Yael gnaws on their bottom lip. "I'm not actually great with magic."

"You said that, after—" She cuts herself off, flushing pink beneath a streak of soil on her cheek.

"After I woke up in your bed," Yael finishes with a teasing smile.

Her blush deepens. "Speaking of which . . . Yael, we both understand that can't happen again, yes? If we're going to work together, if you're actually going to stay, we won't be repeating what we, um, almost accomplished."

This feels like a tremendous waste to Yael. The few kisses they managed the other night were nice, if a little fuzzy in Yael's memory, and Margot seemed to enjoy them at the time. She hasn't mentioned a partner in Bloomfield, and the gods know Yael doesn't have anyone waiting in Ashaway except for their family, certainly growing more and more furious with them by the day. Past flings, yes. There've been plenty of friends and classmates and fancy strangers they kissed and danced with and tumbled into bed with after a night at the alehouses.

But when the whole world (or at least the whole of Harrow) knows you take nothing seriously, they expect nothing serious from you. So nobody is sitting up at night in their family's mansion, awake yet dreaming of a future with Yael. Or if they are, it's the Clauneck name they dream of, rather than the Clauneck heir.

Apparently, Margot doesn't want the name or the heir. And that's fine; perhaps she too is waiting for something serious.

"Of course," Yael says, fighting to keep the smile on their face. "Never let it be said that I mix business with pleasure."

"Right. Anyway, that's not how expulsion works." Margot hurries to change the subject. "Or it is, but I'd have to cast it on every individual gnat in every individual pot. It gives me a nosebleed just thinking about it." With a grunt of disgust, she shoves the pot away. "I'll teach you how to make honey traps. A couple dozen will take care of the worst of them without magic. But the strawberry plants are the priority at this time of year. Come on, I'll show you."

In the chamber beyond the shop, a round, domed green-house holds rows of shallow clay troughs full to bursting with small, serrated green leaves and delicate white blossoms.

Beneath the troughs, palm-sized bonfires in their own pots burn every few yards, turning the room a subtle pink to match the flames. "We have smokeless kindling to keep them going," Margot explains. "They help keep out fungus and pests; we've had a weevil problem. The plants need watering whenever the soil feels dry a fingertip length below the surface. And I give them food for every phase: the blooming food now, the harvest food in two weeks. In an outdoor strawberry patch, it'd be too early for blossoms, and even in the greenhouse of your average non-magical non-plant-witch, it would take a month or more for the plants to fruit after they flower. But not here. They'll be ready to harvest in half that time, and I'll have the first fresh heartbreak jam of the season." She gazes out across the plants with a deep and obvious pride.

Yael would love to feel that way about . . . well, something. Anything.

"You know, I actually *can* do magic," they say, reaching out to run a finger along a strawberry trough. The clay is pleasantly warm, and the soil too. "Or I could. A little, anyway. It's just that I need to ask the family's, um, *patron*"—they whisper that word still, after all these years—"and I always put that off."

"If all you have to do is ask, then why don't you?" Margot turns to them with curiosity.

They shake the dirt from their hand to rub the back of their neck, already lightly misted with sweat in the hot greenhouse air. "Every warlock's patron is different, but ours requires . . . promises. Bargains. He makes requests and gives us tasks here and there—usually in service of the family business. You know, *send an inquiry to this timber baron, invest in this inventor, take a meeting with this judge's mistress.* That sort of thing. You could say that we're *his* greatest investment. But anyway, a person doesn't really need magic for law, not even arcana and transmutation law. You just need to know how Harrow manages and regulates its magic users. How it stops folk from turning potatoes into gold or gold into potatoes, thereby ruining the market."

"The potato market?"

"I suppose, but also the general market, which is of more concern to the crown and, thus, the Claunecks."

She snorts. "Sounds like a thrilling program."

"Orgasmically so."

Margot covers her mouth—to hide a smile, they think. They hope.

Encouraged, Yael decides to confess, "When I was at Auximia, we always hoped you'd come back to the capital to study, you know."

Crossing her arms, swathed in an oatmeal-colored cardigan already sprinkled with soil, Margot raises an eyebrow. "Who's 'we'?"

"You know, our old crowd."

"Huh. I suppose Sedgewick Wayanette was just dying to have me back."

Yael grins. "All right, *I* was hoping you'd come back. Why didn't you?"

She squints at them as though some message might be scrawled across their face in invisible script that only she can see. "Yael, can I ask . . . why do *you* think my family left the capital? I mean, did you wonder?"

They try very hard to remember any explanation they might've heard—any scraps of gossip going around the city, any conversation between Baremon and Menorath. Alas, Yael's never been great at paying attention to the troubles of others, especially while preoccupied with their own. Maybe they should work on that. "I— Of course I wondered. If you wanted to tell me, I would—"

"Never mind, Yael. That was a very long time ago." She looks down at her hands, where Yael can see the soil deeply engraved in the lines of her palms. Margot lets her long fingers curl closed, and when she looks back up, she doesn't meet their eyes. Instead, she turns and marches forward between the strawberry troughs. "I'll give you the rest of the tour and then show you where that mix is. Also, the cleaning supplies. All of the glass could use a scrubbing so the light can get in, and I never have the time to spare. Keep up, please. The Spring Fair— that's the festival to celebrate the annual opening of the market square in Olde Post—is in two months' time, and I never miss the opening weekend. Even with both of us working, we'll need every moment to prepare."

Closing their mouth around the question they never had the chance to finish asking, Yael follows.

🌿

By the time Yael makes it back to their room at the tavern, the sun has set and every muscle in their body has wilted. At least, it feels that way.

After a tour of the remaining greenhouses—the herb garden and the succulent grotto, the tropical garden and the butterfly garden, the mushroom ring and the perpetually blooming cherry orchard (but *not* Margot's private workshop, the door to which remained closed)—Yael was put to work cleaning dirt and debris and sap from the outside of hundreds of glass panes. Even the chilly morning soon turned warm under the sun, and hauling a bucket of soapy water and a wooden ladder between greenhouses was surely the most physical labor Yael has ever done in a day. Probably the most they've done collectively in a lifetime.

They've earned the dinner waiting for them downstairs in the tavern, but it's all they can do to haul themself up the stairs, peel off their filthy new clothes, and lie naked atop the quilt on their mattress with the cold evening breeze blowing in through their window. Even the pitcher of water on the other side of the room seems miles away, never mind the tub in the bathing chamber down the hall. So they decide to lie here stinking for a bit longer.

If they were in Ashaway, their second day in the office in the Copper Court would just be coming to an end. There would be dinner at the manor afterward, or in town. Drinking with major investors and high-profile customers, talk of partnerships, shipments, and exchange rates over platters of roast pheasant and gingered pears. Concepts Yael barely understands, yet they would be expected to nod along and agree with every awful or tedious opinion, as they've been trained to do. Instead of lying alone in their small room, Yael would be sitting at a table with every seat occupied, pretending *not* to be desperately lonely and lost all the while.

When they think of the alternative, their little room above a tavern feels more like a home already.

# 8

# MARGOT

*Mid-spring*

"Heartbreak-healing strawberry jam requires several in-gredients," Margot says, feeling a little like Granny Fern as she stands beside the bathtub-sized silver cauldron and brazier that are currently taking up nearly half the strawberry room in the Greenwillow Greenhouses. Margot wears Granny Fern's favorite blue apron, and her hair is twisted into two high buns. The smell of strawberries and sugar fills the warm air, delicate and intoxicating, mixing with the scents of earth, leaves, and growing things. Normally, she would make jam in her kitchen at the cottage, but it's too small for Margot, the cauldron, dozens of jam jars, and the baskets and baskets of strawberries she and Yael harvested. (Thanks to Yael's help around the greenhouses over the past two months, Margot was able to turn her full attention to the weevil infestation and was rewarded with one of her best crops yet.) Not to mention Yael themself, who's currently leaning against a table, holding a paper and a quill.

Outside, rain patters against the long glass windows of the greenhouse—now cleaner than they've been in years thanks also to Yael's efforts—and thunder booms far off, like the rumble of laughter in a distant room. Like Granny Fern's laughter, filling up the cottage as she'd sit with friends, playing cards long into the night while a young Margot dozed in the loft.

"Go on." Yael takes a sip of their tea—freshly brewed ginger and hibiscus, which has become their favorite—and nods encouragingly. They look every inch the eager student, which is doing things to Margot's insides, and to her resolve.

Brushing dirt off her apron and all her treacherous thoughts aside, Margot continues. "Of course, we need fresh strawberries and sugar to make them sweeter."

"Fresh strawberries, check." Yael gestures to the bowls of strawberries covering the long wooden tables that stretch the length of the greenhouse. The berries are washed, and their tops have been chopped off. They just need to be mashed and added to the cauldron, but Margot has discovered over the last eight weeks that unless she explains things very carefully to Yael, their flair for improvisation can cause some exciting accidents.

"Once the strawberries and sugar are simmering, we add the juice of exactly nine lemons that've been soaking up moonlight for two weeks."

"What happens if you use lemons that *haven't* been soaking up moonlight?

"The jam doesn't work. Or it does, if all you want is a delicious fruit spread."

Yael opens and closes their mouth, as if they have competing questions, but they settle on: "Why do you need the lemons?"

"They balance the sweetness of the sugar and berries and speak to the sourness that comes with heartbreak. It's a tricky piece of magic, but one Granny Fern figured out years ago. I found the recipe in one of her books and tried it when . . ." Margot trails off as memories of the dark days after Granny Fern's death fill her mind. Which in turn reminds her that the

Claunecks' deadline is creeping steadily closer, only five months away now.

"When did you get your heart broken? Was it by Sedgewick Wayanette? I knew you'd kissed him!"

That makes her laugh. "I swear, there was nothing between us. Ever."

Yael raises an eyebrow.

Margot glares back. "And if there were—which there really wasn't—I'm not going to talk about it now. Especially when there's so much to do."

The Spring Fair in Olde Post is in three days, and since the last of the berries only ripened this morning, and since tomorrow is for gathering supplies and packing, and then it'll take at least a day to get to Olde Post and get settled, they've got to make the jam in the next few hours.

"Suit yourself," Yael says, grinning. "Though if you won't talk about your heartbreak, how about your magic?"

"It's advanced plant magic," Margot relents. "Accomplished by layering will, technique, intention, and perfectly grown ingredients."

Yael whistles, a sound of appreciation that sends pride whipping through Margot. It's been so long since she's had anyone to share the process of making magical remedies with. Her parents didn't care about the craft. Well, they didn't care until it was too late—

"And of course," Yael says, patting the cauldron's belly like it's a giant dog, "we need a pot."

"Cauldron," Margot corrects. "One made of silver and wrought by a witch in my family many generations ago."

"Just so." Yael jots more notes. Already, they look more comfortable in the greenhouse than Margot has ever seen them. There's dirt in the creases of their palms, she notes with satisfaction, and a bit smeared across their forehead. It's adorable.

"Once we add everything in and it's boiling, I'll complete the spellwork that makes the jam curative."

At least, that's what she hopes will happen. Margot is an excellent plant witch; she knows this. But every time she brings out Granny Fern's cauldron and remedy book, her nerves fray and her palms begin to sweat. There's so much at stake—her reputation, her major source of income, other people's broken hearts, and, in a way, Bloomfield itself—and she quite literally can't afford to mess up this batch.

She lets out a long breath, loosening her white-knuckled grip on the wooden spoon.

Yael tosses a berry into the air, catching it in their mouth in one smooth motion. "So, what exactly is my purpose? Am I here for aesthetics? This *is* the most complimentary of my identical tunics, but I can, I don't know, stir things?"

Margot swats at their arm. "You could *not* eat all the berries, for one."

"Relax, Greenwillow. There are nearly a thousand strawberries here. Not even my parents purchase this many for their spring feasts, though hardly anyone consumes those; mostly they're tabletop decor. Still, they ought to have ordered from you."

Margot exhales slowly, surveying the harvest and the empty jars waiting on another table. "We should have enough for at least three dozen jars. Barely. If you stop eating them."

Yael pops another berry into their mouth. "Make me."

Their grin is all wickedness, infectious as root rot. Despite her intention *not* to flirt with Yael, she's unable to resist the smile that curves the edges of her lips.

"You wouldn't want me to make you," she says, slipping her body between Yael and the piles of berries on the table.

"Don't be so sure of that." Yael reaches around Margot, their arm skimming past her waist. In one quick motion, they grab another handful of berries and dance away. Margot lets out a shout and chases after them, running down the aisles between the strawberry troughs, following Yael as she did when they were kids racing through her family's manor.

"Got you," Margot says, grabbing Yael's arm and spinning them around. Yael's back is pressed against the greenhouse glass, their chest heaving a bit from the chase. Unable to stop herself, Margot plants her hands on the window frame behind Yael. Caging them with her arms.

Yael's eyes sparkle with mischief as they gaze up at her. "So you did. Now, what are you going to do with me?"

Desire snakes through Margot, hungry, edged with loneliness, battling against her good sense. As in so many moments during these last eight weeks, Margot finds herself delighted to be near Yael without meaning to. How does Yael do that? How do they turn every tedious task into something fun? Make the work in the greenhouse less of a burden, even as their inexperience adds the occasional complication to Margot's day?

It's not like they're great with pruning or spellwork, but the plants respond to Yael's presence with giddy enthusiasm, just as Margot does. She swears that earlier this week, when she walked into the cherry orchard, the trees were showing off for Yael, waving their branches in a nonexistent breeze, like women dancing to a song only they could hear.

"I'm going to get my berries," she says primly, though she's biting back laughter.

"Oh? These? You want *these* berries?" Not breaking her gaze, Yael lifts a berry, raising it up to Margot's mouth, as if they're going to feed it to her. Then at the last minute, Yael pops the berry into their own mouth.

Roaring in false outrage, Margot plucks another berry from Yael's hand at the same moment they lift it toward their mouth. Margot's fingertips brush their lips instead.

She goes very still, shocked by the softness of Yael's berry-stained lips. Wondering if they'd taste like berries if she pushed her own lips against them.

From the look on Yael's uptilted face, Margot suspects they might be thinking something similar.

She pulls herself together, dropping her arms and turning to the supply table. "Yes, those berries, you awful goblin of a greenhouse assistant. Now, come on. This is yours." She puts a wooden spoon in Yael's hand. "I'll add ingredients, you stir."

"Yes, ma'am," Yael says, popping one more berry in their mouth, which Margot pretends not to see.

Three hours later, the jars are filled with ruby-red jam and have cooled. Each is sealed and capped with pink cloth, a green ribbon tied around its belly, and they're all packed into the straw- and linen-scrap-filled crates they'll take with them to Olde Post. In addition to the jam, Margot is also bringing her best houseplants, some seedlings, and heaps of cut flowers. All of these will be packed into a wagon early tomorrow before they set out for the Spring Fair.

"That was exhausting," Yael says, stretching out their back. Strawberry juice stains their shirt, and their stomach growls audibly as they walk toward the shop door.

"Be glad we only make this much jam once a year." Margot slips a jar into her basket and locks up the greenhouse. "It'll be smaller batches after the Spring Fair."

"I cannot believe you do this by yourself every spring."

Margot shrugs. "It just takes longer. Thank you for your help."

"You can thank me by joining me for an ale at Clementine's."

"I can do that, but first I have to make a stop." She wants

nothing more than to head straight to the tavern and spend the evening laughing with Yael and Clementine and the gathered townsfolk. But as she does every year on the first jam-making day, she's got to drop off one of the jars at the Bloomfield Care Cottage. It never helps her parents, whose ailment unsurprisingly can't be cured by heartbreak magic, but she has to try. Together, they step outside the greenhouse, and Margot inhales. The rain has stopped; twilight paints the sky in soft pinks and grays like cherry blossoms. The air smells of petrichor and the magic that clings to their clothes after jam making.

"Well, I'm in no rush. I'll come with you." Yael slips an arm through Margot's.

"You don't have to do that." She really shouldn't let them. What is Yael going to think when they see the once dazzling Iris Greenwillow and her husband, Welton Sameshoe, reduced to husks dozing in their beds? What if Yael tells their parents about hers? Maybe that would be a good thing, so they might know exactly what they've done to Margot's family . . .

"I want to come," Yael insists. "Besides, dinner will taste better the hungrier I am. So really, you're doing me the favor."

Margot should tell Yael to go on to the tavern. She knows that. But their company has been so nice these past weeks. So comforting. Would it really be so awful to share this truth of her life? All of Bloomfield knows where her parents are, anyway; Yael's bound to find out sooner or later if they stick around, and they haven't left yet.

Whatever the reason, Margot squeezes Yael's elbow, trying to put a thousand things unsaid into the touch. "This way," she says, walking toward the west end of the village.

✄

Margot's parents have been living at the Bloomfield Care Cottage for three years. Not because Margot doesn't want to take care of them, but because she can't. Not at her gardener's cottage, at least. She tried, but there wasn't enough room for the two extra beds, and she didn't have enough money to send them to a place in Ashaway or Olde Post. Luckily Tulip, a lovely middle-aged woman who had grown up with Granny Fern as her mentor when it came to remedies and healing plants, and her daughter Ruby, a healer with a degree from Auximia thanks to Granny Fern, had space for Margot's parents at the Care Cottage.

The Care Cottage is just that: a large, cozy house in the center of town, built for the sick and the older citizens of Bloomfield as they aged. It has ten bedrooms, a large garden, a fishpond, and lots of space for sitting in the sunlight, passing time with friends.

"Hi, Margot!" Tulip calls out, not looking up from the loaf of bread she's kneading as Margot and Yael walk into the round, yellow-and-blue kitchen of the Care Cottage. Tulip has golden-brown skin and long braids wrapped into a bun high on her head. Soup simmers on the stove, and Margot would bet her entire greenhouse that Tulip has woven all sorts of healing enchantments into the bread and soup.

"I brought jam." Margot pulls the jar from her basket.

"And a friend, I see," says Tulip, finally looking up and smiling at Yael. "We've heard you had some help at the greenhouse. We were surprised but pleased!"

Yael makes an elaborate bow. "Yael Clauneck, at your service."

Tulip's eyebrows shoot up at their surname.

"It's a long story," Margot says quickly. "But Yael's assisting me in the greenhouses for a bit."

"For longer than that, if I'm not fired," Yael puts in.

Tulip looks between them again and then holds out a hand for the jar. "I've seen stranger things for sure, especially in

Bloomfield. Thanks for the jam, Daisy. I'll serve some tonight at dinner."

Margot shifts from one foot to the next, a sliver of sadness piercing through her at the sound of Granny Fern's nickname for her on Tulip's lips. "Well, I guess we'll be going . . ."

"There's been no change," Tulip says softly. "But you should look in on them. Just to say hello."

Of course Margot should. She knows it. What kind of daughter doesn't want to look in on her comatose parents?

*One who put them here in the first place.*

"Thanks, Tulip," Margot says, turning away from the kitchen and all its delicious smells.

"Did she call you Daisy?" Yael asks, following. "That's the sweetest thing I've ever heard."

Margot scowls. "It was Granny Fern's nickname for me. Some of the people in Bloomfield still remember it, and I guess I'll always be six in their minds, making daisy chains for the entire village."

"Can I call you Daisy?"

"Never. It's only for friends and family."

Yael looks almost wounded for a moment, putting a hand across their heart. "I will earn the right to call you Daisy."

Margot smirks at that. "We'll see."

They walk through a living room where an elderly couple dances to music from a gramophone and a young woman does a puzzle on her own near the fire.

"This way," Margot says, pulling on Yael's arm. Her heart hammers as they walk up the wide wooden staircase and down the carpeted hall. She raps softly on the third door on the right. No one answers, of course, and she turns the knob and pushes the door open.

As she does every time, she hopes, just for that first moment, that this might be the visit when she finds her parents awake. Smiling. Greeting her as the beloved daughter they've not seen in many years.

That doesn't happen tonight.

"Oh," Yael says softly as they both step into the room.

The bedside lanterns are turned low, and the curtains are still open, letting in the sunset. Margot's parents lie in separate beds facing the windows, covered with thick blue quilts that Margot took from Granny Fern's cottage. The air in the room is fresh, the product of a cleanliness spell Tulip casts every morning to keep things as healthful as possible, especially on mornings when it's too cold or hot or damp to open the windows. There are flowers on the nightstand between the beds, looking a bit wilted, and Margot makes a note to send more over in the morning.

Margot's mother, Iris, is still beautiful, even though her high cheekbones stand out more these days and her skin is as pale as a winter-frosted window. Her long purple hair—now shot through with silver—fans out on her fluffy pillow, and her hands are clasped at her waist. She breathes softly, a wistful smile on her face. Margot's father's cheeks are ruddy beneath his beard, his hair still curling, though it and his beard are salted with more gray these days. Like his wife, he sleeps peacefully with a smile on his face. Whatever they're dreaming, Margot has no idea, but she hopes it's lovely and comforting.

"Hi, Mom. Hi, Dad," Margot says, walking between their beds. Her feet sink into the thick rug, muffling her steps. She can't look at Yael. Doesn't really want them to see this: the true downfall of the Greenwillows. But also, she needs them to see exactly what their family has done to hers, even if they don't realize it. She needs somebody to know. "How are you both tonight?"

As usual, her parents don't reply. Margot brushes a bit of hair from her mother's forehead. Straightens her father's covers.

If Yael weren't here, Margot would pull up a chair and tell her parents about everything going on at the greenhouse. But tonight, she's self-conscious with Yael waiting in the doorway, limned in the soft light from the hall.

"I left some jam with Tulip," Margot whispers, holding her mother's hand. Her skin is papery thin but soft. "Be sure to try it. I think it's our best batch yet."

Regret surges through her as she kisses both her parents on the forehead. It isn't supposed to be like this, and she has to fix it. She *will* fix it. No matter what it takes.

"See you when we get back from Olde Post."

Yael's usually large eyes are huge in their face as Margot carefully closes the door.

"What happened to your parents?" they ask once Margot has said goodbye to Tulip and they're walking back down Bloomfield's main street.

Anger burns through Margot, fierce as the evening wind that pulls her hair out from its braid. Shame and regret chase the anger, and every emotion flares and flickers out as fast as it appears. Margot is left feeling empty, hollowed out, and so very tired.

That her parents are in the Care Cottage is more her fault than Yael's family's, but how can she tell them that?

"It's a long story," she says. "And not one for the end of such an exhausting day. Let's get dinner, and then we have to get to sleep. Tomorrow's going to be another tiring day."

Margot feels Yael's eyes on her. Feels their questions, their pity, their confusion. But they don't say anything, and for that Margot is grateful.

She really is starting to like Yael Clauneck more than she should.

# 9

# YAEL

Despite their best intentions, Margot's house is on fire.

"Fuck fuck fuck . . ." Yael stamps a boot into the flames beginning to lick across the woven rug, regretting every choice that led them here.

Their plan was simple. The next morning—the day before they were set to leave for the Spring Fair—Yael would rise early (really, inhumanly early) and sneak out to the cottage before Margot woke. When Margot came down the loft ladder, she would find Yael at the bottom with breakfast made (or brought over in a parcel from the tavern, at least) and a freshly poured cup of tea. Her jaw would drop at the sight, and Yael would say, *I know there's much to do today, but sit with me for a moment.* They wouldn't bring up Margot's parents, no matter how desperately curious they were, or pressure her to talk about real things. The fact that Margot took Yael along to the Care Cottage at all feels like a kind of trust, fragile as blown glass, and they won't break it by asking questions. The two of them could just sit together, mutually appreciating Yael's thoughtfulness. Yael would even wash the mugs after.

Alas, things didn't go to plan.

"Yael, what the devils!" Margot cries, dropping down the ladder behind them.

"Margot, I—" They cough, swatting through the smoke in the little living room as they manage to snuff out the rug. "Surprise?"

She looks down to where the woven scraps of multicolored wool have been scorched brown. "Thank you?"

"I wanted to make you tea," they explain. "But I couldn't read the spell on the teapot, so I, um, tried to do it the nonmagical way." Because the little bin beside the fireplace was empty, they'd gone out to the woodpile in the garden, gathered an armful, and set it down as silently as possible. They found a tinderbox on the mantel, then copied what they thought they'd seen Margot do: piled the wood in, scattered scraps of char cloth on top, struck the flint against the fire striker, and let the cloth catch. Then they went for the teakettle in the kitchen. When they came back, smoke was puffing into the cottage, and the rug on the rough wood floor beside the fireplace was ablaze.

"Well, next time you break into my home, put the logs farther back in the hearth so the embers don't spit out into the room." Margot frowns at the fireplace.

They nudge a log that's nearly fallen out of the hearth back with the toe of their sooty boot. "I'd hardly call it breaking in when your door wasn't locked."

"It's never had to be, but perhaps I'll rethink."

"I really am sorry. I was trying to . . . I wanted to do a nice thing for you, because . . ." They make the mistake of meeting her eyes, as gray as the last ice to melt in spring, and know she must see the scene at the Care Cottage reflected in theirs.

"Well, thank you," she says again, stiffly, "but I can make my own tea. If you want to be of use, there's a list of supplies we still need before we set out for Olde Post tomorrow, and I've got to head to the greenhouses to pack the wagon, *and* I've yet to begin preparing for the community dinner tonight." She pulls a list from the pocket of her dressing gown . . .

And Yael just now realizes that Margot is wearing a dressing gown loosely tied over a whispery thin, white cotton nightshirt that doesn't quite reach her knees. She rubs one mile-long leg against the other absentmindedly as she reads over her list.

Catching Margot in her nightshirt was never part of their plan, any more than setting the cottage ablaze or proving themself as useless as ever.

Gods.

"Of course I'll get the supplies." Yael tears their eyes away, holding a hand out for the list.

"Great. Just tell the shopkeepers to put it on my account. I'll come around to settle up when we get back from the fair. Ask for help if you don't recognize an item; you don't need to guess." She says this as though they're a child being given an errand to keep them busy, rather than because they can be trusted to complete a crucial task.

Staring down at the ruined rug, Yael can hardly blame her. "This wasn't Granny Fern's, was it?" they dare to ask.

Instead of answering, Margot rests a hand on their shoulder, shaking them lightly. "This was . . . a nice thing to want to do. Wildly unnecessary, of course. Please don't do it again. But still, nice." Her grip on Yael's shoulder tightens momentarily, fingertips twitching, before her hand slips down their arm (perhaps more slowly than needed) then away. "Come to the greenhouses when you're done, and we'll load everything into the cart."

"Right." They clear their throat.

Margot climbs back up the ladder rungs, her long legs gone in a blink, leaving Yael alone in the ashes of their good intentions.

First stop is the bakery, run by a tiny sprout of an old woman named Estelle, where Yael acquires a few loaves of crusty brown bread for their travels, then Yvonne's butchery for a small parcel of dried and cured meat. The nature of the "meat" isn't defined by either Margot or Yvonne. Whether it's sheep or badger or blood hawk or giant toad, Yael doesn't ask. Next, it's Javril the cobbler's, where Yael picks up Margot's only pair of traveling boots, which have needed to be resoled since last spring.

On their way to Marvel's blacksmithery for a replacement hub band for one of the cart wheels, villagers wave and call out to Yael. How quickly things change. Two months ago, they were a stranger in Bloomfield, met with incredulous stares. Now the librarian/bookshop owner stops them to talk about a romance novel he's just gotten in. "It's a story as satisfying as perpetual stew!" Mike raves, promising to bring it to the tavern tonight.

Unbelievably, they've settled into a routine here. Six days out of seven, they wake just before sunrise to the pounding of a broomstick handle on their floor from below—an arrangement they made with Clementine that first day and have regretted every morning since. She knocks when the morning's delivery from the baker arrives, and Yael goes down to have a bite in the tavern—also included in their arrangement, but much preferable to the alarm broom. Then it's off to the greenhouses, arriving after Margot no matter how hastily they devoured a bowl of current and honey porridge or a cinnamon bun. Once there, they begin their list of daily chores:

1. Check the trellises to make sure the vining plants are growing in the right direction, delicately untwining any

tendrils that have coiled where they shouldn't and adding ties as necessary. Yael enjoys this job; guiding the tendrils of a sweet pea plant to curl around the correct pole, like helping a toddler to grip and pull themself upright for the first time.

2. If Margot's spotted any pests, discolored patches, or fungi in the soil on her own morning walk-through, Yael tends to the simpler, non-magical problems, like replacing soil or plucking ordinary, non-magical, squishable bugs from beneath the leaves. Yael does not so much enjoy the bug plucking.

3. Take a midday survey of any fruits, herbs, or petals that seem ready to harvest, but do *not* harvest it themself; they simply make a list for Margot, as Yael is not yet trusted around the plants with a pair of shears.

After that, it's on to whatever tasks Margot has in mind for them that day, from hauling soil to fetching lunch to weeding the path. After work, it's back to the tavern to wash up and then collapse (or collapse and then wash up, depending on the day) until they head downstairs for dinner. Sometimes Margot will already be there, or she'll join them later, but it's never planned. Except for community dinners, that is, which include everyone in Bloomfield.

The gods know Yael has been to banquets. During the social season, it seems the Clauneck estate hosts more dinner parties than private meals. Elaborate, hours-long rituals for exclusive guest lists, involving opulent table settings of handwoven tablecloths (not Clauneck hands, of course), golden candelabras, and exotic fruits in glass pedestal dishes, destined to rot in the bins after serving their decorative purpose. There are up to a dozen courses, all strictly ordered—salads, nuts, soups, cheeses, fishes, meats, greens, and always some sort of magical elixir to combat the latest illness embattling the capital. There's conversation of the most calculated sort, meant to impress and intimidate but never offend. If children are present, they are silent until called upon to recite some practiced speech or song, as Yael and their cousins often were.

Community dinners are another story altogether. Yael has attended a handful so far, one for each of their eight weeks in Bloomfield. To put it generously, these dinners are gentle chaos. Dozens of hands passing dozens of dishes back and forth with no particular order or logic while children dart between their grown-ups' legs. There in the middle of it is Yael, somehow feeling a part of it all, even if they don't understand half of the jokes being tossed about. They've had their hands in the soil that grew the herbs that flavor the dishes, and that seems to be enough for folk who've known one another for a lifetime to treat Yael as one of their own.

Except, perhaps, for Margot.

Clouds gather overhead, and the noontime sun has vanished from the sky by the time Yael completes their errands. They reach the greenhouses just as rain splatters the road around them and duck inside the shopfront. "I've returned—with unspecified meat!" they call out.

No answer from the empty shop.

They shake the raindrops from their hair, then move through to the strawberry chamber, where, shockingly, Margot isn't. Nor is she in the succulent grotto, or butterfly garden, or any of the greenhouses, until the last option left is Margot's workshop. The painted, peeling yellow door is shut, as ever; they've yet to be allowed inside. She claims it's because the room is a mess and one wrong step might send a dozen pots and delicate cuttings tumbling to the floor.

They hesitate, then rap against it with one knuckle. "Margot?"

No answer.

"Daisy?" they try.

A moment later, the door opens, only for Margot to poke her head out through the narrow gap. "Don't call me that. Found everything on the list?" she asks, brushing strands of violet hair that've slipped loose from her braid out of her face. The night-shirt has been replaced with a sensible pale-green work dress.

Yael peers over her shoulder. "You know, if you wanted help to tidy up your workshop, I *did* clean every pane of glass in this complex without breaking any."

"And yet you set my cottage aflame with a teapot."

"I didn't!" they protest. "I never even got to the teapot."

Margot presses her teeth into her bottom lip (whether she's biting back a smile or an insult, Yael can't tell), then says, "Let's just . . . focus on the work. The cart is out by the shed, but we can't pack it in this mess, anyway." She sighs, glancing up at the rain that beats against the glass roof. "Go and mind the shop for now, just in case somebody braves the weather, and I'll meet you there with tea."

Yael perks up. "Ginger hibiscus?"

"Naturally." With a last worried glance, Margot squeezes back inside her workshop, shutting them out once more.

❦

All afternoon, the rain persists, so that Margot and Yael have to dash through it to get to the meeting hall. Community dinners are held on the village green beside the hall, weather permit-ting, but when it isn't, the hall is the only building in Bloom-field large enough to hold its modest population. They scrape their boots against the threshold so as not to track mud and grass inside, then carry in their offerings: stoppered ceramic flagons of mint lemonade, juiced from the lemons left over from jam making, and pouches of herbs picked fresh from the greenhouses. They set them on the rough wood table the full length of a tree trunk, already piled with bread from the bakery, bowls of salad greens and asparagus spears and snow peas from the village garden, foraged fiddleheads, pitchers of ale and wine and water, and steaming meat pies prepared in the tavern with the help of the butcher. Most of the villagers are gathered already, soggy with rain but chatting happily. Poppy and Clementine chat in a cluster with neighbors Kate and Eric as they work together to arrange a motley collection of chairs. The handful of young children in the village dash about, chasing one another around the table, scream-laughing as children do.

Yael pauses to watch, thinking of themself and Margot and their pack when *they* were little. The freedom they didn't have, and the people they all might've become had they lived in Bloomfield. Margot had summers here, at least; perhaps those summers were why she grew up to be the best of all of them.

"There's Javril," Margot says at their side, and Yael lets the memory of the children they'd been fade away again. She waves to Bloomfield's cobbler, who stands across the room. "I've arranged for us to borrow Sunny for the trip, and—"

"Wait, not Sunny!" Yael protests. Javril's stocky, gray-haired cart horse is known for escaping his paddock—really just a mossy, knee-high stone wall—and ranging the length of Bloomfield until somebody leads him back, where he can stand around munching grass until the next jailbreak. "Why don't we take Sweet Wind instead?"

Her lips pucker, perhaps remembering the circumstances of her one and only ride on Sweet Wind. "I don't trust it. I'm not a tinkerer, and I've no idea the spellwork required to keep it going or how to fix it if it breaks on the way."

"What if Sunny slips his lead and gallops off a cliffside while grazing? Can you fix that?"

"Maybe I could." Margot lifts her chin.

Yael wouldn't put it past her; Margot can do almost anything, it seems. Grow an orchard indoors, mend hearts with jam, find room and board and employment for a runaway heir with no practical skills to speak of, boil water . . .

"All right," Yael concedes. "How about we take both? If Sweet Wind throws a shoe halfway to Olde Post—or a bolt—we've still got Sunny to get us there. Hopefully."

"Sunny's never been a problem before," Margot insists, bristling, "and we can't just leave a mechanical steed on the roadside. How will you get back to—" She cuts herself off, but Yael hears the rest of her question anyhow: *How will you get back to Ashaway?*

Overhead, the rain begins to beat even harder against the roof.

"I don't intend to go back." They step closer to be heard over the storm and the surrounding village chatter, close enough to count the faint springtime freckles on the bridge of Margot's nose.

Margot looks away, glancing around them, perhaps anxious that they're being watched. "Not today, you don't. But, Yael, do you really think you can stay away from home forever? I know life here seems easy, but—"

"You think cleaning eight greenhouses in a single day is easy?" They grin. "Not to mention the sheer amount of potting soil that washes off me in the bath each day. I swear it gets *everywhere.*"

"Yes, all right, I just . . ." Margot stammers, flustered, searching for the words. "I mean that you might like your life here now, while all of this is still an adventure to you, but eventually—"

"Isn't it to you? Everything used to be an adventure for Margot Greenwillow."

Emotions shift across her face like the fluttering pages of a book, moving too quickly for Yael to read. "There has to be something you miss about Ashaway," she insists, peering at Yael as though she can see the capital city through the dark window glass of their eyes. "You can't just be perfectly fine with leaving it all behind."

Does she think Yael fled Ashaway lightly, on a whim (fair enough, they did), and so will flee Bloomfield just as lightly? Is Margot actually worried that they'll leave? Promising, if true.

"Whatever I left in Ashaway, it comes with a higher price than I'd pay to get it back," Yael vows over the storm, certain that they mean it. Pretty certain.

Margot blinks down at them, still unreadable.

"We'll leave Sweet Wind here, all right?" Yael surrenders. "Probably a magnet for highwaymen and marauders, anyhow. I'm sure Sunny will be . . . great. It'll be an adventure of a different sort, ey?"

"Yes, right. An adventure." Margot clears her throat and nods sharply, taking several steps back before crossing to Javril. Of course she doesn't believe them.

Fine, then. Yael will just have to prove it on the road to Olde Post. Prove that they can be useful; that they can be serious; that they can succeed at this life. Or if not this *exact* life (because who can promise to remain forever in a place they drunkenly stumbled into two months ago, no matter how lovely the community dinners, and the local wine, and the . . . Margot?), then at least a life of their choosing. Any life but the one that's been picked out for them since birth and never tailored to fit them even as they failed to grow into it.

They are almost completely, deathly certain they can do that.

# 10

# MARGOT

Despite the storms of yesterday, the morning they set out for Olde Post surprises Margot. The sun shines golden and warm, dappling the forest path that winds through a deep ravine. A soft breeze caresses her cheek, and birdsong surrounds the wagon in a curtain of music. Everything is perfectly lovely—except for the mud. The inches-deep, sticky-as-glue mud that is currently slathered on their cart wheels.

"Oh gods," Margot says as their progress grinds to a halt yet again. Sunny snorts, stomping his heels, either unable or unwilling to go a step farther in the muck that's up to his fetlocks.

"Maybe we shouldn't have taken the shortcut?" Yael offers unhelpfully, peering down from the wagon's seat. They've got a flask of tea in hand and biscuit crumbs on their vest. "Or perhaps we should've taken Sweet Wind, after all. Bet it could've gotten through this mud."

"Mechanical horses still get stuck in mud."

"Sweet Wind is a champion among mechanical steeds. Probably."

Margot lets out a very slow breath, counting silently to ten.

She loosens her death grip on Sunny's reins and hops down off the wagon's seat, her boots sinking into the muck. "It wasn't my best idea. But I swear, this has never happened to me here, not even after such a heavy rain. Normally, the canopy keeps this part of the path relatively dry." They'd cut southwest through the forest from Bloomfield to Olde Post rather than spending the extra hours riding west to the Queens' Road, then due south. It really ought to have been quicker, as it's been many times before.

Yael hops down beside her. "Nothing a little plant magic can't fix, right?"

"Mud isn't a plant."

"But it's plant-adjacent, like tea, surely?"

Margot wishes that were the case. "Nope. Mud is just mud." She swipes a hand over one of the wooden cart wheels. The mud clings to her fingers—sticky, dense, and stinking.

Up ahead, the path twists, disappearing behind towering rock faces. Olde Post is only a few miles to the east. Behind them at least a mile back, the Queens' Road waits with its wide stones and straight paths, but between either of those is a muddy morass.

How are they supposed to get out of this?

"Well, we wanted an adventure," Yael says, walking around to pet Sunny on the nose. They pull some sugar cubes from their pocket and feed one to the horse.

Had Margot really wanted that? It had sounded nice enough yesterday evening over community dinner, and again this morning as they set out and the road stretched before them, open and full of possibilities. But now it seems so much less exciting. Like so many other things, it's just a hassle, requiring time and energy and talent she doesn't have.

But maybe Yael's right, and this is a problem that can be solved with magic.

"I have an idea," Margot says, brushing more mud off the cart wheel. In her mind, she flips through the spellbooks she studied in college. And the tomes piled in her workshop. And Granny Fern's remedy book, which she was studying yesterday to give the energy elixir another try. There's something in her notes, something to do with wildflowers . . .

"Is it spreading out a blanket under that pine over there and having a picnic, then a nap?" Yael yawns. "Because sometimes I find problems can solve themselves while I nap for a bit."

"We're not infants," Margot snaps, more bite behind her words than intended. "Now help me clean off these wheels. I'm not sure, but I think they'll need to be free of mud for this to work."

At Margot's direction, they lay long strips of bark Margot whispered off a tree under each of the wheels. She also manages to get Sunny to take one step forward, just enough so the wheels are resting on the bark. Using sticks, Margot and Yael scrape as much mud off the cart wheels as possible. Then they rinse the wheels with water from the small barrel Margot brought along for the journey, and after that, they dry the wheels with packing linens from the crates.

"We're just making more mud." Yael points to the puddle beneath each wedge of bark.

Margot allows herself a small, secret smile. "Trust me on this."

Once they unharness Sunny and lead her out of the way, Margot looks at the wagon, at the ferns and mushrooms growing alongside the path.

"Are you sure this will work?" Yael feeds Sunny another sugar cube.

"If it doesn't, then we're walking the last few miles to Olde Post, carrying the supplies. And possibly Sunny. Now hush, this takes a lot of concentration."

Yael pops a sugar cube in their own mouth and nods. Margot pulls from her pocket a small packet of wildflower seeds that she was going to sell at the fair, emptying the contents into her hand. She closes her eyes, breathing deeply, letting the magic of the trees, the bracken, the woods, the wildflowers fill her.

*Wind through the trees. Water tinkling in a stream somewhere nearby. Air moving all around them in invisible currents. And plants, everywhere, yearning to burst forward into the sunlit spring air.*

She takes another deep breath before her exhale sends the wildflower seeds in her hand tumbling forward into the muddy path. Margot breathes in again, reaching into the well inside her where magic waits. At her urging, the magic rises, and she breathes it into the air as well. It spreads, a purple stream drifting from her fingertips. She can feel it coat the muddy path, and she whispers a spell to the seeds and all the growing things around them.

*Grow, little ones. Make your way into the world. I need you here now.*

The magic flows and flows, and sweat rises on Margot's brow.

*Please make us a path. Please, please, just long enough for us to pass through.*

She knows exactly when the spell takes hold. It's like slipping on ice and then feeling the grip of strong hands catching you and holding you up.

There's a great rustling sound, then a pop. Yael exhales sharply beside Margot, and her eyes fly open.

Where a muddy stretch of road was moments ago, there's now a lavish carpet of dense moss, woven with tiny green plants, and millions of small purple flowers, each of them the exact shade of Margot's hair. The plants and flowers make a living indigo ribbon though the ravine, inviting them forward. Flowers and plants also grow under the bark supporting the wagon wheels, and it now sits on top of the path, steady as if it were resting on the Queens' Road.

Margot lets out a loud whoop—perhaps she does have potential after all, even if she can't make remedies as well as Granny Fern. The noise shatters the stillness of the forest and sends Sunny dancing backward.

"You did it!" Yael crows, pulling Margot into a hug. "Holy shit, you amazing witch! That was the most incredible casting I've ever seen!"

"It's not going to last very long, so we better get going." Margot enjoys the hug for just a second before shrugging out of it and taking Sunny's reins. But exhaustion makes her stumble. "Oh . . ."

"Margot? What's wrong?" Yael reaches out to catch her.

"I've never done that much magic all at once," she says weakly, her voice shaking like her suddenly trembling legs. "Guess I wore myself down."

The color drains from Yael's face. They look around, frantic. "I can do something about this! I will . . . I know . . ."

"You don't need to call your patron or whatever you Claunecks do. Just give me a sugar cube and get the energy potion out of my travel bag." Wearily, Margot points to the green woven bag below the wagon's seat. "I finally got the formula right last night, and it should restore me."

Embarrassment flits across Yael's face, followed by a smile like a sunbreak during a storm. They hand her three sugar cubes. "Of course you have an energy potion. Silly me."

As the wagon trundles out of the woods an hour or so later, Margot is no longer sure she's hungry for adventure. Her back aches from sitting atop the wagon's wooden board seat, and though the energy potion perked her up, she's still weary. Mostly she's just hungry, and her stomach rumbles as the smell of roasted meats wafts toward them.

It's after sunset and torchlight flickers, illuminating the cobbled streets of Olde Post. It's a middle-sized city—far bigger than Bloomfield with its few dozen households, but nothing compared with Ashaway and its social-climbing upper classes. If Olde Post feels like anything, it's *trying*. Trying to be bigger, as its leaning narrow houses multiply with each new addition. Trying to have a good time, with the noise and laughter and twisted-together bodies that tumble out of taverns. Trying to bring in new ideas, with its community magical college and non-magical scholars' havens. And trying to remain true to its roots as a small rural village that has a steadily growing country fair every spring.

The heart of the Spring Fair is the village square in the middle of town, where the market will take place tomorrow, when vendors from outside of Olde Post will open their booths and carts to sell their wares. The celebration always begins the night before, though, and already people of all ages walk the streets eating golden twirls of pastry or cones of chili that make Margot's mouth water. Pipe and fiddle music dances through the air from the stage area, and gaming stalls—ax chucking and archery among them—are already set up and full of customers. These gaming booths open a day early to feed and entertain folk. Margot waves to a few people setting up their booths for tomorrow, then steers the wagon to their assigned spot, a selling space not too far off the main avenue. They've got room for the wagon, their selling table, and a small canopy, which Margot plans to decorate with flowers.

"This is good," Yael says, looking around. "We're going to be absolutely cleaned out by sunset tomorrow, I'd wager."

"That's the goal." Margot clambers off the wagon and helps

the horse back it into place. She'll get Sunny stabled, leaving everything in the wagon packed for tonight, and set up her table first thing Saturday. "Then we can do some supply shopping, rest, and leave when the market closes on Sunday evening."

"Wait. Daisy—"

"Don't call me Daisy," she says—a habit.

"Surely we're friends by now?"

Margot thinks long and hard before relenting. "Fine, just this once."

Yael looks inordinately pleased. "And surely, Daisy, we're not going to leave this place without having some fun?"

Margot blinks at Yael. She isn't here for fun. She's here for selling and restocking and perhaps comparing spell notes with a few fellow plant witches, but that's it.

"You do remember fun?" Yael prods.

"Of course I do."

"Prove it." Yael hops off the wagon and stands, arms crossed. "Prove to me you know how to have fun by coming with me to the fair tonight. I'd even wager I'll be able to beat you at ax chucking."

Margot really should spend the evening checking on the seedlings and rearranging the cut flowers one more time. It needs to be done. Just as something always needs to be done. But the thought of spending that time with Yael instead, exploring somewhere new, is exhilarating. It feels like an adventure in and of itself.

"Fine," she agrees as she unhitches Sunny. "First let's drop our stuff at the inn, and then I'm warning you: I'm a dead shot with an ax, and I'm betting dinner that I'll beat you."

"Prove it," Yael says again as Margot leads the horse away from the wagon and toward the inn.

As it turns out, there's more than just dinner at stake.

"Why don't we have two rooms?" Yael asks as they walk out into the crowds once more. "Not that I'm complaining, but . . ."

Scowling over her shoulder at the Abyssal Chicken, a two-story inn with a wide porch and green-and-white-striped shutters, Margot huffs in annoyance. "I worked out a reservation with them years ago so as not to be crowded out when the fair grew. But this year I forgot . . ."

"That I'd be coming along?" Yael is so decidedly cheerful, Margot can't help but smile. Especially as they stop outside a hat shop next to the inn, where there's an outdoor table set up to take advantage of the extra foot traffic in town, and try on a floppy hat that looks like a giant purple pancake with a feather stuck through it.

"How could I possibly forget that?" Margot makes a face at the hat.

"I am truly unforgettable." Yael sweeps off the hat with an elaborate bow. "Do I need this hat?"

"Decidedly not." Margot giggles.

"I'm getting it, and one for you as well."

Margot starts to protest, but Yael is already handing over money for both the purple hat and a matching green pancake-shaped one for Margot.

"Now," Yael says as they walk away from the hat vendor, "we have matching hats and a wager. Whoever can sink the most axes into that"—Yael points to an ax-throwing booth near an enormous oak tree with a target painted onto its trunk—"wins both dinner and the only bed for the evening."

"Agreed, but I'm not wearing this hat."

Yael frowns. "I insist. I'll let you have the first ax throw."

"Done," Margot says with a laugh as she settles the floppy hat over her braids.

Yael grins back at her as they walk toward an ax-chucking stall.

Three quick rounds of ax flinging fly by—a blur of steel and hefty thwacks as the blades sink into the target fastened to an oak tree. Margot's axes splay out from the center, while all of Yael's are settled firmly near the roots of the tree.

Yael groans as Margot's last ax joins the rest in the middle of the target. "You did warn me you were good at this."

"I did. Now let's find dinner. What do you feel like buying me?"

"Giant spider legs?"

Margot shudders. "Never again. What about a chili cone?"

"I'm not sure I understand the logistics of that exact food."

"Didn't come up much in your parents' kitchens?"

"Nor in Auximia's dining halls, I'm sorry to say."

"Well, you have truly missed out. Follow me. The best food is back this way, near where the artisan booths will open tomorrow morning."

They walk through a maze of stalls that smell like metal and lamp oil. The hum of magical machinery fills the air, louder even than the music from taverns and stages set up around the fair.

"Is that Poppy?" Yael asks, pointing to a familiar face in a booth across the grass lane. "The inventor from Bloomfield?"

"It is! I wasn't sure I'd see her this year."

Margot waves to Poppy, who stands behind a table at her stall, setting it up for tomorrow. Before they can go over to speak with her, a pair of young women, artisans Margot recognizes from previous fairs, approach her table, one of them clutching a broken clock. Poppy waves back and calls out,

"Catch up with you later, hopefully!" and then turns to her colleagues.

"Are there many people from Bloomfield here?" Yael asks
after they've secured two golden waffle cones full of a fragrant,
spicy chili and large tankards of honeyed mead. Yael holds their
cone at a distance, as if the chili will jump out to bite them
rather than the other way around.

Margot shrugs. "Likely some have come to see friends, but
Poppy is the only one I know of who's here selling things. She's
more . . . ambitious than many in Bloomfield. She's lived with
her sister, Dara, for as long as I can remember, but Poppy has
always wanted to travel to the Inventor's Guild in Kingfisher.
Not sure why she's not done it yet . . ."

Her stomach grumbles, and Margot interrupts herself to
take a huge bite of the chili cone. A rush of flavor—garlic, pa-
prika, chili, and something just a hint earthy and magical, like
mushrooms that have been growing at the roots of a willow tree
and picked under a full moon—hits her all at once, and she
groans happily.

"Is it really that good?" Yael stares skeptically at the dripping cone.

"Just trust me, please."

Yael takes a small, tentative bite and then makes an appreciative noise.

"Told you," Margot says, smirking. "Now let's walk. I want
to show you the night-blooming flowers, and there's a band
playing near the lake that I love."

"Lead the way," Yael says through another bite of chili cone.

Happily, Margot does just that.

# 11

# YAEL

On the morning the market opens, Olde Post is busy as a beetle colony. Up even earlier than they would be in Bloomfield, Yael watches the sunrise between bites of a cheese and chive scone and sips of strong black tea. It bursts over the canvas-covered wagons and striped silk tops of the vendors' booths into a gold-and-lilac sky, sparkling diamond-bright off the dew-covered grass. They tip their face up toward the warming light, which does a better job of waking them than the tea. "Margot, come and look at this!"

Behind them in the tent, Margot sets a crate of jam on the counter with a tinkling of glass and a grunt of frustration. "We open in an hour, Yael."

"Sunrise will be over by then!"

"There'll be another tomorrow, fingers crossed. But there won't be another chance to catch this season's opening of the market square. I do a lot of business with the tavern owners and grocers and merchants who show up first thing, and every missed sale hurts the greenhouses for the rest of the year."

Regretfully, Yael drains their mug and stuffs the last half of the scone between their teeth, then turns back to the work at hand. Margot seems particularly anxious this morning. A shame when last night at the fair was such fun: the colorful blur of the crowd, the music of the fiddlers, the fruit tarts and chili cones and glass jugs of honeyed mead, not to mention their ax-throwing competition. Yael suspects that plant magic was involved in Margot's victory—some whispered plea to the moss or the bark still clinging to the outside of the slabs—but they didn't press. It was nice enough to fall asleep in a nest of spare blankets on the floor, listening to another person's breathing in their small room at the Abyssal Chicken. Yael can't say they truly miss any of the socialites or heirs or princelings they tumbled with during their years at Auximia, but it turns out, they've missed that a bit.

Not that Margot is *just* another person.

Anyway, they woke alone, with Margot gone already to the communal washroom down the hall and an ache in their hips from rolling off the blankets and onto the floorboards in the night. Now it's back to business as usual.

"Did you come here when you were little?" Yael asks, lifting a crate of jars out of the cart. Their hips twinge in protest.

"Sometimes, when Granny Fern could steal me from Ashaway." Margot takes the crate from them to set it on the ground beside the tent for sorting. She has a system going. In addition to the jam, there's crate after crate of plants both common and exotic, mundane and magical, with rolled linen packed between the pots to keep them safe for the journey, and narrow-necked water jugs with cut flowers in every color of the rainbow. They'll be sold alone or by the bouquet to anybody hoping to woo a companion at the fair. (*Woo* was Margot's word for it, and she rejected every word Yael countered with.) "But it wasn't so big back then. I like to think Granny helped it grow, as she did Bloomfield; a famous plant witch selling her potions definitely drew people in. And by the time she . . . Well, when I took over a few years ago, it had turned into a real event. Now we're a little fish in a big pond, which is why everything has to be perfect."

"It will be perfect," Yael insists. "You're Margot Greenwillow!"

"Exactly." She rubs a palm across her forehead, frowning down at her own wares. "I'm not Fern Greenwillow. My name doesn't sell products the way hers did. We're not spoken of by the elite and the wealthy the way we once were, and I'm so busy keeping the business afloat, I haven't been able to get it back there. I'm not . . . The merchants don't know or respect me like they did Granny. They know I don't have her gift for potion making."

"Not *yet*," Yael insists. They reach for her but pause just short of laying a hand on Margot's. "But they won't be able to stop talking about you after this week. Not even the so-called elite, who wouldn't know a rose from a . . . a kind of flower that isn't a rose."

For just a moment, Margot's berry-colored lips tug up in a faint smile. "I suppose with you as our barker, we stand a chance."

Yael bows elaborately. "My skills and services are yours, Daisy."

"Stop flattering and start unloading," Margot says, but she struggles and fails to stop a full smile from lighting her face like the sunrise.

❦

By the time the gates of the square open and the first merchants pour down the rows of booths, they're more than ready. Between customers, of which there are a decent number, Margot continues to fuss with their wares and adjust the flowers in the archway. Folk who haven't been to the fair every year might not recognize the young woman behind the counter, but plenty pause when they see the sign for GREENWILLOW REMEDIES AND BLOOMS on the booth. And Yael likes to think they're helping. They stand outside the tent, calling to passersby the way they've heard proper barkers call out to them at fairs and festivals.

Back at Auximia, Yael once piled into Barnabus Silverly's carriage with some friends to attend a sheep-shearing festival in one of the villages just outside Ashaway's walls. They drove into tiny Higley Brook, where the streets were barely wide enough to accommodate their war-camel-drawn carriage. It was a joke, really—something to do when they'd declared themselves bored of the alehouses and art galleries of the capital. So they amused themselves by dropping ridiculous amounts of gold into the villagers' palms for an ear of corn or a hand-knitted cooking pot cozy, though none of them owned a cooking pot. Yael had bought a little glass orb with a stuffed silk goldfish inside, spelled to move as though it were swimming, and to blow occasional bubbles. A child's enchantment, but Yael was genuinely sad to discover it had somehow fallen out of their pocket once they got back to the capital. They'd never had a pet of their own.

Olde Post's Spring Fair is nothing so big as Ashaway's street festivals, with their silk merchant tents full of goods from every kingdom with a port to its name, but it's the closest Yael's come to city life in weeks. And it's *exciting*. Around noon, Yael heads off down the rows to find lunch for them both, and they spend altogether too much time drinking in the sights. On their side of the village square, the booths are staffed by cobblers and leathersmiths, tinkerers and inventors, weavers and glassmakers, blood witches and bone readers, booksmiths and soapmakers. To the west are the livestock stalls and tents, where Margot says that beasts ranging from snarling worgs to snow rabbits are shown and sold. But Yael heads east to the food booths and the lanes full of fairgoers holding roasted potatoes and pickles, pies-on-a-stick, honeyed fruits, and fried giant spider legs.

Yael pauses in their quest to admire a butter sculpture of the royal family of Harrow—the likeness truly isn't bad, given that the butter is starting to sweat and melt under the midday sun—when their blood goes cold as cream. Just beyond the dairy princex's shoulder stands their cousin Araphi.

What in the devils is a Clauneck doing in Olde Post?

Araphi hasn't spotted them yet; their cousin stands arm in arm with one of the younger daughters of Yael's parents' peers (Marisol? Marigold? It hardly matters), both gaping open-mouthed at the booth selling giant spider legs. Perhaps they're here for the same reason Yael and their classmates went to Higley Brook, though it's a much farther journey for the sake of a joke. And truly, the Spring Fair isn't that funny. Not when Yael knows how the cooks and craftsfolk and the artisans from small surrounding villages count on their income from opening weekend year-round.

Though maybe the sheep-shearing festival wasn't funny either, in hindsight. Maybe Yael was just being an ass.

Whatever brought Araphi to Olde Post, Yael isn't about to be seen here. Their cousin is decent enough (for a Clauneck) but still under her parents' thumbs. If Baremon and Menorath find out they were in Olde Post, they mightn't think to look in such a small and faraway place as Bloomfield. But if Yael's presence here were traced back to Margot . . . Well, they would like to keep Margot as far from their family as possible.

The Claunecks have a tendency to salt and burn where they can't purchase and profit.

Ducking low behind the butter royals, Yael makes a beeline down the lane in the opposite direction. They squeeze between a wagon selling frybread and a bright-blue tent with a sign posted for an upcoming oyster-eating contest, spilling out into the next aisle over . . .

Where they find themself face-to-face with Rastanaya.

Quite literally, at that. One of the most sought-after designers in Harrow is of near-equal height to Yael, though the top of her halo-like crown of tight curls far exceeds Yael's hair at its most fluffed up. The pale-purple blossoms studded throughout her curls match her dress—a frosty lavender silk with a tight bodice and a bell-shaped skirt propped up by layers of petticoats, all hemmed at the calf to keep them out of the dust. It perfectly complements her cool, deep-brown skin even as it takes up half the lane. The crowd is forced to flow around this small woman in her forties, like a stream split by a boulder, which might be the whole point. "Sweetheart!" she shrieks, clasping her hands beneath her chin. "You've recovered!"

"I've . . . What?"

"Did your parents pass along my well wishes? I heard you'd taken a horrible fall from one of Oreborn's steeds at his compound and were recovering in the country, but I'm so pleased to see you up and about. And, well, *here*." Rastanaya trails off, probably realizing the unlikeliness of their meeting. She eyes Yael's unadorned violet shirt and plain brown vest and trousers: the finest of the clothes they bought in Bloomfield. "You look . . . at ease."

"Yes, er, the healers thought the country air would be restorative," they're quick to respond; they can guess what's happened. If word is circulating that Yael was injured, it can only have come from Baremon and Menorath, who would've stamped out any rumors that didn't benefit them. This must be the story they've told, rather than facing the shame and scandal of the Clauneck heir galloping off from their own graduation party. "But it's not been nearly so restorative as seeing you, darling."

Rastanaya's plum-painted lips curl into a knowing smile. "Flatterer. Keep going; it will get you everywhere." She holds out an arm and Yael obediently takes it, though the bell skirt prevents them from walking directly side by side.

"Now that we know what *I'm* doing here," Yael says, leading her toward what they hope is the opposite end of the lane from their cousin, "whatever are *you* doing here?"

"I've come with Araphi, would you believe it?"

"I would not!"

"We've just had a fitting for her engagement banquet, but of course you'll know about that."

"Of course."

But Yael did not know. How could the little girl who once swallowed a lightning bug, hoping to glow, be ready to wed? Has she truly fallen in love in the two months that Yael's been gone?

Or was the family so eager to distract from Yael's failures that they turned to their next eldest asset?

"Araphi mentioned her plans to get away from the fuss of wedding planning for the weekend with a friend or two," Rastanaya continues. "Well, I'm in the midst of arranging the debut of my summer collection, and I decided I could do worse than a weekend's adventure for inspiration. Our theme is *the wild places,* you see. I've drawn my aesthetics from those still untamed pockets of Harrow. The Dire Swamp where the bog creepers grow, the forests in the Northlands, the gardens of the fae where even rangers won't tread. And so on. There's no place untamed in Ashaway, so I thought, why not? Alas, there doesn't seem to be a surplus of magic in Olde Post either." She frowns as she looks about. "They say there are fewer natural casters born in Harrow with each generation, and it seems it's true. We've plundered and conquered what we ought to have let grow wild and die wild and grow anew, and now there's little left. Or so they say." Rastanaya waves a hand.

"There's still magic if you know where to look," Yael protests. "There's a natural spellcaster just a few aisles over, at the Greenwillow Greenhouses booth."

"Not Fern?" Rastanaya gasps. "I've based an embroidery pattern or ten on her creations, especially when I was coming up. But I'd heard she passed away years ago, out in the middle of nowhere."

*It was very much somewhere,* Yael wants to object, though it would mean little to Rastanaya. But now Yael's wheels are turning. Because didn't they promise that soon people would recognize and respect the name Margot Greenwillow? And apparently, their parents are more concerned with covering up their absence than tracking them down, anyway. "Not Fern, no, but her granddaughter, an equally talented plant witch. With living creations worthy of your summer collection, I'd wager. If you promise not to tell the world where you heard of her—I'd rather *not* be found by my many admirers until I'm back at peak form, you see—I'll show you."

Rastanaya raises an immaculately shaped brow, brown eyes glittering. "Show me, and I'll keep your secrets. Only I insist you let me dress you once you *are* back at peak form. You look happy, my love, but the rustic look doesn't quite suit your skin tone."

Yael wrinkles their nose and leads the way.

# 12

# MARGOT

Where is Yael?

Margot peers through the clump of customers waiting at her sales table, looking for her missing assistant even as she discusses orchid care with the man in a leather apron in front of her. He's a cobbler, as he's explained three times, but his passion is orchids, as the four orchid tattoos on his forearm attest.

Margot nods, still listening, but her attention is caught by the green silk canopy overarching her table as it flutters in the breeze, twisting the blooms and vines hanging from its support beams.

Margot had some vague idea about decorating the sales tent with fresh flowers, thinking to pull people in and increase sales. But she was imagining something simple and practical, something not-fancy that got the job done. The Spring Fair stall equivalent of her garden boots, not a pair of silk slippers with silver accents. When she mentioned the idea and the shoe comparison to Yael, they laughed and dared her to dream bigger. "Fake it until you make it," they'd cheerfully declared. And so she let her creativity run wild. Now the sales tent is more like a dreamy floral carnival or a woodland ballroom than a fair stall, and it's been pulling people in by the dozens. At the entrance, there's a wooden archway Yael found (or traded for, or charmed out of another merchant?), which Margot wove with honeysuckle, purple wisteria, delicate pink cherry blossoms, blue morning glories, and lush clusters of bougainvillea. The table where Margot stands is at the back of the tent, covered in slim silver buckets full of cut flowers and an artfully arranged basket of strawberry jam. Along the sides, Yael has found (borrowed?) rows of simple wood ladders, and Margot managed to make the pots of flowers cascade down the rungs, their blossoms like a rainbow-colored waterfall running down a hillside. There are small flowering trees and bushes on one side of the booth, which Margot arranged into a miniature forest complete with blankets of moss and mushrooms on small logs. The air is heavy with the scent of blossoms mixing with the smell of the pie-on-a-stick stand just across the grassy lane, along with the goat yard a bit farther on.

It's all exquisite, and Margot is quite pleased with her efforts. Perhaps she should put Yael in charge of something other than window washing; maybe promotion of the greenhouses?

"Hello," a wide-eyed teenage girl says, stepping up to Margot's table and interrupting her thoughts. Her voice is soft, hopeful. "I need something to catch a girl's eye and make her remember me."

"I have just the thing." Margot gathers irises, lilacs, tulips, and foxgloves into a colorful bouquet. "This will get you started." She ties a ribbon around the flower stems. "But the rest is up to you. I suggest talking to her about something she loves, and perhaps also learning her favorite pastry."

This was another one of Granny Fern's traditions—selling custom bouquets and offering a small piece of advice for the buyer.

"Thank you, Ms. Greenwillow." The young woman clutches

the bouquet to her chest. "It's perfect. So much like the one your grandmother made for my father to woo my mother. She keeps the dried bouquet in a vase to this day."

Before Margot can reply, the girl drops some coins into Margot's hand and hurries away, a smile on her lips. Margot smiles too, loving this work of connecting people with the plants she's worked so hard to grow. In the morning's bustle, she feels Granny Fern at her side, gently guiding her, encouraging her, telling her it'll all work out. She really, really hopes it will.

It has to.

Margot turns to the next customer, a gray-haired man in a suit that's far too buttoned up for the Spring Fair, holding a drooping jade plant. As he talks about the challenges of raising a plant that seems constantly on the verge of death by overwatering, underwatering, and one wrong glance, she resumes her search for Yael.

Finally, the crowd shifts as a troupe of musicians threads through the lane playing a merry tune, and Margot sees Yael strolling toward the flower stand. They're confident, grinning, with their arm looped through that of a beautiful middle-aged woman. The woman's extravagant dress is purple as the allium and lavender in a jar in front of Margot, and it looks more suited to a drawing room in Ashaway than the trampled grass lanes of Olde Post's Spring Fair. A spike of something (jealousy? Surely not—why would Margot be jealous? Yael can talk to whomever they want) shoots through Margot at the way Yael inclines their head, whispers, and then laughs along with the woman.

As they approach the entrance to the stall, Yael waves to Margot. She waves back, wondering despite herself what new surprise Yael is bringing into her life. The man with the jade plant moves away, pocketing the bottle of homemade plant food Margot's sold him. The next customer slides into his place, asking for a large bouquet of sunflowers. Before she can gather them, Yael steps behind the sales table, bumping Margot playfully with their hip. The woman in the purple dress stands in front of a waterfall of flowers, one eyebrow raised, her elegant hand outstretched to touch a pale-pink hydrangea blossom.

"Where have you been?" Margot asks. "And where's our lunch?" Suddenly, the smell of the pies across the way is overwhelming, and Margot's scone at dawn feels entirely inadequate.

Yael beams, clasping Margot's wrist for a moment in excitement and then releasing her. "I've done better than lunch. That vision in purple over there is Rastanaya."

The name sounds familiar, like a whisper from a different lifetime, but Margot's head is full of seed prices and bouquet arrangements. It's stuffed with the dozens of plant-related questions she's been answering and the snippets of customers' stories she's been told. For the life of her, she can't place who Rastanaya is or why it matters.

She stares at Yael blankly.

"Rastanaya!" Yael exclaims, still whispering, practically vibrating. "The famous designer! She's looking for inspiration for her summer collection, and I told her all about you. She was keen to meet Fern's granddaughter."

Ahhh, that's why she sounds familiar. Margot looks again at Rastanaya, taking in the unique tailoring and the skillful drape of her dress. She's the embodiment of chic in so many ways, and now Margot remembers that her mother had loved wearing her ballgowns back in that other life.

"I'm sure she doesn't want to see my flowers." Margot smooths a hand over her messy braid and her soil-stained apron.

"Of course she does. She's here for you!"

Margot furrows her brow. It seems more likely that she's here for Yael, but perhaps this is what opportunity looks like: a renowned designer and darling of Ashaway in *her* Spring Fair tent. "Fine. I'll go talk to her. But you have to watch the counter."

Before Yael can agree or Margot can approach, Rastanaya turns, holding a bundle of onyx tulips and eyeing them critically. "Yael, darling, introduce us already. I'm meeting your cousin at the Wilting Bear Tavern soon, but I must know more about these divine blossoms."

Yael bows. "This is—"

"I'm Margot Greenwillow," Margot says, cutting off Yael and offering Rastanaya her hand. "Honored to meet you, sir'ram."

Rastanaya smiles and takes Margot's hand, her smooth palm against Margot's callused one. "No need to be so formal, darling. Yael here was telling me about your exquisite blooms, and I came to see what they were on about. Your grandmother's greatness continues in you!"

Margot can feel her cheeks heating with a blush. If only that were the case. She releases Rastanaya and fiddles with one of the flower buckets in front of her, fighting the urge to reach for the ever-present letter in her pocket.

"You haven't seen anything yet," Yael chimes in. "I wish you could visit the Greenwillow Greenhouses in Bloomfield; that's where Margot's family's estate is. If you think this stall is incredible, the greenhouses will inspire you!"

Margot steps on Yael's foot for complicated reasons she's not entirely sure of. She wants them to hype up her greenhouses, yes, but it feels awful to hear them talk of Greenwillow Manor without knowing the whole truth.

"I'm already inspired." Rastanaya hands Yael the tulips to hold, then lifts a bouquet of plate-sized blue hyacinths to her face, inhaling. "These are decadent. Just the wild extravagance I love to see in nature." She looks upward at the flowers hanging from the ceiling and taps her lip with one polished fingernail. "Yes, imagine it . . ." she murmurs.

Yael rests a hand gently on Margot's lower back. "Go on,"

they urge in a low voice. "Tell her more about your work. Sell her on *you*. Clearly, she's ready to buy!"

Margot can't do that, can she? But how often will someone like Rastanaya stand in her flower stall, waiting to be impressed? Margot has to try.

Her heart races as she steps away from the counter. "Don't give anything away for less than the stated price," she whispers to Yael. "And please, don't offer horticultural advice. Just come ask me if you have any questions."

Yael salutes Margot with Rastanaya's tulips and turns to the customer at the front of the line. Pausing in front of the table, Margot touches one of the tattooed strawberries on her arm for luck and picks up a jar of jam so she has something to give Rastanaya to remember her by.

"Stay with me, Granny Fern," Margot whispers as she walks forward.

"That was incredible!" Margot says for what's got to be the tenth time in the last hour. Her words are a bit sloppy from the bottle of wine she split with Yael, and as they approach the Abyssal Chicken, she does a little happy turn nearly on beat with the fiddle music floating down the street from the fair. It's long after midnight, but the inn is still full of people eating, singing by the fire, and talking to one another at drunken volumes. Margot wants to go up to each of them, pull Rastanaya's perfumed card from her pocket, and tell them the good news: She is going to help with Rastanaya's next collection!

Well, *she* isn't going to help, but her flowers and plants will be the inspiration behind a few late additions among the garments Rastanaya's set to debut just about two months from now, at summer's start. (Margot refuses to contemplate how soon summer will be upon them; it would only bring her crashing back to earth. She wants to float for just a little while longer.) And the amount of money she's paid Margot for nearly half the stock she brought to Olde Post? It makes Margot's head spin more so than the wine.

"*You* were incredible," Yael says. "You charmed Rastanaya entirely."

Margot waves a hand as they walk through the common room of the inn, heading upstairs to their room. "It was all your doing. You may not be able to make tea, Yael Clauneck, but you have an excellent eye for opportunity."

Yael holds one hand over their heart. "And you for flower arranging."

"And me for flower arranging," Margot agrees, because if she hadn't decorated the stall as she had, Rastanaya would've never seen the possibility in her work.

Yael kicks the door closed behind them, and despite the noise drifting up from downstairs and their ebullient, tipsy conversation, it's suddenly too quiet in the room. There's just the sound of their breathing. The one bed. Yael's nest of blankets on the floor.

"Well . . ." Margot says through an enormous yawn.

Yael catches the yawn and stretches as they yawn too. "Well indeed. I'd love to stay up, charm you some more, drink another bottle of wine, but do you want the truth, Daisy?"

"Of course, always the truth," Margot says before she can help herself. The truth is not her custom when it comes to Yael, but no reason to get into that now. Plus, it turns out it's adorable when they call her Daisy. She enjoys that very much after all and has decided not to fight it any longer.

"The truth is, I've never been more exhausted in my life." Yael flops onto their pile of blankets, groaning.

Margot understands. She sits down on the bed, slipping her shoes off. Another yawn overtakes her.

They'd sold through most of their flowers, seedlings, and strawberry jam before sunset, thanks in large part to Rastanaya, and spent the rest of the evening restocking what few wares they had left for their second and last day of selling tomorrow. Since they'd gotten up so early and worked so hard, now—as she's finally sitting still on a comfy bed—Margot's exhaustion crashes down on her. Not bothering to undress, she falls back on the mattress, sinking into the feather pillow. A moan of tired happiness escapes her lips.

"Oh gods, I know it's late spring, but this floor is freezing." Yael pulls more blankets around themself, making the floor creak as they burrow in.

"Get in the bed, then," Margot suggests before she has the chance to stop herself. She shifts over, making room on the side closer to the window. It's the best idea she's had all day, she thinks sleepily.

"Margot Greenwillow, are you trying to seduce me?" Yael's voice is all testing and teasing.

"Perhaps, if I weren't so tired and we weren't such good friends."

"So we *are* friends now?"

"Yes," she admits. "And I don't seduce my friends."

"Why not?"

"Because it never works out." Margot takes two extra pillows and rests them between her half of the bed and Yael's, making a plump, feather-filled barrier between them. "I've seen enough proof from the very small pool of Bloomfield's population who's eligible to date. Dara had to move and build a whole new cottage for her and Poppy when her romance with Genevieve ended, you know. It simply isn't worth it."

Yael slips into bed, propping themself up on one elbow. "I'm not sure I like this rule."

Margot isn't sure she likes it either, but she's in no position to untangle her complicated feelings for Yael tonight. "Let's talk about something else, please. Was it strange to see Rastanaya here, in Olde Post?"

"Very." Yael pauses, and Margot hears a hundred unsaid things in the pause that follows.

"What is it?"

Yael fluffs their pillow, restlessly sitting up and then lying back down again. "It's just . . . well, seeing Rastanaya reminds me of my life in Ashaway, of course. But also, it's my parents."

"What about them?" Margot prompts, unable to keep a note of interest from her voice. The last thing she wants to talk about after such a happy day is the Claunecks, but her curiosity is overpowering. Besides, if she's ever to finish this mysterious remedy they think she's capable of making, eventually she'll have to become . . . reacquainted.

"Apparently, they've told everyone I fell off a mechanical steed while out riding at Oreborn's city compound and was badly hurt. They've said I'm now recovering in the countryside." Yael flings the pillow at the wall between them, causing a minor explosion of feathers. "I suppose I am in the countryside recovering from, well, life in Ashaway. But it seems I'm such an embarrassment to them that they would rather lie to the world than come find me and ask why I ran off in the first place. I should be grateful they've let me be. I've always known I'm not what they expected from an heir, or wanted . . ." Yael's voice breaks on the last word.

Margot feels a surge of compassion. If there's anything in the world she understands, it's not living up to who she's supposed to be. But for Yael, it's different. They haven't got their family's entire future on their shoulders, no matter what they've been made to believe as the Clauneck heir. "Yael. Hear me." Margot lightly rests a hand on their arm. "Your deviation from your parents' expectations of you is not a failure on your part.

It's a failure of imagination on theirs if they can't see you for who you are. And . . . well . . . you're pretty spectacular. Not just at washing windows or wrangling famous people to our fair stall."

Yael looks up at Margot, dark eyes wide. "I . . . that's the nicest thing anyone has ever said to me."

"I'll tell you a secret." It's not the biggest secret of her life, but it's a close one.

"What?" As Yael moves to settle back against the headboard, their shoulder brushes hers, and they seem to take their sweet time shifting away again.

"I've also disappointed my parents."

"Oh." Yael exhales. "Margot, how is that possible? You're so good at everything."

She can't help cracking a smile. "Well, I may not have a fancy degree from Auximia, but I know a few things."

"You know everything, and you're good at *all* of it. Trust me, you're going to be huge, especially after Rastanaya tells everyone about her inspiring visit to the Greenwillow booth. You're amazing, Daisy. Your parents will be so proud of you when they wake up."

The words cut through Margot, the truth of her life and how her parents ended up in a magical sleep warring with the force of her ambitions to save the people and the village she loves. "I don't know about that," she admits. "What if they never wake up?"

"They will." Yael sounds so sure. So fierce.

"But what will they say when they see I've not fixed anything for my family?"

Yael gives her a long, appraising look. They take her hand from where it rests on the mattress beside them, holding it close. "Margot Greenwillow, you hear me. If your parents wouldn't be proud of the life you've built and the people you've helped—

people like yours truly—then that's their mistake. You're allowed to make your own way."

Tears rise at their words. "Thank you," she whispers, overcome, even if it can never be true.

"Of course," Yael says through an enormous yawn. They release Margot's hand, and she misses the contact immediately. "Now I'm going to sleep. This is enough adventure for one day, even for me."

Margot turns away, leaning toward the bedside lamp to blow out the flame. Outside, an owl hoots, and noise from the fair and the inn floats upward. As the moments pass, the bedroom fills with the sound of Yael's steady breathing, their words still dancing through Margot's mind.

*If your parents wouldn't be proud of the life you've built and the people you've helped—people like yours truly—then that's their mistake . . .*

It's perhaps the most freeing thing she's ever heard.

"Yael," she whispers into the dark.

They're quick to reply. "Yes?"

"I'm glad you're here."

And she is. Glad they're in this bed with her, even with the pillows stacked between them and her own rules firmly in place. Glad to finally tell someone at least some small truth about her. Glad to rest here, in the darkness, with the easy companionship of Yael Clauneck, who somehow understands her better than anyone since Granny Fern.

"I wouldn't be anywhere else in the world," Yael says, their voice sleepy but intense.

Margot smiles and pulls the blankets to her chin, fighting herself not to cross the pillow barricade and curl around Yael and just hold on to them until they're both asleep.

# 13

# YAEL

*The end of spring*

In the weeks that pass after their triumphant return from Olde Post, spring blushes toward summer. The community garden flourishes, kale and beets and peas giving way to melons and tomatoes, cucumbers and currants. Yael pitches in with the villagers in their off hours to prune and harvest herbs, berries, and all manner of non-magical but delicious plant life. Beyond Greenwillow Greenhouses, the flowers bloom—none as spectacularly as Margot's, but the grass is splashed with wildflowers and the lilac bushes outside of Clementine's tavern blossom, their strong, sweet scent drifting upward to perfume Yael's room each morning. The wife of Astrid the healer returns from her pilgrimage, and the fish in the pond seem to double in size overnight. They shine in the sun through the tea-brown water as though their scales were polished plate armor.

Not that the countryside is a total paradise. The bugs are devils; during summers in Ashaway, they hang spelled braziers about the city to keep pests away, but not in Bloomfield, where pollinators are a necessity and magical objects few and far between. And then there's Margot and Yael, or the lack thereof.

That night in the Abyssal Chicken, it had seemed as if

things might change between them—or perhaps as if things had been changing all along, the two of them sliding from once-upon-a-time friends to failed lovers, to employee and employer, to proper friends who sometimes wondered how the other would taste (at least, Yael wondered), and perhaps, finally, to something *else.*

But no. Margot doesn't even invite Yael back to her cottage at night, never mind into her bed. And though Yael happily flirts with tourists and travelers passing through Clementine's Tavern (and with Clementine occasionally, and once, Mike the librarian) over a late-night ale and games of chess and knuckle-bone, inevitably, they climb the steps to their room alone. Unlike in Ashaway, there are consequences for dalliances in Bloomfield, where everyone knows the business of everyone. Margot wasn't wrong about that.

It shouldn't matter to Yael that Margot would find out. Really, it shouldn't.

Alas, what Margot thinks of Yael—and whether Margot thinks of Yael at all, and how often—has come to matter. Probably too much, considering how little progress they make after Olde Post. So Yael goes to work in the greenhouses, and goes to bed by themself, and all the while, a new, impossible kind of wanting blooms under Yael's skin like lilac, scenting and coloring everything around them.

⚜

Five weeks after the Spring Fair, Yael is returning from the baker's with a pouch of yeast for Margot's home-brewed cherry cider when they see a rider in Ashaway's courier livery waiting beside a saddled mastiff at the entrance to Greenwillow Greenhouses.

Caught between diving into the bushes that grow along the road or bolting back the way they came, Yael freezes in the middle of the lane. Have their parents tracked them here, after all? Despite her assurances that she would keep her source a secret, did Rastanaya report to Baremon and Menorath immediately upon returning to the capital?

*Oh, Yael. You can't believe you've been that hard to find for anyone who wanted to find you. If anyone had wanted to find you.*

Yael slaps at their own head to rid it of their patron's unwelcome voice, and the movement catches the courier's attention.

"Sir'ram!" the courier hails. "Do you know where I can find . . ." They peer down at the envelope clutched in their riding glove. "Margot Greenwillow? The young woman at the tavern sent me here, but I've been inside the shop, and there's no one there."

Likely, Margot is still busy in the perpetually blooming cherry orchard. A local would've known to wander deeper into the greenhouses or try again later. "I'll take the letter," Yael says, eager for the courier to leave. Whether they're here for Yael or not, nothing good can possibly be coming from Ashaway.

The courier frowns. "I was paid to give this directly to the proprietor of Greenwillow Greenhouses."

"Well, you've found them," Yael says with a bright smile and a quick bow.

The courier eyes them up and down.

Just three and a half months ago, few people would've believed that Yael had worked a day in their life. Those people would've been right. But now Yael stands in the dust in trousers with soil-stained knees, their simple tunic untied in the very late-spring heat. And if they were to run their fingers through their hair, grown nearly to their cheekbones by now, they would probably find a twig or two tangled in the dark strands.

"Very well," the courier says, handing them an envelope nearly as fancy as the ones sent out for Yael's graduation party.

"My thanks, sir'ram." Yael fishes in their trouser pocket for any coins and comes up with two copper denaris and a fistful of cherries, which they'd swiped from the picking baskets in the orchard and were saving for a snack. They drop the whole lot into the courier's waiting palm.

"I— Yes, my thanks to you as well." Awkwardly, the courier tucks the coppers and the cherries into their breast pocket and remounts their steed.

Yael lets out a breath of relief, not turning their back until the mastiff has galloped down the lane and out of sight.

As they expected, they find Margot in the indoor orchard, still sifting through the picking baskets. "Good, you're back," she says without looking up. "Why don't you start coring these cherries? I'd like to get them in the fermenter this afternoon if this batch is going to be ready by the summer festival."

They would much rather be elbow-deep in cherries with Margot, their hands *accidentally* brushing when they plunge them into the same basket, than stand here clutching a message from the capital. Best to get it over with, whatever it is. "You have a letter. It's from Ashaway; a courier gave it to me outside."

Margot turns to them and lifts an eyebrow. "Who would be writing to me?"

Yael shrugs. "A secret admirer?"

"Quite a secret, if so." She takes the envelope, breaking the mulberry-colored wax seal to slide out the parchment.

A familiar seal, now that Yael looks at it, like something they would've seen among their mother's letters—

"It's from Rastanaya," Margot announces. "She . . . gods, she wants to come to Bloomfield!"

"What? What for?"

"Her summer collection," Margot says as she reads, a slight tremble in her voice. "She wants to preview it here for a small, select audience before its debut in Ashaway. She says . . . she wants to use the greenhouse's plants, my plants, as her stage. Something about . . . about the wild places of Harrow, and my work being magical. She'll be here in a matter of weeks, and wants my recommendations for a staging ground . . ."

"*What?*" they ask again. "Margot, let me see." After a moment, they gently pry the letter from her hand, which has gone limp at her side, to read it themself. "This is amazing! Truly, this is just the opportunity Greenwillow Greenhouses needs. This is going to change everything for you!" they cry even as, selfishly, they're not sure they want everything to change.

But instead of looking thrilled as she should, Margot looks utterly panicked. "We can't, Yael. This is impossible. She wants to bring the peers of the realm to *Bloomfield?* They won't come."

"They came for your parents," Yael points out. "Even my parents came out that one summer."

"Sure, to the manor house. But what are we going to do, put Rastanaya and the richest folk in Harrow up in Clementine's Tavern?"

"Why not? I live there. It's good enough for me."

"Well, but . . ." she splutters. "All right, then where will she have the show, in the sheep fields? If the queens' personal bard is gored by one of the mammoths, you think that'll endear me to high society?"

So the weaver *does* have mammoths, after all.

"Why not host it at the manor house, then?" Yael suggests, making a mental note to wander out to the fields north of the town; they've never seen a mammoth up close, not even in Perpignan.

Margot grimaces. "There's no way. Nobody's been inside for three years. I'm sure it's an absolute mess, and anything of value was sold off, the furniture included."

"So? They're not coming for dinner. They're coming to see Rastanaya's work—and yours too. Let her worry about where to put everyone up for the night. She's an icon, so if she tells people that it's the height of fashion to sleep in a potato sack in a hollow tree, they'll probably believe her. All we need to worry about is a staging ground, and why not use your manor?"

"Because it isn't mine, for one."

"All right, maybe it technically belongs to your parents, but I'm sure they'd—"

"It isn't theirs either." She turns on them, squaring her shoulders, which makes Yael want to sink into themself on instinct. But she doesn't tower over them or berate them—of course not, she isn't Baremon—even if she does speak to them slowly, like they're a child who's neglected their lessons. "Why do you *think* I live in the cottage and not the manor house? Why do you think my parents are in the care home instead of cozy in their grand bedroom with a hired private healer?"

"I . . . I suppose I thought you preferred it that way. Though nobody could blame you for needing help, Margot. Everybody does."

"That's not what I meant!" she snaps, snatching back Rastanaya's letter and dropping it to the dirt in disgust. But she takes a deep breath and says simply, "The estate doesn't belong to my parents anymore. It belongs to yours."

There's a terrible sensation rising in Yael's stomach, as though the floor of the greenhouse has fallen away to reveal a whirlpool, and it's about to pull them down. "To mine?" they repeat helplessly.

"Well, to the Clauneck Company, so as good as."

"But . . . how?"

"Soon after Granny Fern died, my parents gambled the fortune they'd inherited on ventures that were meant to expand Greenwillow Remedies—she'd died without a will, you see, so everything had gone to them—but it all went bust. They commissioned adventuring parties to chase down rumors of supposed cure-all plants that only grew in the coldest and most desolate pine forests of Thorn, and the parties came back with nothing time and time again. They bought huge amounts of stock from a so-called plant witch for a strengthening potion that turned out to be mostly fermented yeti piss. Within a year, her remedies business was mostly dismantled, and the manor house was sold off and stripped for anything of value to pay down their debts. But it wasn't enough. So they reached out to the Claunecks to beg for an extension. We all moved into the cottage together, and I *tried* to help them salvage Greenwillow Remedies before . . . before they got sick. And I haven't been able to do it on my own since. So *that,* Yael, is why I live in a cottage. And that is why my parents are in a care home. And that is why I can't throw a fashion show in an estate that should've been my birthright but now belongs to a company that scraped it for parts and abandoned the shell."

By the time Margot finishes, her chest is heaving and her cheeks have gone bright red, and Yael feels a kind of kinship with that hollow shell of a once grand house out in the woods.

Everything is their family's fault.

Margot's quiet country existence, which Yael had envied and thought of as some quaint little storybook life, is simply what's left after the havoc their own family wreaked. This whole time, Yael's fairy tale has been Margot's unhappy ending. They feel numb, and foolish, and despise themself just as much as their family's company for daring to feel sorry for themself.

"Margot, I—I didn't know."

Margot sighs and sags back against the worktable, winding

down from her anger. "I wondered when you first came to town, but I believe you. And I didn't mean to blame you. You aren't your parents, Yael. I know you aren't responsible for their actions. You're just doing the best you can."

It is more gracious than Yael deserves, and in that moment, they decide to be worthy of Margot's grace. "Well." They straighten their tunic as though it's a fine silk suit. "I may not be my parents, but I am their heir, as they keep insisting. The heir to the Clauneck Company and a representative of the bank, as its employee." That Yael has yet to work a single day at the bank (and never intends to) is another technicality. "So, as the heir and representative, I hereby give you permission to use the company's ill-gotten assets. They are at your disposal, as am I." Yael holds out a hand for hers. "You're going to put Green-willow Greenhouses back on the map, Margot, so let's get started."

In truth, the house isn't nearly as bad as Yael thought it would be. The front walkway is overgrown with grass and weeds, and the steps are plastered with forest debris. Climbing ivy has crawled its way up the bricks, which could certainly use a washing. But inside the wide front doors, it's simply dusty and empty. Yael's sneeze echoes wildly around the marble foyer when they enter and stir up dust bunnies, as does Margot's nervous giggle. After that, they walk through the rooms stripped of their fine woven rugs and carved furnishings and collected treasures. Only small piles of useless things remain—a chair badly broken by hasty agents of the bank here, a gray discarded mop there.

"Well, I suppose there's room to fit everyone in," Margot jokes sourly.

Yael is silent beside her, touring the remains of her former life.

They wander from room to room, peeking into what might've been a sitting parlor, the way it's traditionally positioned in the house. On the far end is a pair of stained-glass doors, the pictures of climbing roses and briars lit from without.

"What's through there?" Yael asks.

"My mother's private courtyard. She wanted to throw garden parties out there, though the garden party set would rarely travel so far to see her. I know it disappointed her."

Yael crosses to the doors then looks back to Margot for permission. She shrugs, and they push through.

Out in the courtyard, a set of marble stairs leads down to a small terrace made of the same, heavily scattered with dried leaf litter and dirt. From there, a narrow walkway winds around the garden, though its exact path is hard to trace as it vanishes into shin-high grass dotted with wildflowers. (Or perhaps they're weeds; Yael never can tell the difference.) In raised beds, rosebushes burst from the earth. Years without pruning have left them thick and tangled at ground level, long-dead canes spilling out. Some have overgrown their own beds and matted together. But they're flowering and still beautiful, the blossoms varied among deep wine red, and peach, and pale lemon, and blush pink. An arched trellis in the middle of the courtyard has practically become a private chamber, with tendrils hanging down in a flowering curtain, swaying gently in the breeze.

"This is it," Yael declares, their footsteps echoing off the marble as they take the stairs down to stand amid the lovely mess of it all. "Rastanaya said she wants to evoke the wild places of Harrow, right? The magic we haven't mastered? The show has to happen here. This *is* magical, don't you think?"

"I don't know." Margot glances around the courtyard from the top of the steps, and Yael can tell she's trying to see it as the designer might, or as the peers of Harrow might. "It feels strange. This was my home, at least in the summer. And then for a while before the bank came to claim it. Maybe it never felt exactly like a home, but to let rich and famous people come traipsing through, talking about how ruined and wild it is, like my family manor is some kind of art project or statement piece . . . I just don't know, Yael."

When she puts it like that, it does sound horrible. Yael hurries back up to stand on the step below Margot and slips their hands into hers so she's looking down on them and not the untended garden. "We'll fix it up. *I'll* fix it up. Clear a path from the front entrance to the courtyard. I'll come here after work each day. We'll put your flowers everywhere, and nobody will see what this place *used* to be. They'll only see you, and everything you can do, and how everything you touch grows better because of you."

"Not everything." Margot's eyes turn shadowed in the bright sunlight, and though she presses her lips together to steady them, her chin trembles.

Somehow, Yael has made Margot Greenwillow cry—made the strongest person they know cry—and it feels like the worst thing they've ever done. "I'm sorry, Margot, I shouldn't have pushed. I should've thought . . . Gods, I'm an idiot." *You never do stop to think, Yael.* "Here I am blathering when this is all my family's fault."

"No, it's not. Not all of it. It's . . ." She looks around the courtyard one more time. "There's something I need to tell you. But not here, all right?"

"Anywhere," Yael promises.

She sighs and drops their hand, turning toward the manor's interior, the dark and dusty halls, the empty rooms.

Yael follows Margot up to the second floor, then the familiar stone staircase spiraling up into the tower they stood in ten years ago. It feels smaller than it was, even if Yael hasn't grown much bigger since then. It's empty now too. Of course it is; Margot wouldn't have left her strange prized possessions behind.

She crosses the circular floor and stands at the window with her back to them, looking down on the treetops between the mansion and the town. Her shadowed silhouette against the bright-blue sky outside is an actual work of art, cardigan and all. But this is clearly not the time to say so.

*Be sensitive,* Yael commands themself, stepping on their own foot with the other, grinding the boot heel down on their toes. *Be serious, for once. Do something right.*

It's unnerving how that last part might've been someone else's words echoing in Yael's head. But no, the words are their own.

"This isn't all your family's fault," Margot says again. "A lot of it was, obviously. But my parents made their choices. And your parents didn't put mine in comas in the care home. That . . . that was all me."

"What do you mean?"

Margot turns halfway toward Yael so her profile is outlined in the window as she exhales. It's an ancient sound—somehow decades older than her twenty-two years—and carries more grief than Yael has felt in their entire life.

"It happened a few months after we moved into Granny Fern's cottage," Margot says, staring intently at a patch of wall, "after we were kicked out of the manor house. My parents were a mess—arguing constantly about whose fault it was that they'd lost the fortune, spinning from one scheme to the next, dashing off letters and sendings to old 'friends' who wouldn't write or speak to them. I remember my mother sobbing as they had to sell the last of the jewels and furs they'd smuggled out of the estate." Margot turns to Yael at last, meeting their eyes. "I couldn't stand to be around them, so I fled to the greenhouses as much as I could, sleeping there sometimes. I was trying to help. I thought I could . . . find something in myself that Granny Fern always swore she saw in me. I started messing around, hoping to discover some new remedy that would recapture the world's attention. It was a silly dream, but it was something to do.

"Meanwhile, I didn't know my parents were begging for time by talking me up to the Clauneck Company, claiming I was as powerful a plant witch as Granny Fern, and that I was *this close* to cracking a brand-new remedy they thought would be of particular interest to your family. They swore I was capable of finishing this potion that even Granny Fern hadn't been able to crack."

"What sort of potion?"

Margot hesitates, biting her cheek. "I don't, um, I don't really like to talk about my work in progress until it's ready. Though I don't think it ever will be." She laughs, quick and brutal. "My parents were lying, obviously. I never had Granny Fern's talents. And without investors or the assets my parents had lost, I didn't have her resources. But I was desperate, so I tried to complete her work anyhow. I shouldn't have done that." Margot turns to stare out the window again, fiddling nervously with her braid.

Yael takes a few steps closer. "It sounds like an awful time to live through," they say softly, "but hardly your—"

"One day," Margot cuts in, "I got up before dawn and left the cottage. My parents were sleeping off their night at the tavern—they were always there in those days, and Clementine had to cut them off more than once. That morning, I had a particularly volatile potion brewing, something I thought might crack it at last. I buried myself in my notes and lost track of time; then it was midday and my parents were strolling into the workshop. My mother asked how it was going, and without paying them much mind, I explained my latest theory. When I looked up, she and my father had goblets in their hands."

"Margot . . ."

"I told her not to drink it! That it wasn't ready. I hadn't tested it properly. But my mother . . . gods, she trusted in me, if you can believe that. She thought it was exactly what she and my father needed to get back on track and revive their business. She—she said if it came from me, it was as good as a Granny Fern recipe, and the Claunecks would be thrilled."

"What happened?" Yael hardly dares to ask.

A long silence fills the tower as Margot swipes angrily at the tears gathering on her cheeks. "My parents drank. They went wild over it at first—the way they felt invigorated, the confidence they'd regained all at once. And then they promptly collapsed, and have been asleep for the past three years."

Yael considers this. "That's . . . that's a lot to deal with," they say inadequately.

"It is." Her voice is flat, lifeless. "Their ambitions and my failure were a deadly combination. Or nearly deadly."

"But Margot—and I don't mean to make light of how hard this has been on you—did *you* demolish the empire your grandmother built, or squander the fortune she didn't seem to want, anyway?"

"No, but—"

"And were you truly trying to help your parents with your experiments?"

"Yes, but it doesn't change—"

"And listen, Margot, because this is an important one: Are you, in fact, Iris Greenwillow or Welton Sameshoe in disguise?"

She sniffs, letting out one strangled burst of laughter in the same breath. "No, Yael. Where is this going?"

"Here, where I tell you that you aren't your parents." They repeat her own words back to her, carefully and deliberately. "And you aren't responsible for their actions. You're just doing the best you can."

Margot gives a little sob, slumping forward to rest her forehead on Yael's shoulder, and Yael plants their boots on the floor to support them both. But they want to do more.

They can't give her back what the Claunecks took, but they can give her some part of themselves, at least. Margot's perfectly positioned for Yael to whisper in her ear, "Now that you've told me a secret, it seems only fair that I tell you one. My patron's name, it's . . ."

Perking up, Margot peers at them through tear-clumped lashes but with curiosity in her cool gray eyes. "Yes?"

"It's . . . Clauneck," they confess with a full-body shudder.

Margot's brow furrows. "It's what?"

They clear their throat. "It's *Clauneck.* My family patron is, well, my family. Or my ancestor, anyway. Seems there's some demonic blood way back in the line—way, *way* back, too far to cast with magic of our own—and that's who we beseech. The more prosperous our family, the more our empire grows, the more we spread his name across the kingdoms, quite literally. He gets the worship, even if our clients and admirers aren't *entirely* aware of the nature of the relationship, and we get his patronage and the ability to do spellwork."

"So . . . sort of your great-great-great-great-grandfather is your patron?"

"Yes. But I don't like to call on him. He's not very nice. I hear his voice in my head sometimes—I have since I was a child, as all Claunecks do, or so I assume—usually when I've disappointed him in some significant way. I suppose that run-

ning away from home to become a greenhouse assistant quali-
fies."

For whatever reason, this sends Margot into a fit of hysteri-
cal laughter, until she falls against Yael for support once more.
Only Yael wasn't braced this time. The two of them go tumbling to the tower floor, Margot still cackling. Yael leans back
on their elbows to watch her, their heart swelling even as their
rear end aches from the impact.

"It isn't funny," they giggle.

"It is a little." Margot wipes the tears from her cheeks, flop-
ping over to lie on her back on the floor and gaze up at the
conical rafters of the tower roof.

Lying back, Yael joins her. They decide that they could lie
here next to Margot for hours. For days. For another decade,
happily surviving on strawberry jam while the world spun onward without them. Yael has all the world they need up here,
and Margot Greenwillow has somehow become its core.

# 14

# MARGOT

*The first day of summer*

lmost exactly three weeks after the arrival of Rastanaya's letter, and Margot's almost full confession in the tower of Greenwillow Manor (she couldn't bring herself to tell Yael about the Claunecks' claim on Bloomfield—her parents' last secret, the heaviest burden she bears, and one she doesn't know how to share with anyone, especially with the deadline a mere season away now), she finds herself standing in front of the only mirror in her cottage, fidgeting with the low, low neckline of an absolutely stunning, entirely impractical dress. It's an elegant confection with a shimmery blue-and-purple bell skirt that looks like it's made from starlight-kissed hyacinths, along with a gold-and-purple-corseted bodice that accentuates her curves and plunges deeply, leaving a swath of creamy skin exposed.

Rastanaya, who has been in town for nearly a week to prepare and set up with her entourage, presented both Margot and Yael with gold-wrapped boxes after dinner at the tavern last night. She declared that the manor and Margot's flowering arrangements had "exceeded her wildest whims and most fanciful dreams." Yael had tried desperately to peer inside her box, but

Rastanaya chided them, telling them both to open their gift only when they were alone so that it was a surprise.

Yael is certainly going to be surprised. Whether that's a good thing or not, Margot's not sure. But really, when it comes to Yael Clauneck, there's much she's unsure of, so this feeling is nothing new.

Pushing thoughts of Yael away for the moment, Margot turns, examining herself from all angles. Her purple hair is swept up into a pair of elaborate five-strand braids and pinned into place with her mother's silver combs—another small memento Margot found in her mother's things after she'd slipped into the coma, and that Margot couldn't bring herself to sell. Her tattoos are fully on display, and Margot feels powerful, lovely, and entirely not herself. Perhaps she should wear her garden boots under the dress just so she doesn't get swept into the fantasy of this day? After all, when the guests go home tomorrow and the flowers are cleared from the manor, Margot will be right back to working in the greenhouses with Yael.

She's not even sure about that, though. How will Yael feel seeing all these people from their old life? How will Margot feel? After all, she hasn't seen or been seen in high society for years. What will they think of her now? Her stomach flips at the thought, and she takes a sip of tea—fortified with brandy—leaving a ring of purple lip stain on the edge of the cup.

She's going to be fine. This will be fine. Seeing people from her old life is fine, and if they ask questions about Margot's parents, well . . .

She isn't quite sure what she'll say, but she'll think of something that doesn't involve the truth or the contents of the letter that's now tucked into a box under her mattress. For tonight, at least, she can leave it here. Doesn't she deserve one fantastical day free from it?

A small tinkling sound startles Margot out of her thoughts.

She looks around for the source, expecting to find someone walking through the cottage door, but no. It's just the enchanted compact Sage gave her, resting on the table. It trills again and Margot flicks it open. A message in Sage's handwriting scrawls itself across the mirror glass in silver ink.

*Don't even think about wearing your garden boots today. Or anything with a strawberry on it.*

And then a second later: *I'll be there before the show starts. My horse threw a shoe, and I'm running late.*

Margot still can't believe Sage is coming to the fashion show. To any fashion show, really. It's entirely not her scene, but when she'd messaged Margot a few days ago, fresh off her latest adventure in the Swamplands and suggesting that she come to Bloomfield for a quick visit before the next two-month expedition she had lined up, Margot told her everything. Well, almost everything. She'd told her about Yael Clauneck (Sage swore prolifically when she heard the Clauneck name) and how they'd found their way to Bloomfield. About working in the greenhouses together for the last few months, and how the fashion show was being held at the manor now that Yael had introduced her to Rastanaya. Margot very deliberately did not mention the way that Yael made her laugh. Or the extremely complicated mess of feelings they inspired within her.

Sage promised to be at Rastanaya's show, declaring herself *more than able to sit through a few hours of high-society nonsense in order to meet this Clauneck . . .*

*They're not so bad,* Margot had insisted. *Really. You might even like them.*

*We'll see.* Sage had signed off then, since a fight was breaking out behind her in the tavern.

Margot just hopes Sage doesn't want to fight Yael for some reason. (There are so many reasons Sage might want to fight Yael. Perhaps it'd be best never to leave the two of them alone.)

Margot finds a scrap of paper on which to scribble her reply to Sage: *Don't be late! And don't worry, I'm not wearing anything you've seen before, I promise.*

As she's putting the compact into her dress pocket, a knock sounds on the door. "Margot?" Yael's voice drifts through, eager and tentative all at once.

Margot smiles to herself. Casting a final, satisfied look in the mirror, she flings the door open.

Yael stands out in the garden, wearing their own gift from Rastanaya: a formfitting merlot-red suit embroidered with a pattern of black vines and nearly black plum roses. A single low-placed button holds the jacket closed, revealing the lack of any shirt beneath, just a black swath of fabric across their chest. The suit clings to Yael's narrow hips and accentuates their shoulders in the most delicious way. Their dark hair hangs loose, waving about their face, grown out past their cheekbones after these months in Bloomfield. They hold a bottle of wine and lift it as they start to speak, but their mouth only hinges open as their eyes roam over Margot, something boiling in their gaze.

Unable to stop herself, Margot smirks.

Yael makes a small, helpless noise. "What are you wearing?" they ask, their voice jagged, as if in physical pain.

"Do you like it?" Margot spins, letting her skirt billow into a bell around her waist.

"You are . . ." Yael swallows hard. "It's a very, very good dress."

Margot fights every part of herself that suddenly wants nothing more than to pull Yael Clauneck into her cottage and kiss them.

Where are such thoughts coming from? It has to be the dress. The excitement of the day. Her nerves. Well, that's not all. It's also the way Yael's changed in the last few months, the way Margot feels seen by them. They way they're looking up at Margot right now.

She brushes these thoughts away along with a loose strand of hair. There'll be time to puzzle out her feelings later.

"Let's go," Margot says, offering Yael her arm. "The show starts soon, and I want to see the guests as they arrive at the manor."

Though Rastanaya described the crowd she'd invited as "intimate," there still wouldn't have been room for them all to stay at the tavern. And anyway, the designer wanted her audience's arrival in Bloomfield, passing through its open stone gates and riding into the quiet woods, to be part of the magic of the show. They'd stayed at an inn at a crossroads up the Queens' Road instead. It's probably better that Margot's former peers are seeing her for the first time after all these years, resplendent in a ballgown rather than in her typical work clothes following a day in the greenhouses.

At least Yael likes the dress, and Margot inside it, she thinks with a private smile.

✗

Margot and Yael walk in companionable silence, arms linked as their shoes crunch over the now weed-free gravel path between the cottage and the house.

"Wow," Margot breathes as the house comes into view.

"We did good work," Yael says.

They really have, and Greenwillow Manor is nearly unrecognizable. Well, that's not exactly true. Margot recognizes it, because it looks like it did when her parents had a full staff to help them run it, and not like the run-down shell it's been for the last few years. Thanks to these weeks of Margot's and Yael's efforts, Rastanaya's limitless budget, and the labor of the designer's assistants over the past few days, Margot knows that behind the front doors, the public rooms of the manor have been scrubbed and filled with borrowed furniture. Cut flowers from Margot's greenhouses also decorate the first floor, spilling over in extravagant arrangements that she and Yael have worked on for the last week. There will be waiters moving through the crowds with trays of champagne, as well as a reception afterward in the house.

Rastanaya's preview show is called *Wild Places at Gloaming,* and, fittingly, it starts at sunset. It's evening now, and the sun is already painting the horizon pink and orange. Flickering torches line the manor's driveway. People in outfits as lavish as Margot's and Yael's gather in clumps outside the manor, leaving their carriages, horses, and other exotic mounts parked in front of the house. Two women in glittering silver and blue dresses, respectively, climb out of separate carriages and meet by the front door, kissing each other's cheeks and exclaiming loudly. More guests join them as they arrive, a few whom Margot recognizes as her parents' former friends, and her stomach lurches. Can she really do this? It's too late to be asking that question, but the sight of all these people sends fear snaking through her.

"Can we go in through the garden door?" Margot grips Yael's hand. Suddenly, her corset is too tight. Her mouth is too dry. All she wants is to flee back to the gardener's cottage.

They squeeze her hand back. "Of course."

Avoiding the crowds, Margot and Yael dart through a side corridor of the manor to leave through a servants' entrance rather than the main stairway. They slip through a break in the hedges, and Margot relaxes as the garden comes into view.

She really has outdone herself this time.

As per Rastanaya's instructions, the fashion show will take place along the marble path under the arched trellis that stretches from the terrace at the back of the house to the fountain at the southern end of the garden. Rastanaya asked Margot not to clean up any of the overgrown garden beds, but Margot couldn't help herself. She pruned a few of the wild roses, though they still sprawl, and she cleared the soil and debris out of the garden fountain and got it running again. She also wove small, glittering lights through the tree canopy—they're powered by a simple spell that Clementine taught her to keep candles burning all evening—and she used her own magic to convince the neglected jasmine that grows along the garden trellises to flower. Its scent wafts across the garden, filling the night with perfume.

"This looks astonishing," Yael says. "You really are a genius, Margot Greenwillow."

She laughs and takes a flute of champagne from a passing waiter. "I couldn't have done any of this if you hadn't been helping in the greenhouses."

"I think we might be an amazing team."

"I think you might be right."

Yael clinks their own glass of champagne against Margot's, and they walk toward the runway.

Rastanaya's team has set chairs along both sides of the garden path, and people are already taking their seats. The terrace at the back of the house is also full of fashionable people who look vaguely familiar to Margot, though she doesn't recognize anyone. Also on the terrace is a small band of fiddlers, lutists, and horn players—something more suited to Clementine's Tavern than a fashion show for Ashaway's elite—and they play a rowdy tune. Rastanaya stands at the top of the terrace steps, wearing a stunning green dress and a tall, magical vining headpiece that Margot created for her, the vines braiding and shifting and rebraiding themselves atop her curls. She greets her guests as they appear outside, like a queen holding court. For a moment, Margot sees a vision of her mother, standing in much the same way on the terrace and presiding over a party full of her friends. Iris Greenwillow would love to know that all of these guests who merited an exclusive invitation from Rastanaya were here, exclaiming over her gardens.

*Except they're not her gardens any longer, are they?*

"Where should we sit?" Margot wrenches her gaze away from the terrace as she and Yael pause at the end of the runway, standing near enough to the tinkling fountain that a few drops of water splash onto them.

"Rastanaya told me we have seats in the front row." Yael points to a set of open chairs draped in garlands of ivy so that they appear to be growing out of the ground beneath them.

"Up front?" Margot squeaks out. "Where everyone can see us?" She'd imagined they'd be tucked away, like the rest of the designer's assistants, somewhere they could watch the show without being watched.

"It would be a waste if I was the only one to see you in that dress."

Before Margot can reply, a loud, high-pitched voice calls out from the terrace. "Yael? Yael, is that you?"

"Oh no," Yael mutters, dropping Margot's hand as they look up. They take a long swig of champagne.

A tall, elegant young woman hurries toward them. Black ringlets hang over her pale shoulders, above the severely cut neckline of a red dress woven with dark floral motifs. A silver corset accentuates her narrow waist, and an enormous ruby necklace sits like a duck's egg in a nest at the base of her throat. Everything about her screams money and power.

"Who's that?" Margot asks, taking a fortifying sip of her own champagne.

"My cousin Araphi Clauneck. You won't have seen her since she was a child, and too young to run with us at parties. She's—"

Before Yael can reveal what Araphi is, she's standing in front of them, beaming. With another squeal of delight, she pulls Yael into a hug.

"Yael! You evil thing!" she gushes. "Where've you been hiding? I've heard the most surprising rumors about you!"

Yael shrugs, making a noncommittal noise. "Well, you know me, Phi; I'm sure every one of them is true."

She barrels on, tugging one of Yael's lapels. "Have you missed us terribly? Rastanaya told me she saw you at that sweet little fair in Olde Post. We must have just missed each other, can you believe it? Have you been bored out here in the country, all cooped up recovering?"

Something about the coy smile dancing across her painted lips plants a seed of doubt in Margot's mind. Does Araphi know more about Yael's exit from society than she's letting on?

But before Margot can wonder further, Yael replies with a coy smirk of their own. "I take it you haven't been bored without *me,* what with all the wedding preparations, hmm? I hear congratulations are in order."

Araphi's dark, sparkling eyes seem to dim a bit, her lips pressing flat. But the change in her expression passes quickly as she turns to smile brightly at Margot, and she presses a hand to her corset, above her heart. "And who's this vision?" Araphi exclaims. "What a treat you are in this dress! Clearly another Rastanaya creation, and you wear it beautifully, but I'm sorry I don't know your name."

"I'm Margot Greenwillow," Margot says quickly, as Yael is too busy swallowing champagne to introduce her. "I . . . well . . . I set up the gardens for Rastanaya's show."

Margot can feel Yael giving her an exasperated look, implying that she's so much more, but what else is she supposed to say? That they're standing in the very spot where Granny Fern taught her the importance of soaking oak leaves overnight when making a poultice to cure a lack of insight? Or that she actually does remember Araphi from a party long ago, when Margot and Yael were kids, and Araphi seemed so much younger than they were? And now she's grown and seemingly thriving among the Claunecks.

"Greenwillow?" Araphi says, her forehead wrinkling. "As in *the* Greenwillow Manor Greenwillows? I thought . . . I had heard—"

Thankfully, Araphi is interrupted (and Margot is saved) by the arrival of Sage bounding down the terrace steps. Of course she's not wearing anything by Rastanaya, and her simple leather pants, her half-laced tunic, and the shortsword belted at her hip cause quite a stir. Margot can hear the fine people of Ashaway whispering about her friend, even over the strange band's music.

"Am I glad to see you," Margot whispers as Sage lopes over and opens her arms for a hug.

"Wouldn't miss it for the world," Sage says, squeezing her for a moment and then releasing her. She takes two flutes of champagne from the nearest waiter and polishes them both off in a few seconds.

Yael makes an appreciative noise at Sage's drinking prowess, and Sage glares in their direction, narrowing her eyes. "You must be Yael."

Yael bows. "And you're Sage."

At the same time, they say, "I've heard so much about you," which makes both of them turn toward Margot.

Her cheeks heat. Really, *must they* have met tonight? What was she thinking, inviting Sage to Rastanaya's show, thrusting Sage and Yael together in full view of the public?

"And I'm Araphi," Yael's cousin says, stepping forward. She raises one eyebrow at Sage, appraising her, then smiles wickedly. "I like your sword." There's a gleam in her eye that makes Margot feel a sliver of pity for her friend. She never has been able to resist beautiful women in any context, and—engaged or not—Araphi looks like she'd like to have Sage for breakfast.

Of course, she should've expected that Sage was more than up for the challenge, and her friend steps forward to take the hand Araphi offers. "It's a very sharp sword," Sage says, in a tone that brooks no confusion about where the two of them might have ended up after the fashion show, were both of them free.

Araphi's gaze darkens, but before she can say anything else, the music stops. Rastanaya claps her hands and announces that they should take their seats, as the show is starting.

Margot loses track of Sage as she and Yael find their chairs and the crowd settles. Then, right as the sun sets and the first stars come out against the navy-and-purple sky, an exquisite-looking person with pansies sewn throughout their reddish-brown braids walks in one of Rastanaya's magnificent summer dresses down Margot's former terrace stairs.

⚘

The show is divine. Models in dresses, suits, and cloaks stroll beneath the oak tunnel, their outfits embellished with heavy floral textiles that match the gardens, or woven twigs and leaves that make the wearer seem like a forest creature walking the runway, or other variations on the theme of wild places at gloaming. They are dazzling and mysterious. Margot's head spins from the three (five? six?) glasses of champagne she's had, and much to her surprise, at the close of the show, Rastanaya pauses at the end of the runway to hold out a hand in Margot's direction.

"None of this," Rastanaya says, "would be possible without the sublime Margot Greenwillow, who not only inspired me with her flowers and plants when we first met in Olde Post but also generously lent us use of her family's estate and made the garden so very magical. Please, Margot, take a bow."

Margot freezes. It's not her family's estate, and claiming it seems like tempting fate. Should she correct Rastanaya? Or sprint away to hide behind the closest tree?

Yael gives her a little shove, and Margot stands. Sage lets out a loud, earsplitting whistle as Margot bows and the crowd explodes with applause. Rastanaya blows her a kiss, and then, as she turns to walk away, it's all over.

The next half hour is a blur of people coming up to Margot, introducing themselves (some of them pretending it's for the first time), telling her she "simply must come visit them the next time she's in Ashaway," and asking for her to decorate their next party. Sage says goodbye—she's riding through the night to meet up with another adventurer staying in Olde Post—though not without casting Araphi one last, sizzling look.

"Perhaps you're right about this particular Clauneck," Sage says to Margot before she goes. "They are rather glamorous, and I love seeing you happy."

"I'm not *that* happy."

"You're glowing, friend. Especially when Yael's around."

Margot glances toward Yael, who stands a few feet away talking with Araphi and Rastanaya. Her cheeks heat as Yael's eyes find hers for a moment.

"Maybe I'm a little happy," she concedes.

"Just be careful," Sage says.

"I will, I promise."

But the truth is, as Margot's eyes linger on Yael, she's feeling anything but careful.

She snags their hand a few minutes later as they walk toward a waiter with a tray of drinks. "Save me," Margot mouths, nodding toward the pair of women who've held her hostage with their compliments on the garden and questions about her parents—all of which she's deflected with a quick, "They're traveling, of course, it's so lovely this time of year!"

Yael grins. "Gladly."

With apologies, they slip away from the oak-lined garden path. They skirt the party on the terrace hand in hand, then stumble into the shadows at the back of the garden now that night has truly fallen. Yael laughs as they leap over a miniature rhododendron shrub together, and the sound makes Margot's heart race.

She wants to kiss Yael so badly she can barely think.

Yael Clauneck, whom she's wanted to kiss since she was old enough to know what it meant to want to kiss someone. Yael Clauneck, whom she should really hate, but whom she likes entirely too much.

Yael Clauneck, who looked at her with wonder long before this triumph of a show.

Margot takes a ragged breath, pausing.

"Daisy," Yael says, stopping beside a towering hedge. "What is it?"

Yael Clauneck, who's friend enough to call her Daisy but also someone she's ready to break all her rules for.

Margot pulls them onto a stone garden bench, hidden away from prying eyes. She leans toward them, strands of her hair that have come loose brushing their cheek. And then, suddenly, they're not just holding hands. They're crashing together. Yael's hands find Margot's waist, and heat floods her belly. She cups their jaw, leaning in. Their lips are so very close, and Margot asks, her voice barely a whisper, "Can I please, please kiss you?"

"Gods, yes," Yael rasps out.

Margot's lips find Yael's, and as the noise from the party grows louder beyond their hiding place, she kisses Yael until they're both breathless.

# 15

# YAEL

"Shall we go to the cottage?" Yael murmurs into Margot's hair what feels like hours later, their lips brushing the soft skin behind her ear.

She drops her head back with a quiet groan, protesting, "There will be socialites roaming the grounds for hours yet. I wouldn't put it past them to come bursting into the cottage, assuming it's an outhouse. Rich people are like that."

Yael doesn't take offense, as technically, they are no longer rich. Besides, she isn't wrong. "My room at the tavern, then?" They slide even closer on the bench to trail kisses up the exposed arc of her throat.

"Everyone in Bloomfield will be piled into Clementine's after today's tourist windfall."

Her voice barely wavers . . . but it's enough that Yael grins against the slope of her jaw. "Then name a place. Because, Daisy?"

She shivers. "Yes?"

"I'm about to peel this exquisite dress right off you and have you in the flowers and the dirt. Truly, I will ruin your gown without regret, and I don't care who sees us."

"The greenhouses," Margot gasps out. "There's . . . there's a bottle of Granny Fern's home-brewed mead beneath the shop counter. I've been saving it for something to celebrate. We could, um, have a toast. To the show. To us."

"To us," they echo, kissing down the long line of her neck.

Margot gently pushes them away, but her eyes glow like lanterns in the twilight. She takes their hand and tugs them along after her, and Yael finds themself nearly sprinting out of the garden to keep up. The two of them head for the cottage just long enough to gather Sweet Wind at the garden gate. Yael hops astride the steed, holding a hand down for Margot. She clasps their forearm and swings up behind them, threading her arms around their waist. Now it's her turn to lean in and say, "Ride."

They gallop into Bloomfield. Down the main road, locals hail them as they pass. Maybe they're going too fast and night has fallen too far for folk to notice Margot's hand as it works its way beneath the lapels of Yael's suit jacket, her callused fingertips gliding below their bindings, across their lower ribs. Or maybe they're perfectly visible. Yael could not give one single fuck either way. Thank the gods that the main road is fairly straight, for all the attention they're not paying to the path ahead.

When they reach Greenwillow Greenhouses, it's Margot who hops off first, practically pulling Yael down after. Her larkspur hair has come partially out of its elaborate braids, windblown tendrils clinging to her flushed cheekbones.

"You're so beautiful," Yael says. "I've no artistic talents whatsoever, I swear, but I'd learn how to paint so I could paint you."

She blinks back at them. "I bet you've said that to half of Harrow."

They frown. "Margot, how many people do you think I've slept with?"

"I . . . I don't know. A lot more than me, though that's not much of a feat."

"Well, maybe." Yael reaches up to frame her face between their palms. "But how many people do you think I've washed windows for, filled pots for, and pruned trees for? How many people have I trod through mud for and worn *boots* for?"

She bites her soft bottom lip (they wish it was them doing the biting, are tempted to tug her lip out from between her teeth with their own, but this feels important). "That was work, Yael. You didn't have a choice."

"Margot Greenwillow, I have been choosing you every day for four months now. And if I haven't made that obvious—if you haven't felt chosen—then clearly I've work to do yet. Come inside, and I'll show you." They drop their hands to hold one palm out for her and keep very still while she considers them, looking just as vulnerable as she did fleetingly in the Care Cottage.

"Yael, if this isn't real, you don't have to—"

"Can I kiss you again?" Yael interrupts.

"I— Yes . . ."

They move closer and let their mouth part around hers, meeting her tongue with their own. She still tastes of champagne, and she smells like jasmine in bloom. Pulling back after a moment to hover inches away, they ask, "Can I touch you?"

"Gods, yes."

On the dark path in front of the greenhouses, they trace their fingertips down the low, *low* neckline of Margot's gown until they've gone as far as they can, where the fabric gathers at a point just above her navel. They hook their fingers inside so she can't back away without meaning to. "And can I take care of *you*, Margot, just this once?"

She swallows roughly, throat bobbing. "I suppose . . ."

"Only if you want it." Yael tugs her close again so they're

flush together. Slowly, they glide their other hand up her neck to cup her jaw, and tilt her head just so, and whisper against the shell of her ear, "You have to tell me that you want it."

"Fine, then." Margot reaches around them to fist a hand in the fabric of their suit jacket, pressing them impossibly closer still. "I want it."

Inside the shop, Margot checks that the sign reads CLOSED though business hours have long since ended, then latches the door behind them. She draws the curtains across the door and glances around for a likely place to . . . well . . . but Yael doesn't linger in the shop. They lead Margot by the hand through the strawberry greenhouse and into the cherry orchard. After their last harvest, the trees are flowering again, surrounding them with baby-pink blossoms and the delicate smell of growing things. It's warmer even than the newly summer evening outside, with the heat still trapped from the day. Yael has been in Bloomfield for over a season now. The old itch under their skin flares up, a lingering doubt, that piece of them that still isn't certain they can do this, that they can be good at this . . .

But they push it away as they spin Margot around to face them. Yael truly cannot paint Margot, or start a fire for Margot (well, not on purpose), or cast spells to save Margot from a muddy forest path, but Yael can do *this*. And they want to, with her and for her. *This,* they know. The bedroom—or anyway, the metaphorical bedroom—is the one place where they're never selfish. "Tell me what you like, Margot."

Her eyes dart among the potted trees before settling on Yael's. She's nervous, they think, though not of Yael.

Well, they can help with that.

Yael undoes the single button holding their beautiful suit jacket in place and shrugs it off so that they're topless except for the hand-width strip of black linen. "Tell me what you like," they say again, "and where you want to be touched." They drop their jacket into the petal-sprinkled mulch.

Margot licks her lips as her eyes skim across them. "Where do *you* like to be touched?"

Grinning, Yael reaches for her hand, and she places it in theirs. "Here," they say, gliding across their collarbone, pressing her hand to the dip between, so the wonderfully rough pads of her fingers rest against their throat. "And here." They lift her hand to skip over the tightly tied bindings, then slowly trail her fingertips down the flat of their stomach, until their hands rest at the waistline of Yael's trousers. "I like that."

Her fingers flex within their own. "Where else?"

Yael unbuttons their trousers with their free hand and guides her between the tight-fitting fabric and their underpants.

Margot seems in danger of biting through her bottom lip. "Outside or . . . or inside?" she asks.

"Oh, inside." With a light grip on her wrist, they guide her hand inside the waistline and down between their legs, her fingers stirring once, twice, until they buck against her. "There," Yael confirms, groaning. Then they remember themself and peel her hand out from their trousers to press a kiss to her palm. "What about you?"

"The same," Margot says, sounding out of breath while standing still, "but you should touch me here." She wraps her strong fingers around their wrist and guides them to her breast, deliciously weighty beneath her dress.

Yael smirks. "Outside or inside?"

"Definitely inside."

"Fantastic. If you really want to preserve this dress, then take it off before I chew through it out of sheer frustration. Do you need help with the buttons?"

She shakes her head enthusiastically, lifting an eyebrow in her familiar Margot way. "And what are you taking off?"

They slide their already unbuttoned trousers down their legs, prying off the velvet shoes while they're at it and kicking everything to the side. Standing in the mulch in their bare feet, their underwear, and bindings while Margot's still fully dressed, Yael should feel overly exposed.

But this is a kind of care: the willingness to be vulnerable first.

Satisfied, Margot reaches behind her neck to undo the tiny trail of buttons at the nape. It takes a moment for her to slide the formfitting bodice down her body, the vast skirt pooling at her boots. She stands naked from the waist up, with a sheet-white petticoat meant to add volume to the skirt of the dress tied around her waist, skimming her knees. She moves to untie it.

"Wait," Yael says. They settle their hands against her naked waist, over her gorgeously round hips, and tug her in so that they're pressed together, her full breasts resting just above their bindings, stomach-to-stomach and skin-to-skin. "Let me."

Margot shivers in the heat.

That's when Yael sinks slowly, kneeling against the warm earth, skimming their hands down the hills of her body to the petticoat's hem as they go. "Shall I?" they ask, craning their neck to look up.

Margot reaches down to brush back their hair, which occasionally falls into their face now that they're no longer determinedly fluffing it up; at some point, they stopped doing that without even noticing. She grips her fingers in the shorter strands at their neck. "You absolutely shall."

They hook the petticoat's hem inside their thumbs to lift it as they slide their hands up her full thighs, then duck under.

Yael takes their time caring for Margot, tasting her, hot and soft and slick. She buries both of her hands in their hair and grinds her hips against them, and it's all Yael can do to hold her in place. When she's finished, tugging at their hair hard enough that they wince (not that Yael gives a damn), she joins them on her knees.

"Your turn?" she asks, pressing frenzied kisses along their lips, their jawline, their throat, her chest still heaving.

"If you wish."

They roll into the mulch together, after Yael takes a moment to spread out the skirts of Margot's gown, wide enough to comfortably fit them both.

"I guess we're going to ruin it, anyway," she says, pale eyes dancing.

"I'll buy you a new one," Yael says, laughing. "I'll buy you a dozen."

"With what fortune?"

"With my cut of the fashion show, of course. Didn't I tell you? Don't worry, I only take eighty percent."

"Yael!"

"Just a little banking humor," they say, and let her push them down.

When Yael arrives, it's panting, groaning Margot's name and *please, gods yes, there.* And then with only a moment's pause, they're rolling over atop Margot, kissing their way down her neck, murmuring, "You've been so good to me, Daisy. Let me be good to you." They fumble to untie and shove away the petticoat at last, and bury themself once again between her strong thighs. Bracing themself with one elbow, they reach up to trace her breasts, her waist, to clutch her hand as Margot practically bends their fingers backward. They cradle her jaw and feel the tendons flex.

"Yael, gods, Yael . . ."

They are good to Margot, as good as they know how to be, for quite some time.

# 16

# MARGOT

Margot's carefully kept record of how many days she's gone without being touched the way Yael touched her last night lies in the dust somewhere, along with her petticoats and her dirtied Rastanaya dress. Not that it matters. Last night was so very, very good. She would ruin a hundred dresses to feel that way again.

Margot's body is curved around Yael's as she wakes. She places a gentle kiss on their bare shoulder. They're still sleeping, curled up in the folds of Margot's skirt that they spread underneath the cherry tree last night. Thank the gods she left the Clauneck letter at home, wanting one night's distance from it. Even that had seemed careless in the moment, but if she'd brought it along, who knows where it would've ended up?

Settling Yael's jacket over their shoulders, Margot sits up. Yael murmurs softly, and Margot brushes a piece of their hair off their forehead. They're so striking, even in their sleep. Perhaps that's what Margot's feeling most deeply this morning: just how much she likes waking up next to Yael Clauneck. Such a huge change from four months ago, when Yael first rode into town and Margot took them back to the cottage as a drunken, one-night fling.

Of course, if she'd known Yael was so good at . . . all the things they'd done together last night, she might have kissed them sooner. Well. There will certainly be time for that, but first, Margot needs tea.

She stands, stretches, pulls on a chemise, and pads on bare feet through the cherry orchard, moving along the winding path in the waterfall room with its hanging arrays of tropical plants to her private mood garden, where she grows whatever flowers catch her fancy. At the far end of the room is her locked workshop. She places a hand on the yellow door, whispering a word to unlock it.

She lets out a contented sigh as she steps inside, leaving the door open behind her for the first time since Yael started working in the greenhouse and letting the cinnamon-laced smell of the workshop wrap around her. It was here where she spent hours at Granny Fern's side, learning how to feed plants and encourage them to grow. She also learned to draw plants—one of her sketches of a fern that she gave Granny Fern for a long-ago Solstice present still hangs on the wall—and to prepare potions with exacting requirements.

It's where she keeps the tea as well. Using a spelled kettle like the one she has at home, she gets two cups steeping and settles down at the table. Soon, she's lost in the notes she was taking a few days ago on the Natural Caster Potion. Her neat handwriting fills many pages, and she turns to where she left off:

Problems: Not really sure how to make this or even what I'm looking for. (Ha. Fabulous.) Have made most of the potions in the book, many of which might replicate a single effect but not the sum needed for a potion of this magnitude.

Maybe the Natural Caster Potion is a combination of all of them?

Margot bites her lip as she re-reads that last note. The thought had come to her a few days ago, as she'd been cleaning out the Greenwillow Manor's fountain for Rastanaya's show. Despite the neglect, there had been several varieties of flowers growing in the cracks in the fountain that had never been planted there. They had found their way to the fountain, creating something beautiful from many other previous plantings. Something about that had struck her, and now she lets her mind consider the possibility.

Hmmm. She hasn't ever tried making all the potions in Granny Fern's book and combining them. That seems foolish, because who knows what effect it might have? But then again, it could be the answer to all her problems. Yes, it would take months—perhaps more time than she has, given the Claunecks' deadline at the end of summer—but it's worth a try.

She looks over her shoulder through the empty doorway and back into the greenhouse. There's no sign of Yael, so she might as well get started.

Flipping to the front of the book, she sets to work on making the first remedy Granny Fern ever became famous for— a simple potion meant to grant the drinker a bit of courage. It was wildly popular with adventurers and nervous students, though Margot's version of it only lasts about three minutes rather than the three hours Granny Fern's promised. (Which is why Margot had never offered it to Sage; her best friend was brave enough as it was, and imagine if she drank Margot's courage potion, pushed beyond her usually outrageous limits, and got eaten. Margot refused to think of it.)

Humming to herself, Margot fills up a small glass bowl

with rainwater from one of the bottles on her shelf. The bowl, she sets in a beam of sunlight. Then she chops up three tiny red cap mushrooms—only just deadly enough to encourage bravery—that she grows in the greenhouse. These go into a mortar, and on top of them she adds ten fresh lilac blossoms, which will ease some of the effects of the mushrooms but not make the drinker too complacent. Next, she adds a dried orange peel (for brightness), ten peppercorns (for gusto), and exactly fourteen drops of morning dew that she's harvested (for clarity of mind).

Of course, her dew supplies are running low, as she was too preoccupied to set the bottle out last night, and she ends up with only eight drops, but that shouldn't be too much of a problem.

A handful of other ingredients—bees' wings, an acorn cap, ten bitterroot shavings, and several other things from Granny Fern's notes—also go into the mortar. Then Margot picks up a pestle and begins to grind everything together. As she does so, she thinks of Yael, of the way they looked in their suit, of the way they kissed her, of—

A soft knock sounds on the door. Margot turns to see Yael standing in the doorway, wearing one of Margot's oversized cardigans she leaves around the shop, which hangs to their knees, and their own garden boots, which they keep at the greenhouse. They look sleepy and adorable. Margot immediately longs to kiss them.

"Good morning," she says, putting down the mortar and closing Granny Fern's spellbook.

"Morning, lovely. I smelled tea. Need any help?" Yael stands in the doorway, waiting.

"I don't." Margot dumps the mostly crushed ingredients into the water. They'll need to soak for ten days, but then the potion should work. If she's ground them finely enough. And if the missing dewdrops don't matter, as she's guessed. And if she remembered to add everything in the correct order . . . (No wonder her potions never work as well as Granny Fern's did. Well. A problem for another time.) She turns her full attention to Yael. "Come in. Please."

Yael smiles at the invitation. This is the first time Margot's invited anyone into her workshop since her parents barged in and drank the potion on that awful day, but somehow, it feels like exactly the right thing to do. She *wants* Yael to join her this morning. Maybe every morning.

Yael steps across the workshop threshold, their dark eyes on Margot. "I'm honored, Daisy."

She lifts her teacup, blowing off the steam. "I feel like you've earned it after all the hard work you did last night."

Yael chuckles, sending heat through Margot's lower belly as they step closer, pinning her against the workbench when she spins around to face them. She has no choice but to put her teacup down and kiss them.

It's a sweet, slow kiss, gentler than Margot has ever had and somehow perfect after the . . . energetic night they shared. Margot lingers in that kiss, threading her hands through Yael's already mussed hair.

"What do you work on in here?" Yael asks against Margot's lips before they pull away at last.

They take the tea Margot offers, and she draws herself up. Yael knows so many of her secrets now; what harm is there in telling them another? Even if she doesn't tell them the full secret of how she's trying to save Bloomfield.

"Remedies mostly," she says, sipping her own tea. "This is Granny Fern's book." She touches one finger to the green leather journal, which is nearly the size of Harvey the cat, who has wandered into the workshop and now curls around Margot's legs.

Cautiously, Yael touches the spine of the book. "So this is where it all began? The entire Greenwillow empire?"

Margot nods. "I've made every potion in that book—well, most of them—with varying degrees of success, along with a few of my own."

"Do you like making them?"

"I . . . think so?" Margot has never asked herself this question. Why would she? Making remedies was what she was taught. It's what she was expected to do. "I was trained by Granny Fern. Then, once she was gone and we moved in here, I dove into re-creating them . . ." Margot trails off, drinking more tea.

Yael picks up a slim bottle full of emerald-green liquid. "What's this?"

"A potion for getting rid of imperfections—temporarily— but I'm fairly sure you don't need it."

Yael's eyes meet Margot's, the air between them crackling. "Thank you, Daisy. Rest assured, you don't need it either."

After Margot's done kissing Yael again—though will she ever truly be done kissing Yael Clauneck?—she says, "Perhaps I'll be able to restart Granny Fern's business and sell remedies again someday. Or at least I hope to. There's a long road from tinkering in this workshop to carrying on her legacy, but I want to try." Admitting this sends a snicker of guilt through Margot. Her original plan to use Yael to convince their family that she's living up to her potential feels ridiculous this morning, after so many weeks together, and their intimacy last night. But still. Things are complicated between them. Even more so now. Pushing these feelings down for the moment, Margot moves over to a shelf where row upon row of small bottles filled with bright-pink potion rest in a wooden holder. "These are for hangovers. The really vicious kind. They're nearly ready."

Yael picks up one of the bottles of pink liquid, holding it up to the morning light and considering the contents. "Hibiscus?"

"And strawberry. I just got the formula right last week. Clementine is eager to keep them in stock."

"Fabulous. I may need it after the next community dinner."

"No. Never." The words leave Margot's lips too quickly, out before she really even considers them. Because she can't let Yael try her potion. Never mind that Margot tested it on herself after *last* week's community dinner, when she and Yael and a handful of Bloomfield friends had ended up at Clementine's, singing the night away and drinking too many ales. It had cured her hangover with the first few sips, giving her more energy than she'd had in days. But there was a tremendous difference between sampling her own potions and letting Yael drink one. What if something went wrong, as it had with her parents?

"I'm sure it works perfectly," Yael says, putting down the tiny bottle. "Mind you, I was mostly sober last night, and I'm in ideal health today, but I wish it could cure my morning breath, which is horrific."

"I'll be the judge of that," Margot says, delighted to have an excuse to kiss Yael again.

The morning is busy in Bloomfield as they walk hand in hand back to the cottage, having left Sweet Wind outside the greenhouse, as Yael absolutely insisted they enjoy the morning air. They walk past the northern field so Yael can see the mammoths for the first time, to their extreme delight, then head back into the village. They wave to Mike, Dara, Clementine, Estelle, Javril, Astrid, and Rosiee, all moving through their daily stretching routine in the town square. Affection surges through Margot as they stroll the village.

"What are you smiling about?" Yael asks as they round the bend past the tavern and start toward the cottage.

"I'm just . . ."

"Happy?"

"Yes," Margot says softly. "I feel like we're exactly where we need to be. This feels like home."

And for the first time in a long time, with Yael at her side, she feels like it might be possible to save the village and all the people in it.

As the front gate of the gardener's cottage comes into view, Yael pulls up short. "Oh no," they whisper, going pale.

Margot follows their gaze to the envelope affixed with ribbon to the gatepost. Yael's name is an elegant flourish in green malachite ink across the cream-colored paper.

"Who's it from?" Releasing Yael's hand, Margot steps forward to take the letter. "And why would they tie it to the gate?"

She turns the letter over to open it, but Yael takes it from her with trembling fingers. "You don't recognize the seal?" they say wryly.

Of course she recognizes the little picture stamped in deep-green wax, now that she looks: the façade of a tall stone building with a C turned horizontal at its peak, almost like a pair of horns rising from the roof to spear the sky. She saw it on the letters her parents used to pore over again and again until the ink faded beneath their fingers, as though they were searching for some clue or key to free them from their own doom. She knows it from the letter tucked away in the loft.

The seal of the Clauneck Company.

Yael breaks the wax and removes the message. "It's an invitation." They sniff then clear their throat to read aloud in an uncharacteristically flat voice, with none of their usual flair: "'Mr. Baremon Clauneck and Mrs. Menorath Clauneck request the honor of your presence at their Midsummer Masquerade, to be held at Clauneck Manor.' And ah, there's a postscript. 'Enough of this, Yael. It is time to come home. We're sending a carriage to pick you up in three days' time, which will arrive at the outpost gate at noon. Don't miss it.'" They scoff and toss the letter into the dirt with an attempt at bravado Margot doesn't quite believe. "Chaotic of my parents to send out invitations a mere week in advance, but perhaps I was an afterthought. How flattering to have made the C list."

Margot opens and closes her mouth, not quite sure what to say. After a long moment, she manages, "What will you do?"

Yael shoves both hands through their hair. "Nothing. This changes nothing."

"They know where you are, Yael. Do you think Rastanaya told them?"

"I don't know. If not, then someone must have. Once I was spotted in Olde Post, it was only a matter of time until word traveled back to them, and we weren't exactly discreet yesterday evening." Crossing their arms over their chest, Yael starts pacing back and forth on the garden path. "But you'll notice they've sent a messenger rather than traveling themselves. Well, they did swear they'd never come back after the first visit."

Margot can't tell whether Yael is relieved by their absence or stung by it. Perhaps both, and she's not sure how she feels about that. "May I?" she asks.

"Of course."

When she stoops and picks up the parchment to re-read the invitation, she nearly drops it again in shock. The Claunecks' brusque postscript isn't the end of their message. There's more, written in plain letters and shimmering silver ink unlike the bright-green calligraphy of the invitation and postscript. And it's addressed to her.

We request your presence as well, Margot Greenwillow. Say nothing of this personal missive, but bring our heir back to

Ashaway where they belong, quickly and discreetly. Baremon and I know you're capable of this and a good deal more. My husband and I place our faith in you.

However, should that faith be misplaced, you may expect a summons to discuss the willful and unauthorized use of company property that no longer belongs to you, as well as the future of assets we have been gracious enough to allow you to continue to occupy. An outcome neither of us wishes, I'm sure. We look forward to your immediate presence in Ashaway, along with Yael, lest your absence be considered your response, and our previous agreement considered void.

> *Best Regards,*
> *Menorath Clauneck*

Margot makes herself keep hold of the invitation, though her nerves threaten to abandon her. The note must be written in invisible script, spelled so it's only visible to her. She skims the letter again, hating herself as her heart leaps at Menorath's words and at the threat within them.

> My husband and I place our faith in you. However, should that faith be misplaced, you may expect a summons to discuss the willful and unauthorized use of company property that no longer belongs to you, as well as the future of such assets we have been gracious enough to allow you to continue to occupy.

It's Margot's worst fears laid bare on the page. The Claunecks are willing to take the cottage, the greenhouses, and Bloomfield, unless she gets Yael back to Ashaway *and* somehow convinces them that she's on track with the Natural Caster Potion. That their faith in her is not misplaced. But can she still hold on to Yael's friendship if she's also working for their parents?

Does she have a choice?

Clearly not.

Margot blows out a breath, running her gaze over the wild-flower garden, Granny Fern's wind chimes, and the peak of the tower of Greenwillow Manor in the distance.

There's really only one choice to make, even if her reasons for it are as tangled as the ivy that crawls up the front of her cottage.

She hands the letter back to Yael, who shoves it into their pocket. "When you go back—"

"*If* I go back," Yael interrupts bitterly.

"Or if you go, let me go with you?" Margot weaves her hand through Yael's again.

"Really?" Yael says. "You'd do that? For me?"

"*With* you." Margot has to look away as she says it, her treacherous heart cracking at Yael's hopeful expression.

"Even if it means seeing my terrible family?"

"Even if it means that. You . . . you owe yourself the chance to confront them, don't you think?"

Yael pulls Margot to their chest, hugging her tightly. "You are a magical human, Margot Greenwillow. I—I'm just so very glad to have found you again."

She is so very glad of that too, even if she isn't sure what being in Ashaway with Yael—and their parents—will bring, or what it will do to the fragile thing growing between them. Alas, she has no choice but to find out.

# 17

# YAEL

nder the high-noon sun three days later, a carriage arrives just as Yael's parents promised—or rather threatened. It appears from the distance as a black spot against the gently sloping countryside. Its ebony wood is polished to a high gloss and crowned with sharp gold trim. On one door panel is a golden Clauneck seal, and on the other, a painted panorama of the Copper Court with the vast Clauneck Company offices at its center, twin-peaked towers rising from the roof akin to horns. Perched on the raised box seat, a coachman Yael recognizes from their family's employ but couldn't possibly name holds the reins for a pair of giant boars, with shaggy black fur and eyes like fiery coals sunk deep into skulls as large as carriage wheels.

"Nice, Father," Yael mutters, scowling.

If only they could have ridden Sweet Wind. But returning to Ashaway with the steed would most likely mean returning the steed to Oreborn. At least they were instructed to wait at the outer gate; Yael is grateful for that, though it meant half a mile's walk with their trunks. Devils forbid the carriage had driven into Bloomfield to pick them up, terrorizing everyone in its path. Even Margot looks like she would rather walk the rest of the way to Ashaway than climb inside this monstrosity.

Yael reaches for her hand. "My family never was subtle in their villainy. But it's actually quite nice inside. There are curtains for privacy, and there's very comfortable seating. There may even be snacks."

Margot looks nervously at the boars. "Do they bite?"

"Not as hard as I do."

This earns a burst of laughter. "Thank gods you've managed to restrain yourself so far."

"Just barely."

Yael opens the carriage door for her to climb in before the coachman can hop down to do it. They settle across from each other on the plump, purple velvet bench cushions, the cabin wide enough that they could only just touch fingertips if they leaned all the way forward toward each other. The coachman slaps the reins to start the boars moving. The carriage churns down the dirt lane away from Bloomfield, and Yael watches from their backward-facing seat as the old outpost walls disappear past the rolling horizon line.

Margot never turns around to look, only staring past Yael at the path in front of them.

They reach the Queens' Road, and the carriage turns north toward the capital. Yael watches out the window as they retrace the miles Yael barely remembers from their months-ago drunken sprint through the dark. They wind alongside a sluggish river where gold-plated fish flash through hazel shallows. They pass fields of waving grain, then meadows of parti-colored wildflowers where mountains rise in the background like sleeping mammoths.

Occasionally they pass fellow travelers in carriages and carts and on beast back, all of whom goggle at the Clauneck carriage then quickly avert their eyes—because they either recognize the family seal or have the wits to sense danger when it meets them on the road. Margot speaks less and less the nearer they draw to Ashaway, despite Yael's jokes and attempts to crack the strange ice that's settling across the cabin between them.

Perhaps she regrets offering to come with Yael. They know she's worried about the greenhouses, though Clementine and the townsfolk have promised to take turns tending them until Margot and Yael return, and she's cast spells to keep the soil damp and the vines winding upward. Besides that, being thrown together with the family that ruined hers is probably the last thing in the world she wants. Still, selfish as it is, Yael feels enormously grateful not to be churning toward Ashaway alone. They'd *like* to think they're capable of telling their parents off and turning right back around for Bloomfield after the damn masquerade . . . but they've never been very good at standing up to Baremon and Menorath. Disappointing them? Easily done. Denying them? Not so much. Last time, they had to sneak away in the night. Without Margot here to keep them from falling back into the Claunecks' trap, who knows if they'd be strong enough to slip out again?

"Have I thanked you yet for coming with me?" Yael asks to break the silence.

Margot doesn't look away from the landscape beyond her window. "About fifty times."

"Have I thanked you yet for last night?" Sprawling decadently across the bench, they prop one dusty boot on the velvet cushions and raise an eyebrow.

Margot grins, remembering. "You did most of the work."

"That's not true."

"It is. It's been true every time since the first."

"Well then, my father will be thrilled to hear I've finally developed a work ethic."

"You know I'm perfectly capable of leading, right?" Margot rolls her bottom lip between her teeth.

"I— Of course. Anytime you want."

"Now," she says urgently, meeting their eyes at last.

"What?"

Margot shifts on the bench, clutching the green linen of her traveling dress. "I need a distraction. Badly. But if you don't feel like—"

"Oh, I feel like."

"How far are we from the city?"

"Hours yet." Yael sits upright, reaching across the cabin for her. She ducks past their outstretched hand to kneel on the embroidered rug between Yael's legs. "And it's my turn to take care of you?"

They gaze down at her as she peers up at them and feel the breath leave their lungs. Nobody in the kingdom could be as beautiful as Margot is right now. Her hair is twisted and pinned into crown braids the color of the wild indigo that grows around the cottage (see, Yael listens when Margot talks about plants), and her mouth flushes red where she sinks her top teeth into her bottom lip.

Still, Yael hesitates.

It's not that they *need* to lead in the bedroom. Or the greenhouse. Or the carriage. They've had lovers who preferred to take charge. At least, they preferred to think they were in charge. It's just that Yael is so good at this. They don't have many skills or talents, but divining what or who their partner wants them to be, and performing the role as lavishly as possible, is a talent of which they're particularly proud. Even when they've felt like they had nothing else to offer, they had this.

But Margot knows them, doesn't she? She knew them for years before they found each other in Bloomfield, and for months before they found their way into bed together.

She must see something more.

"Yes, Daisy." Yael reclines against the bench back, resting their arms atop the cushion. "It's your turn."

Her wide gray eyes turn storm-dark just as the carriage hits a particularly deep rut, rocking side-to-side, and Margot grabs Yael's thighs to brace herself.

Yael's fingers twitch against the velvet as they struggle not to grab the back of her neck and guide her lips to theirs. They can admit to themself that the sight of Margot between their knees is something they'd imagined in their room above Clementine's tavern, usually while sliding their own hand inside their underpants. To stop themself from reaching for her again, they shift just enough to close the thick privacy curtains across each window, blotting out the world beyond.

Margot grabs the buckle of their trousers, undoing it, and begins to tug downward. "Since it's my turn, I'll tell you what *I* want, yes?"

Yael lifts their hips to make it easier for her to slide their trousers and underpants down until their clothing catches on their boots. "Tell me."

She pulls their boots off to finish the job, tossing the bundle across the carriage floor, then sits back on her heels to consider. At last, she declares, "I want to hear the sounds you make when I'm inside of you."

"Gods, Daisy." Their belly clenches.

With a villainous grin, Margot pushes their legs even farther apart and dips forward, her tongue finding them.

"Fuck, oh fuck," they grunt as they try not to grind into her mouth; they really do. They shouldn't be surprised by how good it feels; in all things, Margot is competent, confident, magical. But *godsdamn.*

Some number of blissful moments later, she surfaces, slipping two fingers inside of them in place of her tongue. "Do you know what I thought of you the moment I saw you in Clementine's Tavern?"

"What?" Yael breathes out, somewhere between a grunt and a moan. It's hard to focus while the pace and pressure of her fingertips continues to stoke the swelling heat between their legs.

"I thought that even after years apart, you were still the most beautiful person I'd ever seen. And I remembered that when I was young, before I even knew about . . . about all of *this* . . . I'd looked at you and dreamed about burying myself in you, and coming out as somebody new."

"But why would you want to be—" They're cut off by the insistent slide of her fingers inside of them, stirring harder and faster now. "Gods, Margot!" It's becoming impossible to keep still.

She laughs, reaching up with her free hand to cradle their jaw and press her thumb across their lips. "Do you want the coachman to hear you?"

Yael shakes their head once.

She tugs at Yael's bottom lip with the pad of her thumb. "Well, I do," she says, gray eyes sparkling.

Yael obliges.

Their feet skate against the cushion and their back arches above the bench as the climax rolls through their body like a warm sea wave, filling every part of them before it breaks. How many times has Yael sat in this carriage with their family, fidgeting anxiously as they rode toward some ball or business dinner they dreaded attending until they were scolded to *just sit still,* to *just keep quiet.* For twenty-three years, this cabin (or one exactly like it) has witnessed Yael's silence and dread and shame. Even now, moving toward Ashaway, they should feel nothing but miserable.

But because of Margot, they feel good. They feel so *good.*

Like a disciple of one of the gods of the plane besides their own might bless a haunted field or manor house, Margot's cleansed this carriage, and Yael inside of it.

Yael really doesn't deserve Margot Greenwillow.

꧁

They blink awake some hours later to the coachman's shouted warning.

"City gates ahead, sir'ram!"

Yael stretches where they lie entangled on the narrow bench cushion with Margot, who stirs against their body, yawning. Neither of them bothered to straighten their clothes before napping, and in fact, they took off a good deal more between them. Margot's dress and Yael's shirt and trousers lie crumpled on the rug under their dust-caked boots, which is not the impression they'd planned to make on the capital after months away. Maybe Margot can magic away the wrinkles and dust. They'd do it for her if they could, they think sleepily; they hate to wake her to ask.

*Now you long for the family magic? You've wanted nothing to do with this family for more than an entire season, but suddenly you're in sight of the manor, and you can't manage without us.*

Yael freezes mid-stretch. They haven't heard Clauneck's voice in their head—like the sour, off-key peeling of a dented bell—for weeks. It was foolish to think they'd never hear it again. But after confessing to Margot about their patron, Yael had hoped there was no corner of themself for Clauneck to hide in.

"I don't need you," Yael mumbles back, too low to disturb Margot, at least no more than the noise of the carriage and the pounding of the giant boars' hooves against the Queens' Road.

*We'll see, shall we?*

Sitting bolt-upright (startling Margot in the process despite their intentions) Yael moves to the window and yanks back the curtains, watching the nearby settlements of Higley Brook and Poppler approach, and the vast black city walls and southern gate grow larger and larger as they churn unavoidably forward. "Once we're inside, ride on," they shout up to the coachman. "We won't be staying at the manor. Take us into the city proper, where we'll secure lodging for ourselves."

Margot blinks, looking up at them curiously.

"I've instructions to deliver you both to the estate," the coachman calls back, uncertain.

"And what if we jump from the carriage and sprint down the Queens' Road, shouting, *Kidnap!* I'm sure I could cause quite a scene if I tried. I'm actually known for it."

Reaching across the cabin for her dress, Margot slides it over her head, still staring at them.

There's a long beat of silence before the coachman sighs defeatedly. "Where to, then, sir'ram?"

"As I said, take us to the city, to the Glowing Coin." They turn back to Margot, explaining, "It's right on the edge of the Golden Court, with the best view of the palace in the city. And the best chef outside the palace itself. You'll love their spiced bat."

She frowns. "I'm not sure I've been paying you high enough wages to afford the Glowing Coin, and nearly all the gold Rastanaya gave us is back in the greenhouse till."

"Never fear." Yael waves away her concerns as they shrug on their shirt then reach for their trousers. "We'll purchase our room—our *rooms,* if you prefer—on Clauneck credit."

"And your parents will allow that?" Margot asks, seeming dubious.

"By spreading rumors of my supposed injury, my parents have made it clear they're trying to keep our family business out of the public eye. They won't risk creating a spectacle by cutting me off in front of the whole capital."

*Thinking like a Clauneck all of a sudden? Interesting . . .*

For perhaps the first time ever, their patron sounds as though they *have* found something of interest in Yael.

They would prefer not to think about that, so they press on. "Besides, I'd sleep on a bench in Coult Park before I put us in the same house as my father and mother, after what they did to yours."

"Yael . . ." Margot starts, "your mother . . ."

"Yes?"

Pressing her lips together, she shakes her head, then says, "I don't think Menorath is going to like me much."

Laughter bursts out of them, and they fall back against the bench. "The fact that my mother may hate you is one of the many reasons I love you."

Margot freezes halfway through retying the bodice of her dress, knuckles turning white around the laces, lips parting as if to protest, but nothing comes out.

Recognizing panic when they see it, Yael rambles, "Not that I'm some angry young person trying to piss off their parents in return. I swear I'm not. I mean, I *am* angry at them, but I just meant to say that you're nothing like my mother, and that's why—"

"Why you love me?" Margot whispers, her gray eyes wide, looking like a cornered cat.

She looks the way Yael feels whenever they think of returning to Ashaway: like they're strolling into the mouth of a beast, having narrowly escaped its teeth once before.

"I . . . I . . ." The carriage is stifling all of a sudden, the air sucked out by Yael's obvious mistake. Of course she doesn't want to hear their accidental admission just as they're about to ride through the capital's gates, placing her back within the reach of the people (*Yael's* people) who took everything from her in the first place. This is hardly the time to talk of love.

Gods, they never do stop to think.

*Oh, Yael. Do you believe a time will come when Margot Greenwillow looks into your eyes and does* not *see everything she's lost? Do you believe you've anything to offer that will persuade her to see a lover—a beloved, even—before she sees a Clauneck?*

"That's not true," Yael insists.

"What's not? That you—"

"No, I didn't mean . . ." Yael grinds the heel of their palm into their temple, but Clauneck has fallen silent. "I mean that . . . You know, I've just been really thoroughly fucked, so I wouldn't take my word on anything right now." A flimsy excuse, and a cowardly path out of the conversation.

But Margot takes it. She hesitates for only a moment longer, then goes back to tying her laces, perhaps tugging more roughly than necessary (certainly, Yael would've treated her more gently). "Well then, we'll write it off to being thoroughly fucked and save our words for the innkeeper, if you think you can convince them to give us a room."

"Not a doubt in my mind, Daisy." Yael sprawls out on the carriage bench once more, the very picture of calm, cool, unbothered.

They tell themself that Margot will soon forget their mistake.

They tell themself that all of this—leaving Bloomfield, letting Margot accompany them, and placing them both back under Yael's parents' influence—isn't one huge mistake that they'll live to regret.

# 18

# MARGOT

An apricot slice of early-morning light shines through the crack in a pair of thick, velvet drapes, beckoning to Margot. The evening before, she and Yael were given the Glowing Coin's finest room, because, "nothing but the best for Yael Clauneck and their guest!" It's an extravagant suite with violet-and-silver-patterned wallpaper, a burbling ornamental waterfall in the bathing chamber, and crystal chandeliers throughout. Not as fancy perhaps as the way Margot's mother had decorated, but after all these years in Bloomfield, it looks like a queen's bedroom to Margot. Not that she's ever been in a queen's bedroom. Yael probably has. She'll have to ask them . . . or maybe she won't. It's not like she needs to know.

She shifts under the silk covers, her knee brushing against Yael's bare thigh. The touch starts a fire low in her belly, and she plants the lightest of kisses on their shoulder.

Yael murmurs, then burrows deeper into the piles of pillows. Margot could keep kissing them, but she lets them sleep. She's been awake since before dawn—greenhouse habits don't disappear simply because she's traveling—and she's been replaying their journey from Bloomfield to Ashaway over and over in her head, lingering on the steamy parts, while hoping sleep might find her again. But it's a lost cause. Fully naked, she slips out from under the coverlet, careful not to disturb Yael.

Margot's bare feet whisper across the marble floor as she searches for her hastily discarded traveling dress, which is piled somewhere near the bed . . . maybe? Or in the bathing chamber, where she and Yael took the longest, most delicious bath of Margot's life. But it's not there, nor slung across the back of a chair, nor under the inlaid table where the remains of their dinners still sit under silver cloches.

After several minutes and more than one stubbed toe, she finally finds her dress and underthings discarded along with Yael's travel clothes in a lump beside their trunks, which a porter placed near a sitting area stuffed with velvet sofas and cut-glass decanters. She picks up Yael's jacket, running a hand over the lapel as their words from yesterday's carriage ride rise in Margot's mind.

*The fact that my mother might hate you is one of the many reasons I love you . . .*

*I love you.*

Margot drops Yael's coat and pulls clean undergarments from her own trunk roughly, as if the force of the movement could shove away Yael's words along with their love—if it even is love. Which Margot doesn't want to consider.

*Because you might love them back?*

Ridiculous.

Margot slips into her undergarments, desperately ignoring the voice in her head.

*. . . one of the many reasons I love you . . .*

If only Yael knew what their mother actually thought of Margot. How had Menorath spoken of Margot in her secret note? *A capable witch can accomplish much in the capital, especially with patronage such as ours. My husband and I place our faith in you . . .*

Is that who Margot is? A capable witch in need of a patron? Or is she Yael's favorite form of rebellion? Or just someone doing their best with what they've been given? Which version of herself does she even want to be?

The questions spin through her head as she digs into the trunk again, sifting through layers of cardigans, stockings, petticoats, and her three best dresses, until she finds a hyacinth-blue day dress she'd bought from Arnav. It's not fancy, but it's certainly nicer than her faded strawberry-print frock or her garden boots. As she twists her hair into a simple braid—something much more suited for Bloomfield—Margot takes in the sleeping lump of Yael burrowed deep in the covers, practically hidden, just as they had been that first morning in the cottage's loft.

How has it been four months already? If you'd told Margot back in February that she'd be in Ashaway, sharing a room—and a bed—with Yael Clauneck by the start of summer, she would've laughed out loud. But here she is, in Ashaway, listening to the soft way Yael breathes in their sleep.

Of course, four months with Yael also means there's only a season left until her deadline.

Life is surprising, and often nothing happens like you've planned. Margot knows this. But that doesn't mean she should give up, right? After all, she's in Ashaway with dreams beyond accompanying Yael to the masquerade ball. She knows what she has to do—convince the Claunecks she's living up to her potential as a brilliant remedy maker so they'll extend her grace period awhile longer—and now it's time to make it happen.

*But . . .*

*What if you can't do that?*

She drops into the closest chair, swearing under her breath. Her fingers are still tangled in her hair, the braid half completed. It had all been so simple in Bloomfield, when it was just her and Yael in the greenhouses, but now everything is a mess.

Her ability to make a godsdamn impossible potion is still her only hope for the future of her business and Bloomfield. But also, she has very real feelings for Yael. And along with those feelings, there's guilt over the way she talked Yael into coming to Ashaway under false pretenses. And then there's Menorath's threat of the Claunecks gathering up assets they'd overlooked, which means Margot may be out of time sooner than expected.

Margot buries her head in her hands, wanting nothing more than to crawl back into bed with Yael and stay there. It's all such a tangle. More knotted than the ivy that covers the cottage she loves so much.

The cottage she can't lose just because Yael Clauneck strolled into her life and kissed her like she mattered to them.

Margot takes a shaky breath and stands, finishing and tying off her braid. She can't give up on her family or her village. Crossing to the window, she pulls back one of the heavy curtains to peer through the leaded-glass panes into the city. She undoes the latch and lets it swing open just a crack. A warm breeze that smells of fresh bread and river water fills her nose. She inhales deeply, feeling like she's twelve again and standing on the balcony outside her room in the city. *Is* this what it feels like to come home? She'd thought it would be, but Ashaway is just loud, busy, and enormous.

From their high vantage point, she peers across the burnished rooftops of the Copper Court, the golden ones of the palace, and red-clay-tiled ones that cover the many buildings spreading through the city between the courts. The house she grew up in is somewhere east of the Glowing Coin, on a street with other packed-together mansions. Margot turns away and looks instead to the west. Coult Park is only a few blocks from here, and the Willowthorn River winds like a silver ribbon through the city in the distance. Swallows and tiny pixies dart through the air, chasing one another around the eaves of a building across the street from Margot's window. It's lovely, but the trees only remind her of Bloomfield.

She pushes down the thought, watching as a pair of wagons trundle over the cobblestone street. The cries of vendors fill the air as they pass one another, competing with birdsong and the bells from a longboat floating along the Willowthorn.

"Morning," Yael says behind Margot, their voice laced with sleep.

Margot turns, smiling to see the many directions in which Yael's hair is standing. "Morning. Sorry if I woke you."

Yael yawns as they sit up. "Not you so much as that racket. I'd forgotten how noisy Ashaway is in the morning. I'm not sure I enjoy it."

"Yael Clauneck, I do believe you might be a country soul after all these months."

Yael gives an exaggerated shudder. "Nonsense. I'd forgotten just how loud it gets near the Copper Court. Why don't you come back to bed?" They pat the space beside them.

Margot walks over to them. "Normally, I'd like nothing better, but I'm already awake and restless. I'm going to find us some tea." She kisses them on their forehead.

Yael tilts their face upward, closing their eyes.

She cups their cheek, tenderness filling her as her lips find Yael's. "I'll be back soon," she murmurs after they kiss for a long moment. "You sleep."

"That I can do." Yael tugs lightly on Margot's braid and steals one last kiss. "And shut the window before you go?"

They're already sliding under the covers as Margot closes the window and slips out of the room.

Outside the Glowing Coin, the streets are even louder than the noise that filtered through the window would have Margot believe. A stable hand leading a horse nearly flattens her as she moves through the courtyard and down the nearest lane. She has no idea where she's going. Yes, she grew up in Ashaway, but she's never been down this particular street, and the city has changed so much in the years she's been hiding in Bloomfield.

No, not hiding. Creating a new life for herself. A life she was exiled to, but still, one that she has managed to make her own. A life she desperately hopes to keep.

If she knows Yael, and she thinks she does fairly well by now, they'll sleep for hours yet without the pressing concern of their chores in the greenhouses. Which means Margot is free to wander the city. If she gets too lost, she can ask for directions back to the Golden Court and the Glowing Coin. It's not like Yael put them up somewhere subtle. Even as she thinks it, Margot turns to look back at the inn.

Really, to call it an inn is ridiculous. It has no more likeness to the Abyssal Chicken than a strawberry plant does to a cherry tree. Beyond the basics—all inns being buildings where people rent rooms for the night—there's no resemblance. The Glowing Coin is a four-story confection with marble porticoes and columns. Its leaded-glass windows on the first floor are shaped into whimsical designs: swans and tulips and the like. A motif of shining coins tiles its façade, and the guests standing around its lobby this morning had all given Margot sideways glances, as if she didn't belong there in her dusty boots and simple blue dress.

She wishes that she had spent some of the money from Rastanaya on fancier clothing before they'd left, but where in Bloomfield would she have purchased such items? She still needs to find something to wear to the Claunecks' ball because, although the dress Rastanaya gifted her for the fashion show would've been perfect, she and Yael had promptly ruined it— albeit for a worthy cause.

*Gods. The Claunecks' ball.*

Swearing under her breath, Margot turns away from the Glowing Coin. She leans against a nearby ivy-covered brick building, running a finger over the leaves. Her heart races at the thought of seeing all those people, talking to them, wearing a fine dress, being expected to dance with Yael with everyone watching.

"Maybe it won't be that different from Rastanaya's fashion show?" Margot whispers bracingly to herself.

But of course it will be. Because the show was a chance to play pretend for an evening. It was one night of magic, and Margot was still a gardener who lived in a cottage at the end of it. Here, as the noise of the city rises around her like a living creature that could swallow her up, she knows that in order to get what she wants, what she *needs,* she must become someone else. Someone who belongs in Ashaway.

As her thoughts race, she twines the ivy through her fingers. It responds to her touch, and a riot of tiny purple flowers breaks out along the vine, looking entirely out of place against the otherwise stoic façade of the building. The purple is the exact shade of Margot's hair. Before anyone can see, she untangles her fingers and rushes away. She knows exactly where she needs to go. Back to where it began and who she was supposed to be before everything fell apart for the Greenwillows.

As the sun settles higher in the sky, Margot walks along a mess of familiar and not-so-familiar streets, asking directions a few times until she's standing outside a tall, sprawling mansion that takes up half a city block. Greenfield House, her childhood home where she lived for eighteen years, not counting summers, until she rushed back to Bloomfield to mourn Granny Fern.

She's filled with a strange, disconnected feeling—half regret and half repugnance—as she wraps her hand around one of the

gilded metal flourishes on the gate. Her parents had always re-
ferred to Greenfield, with its four levels and façade of green
marble, as a cottage, but that was just an affectation. A bit of
rich people's whimsy, like a queen playing at being a shepherd-
ess. Margot's childhood home in Ashaway is no cottage. It's a
place built to impress behind its golden gates. Margot resists
the urge to demand entrance. She isn't even sure who lives there
now. Maybe the Claunecks sold it to a family friend in better
graces than the Greenwillows or an investor in their company.
It doesn't really matter who owns it now; it's more about who
doesn't own it, which is Margot's family.

 *But would you even want it back? If that is an option, would you
want to live here again?*

Yes? No? She isn't sure.

She knows Yael's family home—a dragon of a mansion
that reeks of old money—is set away from the center of town
because they have land. Lots of it. And stables, and all the
things Margot's parents tried to emulate in their own country
estate.

A carriage rolls past, and Margot shrinks up against the
gates of her former home, making herself small. Desperate not
to be recognized.

It was a mistake to come back to Greenfield. She doesn't
need to focus on the past. She needs to focus on the future. And
there won't be any future for her and Yael, or for Bloomfield,
unless she makes good with the Claunecks.

Turning away from her childhood home, Margot heads back
into the city. On the way, she stops at a pastry shop and leaves
with two bags full of iced buns, fruit tarts, and golden-papered
chocolate treats. When she makes it back to the Glowing Coin,
she stops by the front desk to order tea for their room.

"Ah, Miss Greenwillow," the person behind the counter says
cheerfully. "I was just about to send this up to you." They ges-

ture to a small envelope on the counter with Margot's name written across the front.

Margot hadn't given her name last night when they checked in, and now she eyes the clerk and the envelope suspiciously. "How do you know that's for me?" she asks.

"The letter was left for you by Lady Clauneck herself." The clerk beams. "She said you'd be staying with the young sir'ram, and that you had the loveliest purple hair. That has to be you, yes?"

Margot's stomach sinks at the mention of Yael's mother. She touches the tip of her braid self-consciously. "Thank you?" she says weakly, taking the letter.

"Of course!" says the clerk. "I'll send up some tea now. Will that be all?"

Margot nods, fighting the urge to rip up the letter. Instead, she takes it to a tucked-away alcove in the lobby and opens it.

The script is elegant and the message simple:

Menorath Clauneck invites you to an exclusive fitting at Rastanaya's dress shop, in preparation for the upcoming Midsummer Masquerade. All costs will be covered by the Clauneck family. We look forward to seeing you on Tuesday morning at 10 A.M. sharp. Come alone. We've much to catch up on.

Margot crumples the letter in her fist.

"You have to meet her," she whispers to herself. "Charm her, and perhaps she'll believe you're greater than you really are. Just buy yourself more time to save . . . everything."

It's possible, isn't it?

She tucks the balled-up note into her pocket beside the original letter from the Claunecks, forever on her person, and heads back to her room, ready to lose her worries in Yael's arms, a pile of pastries, and many cups of tea.

# 19

# YAEL

"So this is where you spent your scholarly years?" Margot asks, gazing up at Hair of the Dog. The iconic tavern was built to look like a ship beached on a cobblestone street bordering the Ivory Court, complete with a crow's nest where a continual flame burns without ever scorching the wood, casting its fantastical glow into the night air.

"As far as I can remember," Yael answers.

She turns toward them, lifting a brow.

Yael spreads their hands. "What can I say? Half the point of Auximia was what happened at night after classes ended, and we often washed up here. It was far enough from the Copper Court that most of our parents wouldn't deign to come here, and close enough to the student chambers to crawl home after. You know, I always hoped I'd run into you out on the town. I would have remembered *you* the next morning."

"Your flattery overwhelms my senses," Margot deadpans, rolling her eyes.

Yael grinds their tongue between their teeth. Though there's truth buried in there like a seed in soil, it does sound like shameless flattery, even to their own ears. They should have said, *If only I'd found you sooner, I wouldn't have spent all that time feeling lost.* But the words wouldn't come.

Anyway, who is Yael to speak those words to Margot? Who will Yael *ever* be to Margot Greenwillow? A friend? A lover?

Or just another Clauneck?

It was easier to pretend otherwise in Bloomfield, all-but-naked with their bare feet planted in greenhouse mulch, than it is while wearing this exquisite, olive-colored silk suit. A trunk full of clothing from the wardrobe Yael left behind was waiting for them at the inn when they rose this morning, sent over by their mother with a note that read: *If you're going to exploit our family name and fortune, then you had better dress appropriately to reflect both.* The jacket's a bit tight in the biceps and shoulders now, but not as much as they might have guessed it would be, or hoped. Aside from that, the fit is near perfect.

It's Ashaway, Yael decides. This city makes it disconcertingly easy to slip back into their old costumes.

"Shall we?" Margot knocks them loose from their spiral before they can really get going.

Thank goodness for that. They've promised her a pleasant night out in the capital, not an identity crisis. "We shall."

They offer Margot their arm—a habit now—and approach the door with its porthole window. Charmed to admit anyone with a pocketful of denaris, it swings open before Yael, just like old times. The tavern's interior seems unchanged as well. Built to resemble a sprawling and luxuriously appointed captain's quarters, its walls are pinned all over with nautical tapestries, maps, and illustrations of sea monsters curled among the waves—though as far as Yael knows, there aren't any leviathans off the shores of Harrow. Certainly not in any mapped waters. They vanished generations ago, along with their dragon brethren. Patrons sit in overstuffed leather armchairs and rest their drinks on small side tables draped with jewel-toned velvets and silks. In the large stone hearth, a fire flickers in pale rainbow shades, like an opal enchanted to burn. Margot stops in the doorway to watch it, mesmerized.

"Well, gods be damned!" a familiar voice bellows. Alviss Oreborn—the last person Yael expected to find hanging around the Ivory Court—levers himself out of an armchair, hoisting his signature tankard to hail them from across the tavern. He splashes a bit of ale on his steel-studded tunic, which has the look of plate armor despite its fine fabric and shortened sleeves. "Yael Clauneck, a handsome sight for these old eyes!"

Yael sighs.

"Isn't that the mine owner?" Margot asks. "I remember my parents going in with him on adventuring expeditions, sending parties out together, since they weren't competing for the findings."

"That's him."

"He gave them a fully kitted warhorse for my birthday. My eighth birthday."

"Oh, Mulligan!" Yael exclaims.

"You remember Mulligan?"

"Of course; your parents regifted him to mine. He was a mean thing."

"Truly a villain of a horse," Margot agrees.

"Well, Oreborn has always been . . . colorful. And that's his son."

Denby is wedged into the chair beside his father, looking broad and bored as ever, each of his biceps like a cask of wine. Even when he's seated, the top of his plaited blond head is nearly level with his father's.

"I should probably go over," Yael concedes. "I might owe the Oreborns a steed, which I'm *not* giving back. But if you want to wait for me by the bar—"

"No," Margot says, plastering on a smile that looks only a little strained at the corners. "Sweet Wind has carried me around too, remember? Where you ride, I ride."

If Yael could peer through a porthole in their own chest to see their heart, they're sure it'd be glowing opalescent as the hearth fire.

Oreborn grins as they approach. "Wonderful to see you well, Yael," he roars, wrapping thick, freckled arms around them and pulling them close. "Such a nasty spill you took off one of my own horses. I was sick with guilt, just sick," the man declares, loud even for Oreborn.

Yael doesn't hesitate before playing their part. "The fault was none of yours and all of mine. Never ride a mechanical steed after finishing off a Copperhead or four at brunch." They laugh just as loudly, shoring up the lie to anyone listening in; inevitably, someone will be.

"Ah, that's kind of you to say. Your parents were equally gracious. Paid me well for the horse that was harmed in the fall." From beneath monstrously bushy brows, his crystalline-blue eyes meet Yael's, twinkling with shared, secret meaning. "There's no debt between us two. None but the drinks I owe you now that you're back home." Pulling away, Oreborn winks theatrically and turns to Margot. "And this beautiful lass is . . ." His grin slips. "The Greenwillow girl, isn't it? I'd know you by the hair, just like your mother's. Haven't thought of you since—"

"Since word reached Ashaway of Rastanaya's triumphant showing on Margot's family estate, starring Margot's own botanical creations and arrangements?" Yael interrupts, threading their arm around her waist. "You really should see her work, Oreborn. It's soon to be found in every estate and household of importance in the capital, I'm sure of it. Margot's the brightest star rising on Harrow's horizon, and she has been a dear friend to me during my recovery, with her incredible talent for remedies."

Margot tenses against them; perhaps they're laying the praise on a bit thick for her tastes?

After only a moment, Oreborn nods, eyes sparkling like gems. "Aye, that's exactly it. That's where I heard your name last. Well then, maybe we'll send around for flower arrangements. Denby's got an engagement party coming up this autumn, and that's what the gentlefolk do, ey? To think, Yael, you two will soon be cousins!"

"I . . . excuse me?" For the first time, they stumble to catch the man's meaning.

"Well, near enough to cousins, once Denby and Araphi tie the knot. Lucky you've recovered in time for the wedding."

Yael looks to Denby, who scowls up at them from the chair, his only contribution.

It can't be . . .

"Congratulations to you both," Margot says, leaning in to save Yael.

"Yes . . . yes. Apologies, it's the fall . . . from the horse. Sometimes I . . . forget." They pat their head, a weak pretense.

Oreborn claps them on the shoulder, and the blow stings as always. "A drink will help with that. Fetch yourselves an ale and tell the barkeep to put them on my coin."

Yael bows lightly and leads Margot away to the bar counter, built of polished wood planks enchanted to smell faintly—but never unpleasantly—of brine and sea vegetation, as though they'd been fished from a sunken ship the day before. Yael easily summons the barkeep with a raised finger and orders two overpriced ales on Oreborn's tab. The man insisted, after all.

"Me and Denby Oreborn, soon to be family," they mutter as

the barkeep moves away. "Curious, Araphi never did mention the name of her fiancé at the fashion show."

Margot shrugs. "Maybe she didn't have the chance. If she's marrying him, she must be happy about it."

Yael's lovely, flighty cousin, happy to hitch her carriage to that sour storm cloud? "Impossible."

"Not everyone wants what you want, Yael," she snaps back at them.

They've said something wrong, clearly, and must repair it. "Untrue," they say smoothly, leaning against the counter and tilting their head to face her. "Everyone in this tavern right now wants *you,* unless they're too drunk to see farther than the nose on their face."

With a sigh, Margot yields. "You're very charming, but—"

"How charming, Daisy?"

"*Very.* And I do appreciate your attempts to talk all of Ashaway into forgetting my family's scandal, though I'm not sure that's within even your powers of persuasion."

"Oh, I assure you it is. I've heard I'm very charming."

"But Yael . . . doesn't it bother you, going along with your parents' lie? Every person we've passed in the street who recognized you, it was like . . . like you were both performing in a play and had already memorized your lines."

"I suppose we had. It's just, well, it's easier than telling the truth, isn't it? Seeing as we're only in Ashaway for a few days. Why complicate our lives?"

Margot looks at Yael with inscrutable eyes for long enough that they start to squirm. Then, reaching over to brush their cheek, she says, "Of course. I guess I'd just forgotten what this city is really like, that's all."

They lean into her touch the same way they've seen that monstrous cat Harvey do, suppressing the urge to purr.

As soon as the barkeep returns, she drops her hand and turns from them. "Let's have our drinks and head out, all right? It's been a long day, and I'm suddenly dead on my feet."

Yael's just about to ask whether she'd like a ride back to their room at the Glowing Coin, or a ride after they've reached it, but they bite their cheek to stop themself. They've got to stop behaving like the same decadent disaster they were when they left home. No wonder Margot froze with panic in the carriage after Yael's accidental confession. Yael had hoped it was only a reaction to their parents' proximity as they rode toward Ashaway. But maybe Margot sensed Yael's old self drawing nearer and nearer as well, approaching as surely as the black basalt walls.

This isn't a pleasant thought.

With every swallow of ale, Yael tells themself that it'll be fine. The problem will resolve itself the moment they leave the city to return to Bloomfield after the masquerade. And if Yael has to play the role of the rakish Clauneck heir until then, so what? Especially if they're putting Margot's name on everyone's lips while they're at it.

It's the least Yael can do for her when she's already doing so much for them.

# 20

# MARGOT

Well before ten the next morning, Margot strolls along an elegant, tree-lined boulevard just a few streets south of the Golden Court. She's heading for Rastanaya's shop but also anxious to delay her arrival. Her nerves tingle with each step, and she takes a long steadying breath as she passes under the cool shade of a maple tree. Birds chirp overhead and several pixies—city-dwelling creatures Margot remembers from her childhood, though she's not thought of them in years—sit on the edge of a nest built into a streetlamp. Above the city, the early-summer sky is blue, cloudless, and calm.

*It's not a big deal. Just dress shopping.*

*With Yael's mother.*

*Your worst enemy, one of two at least, and the woman who holds the fate of Bloomfield in her hands.*

Clutching her small purse—which, like her purple day dress, looks entirely too plain compared with the outfits of the other early-morning shoppers strolling the boulevard—Margot keeps walking, searching the street for the gold-and-white-striped awning Yael told her marked Rastanaya's shop. There it is, jutting out from the front of a building at the end of the block like the prow of a queens' barge. Two enormous golden urns, both taller than Margot, stand on either side of an amethyst door, and even from here, Margot can feel a forbidding aura of sophistication and elegance wafting off the place. Well, Yael did tell her the door was carved with runes for the protection of the shop's expensive wares; perhaps that's what she's picking up.

Not for the first time that morning, cold dread steals over Margot. What is she doing here? Why is she doing this?

She's here because she has to be. Because one does not ignore a summons from a Clauneck, especially when they hold the deeds to everything that matters. And because she must convince Yael's mother that she's close to creating the Natural Caster Potion, which she'll surely agree is worth waiting for. Yes, of course. She knows this.

If only she didn't have to lie to Menorath Clauneck.

"My mother's a beast," Yael had said that morning as Margot kissed them goodbye over breakfast. She had told them about dress shopping but kept the rest of her worries from them. "But a subtle one. She won't cast dark magics on you in the middle of the shopping district. Really, she's no worse than strawberry weevils or grumpy cats. You can handle her, Daisy. Trust me."

Margot is trying so hard to believe it. She wants it to be true.

It's just . . .

"It's just dress shopping," she whispers bracingly under her breath. "You've lived on your own for years. You can survive *dress shopping.*" Steeling her resolve, she approaches the shop.

A lovely, lilting ballad fills the air as Margot draws nearer to Rastanaya's doorway—some busker close by, she supposes, but there's no hired band to be seen, nor a singer with hands outstretched for coins in exchange for a tune. The song is unlike anything Margot's heard, aching with sadness and bursting with hope at once. It reminds her of being young, standing in the tower of Greenwillow Manor and looking out across the fields, longing for an adventure and believing she would find it in the world someday.

Perhaps there's still a bit of adventure to be found here in Ashaway, after all.

The song stops abruptly as a dark-haired young woman pops out from behind one of the urns. Margot lets out a small squeak as Araphi stands in front of the amethyst door.

"Margot! I'm so glad to see you again!" Araphi exclaims. She wears a confection of purple and black lace, with a tiny top hat resting on her pinned-up hair, and she's draped in ropes of pearls.

"Were you hiding back there?" Margot points toward the narrow, shadowy nook behind the urn.

Araphi brushes a dried leaf from her skirts with a shrug. "Yes."

"Why?"

"I wasn't sure how early you'd be, but I wanted to catch you before you went inside. Though I had hoped that Yael might walk you to the shop, at least." Araphi winks. "My dashing cousin is quite fond of you, Margot. And I thought I might wait for you because—as much as I know you're a formidable woman—I didn't want you to face the dragon alone. I mean my aunt, of course."

The dragon? Facing a dragon is very different from facing a strawberry weevil or house cat, as Yael would have had Margot believe. Margot's heart starts to race again. Still, even through that panic, some small part of her is immensely grateful to see Yael's cousin. In the shifting landscape of Ashaway's high society, she is the perfect person to accompany her. If only Yael were here too.

Yael had volunteered to come, but Margot had insisted they stay back at the inn. Menorath's note made it very clear that Margot was to come alone; a separate appointment would be made for their heir. Besides, she couldn't lie to Menorath about the Natural Caster Potion if Yael was standing right there. They'd want to know what the potion was and why their family was interested in it, and why Margot felt so compelled to create it, which would lead them to the threat of eviction hanging over Margot and the town that Yael was now a part of; the last secret Margot has to her name—

"So, what *exactly* is going on between you and Yael?" Araphi asks as she rests a hand on Margot's arm. She leans in conspiratorially.

"Oh . . . well . . ." Margot trails off. "We're . . ."

She's not sure how to answer, or how much to tell Araphi, who might report back to Yael's family. Margot and Yael are together for now, but they haven't really dug into what it all means *exactly*.

"Yael never mentioned that you sang," Margot says instead, desperate to change the subject.

Araphi holds a finger to her lips as if she's shushing a child and looks around. There's a group of well-dressed people farther down the block, but no one near enough to hear Margot. "The acoustics are great right behind the urns, as I discovered long ago when I'd accompany my mother and aunt to this shop. They'd be in there for hours, and I'd sneak outside to keep myself busy. Though of course a Clauneck scion like myself should never engage in such low activities as singing outdoors—or, really, singing at all, except as a party trick to impress guests or customers. But I've been moonlighting as a tavern singer, you know." Araphi winks. "Nobody else does, not even Yael."

Even through her surprise at the thought of sophisticated Araphi drinking in a tavern, much less singing in one, Margot manages to say sincerely, "That sounds delightful—and you have a magical voice."

"It is, and I know," Araphi says simply, confident enough to take the compliment. "I've loved music my entire life."

"Would you ever pursue it after school?"

Araphi shakes her head and gives a small, bitter laugh. "Oh, that would never happen. Us Claunecks must all end up in the same place, eventually. And I'll be . . . stepping away from school this fall, to attend the many dreadful engagement parties my family has planned. I'll marry Denby next spring, and then . . ." Araphi trails off before adding, "Like my mother used to say. 'I am what I am now, and that is all.'"

Unsure what to say to this, Margot offers the first thing that pops into her mind, "You know, Sage, my best friend—do you remember her from Rastanaya's show?—she asked about you."

At the mention of Sage, the full force of Araphi's attention lands on Margot. Her dark eyes light up. "She did? How is she? Of course I remember her, and I've been wondering about how her adventure is going. Not that it's my business if she's been eaten or stabbed, or anything."

Now it's Margot's turn to smile. Sage's not-so-subtle questioning about Araphi had sounded almost exactly like this when she and Margot had communicated via their compacts the night before.

"She's alive and on her way to the shoreline. I think she'll be back sometime in late summer."

"Well, that's good," Araphi murmurs, a blush pinking her cheeks. "Perhaps we can all get together when she returns. Though of course by then I'll be quite busy. So many engagement parties planned to accommodate my family's many interests, and wedding dresses to buy, and . . . Well, I'm afraid my time won't belong to myself for much longer." She shakes her head as if brushing away a bad dream, and flips a curl over her shoulder. "Never mind all that. The time will take care of itself. Let's get started before my aunt arrives. I'll show you all the dresses she'll hate and Yael will love."

She offers her arm, and Margot links her own through it as they push open the shop's door.

By the time the clocks strike ten, Margot is standing on a platform in front of a full-length mirror, admiring the way a low-cut forest-green silk gown hugs her every curve. Araphi had insisted this was the dress Margot needed for the ball, and she was right. It's spectacular. There are feathers arranged into a collar at Margot's neck, and the gems and beads woven into the fabric of the gown glitter under the shop's chandeliers. Sheer silk sleeves—woven from "the most exquisite enchanted spider silk" according to Rastanaya's top assistant, a severe-looking woman named Nora—cover Margot's arms, veiling her tattoos.

Rastanaya is out of the shop at the moment, but a pack of attendants flitter around Margot like hummingbirds. One of them holds a clipboard and takes notes on the dress's fit; another places a tray of champagne flutes on a table and readies things for the arrival of Menorath; and a third and fourth stand near a silk chaise, holding other gowns for Margot to try on. Araphi sits on a floating couch near the platform, holding a champagne flute and watching the proceedings. When she meets Margot's eye, she winks.

"Can we just choose this one?" Margot asks. "Do we have to look at any others?"

Araphi starts to say something, but Nora jumps in.

"Lady Clauneck has very specific tastes," Nora says as she walks around Margot, assessing every stitch. Her heels click over the star shapes inlaid in the parquet of the dressing room floor, and her eyes narrow as they meet Margot's in the mirror.

"She likes dresses dark in color and elegant but not too risqué—something that makes an impression but isn't overly flashy. I'm just not sure this one will do . . ."

"Lady Clauneck isn't wearing it," Margot mutters, making Araphi giggle.

"What's that?" Nora glares at her.

"I said, 'It's lovely.'" Margot offers Nora a smile as a peace offering.

In fact, it's the most exquisite thing she's ever worn, besides the dress Rastanaya gifted her for the fashion show. It almost—almost—makes her feel like she belongs here. Margot had heard her mother talk about Rastanaya's shop, but she'd never had reason or inclination to visit it when they lived in Ashaway. Even having seen Rastanaya's extravagant garden fashion show had not prepared Margot for the store itself.

Beyond the amethyst doors is a vestibule lined with amber panels, accented with gold leaf and mirrors. Margot had tried not to gape as she and Araphi passed through the entryway into a showroom full of Rastanaya's creations that felt more like a museum—or a greenhouse full of exotic plants—than a shop. Several private dressing rooms, all of them larger than Margot's cottage, are set off the showroom, each of them decorated in the same decadent amber-and-gold motif as the hallway.

"She looks wonderful," Araphi says, her voice full of the assurance and command of a seasoned shopper. "Can you find her a mask to go with that gown?"

An attendant is dispatched to a storeroom, and Margot turns back to the mirror. Her hair is pinned into a hasty updo—a quick mimicry of the hairstyle she might wear to the ball. Eyes on her reflection, Margot runs her hands lightly over the dress. She looks like a proper Greenwillow now. An acclaimed plant witch. Someone worthy of the praise Yael has been heaping on her since they arrived in Ashaway to anyone who would listen.

*Or you look like a corpse flower about to bloom.*

Gods, she wishes Yael weren't singing her greatness quite so much. Yes, she needs to convince Menorath and the Claunecks that she's fully capable of creating the Natural Caster Potion, given enough time, but why does it make her feel awful whenever Yael introduces her to the very same people she remembers from her parents' dinners so long ago?

"Don't overthink it, darling," Araphi says, standing and offering Margot a flute of champagne. "You're a vision, and Yael won't know what do with themself when they see you in that dress. Or"—she grins wickedly—"perhaps they'll know *exactly* what to do."

Margot laughs even as heat warms her cheeks. Some of the tension in her uncoils. Yes, Yael would like this dress very much.

Certainly, they would enjoy helping her out of it.

She takes a long sip of the champagne. It's far earlier in the day than she usually drinks, but this is the capital, city of decadence and extravagance. Besides, she needs courage to lie to Menorath. She takes another sip, and the bubbles rush to her head.

It's not ordinary champagne. The assistant confessed it's been spelled to make the drinker feel lovely, dreamy, reckless—all emotions that encourage patrons to find a dress they adore and help them get over paying Rastanaya's extravagant (but apparently well-deserved) prices.

Margot drinks it gratefully. A heady cocktail of guilt, fear, and worry has been swirling through her bloodstream since they arrived in Ashaway—really since the Clauneck summons. But when she's around Yael, it abates just a bit. If only they were here now . . .

Right as Margot thinks it, the door to the dressing room flies open. She turns as Menorath Clauneck strides into the room.

Yael's mother is a tiny woman—slim, narrow-faced, yet

beautiful—but her presence fills the room like a cloud blotting out the sun. In one quick movement, her eyes move over each of the attendants and then land on Araphi, who raises a champagne glass in her direction. Menorath's eyebrows fly up in what looks like surprise for a moment, but she quickly recovers her composure. She nods coolly at Araphi; then her gaze finds Margot.

Margot forces herself to stand still under the assessing aubergine eyes of Menorath Clauneck.

*You can do this. You can do this. You can do this.*

She pushes her shoulders back and meets Menorath's eye.

"Ms. Greenwillow. You've grown into quite a lovely woman since we last met."

"I believe I was twelve the last time we met," Margot manages. Hastily, she takes another sip of champagne. She's waited so long to face the Claunecks, but in none of her imagined scenarios was she half-dressed and holding a champagne flute.

"Just so. Leave us." Menorath waves a hand at all the attendants. "You too, Araphi."

"But, Aunt Menorath," Araphi protests, "we're waiting on a mask to go with the dress. Don't you think this gown will be perfect for your ball?"

"It's fine," Menorath says, her voice leaving no room for argument. "For now, I need to speak to Margot. Alone."

Araphi shoots Margot a sympathetic look and mouths, "Good luck," as she and the attendants leave the room.

Menorath settles on the floating sofa and gestures to Margot. "Come here, please. Let me see you."

Feeling like a child who's been summoned, Margot steps down from the platform. She totters for a moment in her heels but then steadies herself.

*You're amazing, Daisy,* whispers Yael's voice in her head. *Your parents will be so proud of you when they wake up.*

"I received your notes," Margot begins, crossing her arms, "and—"

"We'll speak on those soon enough." Menorath glances toward the door, checking to make sure the room is truly empty of all but the two of them. She leans forward, clasping her thin hands together. "First, I must know: Have you completed the potion? Can you make those without magic of their own into natural casters?" There's an edge to her voice. Something brittle, hopeful, desperate. Something dangerous.

Everything in Margot yearns to flee or to wilt, but instead, she stands straighter, lengthening her spine. And then she lies with a smile on her lips. "I've had quite a breakthrough recently, and I'm very close to finishing the potion."

Menorath lets out a huge breath, slumping in her seat. "Is that true? How fabulous."

Again, that delicate hope in her voice makes Margot brave. And just curious enough to ask: "What would you do if you were a natural caster?"

"What wouldn't I do?" Menorath declares, rising from the sofa. She starts to pace, her tiny frame more commanding than a general's at the war table. "My husband is simply eager to turn a profit, and this would be a profitable venture indeed. As for myself . . . Do you know what it's like having to ask your in-law for all your power?"

She shudders, and Margot nearly feels a sliver of sympathy.

Menorath continues. "With this potion, well . . ." Here, she stops pacing, standing directly in front of Margot, looking up at her with a glint in her eyes. "Let's just say *my* world would be very different."

Margot swallows. "And Yael's world too, I'd imagine."

Menorath waves a hand and resumes pacing. "Yes, of course. Will you make your deadline? Summer will pass before you know it."

"I hope to have it finished by then . . . but more time will allow me additional tests to ensure that the effects are permanent and the potion is completely safe," Margot says, putting as much confidence into the words as she can muster. "Especially if it's for . . . personal consumption."

"Well, that really depends upon you, Margot." Menorath's shrewd gaze finds Margot's again. "Which brings us to the next piece of business: Yael seems to adore you."

Here, Margot swallows hard.

"Or at least that's what my spies in the city report," Menorath continues. "And I—*we*—need Yael here in Ashaway, not running around the countryside playing at being a farmer."

"A gardener. They've been working in my greenhouses."

Menorath's lip curls ever so slightly. "Yes, of course. But whatever it is, it must stop. The family needs their heir, and for that, I need you. If you can convince Yael to stay in Ashaway, then I will give you as much time as you need to perfect the potion. Because it *must* be perfect."

"And what if they don't want to stay?" A vision of Yael standing up to Menorath flickers in Margot's mind, but quickly disappears as Menorath scoffs.

"Don't *want* to stay here? What a ridiculous thought. I've known my child far longer than you have, my dear. They are a creature of parties and whims, of comfort and excess. Even if they claim to be done with Ashaway, they never will be."

"If you're so sure, why don't you tell them so?"

Menorath laughs. "Because I'm not sleeping with them."

Margot flinches, speechless.

"Oh, don't look so alarmed. Yael has always been susceptible to suggestion, especially when trying to please their amorous partners. You have more influence than you think—at least, as long as your dalliance lasts."

Margot wants to be brave enough to tell Menorath that this

is more than a dalliance—that she and Yael could make a life together—but she's not even sure that's true.

"What do you want me to do?"

"Convince Yael to reconcile with their father and me. They must be ready to play their part in the Clauneck empire. We cannot afford to have people speak of this family as though it can't control its own scions."

"What happens if I can't do it?"

"Then the Claunecks will finish what we started—potion or no potion."

Menorath walks out the door without a look back, leaving Margot standing in front of the mirror, desperately holding back tears.

Menorath is as monstrous as Yael and Araphi had said, but even with the awfulness of this bargain, Margot feels horribly torn.

She exhales slowly, trying to work her way through her snarled thoughts. Yes, Menorath is offering Margot her only chance to save her parents and their legacy, as well as the community that saved *her,* which she loves. And would she and Yael really have a future in Bloomfield? Maybe Menorath is right, and Yael would inevitably have left her to come back to Ashaway, deciding that Margot simply wasn't enough to hold their interest. Maybe this way, if she takes Menorath's offer, Margot's just helping them both become the people they were always supposed to be.

But if that's the case, why does it feel so treacherous?

Margot swipes at her eyes as Araphi and the dress shop attendants come back into the room, ready to help Margot out of her costume for the ball and back into her normal clothes, which no longer feel like they fit her at all.

# 21

# YAEL

After months of living in linen shirts and work boots that never wash clean (soil is practically baked into the scratched leather by now), Yael doesn't expect to recognize themself in their masquerade finery. But the version of themself in the mirror looks terribly familiar. It's the outfit. Yael's mother has consistent tastes, and much like their graduation party, Menorath arranged this ensemble without so much as a fitting or a single opinion required from Yael. She might have had it sewn for them weeks ago, for all they know, anticipating their return.

The suit itself is crisply understated: a shirt, vest, and trousers all in varying shades of black silk. The jacket is glossy, closer to a deep plum in color. The vest is darker, embroidered with black roses, reflecting just enough light to contrast with the shirt—black as the water at the bottom of a well on a moonless night. Over it all, there's a heavy, gold-trimmed black tailcoat that seems mercilessly warm for a summer night in the city, with thickly embroidered gold roses adorning the shoulders like pauldrons and thorny golden vines twining like chains around the buttoned cuffs. Polished, thin-soled black boots complete the outfit, and of course, there's the mask: a golden half mask that covers their cheekbones and the bridge of their nose, with a long ram's horn curling backward from each temple. It's heavy when Yael slips it on; their neck will ache by the end of the night from holding up the horns, they can already tell.

They pluck the last item from the satin-wrapped package a courier delivered to their room—a tiny stone pot of liquid gold lip paint. Yael hates that they *don't* hate the aesthetic. They've just finished brushing it on with one finger when they hear Margot behind them.

Her sharp intake of breath sets Yael on fire before they even turn around.

Margot stands in the doorway of the bathing chamber in her slip, revealing acres of soft curves and smooth skin. Gods, she'd look good with golden lip prints stamped all across her; Yael intends to make that a reality as soon as the night's done. She takes in Yael's outfit with bright eyes and flushed cheeks, her gaze tracing a slow path from the gleaming horns to their painted lips, down the small buttons of their vest and the sharp lines of their slim-legged black, ankle-length breeches, all the way to their boot buckles. Margot licks her lips. "You look . . ."

"Worthy of escorting you?"

"More than."

Yael hopes that's true. "And when do I get to see your gown?"

"I took it out while you were in the washroom, but can you help me put it on? This corset is relentless, and I can hardly bend to pick the dress up. I'm scared to try by myself."

"Of course."

Yael scrubs the lip paint from their hand in the washbasin, flexing their fingers as they trail behind Margot to remind themself that *they're* not allowed to tear the fabric either. Not until afterward. With great care, they pick up the ballgown laid out on the bed—a sleek bouquet of feathers and gems and green silk.

Turning away from them, Margot raises her hands above her head. Yael pauses briefly to press a kiss to her spine above her corset—lightly, so the paint doesn't stain—and she shivers. They stand on their toes and stretch to guide her hands into the sleeves, letting the dress slip slowly down over her body. The clip holding her hair out of the way comes loose, and Yael brushes the waving purple strands over her shoulder to pull the laces tight at her back. She hands them a collar of stiff black feathers, and Yael clasps it at the nape of her neck.

When Margot spins around again, she's transformed into a kind of magical, exotic bird from the raindrop-jeweled forests of southern Harrow. Below the unattached collar, the black sweetheart bodice that dips low between her breasts is covered by black feathers, tiny green gems twinkling among the plumage. Sheer, voluminous sleeves leave her shoulders bare, billowing winglike down her arms. Layer upon layer of green and black silk flows down from her tightly cinched waist, pooling around her delicate heeled boots. She's dangerously stunning.

"That settles it," they declare, sliding their hands to her waist to draw her in. "I am, in fact, *wildly* unworthy. We'll have to find you another date on the way to the estate. Maybe the coachman—"

"All right, all right." Margot pushes them gently away. She's laughing, but when Yael clasps their hands around her wrists to hold her close for just a moment longer, her hands are trembling.

"Margot, are you—"

"It's nothing," she insists, slipping free. "I'm just nervous.

It's a lot of people all at once, and your parents . . ." Margot shakes her head. "Let's just get the evening over with so we can be alone together?"

"Of course, Daisy." Yael would love nothing more.

"I still have to pin my hair up. Can you bring me my mask from the side table? I need to put it on first."

Yael bows deeply, and Margot's gaze settles on their lips for a long moment before she turns and swishes into the washroom to use the mirror.

*It could be just like this,* a treacherous voice inside of them whispers suddenly, and this time, Yael can't tell if it's their patron's or their own. *Margot dressed in gowns befitting her beauty, and you riding beside her in fine carriages, fulfilling a few family duties before collapsing onto silk sheets together every night. Life could always be this easy, this comfortable. All you really have to do is pretend, and you've spent the better part of twenty-three years doing just that. It's not a high price to pay, is it?*

No. No, no, no. All of this is temporary, they remind themself.

It's true that the two of them have passed a generally pleasant three days in the city. Margot seemed quiet and on edge when she returned from her dress fitting—time spent with Menorath Clauneck could do that to a person—but since then, Yael's aimed to make it up to her by properly showing her around Ashaway, from which she's been estranged far longer than they have. She had no desire to revisit the street of boutiques and fine dress shops and haberdasheries, but had no objection to the many pastry and tea shops sprinkled across the heart of the capital. They sampled spiced lavender and honey scones, cheese and black pepper turnovers, cinnamon custard that somehow smelled of sunset, and a pot of rich red tea that tasted just like piecrust. They walked the winding footpaths of Auximia, where Yael pointed out their old dormitory tower but steered well clear of the hall of economics named for their family. They rented horses on Clauneck credit and rode along the banks of the Willowthorn. Or at least the slice of the river that's been built up for promenading; farther east from the Golden Court are the alga-slicked ferry docks that transport residents of the Rookery to and from their day's work, but here, there are clean cobbled paths and a flower hedge to keep loose children from tipping into its fast-flowing waters, with pixies nesting in the foliage.

When it was only the two of them, with no old school acquaintances or Clauneck hangers-on to stop them in the streets or taverns or tea shops, it didn't feel *so* different from their afternoons in Bloomfield. At least they were together, and anyplace with Margot was better than anyplace without.

Still, Yael doesn't belong here anymore. They don't *want* to belong here. They don't . . .

"Yael? My mask please? We shouldn't be late!" Margot calls.

Yael hurries across the room and snatches the mask from her nightstand without truly seeing it.

Their carriage ride from the Glowing Coin is almost a straight path down the Queens' Road, out the courts, through the closely built mansions of the rich-but-not-Clauneck-rich, and into the greenery of the sprawling estates at the southern tip of Ashaway. Along the winding private road to Yael's former estate, palm-sized purple fires burn in iron lanterns strung from the branches of the exquisitely manicured trees lining the path.

Beside them on the carriage bench, Margot fidgets. She hasn't sat still since they left the inn, and even her mask— glittering green and black, with a regal crown of feathers and a miniature flock of jeweled birds rising from it—can't disguise her pale skin or the quickness of her breathing.

Yael doesn't blame her. The closer they've drawn to the ball, the more frantic the butterflies in their own stomach. When they clear the trees and the manor house rises up in front of them— six stories of dark-gray stone silhouetted against the summer-bright evening sky—Yael forgets how to breathe entirely.

*Why* are they so terrified? True, they hardly ever felt a moment's peace with themself in this cold, lonely castle of a home, but that's why they chose to leave it behind. They're grown now, and they have Bloomfield, and they have Margot, and they shouldn't feel like . . .

Like a child again.

Like they're thirteen years old, and all they want to do is sneak away and hide in an attic tower with one of their only true friends, eating strawberry jam and pretending they never have to come back down.

They feel fingers close around theirs and look down to find Margot's gloved hand clasping their own. "Ready for this?" she asks shakily.

Yael squeezes back, and slowly they remember how to breathe again. "Let's go in, and be done with it, and go home."

A butler whom Yael doesn't recognize greets them at the doors. What happened to Flatwater, the stoic figure who, if never a warm presence from their childhood, was at least familiar? This man doesn't seem to know Yael at all until they announce themself and Margot. Then the butler simply nods, signaling a footman to lead Yael and Margot up to the grand ballroom. As though Yael needs an escort.

When they reach the great arched entrance to the ballroom, Yael sees that the purple heartwood doors have been removed from their hinges and an elaborate, wrought-iron gate has been installed in their place. Black iron vines curl and wind among the barbed pickets through which a room half filled with guests is visible. As another pair of footmen swing the gates open to let Yael and Margot inside, the theme of this year's masquerade becomes clear.

The ballroom has been remade into a garden.

The marble pillars bordering a temporary dance floor of pale-pink tiles have been wrapped with mats of forest moss from floor to ceiling. Massive silk butterflies are pinned to the greenery, with wings like stained-glass windows. The cold purple candlelight of Yael's graduation party has been replaced by lanterns full of captured fairy light; they float in clusters above curved settees, where guests lean in to converse under the cover of boisterous music from a hired quintet. Hundreds or thousands of silk flowers half as big as Yael obscure the starred black ceiling. Hung upside down, they create a dome of giant petals and palm-sized stamens, an occasional puff of gold "pollen" drifting down like stardust.

Margot cranes her neck all the way back to stare up at them.

"I've never seen it like this," Yael says, puzzled.

"Why do you think—" Margot starts, but presses her lips together as Menorath slithers in between them.

Yael's mother is dressed to match the massive flowers overhead in a fitted gown that hugs her narrow figure from chest to knees, stemlike, with a skirt that poufs dramatically into layered petals of crepe and satin. But the fabric is all in black, with a mask of sheer gold lace to match Yael as well.

"Mother," Yael mutters as Menorath leans down to press a brief kiss to their cheek.

"So glad you both could join us. What do you think of our garden of delights?"

"It's . . . unexpected," Yael admits. "Aren't your parties usually themed around some stuffy old Harrow legend, or just 'wealth'?"

"We had a different theme in mind, it's true, and had to scrap it all at nearly the last moment, which cost us what some might consider a fortune. But it's worth it to celebrate your companion's reentry to fine society, is it not?"

"What exactly are you up to, Mother?" Yael demands. "Is this some sort of . . ." A bribe? A threat? A gift?

"It's an investment, Yael. Margot made an impression upon a scant handful of Ashaway's elite, and Rastanaya has risked much on this collection. She told me herself. Structure was said to be the trend this season—sharp tailoring and metal embellishments and clean-cut lines. Now, with our taste and position, everyone will be throwing nature-themed balls and bacchanalia, and wanting Rastanaya's pieces to wear. She'll be in higher demand than ever, and Margot, as her muse, will rise into the public consciousness."

Margot's face is half inscrutable behind her mask, but Yael can imagine the furrow in her brow as her lips part speechlessly. There's something off here. Menorath Clauneck isn't the generous patron she's pretending to be. Yael starts to protest, suspicion coiling in their gut like a poisonous snake.

But Margot speaks first. "Thank you for your gracious welcome," she says to Menorath, clearly selecting her words with care. "It's a lovely party."

"And you look as exquisite as expected, dear."

Yael doesn't like the way their mother's looking at Margot, appraising her. They don't like it when she reaches out to adjust the feathered collar around Margot's neck, as though Margot is just another piece of party decor for Menorath to dictate and fuss over.

"I see our guests of honor have arrived." Baremon greets them both in a voice meant to carry as he cuts through the crowd, and Yael is grateful for the mask that hides their flinch. Their father stops beside his wife to wrap a possessive arm around her waist. "How fine you look for your grand reentrance to civilization, Yael." Their father wears no mask—rules are beneath Baremon, even his own—and is clad in a suit in varying shades of black uncomfortably similar to Yael's, albeit with a taller cut and broader shoulders and chest.

"Thank you, Father. It's good to be here," they lie without looking him in the eye.

"And you, Ms. Greenwillow." Baremon holds out a hand.

Reluctantly, as if she's reaching inside the jaws of a coiled fire snake, Margot gives him hers. Their father kisses her knuckles, and a shiver runs down Yael's spine.

"Will you grant me the first dance, Ms. Greenwillow?" Baremon asks. "I've not seen you since you were a child and would cherish the chance to reacquaint myself with such a lovely young woman."

"Father—"

"Of course." Margot cuts them off, squeezing their linked arms before Baremon leads her away from Yael and out onto the tiled dance floor.

The hired musicians strike up an elegant waltz at Baremon's cue. From the edge of the room, Yael watches them, watches Margot's face remain impassive as Baremon leads her authoritatively in the dance.

"She really is lovely, darling," Menorath says. "Country living has clearly done well by her."

Yael can feel their fake smile faltering, and they grind their teeth together to keep it in place. "Yes, poverty is so flattering for the complexion."

"Whatever do you mean by that?"

"I know what you did to the Greenwillows. What our family did."

"What *we* did?"

"Bankrupted them. Took their home in Ashaway and drove

them out of the city, then took the manor in Bloomfield. Forced them into a cottage on the edge of the only land they had left. I *know*, Mother."

"Darling, you can't believe that any of that was personal! That was business. Margot's parents made poor investments, defaulted on their loans, and cost the company money we had to recoup elsewise. Poor choices must have consequences, and you cannot reasonably expect us to bear them. Did she tell you everything, then?"

"Of course she did."

Their mother studies them, dark eyes burning out of her golden mask. They flare a cold, bright purple at the center, and Yael shifts uneasily under her attention, which seems to fill their head with smoke, fogging their thoughts for a sliver of a moment. Then she blinks and smiles, seemingly satisfied. "Well, it's Margot's great fortune that she's smarter than her mother and father by far, and with real talent. A natural caster, darling; this family could do far worse."

"Don't act as though you know the first thing about her," Yael snaps, their façade collapsing.

Menorath laughs, as light as the bubbles in her champagne flute, and waves at a guest in a whiskered dragon mask from across the room. "Someday, Yael, when you're grown, you'll understand that everything this family has done, they've done for you. Every decision of ours that you so righteously spurn was made so that your choices will be easier. And devils know you've always preferred the easier path."

Yael is just about to protest, to find *some* way to object to what feels horribly true, when a familiar voice asks, "Can I claim this dance, cousin?"

Araphi stands before them, radiant in a fluttering, lilac-colored gown. It's a moment before Yael realizes the fluttering is due not to the dress's layers of tulle or wispy sleeves caught in a draft but to silk butterflies sewn along her gown from neckline to hem, each seemingly enchanted to flap its wings independently.

Yael draws in a steadying breath. "You'd better."

As Yael follows their cousin onto the floor, the violin players begin a lively tune, and Yael and Araphi bend the knee to bow to each other.

"What have you been up to this midsummer eve?" they ask, appraising the lace mask made to look like a broad pair of deep-purple butterfly wings resting askew on her lovely face, and the artful pile of dark hair that's come slightly unraveled atop her head, and the glittering blackberry lipstick smudged at the corner of her mouth.

She presses her palm to Yael's as they circle to the right. "A Clauneck never confesses," Araphi answers, smirking.

"Just between us, have you left Denby in a closet somewhere?"

She snorts. "Whomever I've left in a closet, *you* of all people have no right to judge me, Yael Clauneck."

"The heart wants what it wants, I'm sure, and I'll not judge you for it. But . . . *Denby*?"

The pair drift apart to weave among their fellow dancers in the predetermined pattern, reuniting to spin each other in turn. "Alas, the heart has little to do with it," Araphi continues, low enough that the nearest couple can't hear them; Yael can just make her words out over the music. "Alviss Oreborn is the only person who knows what really happened the night of your graduation party, aside from this family. The guests were all told that you'd drunk too much and taken to your bed, and our parents spread word of your supposed accident in the days after. But Oreborn's mount was gone when he and his son went to leave that night, and when pressed, the stable hands admitted they'd not checked on the animals for three hours—just about the time you'd disappeared from the party. He's not a stupid man, however thick his boots."

Yael's impressed with Oreborn, actually, until the implications sink in. "Good gods. Did he blackmail us?"

"Of course not," Araphi scoffs. "And risk being found at the bottom of one of his precious silver mines?"

"They wouldn't . . ."

"Oh, wouldn't they? No, Oreborn swore not to say a word. What happened next was your parents' idea, passed along to mine. The Claunecks don't like debt—their own debt, anyway—and Oreborn's silence was a commodity more precious than his missing steed. Our family thought it needed to be properly purchased."

"So you mean to say . . ." Yael stops in the middle of the floor until Araphi prompts them into their next turn. "You mean they offered you to Denby?"

"They proposed a match," she corrects them, "no less than what Alviss Oreborn intended to propose to them before you fled, only it would've been between Denby and you. Anyway, there were worse bargains to be made. The son of a mining empire is a solid match."

"I'll say Denby's solid."

"Don't, Yael," she scolds, her eyes sharpening behind her mask as she dips in a graceful curtsy.

"All right, all right. But even so, you've not yet graduated from Auximia! You can't possibly want to marry so young."

"Oh, what is the *point* of wanting? We aren't all lucky enough to ride off into the sunset—quite literally—and stumble upon some better, blissful life." Araphi says this not with disdain but as though explaining the world to a very young child, even though she's seen no more of that world than Yael has. "Do you think our family hasn't given me the 'where does the true power in Harrow lie' speech? The Claunecks thought they'd let their heir, their greatest asset, slip between their fingers. They needed to conjure up another, and that's what I was raised for."

So, then, Araphi has outpaced them in seriousness, after all.

"Is that what we are, Phi?" Yael murmurs as they guide her backward across the floor. "Company assets?"

She sighs. "You're asking bigger questions than I can answer after this much wine."

Yael's had nothing to drink yet this evening, they're suddenly and keenly aware. Their mouth feels parched as a dragon's hide. Where are those servants with their champagne trays? Yael could use something strong to wash down the idea that their leaving had consequences beyond their own happiness, for which their cousin is currently bearing the cost. And the pressure on Araphi to perform will only increase once Yael leaves Ashaway again for good.

"Oh, don't look so gloomy, cousin." Araphi breaks their grip to reach up and pinch Yael's cheek. "And don't worry about me. I'll find another dance partner to pass the evening with once you've rescued Margot from your father's clutches." Her gaze darts across the floor toward Margot and Baremon. "And . . . take care of her, all right? I've never been in love before, you know—wouldn't want it if I had it—but I think it looks marvelous on you."

They scoff on instinct. "Phi, I'm not in—"

"Well, she certainly is," Araphi cuts in with a wink. Then she bows and backs away just as the musicians end the waltz, leaving Yael alone and stunned.

Can that be true?

No. What would Araphi know of Margot's feelings? They've gone to one dress fitting together, and suddenly their cousin is

Margot's confidante? She hardly speaks her feelings to Yael, and they're close, aren't they? Childhood friends. Present friends. Lovers.

But . . . *in love?*

Something vast blooms inside of Yael, as though their ribs are garden gates that can no longer contain their own heart. Because of course Yael is in love with Margot Greenwillow. Margot is the tender of every good thing inside of them. They want nothing more than to leave this city and take Margot home, and maybe—just maybe—Margot wants nothing more than Yael.

What an unlikely, unbelievable, magical thing.

Pressing a hand to Yael's cheek, Margot gently turns their head to face her, having escaped their father's clutches all on her own. She leans in close, closer than any of the dancing couples had, her cheek brushing Yael's. "Suddenly it's very warm in here," she murmurs. "I know we've only just begun to dance, but should we get some air?"

Yael shivers as her lips graze their ear. "We should, at once."

They flee the dance floor before the next song can begin.

There's a balcony off the ballroom where they might find a decent summer breeze, but it's currently bustling with guests and clouded by cigar smoke. So Yael leads Margot back through the halls of the manor, up to a seldom-used parlor on the fourth floor that used to be their nursery and has since been converted. There's a small, private balcony where they remember their governess would sit in the sunlight to mend clothing while they played. Menorath would toss away anything with the slightest evidence of repair, anyhow, but their governess liked to keep her hands busy.

Yael leans out over the railing, and the sprawling estate unfolds before them. The sunset, just beginning now, casts its pink glow upon the ornamental pond, the stable roofs, the sharply trimmed hedges. The manicured gardens where nothing to be eaten is grown, nor any flora particularly beneficial to beasts or pollinators. Acres and acres of land, and so much of it comprises shorn grass and packed-down trails for easy strolling or riding; not that their parents spend much time traversing the grounds.

When they peer over the side, they're looking down on the ballroom balcony below, situated so that any guest looking up would clearly see them and hear them. Notes of flirtatious conversation and hard bargaining drift upward on the light breeze. But for the moment, no one looks up.

"Are you all right, Yael?" Margot asks, resting her elbows on the railing beside them.

*I love you,* they could say. They could tell her right now and put an end to their wondering. *I love you, I love you, I—*

"I'm just . . . on edge," Yael says instead: the least part of their feelings, and the easiest to confess. "It's being here, in my parents' world . . . They don't mean any of it, you know? All their talk of feeling glad to have me back? They lied to everyone for months rather than admit that their plans for me drove me away, and they never even cared to look for me until now, all for the sake of keeping up appearances. And I let them lie. Hells, I helped them lie."

Margot sighs deeply. "So did I, Yael."

"You only went along with their story because I convinced you it'd be easier." And what did *easier* even mean? Easier for whom? What's been easy about chipping off a piece of their own heart every time they let Rastanaya, or Oreborn, or even Denby believe the falsehood that the Claunecks were a family before they were a company?

"No, that isn't—"

"Believe me, Margot, you've nothing to do with my parents' schemes. After what my family did to yours, you're the least culpable person here tonight."

She reaches back behind her head to undo the ties of her mask, pulling it free even as it tangles in her spiraling crown braids, tugging strands of hair loose around her temples. Margot tosses the mask to the parquet floor of the balcony. "I'm not as good a person as you think I am, Yael. And you're a better person than you think you are."

Yael sniffs around a tight throat and burning eyes.

"Listen." Margot rests a hand on their shoulder and turns them around so that she can peer through their own mask, still snugly tied in place. "Forget for just a moment what your family, or I, or anyone else wants, and please, just tell me what *you* want."

A dozen glib responses sit on the tip of Yael's tongue.

But no.

Yael has to be serious, because it's possible that no question has ever mattered as much as this one. "I want . . . I want the chance to figure out who I could be in this world without the burden of who my family's decided I'm supposed to be. I want a life of my choosing."

Margot's gaze burns into theirs, her eyes like candles in the twilight. "There's really no part of you that misses *this* life?"

Yael turns the question over in their mind for a long moment before confessing, "I don't know. This is where I was born and how I was raised. But I know that the better part of me would be happier in a cottage in the woods with you for as long as you'll have me there."

That much they do know is true.

# 22

# MARGOT

Yael's words burn into Margot, a wildfire setting everything in its path alight. It's the truth, laid out plainly and painfully clear. It's so simple, it takes her breath away.

But it's not enough. If Yael goes back to the cottage with her, that means she's out of time, out of chances, and everyone in Bloomfield will be evicted. The cottage and greenhouses taken. All that Fern, Margot, and the people in the village have built and grown will be gone.

Margot wants to weep, but instead, she closes her eyes against all the wanting, the knowing, the lies she's told, and the truths she knows. For just a moment, she pushes it all down and lets herself look at Yael.

A warm breeze rustles the flowering vines on the trellis behind her, perfuming the air with the soft scent of jasmine. The hum of voices and the music from the string quintet on the terrace below their balcony floats upward, but in front of her it's only Yael, outlined in the hyacinth twilight, magnificent in their suit and ram's horn mask. A half smile quirks their gold-painted lips as their hair ruffles in the night air.

They are so lovely, so bold, so different than she ever expected them to be. Margot aches to tell them this and so much more.

"Yael," she whispers, her voice catching in her throat. "I . . ." She swallows hard as desire wars with despair.

She wants Yael. That's it. That's all. But how can they ever be together? Life in Ashaway would be a misery for Yael—and likely for herself as well. Yet if they leave the city, they doom the village; there will be no second extension from the Claunecks, no further grace as she struggles to figure out the impossible Natural Caster Potion she isn't close to finishing, despite all her promises, in the next few months. Margot doubts that Menorath and Baremon will even wait out the summer remaining on their deal if she disappoints them. But if she convinces Yael to stay, they doom themselves to a future under the thumb of the Claunecks all the same. She cannot ask that of Yael, and she cannot trick them into it. Not when she . . .

But that's too much to consider at this moment as the twilight shimmers off the golden paint on Yael's slightly parted lips.

Gods help her, she wants Yael Clauneck right here on this balcony.

Forcing herself to take a slow breath, Margot runs a hand over the Claunecks' letter she's carried with her for three or so years, currently tucked inside a hidden pocket in her skirt to keep it safe and to keep herself from forgetting why she came here. Across from her, Yael leans against the balustrade, clearly aiming for casual, but tension is written in the line of their shoulders. In how they cross and uncross their feet at the ankle. In the way their gaze darts away from Margot's as she tries to meet it.

She exhales sharply. "Yael, I want . . ."

*To say yes to you, and to have a life together.*

But admitting that means destroying the lives of so many people she cares about.

*The better part of me would be happier in a cottage in the woods with you for as long as you'll have me there.*

It can never happen, but in this one moment, she will let herself pretend they can have a happily ever after together. After all, how much time can they have left? She should make every minute count.

Margot lifts a hand to Yael's face, reaching up to tenderly cup their jaw beneath the mask. She tries again. "I . . ." She hesitates, not wanting to say the wrong thing.

But she allows the silence to stretch a beat too long. Yael turns away, their shoulders slumping. They shrug and slip their hands into their pockets. "Don't answer now, Daisy. Please. Truly. It's just that I wanted you to know—"

"Yael?" She grips their elbow, turning them back toward her.

"Yes?" The word is so tentative, so hopeful. It breaks Margot's heart as it hangs in the air between them. She takes Yael's hand and bends so her lips are right beside Yael's golden ones.

"I *would* have you there," she says, putting all her hopes into the words, even if they are foolish. Even if it cannot happen, Yael should at least know her heart. "In my cottage, always. But—"

"Daisy," Yael interrupts. Their eyes are dark pools within the ram's head mask.

"Yes?"

"Have I told you how very lovely you look in this dress?" Yael's hands lightly grip her waist, pressing her against their body, tracing the lines of her bodice as they kiss her again.

A whip of desire, hot, hungry, and demanding, licks through Margot's bloodstream. Letting her fingers trail along Yael's shoulders, she releases her worries, her impending heartbreak, the crushing weight of her responsibilities, and allows herself to sink fully into the moment. "Tell me again . . ."

"You—" A golden kiss lands on Margot's collarbone. "Are—" Another kiss at the hollow of her throat. "Magnificent—" Another kiss where her jaw meets her neck. "In—" One more kiss on the edge of her mouth. "This—"

Before Yael can kiss her again, one of their horns knocks against Margot's cheekbone. A small, surprised exclamation slips past her lips.

"Oh gods." Yael pulls away. "This damn mask. I'm sorry." They fumble for the ribbons holding it together behind their head.

"Wait. You didn't do any damage."

"I'm grateful I didn't spear your eye out or something."

Margot scoffs at that. "I am unscathed, except for the kisses you've marked me with."

Yael swears again, starting to rub at the gleaming trail painted above her breasts.

But Margot grabs their wrist. "Leave them. I'll wear them with pride. Now turn around."

"Why?"

"Just do it, please."

Yael shoots her a smirk over their shoulder and turns. "As you insist."

"Thank you." Margot takes a step backward, her hand at Yael's waist, pulling them into her body. As they fit together, Yael's back to Margot's curves, they take another step backward. And one more. When Margot's firmly pressed against the jasmine-covered stone wall of the manor, she slips a finger under Yael's mask strings, untying the knot. The ram's disguise tumbles to the ground, joining Margot's discarded mask on the balcony floor.

"Are you undressing me in my parents' house, Daisy?" Yael's

voice is husky, a touch playful, with an edge of need woven through it. The words send a shiver down Margot's spine. She would like nothing more than to undress them right here and have them on this balcony.

"Perhaps." Margot rests a hand on Yael's waist, pulling them closer to her chest. The silk of their jacket brushes against her bare skin, and she melts with longing. She isn't thinking about the party below or Yael's fine words. Or the life they will never make for themselves in Bloomfield. All she's thinking about is the desperate need racing through her veins.

"You wicked thing," Yael murmurs as Margot whispers a kiss above the collar of Yael's shirt. They taste like the night, with a hint of their own scent that makes Margot feel drunk. She drags her lips up the nape of their neck.

She feels so very wicked, and so very hungry. "I can't help it. You're delicious . . ." She pulls Yael even closer, nibbling lightly on their earlobe.

Yael lets out a low moan, full of wanting. That noise undoes Margot, and she's suddenly desperate to touch Yael. To feel them under her hands. To taste them . . .

"Daisy . . ." Yael gasps as Margot's hand snakes around to the front of Yael's jacket. "As much as I love this, I thought we agreed to not ruin your dress until after the party."

"My dress will survive us." She unbuttons their pants, slipping a hand past the waistline and letting her fingers drift below Yael's silken underwear. Yael's skin is warm, their stomach muscles taut under her touch.

Margot runs her fingers along the arch of their hip bone, inching closer, ever deliciously closer, to the heat between Yael's thighs.

Yael inhales sharply as Margot's fingers slide another inch lower. "What about the people below? They might hear us." Yael's words are ragged with wanting.

Margot isn't worried about the party. "No one will hear us," she assures Yael, leaning closer so her lips brush Yael's ear. "Because you are going to be very, very quiet."

"Daisy . . ."

"Shhhhhh."

She moves her hand a bit lower, her thumb hovering so close to Yael's center, she can feel them tremble. She kisses the corner of their jaw. The side of their mouth. Slowly, oh, so very slowly, she lets her hand slip between their legs. Yael arches to meet her touch.

"Margot—oh gods . . ."

"Hush," she reminds them, murmuring in their ear.

Yael nods, leaning into Margot, their need hot and insistent against her hand. Her fingers are strong from years of work in the garden and greenhouses, and she knows how Yael likes to be touched.

She slips one finger, and then two, inside them, using her thumb to carefully, deliberately stroke the small center of their pleasure. Again. Harder now, and more demanding, until Yael is nearly gasping as they push against Margot's fingers. Yael bites their lip fighting a moan, and heat flashes through Margot. Suddenly, there's nothing more important than Yael's pleasure. Nothing more urgent than Margot telling them with her hands and her body how vital they are to her.

She works another finger inside them, deeper this time, pushing hard with the heel of her hand. Yael trembles.

"Daisy, I'm begging you . . ."

She increases the pressure of her hand, using the other to pull Yael even closer, so their backside grinds right against her own need.

"What are you begging me for?" Another stroke.

Yael makes a strangled noise, squirming under Margot's

touch. "I need you to . . . oh gods, yes, Daisy, exactly like that . . ."

She keeps going. "What are you begging me for?" she asks again.

"To let me kiss you . . ."

"I thought we agreed you were going to be very quiet while I finish you?"

With a whimper, Yael presses themself into Margot's hand, seeking more pressure, and she works them harder. Their head drops back on Margot's shoulder as they keep grinding into her fingers. "But, darling," they manage on the edge of a gasp, "it's so much more fun when we do this together."

Margot can't argue with that. She gives Yael the briefest of reprieves as they turn around so their body is flush against Margot's. With desperate intention, Yael kisses the valley between Margot's breasts, sending an ache through her entire being. As Yael slips a hand under her breast, lifting and freeing it from its corset, Margot's fingers get back to work.

Yael lets another low moan escape them, ragged and even hungrier. "I'm not going to last if you keep that up, Daisy." Their mouth finds Margot's nipple, and their tongue traces the edges, nipping at it lightly.

Neither will Margot if Yael continues to attend to her breasts like they're doing. Yael hasn't even touched her between her legs yet, and still, she's drenched with desire. "I know *exactly* what you mean." She pulls Yael even closer.

Yael's lips find hers, and they kiss her urgently, deeply. Margot takes their hand, directing it to where she needs them.

They tug on her bottom lip with their teeth. "How shall I ever get this damn skirt of yours up?"

Margot should've insisted upon fewer underskirts or forgone undergarments. Then again, they never should've come to the ball in the first place. Why aren't they back in their room at the Glowing Coin, where such problems are easily solved?

Margot pauses in her work just long enough to lift her skirts. She leans back against the jasmine-covered wall as Yael's hand snakes beneath her clothing and into the heart of her desire.

Together, they find a rhythm, each of them teasing, pushing, pressing. Margot wraps one silken-stocking covered leg around Yael's waist, and they gasp.

"Daisy," Yael moans, arching up to her. "I can't wait—"

And then they break, their pleasure shattering across Margot's hand. They shiver as they finish, then their mouth dips to Margot's breast once more. Their hands move under her skirt, insisting she follows them.

She comes a moment later, riding waves of delight. Her head falls back on the trellis, sending jasmine blossoms raining down around her, and she grips Yael's hair tightly with both her hands.

"Oh, darling," Yael murmurs moments later, kissing a path back up her neck. Their lips hover directly above hers as they whisper against her mouth, "I fear neither of us was quiet."

Margot laughs, giddy with sated desire and the closeness of Yael. "I don't believe anyone heard us, but if they did, I don't think I care."

"I feel the same way entirely." Their lips sink into Margot's, drawing her to them again.

When they finally break apart, Margot lets go of her bunched skirts—gods, her dress is wrinkled beyond repair, but she can't bring herself to give it more than a passing thought. Crushed and fallen jasmine flowers litter the balcony floor. Yael plucks one from her hair, and Margot brushes one from their lapel, pouring tenderness into the gesture.

She loves Yael Clauneck. That's the other truth she knows, and it is utterly terrible.

"Yael?" she murmurs.

"Yes, Daisy?"

"Let's get out of here, please? Just for the night? Let's go back to the Glowing Coin?"

"Why not pack our things and leave the city altogether? I've about had my fill of Ashaway, don't you agree?"

Margot wanted one more night, or at least a few more hours to pretend. But she can't have that.

It's time to tell Yael the entire truth.

Straightening herself, she brushes another flower from her sleeve. Reaching into her pocket, Margot hands them the letter.

"What is this?" Yael asks, their eyes running over the Clauneck letterhead. Skimming the words Margot knows so well. "Margot, what is this?" they repeat. They read aloud: "*We are impressed by your generous estimations of your daughter's talents and intrigued by the Natural Caster Restoration Potion you claim she is close to perfecting. In remembrance of Fern—whose legacy looms large over Harrow and its economy still—we have seen fit to offer an extension on said debts. For a period of four years until that summer's end, we will delay the seizure of Bloomfield . . .*"

"It's from your parents."

"Obviously. What do they mean? What is this Natural Caster Potion?"

Taking a deep breath for courage, Margot finally tells Yael the full truth. She shares the little she knows about the recipe and why Menorath wants it, and about the Claunecks actually owning her cottage, greenhouses, and the village of Bloomfield. She confesses to her failed attempts to make the impossible Natural Caster Potion, and the four mere months that are left. On the edge of a sob, she also tells Yael about Menorath's secret message attached to the masquerade invitation, how she persuaded Yael to come back to Ashaway when they didn't want to, and Menorath's offer for a permanent pause on the repossession of the greenhouses, cottage, and town if she convinces Yael to remain in Ashaway and rejoin their family.

"And if I refuse?" Yael says tersely.

Margot feels tears fill her eyes. "Then they take Bloomfield. For good."

When it's all done, all of it finally out of her and in the open, Margot looks up at Yael as a tear slips down her cheek and says, in a small, broken voice, "I'm so sorry about it all. Not that it really matters, but I've been torn and scared and wretched about this for so long. And then you strolled into my life and made everything softer. And lighter, and I loved that so much. And now, even though you know it all, can you possibly forgive me?"

# 23

# YAEL

Can they *forgive* Margot?

How can Yael blame her at all?

*It wasn't your fault,* they draw in a breath to say, the words a prism refracting half a dozen meanings from one simple phrase.

It wasn't Margot's fault that her parents tore to rubble everything that Granny Fern built with their greed and ambition, with their hunger to be just like the Claunecks and their ilk—obvious even to Yael as a child.

It wasn't Margot's fault that her parents left her alone in such desperate straits.

It wasn't Margot's fault that when Yael fled their childhood home, they stumbled drunkenly into her life, following no star but their own desperation.

It wasn't Margot's fault that Menorath had threatened every remaining scrap of happiness that Margot had managed to keep for herself in order to force her hand.

It wasn't Margot's fault that the Claunecks have never sought to grow a single thing—only to consume.

And, Yael thinks miserably, it isn't Margot's fault she's fallen for one of them.

*YOU, YAEL, ONE OF US?*

Clauneck's voice is louder than they've ever heard—a sharply clanging bell—and Yael claps their hands over their ears to stifle the clamor. But they can't stop it, because it's inside of them.

*YOU, WHO HAVE ALWAYS REFUSED TO PERFORM TO YOUR POTENTIAL? YOU, WHO HAVE PRODUCED NOTHING IN SERVICE OF THIS FAMILY BUT DEMANDED YOUR OWN HAPPINESS AS THOUGH IT WAS OWED? YOU, WHO HAVE REJECTED OUR MAGIC, OUR COUNSEL, OUR WAY OF LIFE? WHAT HAVE YOU TO OFFER THE CLAUNECKS, YAEL, IF YOU ARE ONE OF US? WHAT HAVE YOU TO OFFER ANYONE?*

What *do* they have to offer?

"Yael? Are you all right?"

As the ringing inside of their very bones gradually recedes, they realize Margot's palms are on their shoulders, fisted in the fabric of their hastily rebuttoned vest, her concern for Yael burning in her eyes.

They lower their hands, shaking their head to clear it.

"Please, say something? Or . . . or better yet, just come back to the inn with me? We can talk there. It'll be easier to talk to each other away from all of this." She nods toward the manor behind them, music seeping up from the ballroom along with the chatter of the jeweled guests below—every powerful person in Harrow but the queens themselves, who are rumored to be putting in an appearance at some point during the ball. "We can leave, Yael, right now, and you can yell at me as much as you like in the carriage, so long as we're away from here," she finishes with a little smile that's sad and hopeful and heartbreaking all at once. "Even if it's only for tonight. Or perhaps . . . perhaps we can still figure something out together?"

Yael wants to believe that's possible. That there's no problem or power they cannot overcome. Most of all, Yael has never wanted anything more than they want to say yes.

So if any words have ever cost them more dearly than their next, they can't recall. "We—I can't, Margot."

And this too is true.

Because wishing for a happily ever after with Margot Greenwillow is as useless as . . . well, as Yael Clauneck. No, worse than useless. Their presence in Margot's life has already cost her dearly, and it will continue to cost her. Even if Margot wants to believe there's a way to wriggle out from beneath the iron grip of the Clauneck Company, to keep each other and save the village without giving Baremon and Menorath what they want, Yael knows that there isn't. There is no world in which their parents let them go without Margot losing everything she has left out of love for them, including Bloomfield. Yael's family wanted a public reunion with their heir, and they got it. Now they want all Claunecks accounted for and back to business as usual before this potentially disastrous summer ends and autumn sets in.

The only way to protect Margot and the people of Bloomfield—the people who welcomed Yael into their homes without knowing that Yael's family could have them all evicted at any moment—is for Yael to give their family what it wants.

*This* is what they have to offer.

"You can't?" Margot repeats. "But—"

"Rather, I don't want to."

On second thought, this lie has cost them even more than the truth. But they clamp their back teeth together to steady their jaw and shape their face into a mask as lifeless as the one lying on the balcony beneath them, which they bend to scoop up. They tie it back on with shaking fingers they hope she won't notice in the dark, taking the moment to compose themself as Margot fumbles for her reply.

"Because I've hurt you, I . . . I know," she whispers.

"You *used* me, Margot." They make their voice as cold as their false ram's horns. "You never wanted me. You wanted a Clauneck."

"No! It's not like that, I swear!"

"No wonder you found a common cause with my mother," Yael forces themself to say. "You two have much in common. You should go now, Margot."

"Yael, no." She unwraps her arms from her rib cage to hold up a hand. "Please, just come—"

"Go back to the inn." They cut her off, surprising themself with all the power of their family name invested in their command. "I'll stay at the manor. At least here, I've always known to sleep with my back to the wall." The words hurt enormously coming out, very like drawing a dagger from a wound (or so they'd guess) with a fresh wave of blood and pain.

But it does the job. Margot sinks onto her heels on the jasmine-covered balcony floor, no longer reaching for them. She hugs herself around the glittering bodice of her dress as she starts to tremble.

Gods, Yael can still take this back. It isn't too late.

They can fall to their knees in front of her, press golden kisses into her hands, and beg for the forgiveness they've pretended to deny Margot. They can seize their chance to be loved by Margot. And in doing, take back the only gift they have to give her in service of their own happiness.

*You have always been thoughtless, Yael, but are you a coward as well?*

Yael would cut Clauneck out of themself here and now if they could.

But they can't.

They cannot be anything but what they are, and what they are would ruin Margot Greenwillow, and Bloomfield as well.

Yael can't leave with Margot, and Margot can't stay where the Claunecks would soon consume and destroy her, as they do all good things. And they cannot pretend, even for one night, that it isn't true.

So with a last formal bow, Yael turns away from her, striding back into the cold stone innards of the manor house until they pass beyond her line of sight. Then they drop all pretense of calm and break into a run.

# 24

# MARGOT

The glass balcony doors slam behind Yael, the noise shaking Margot to her core. She crumples the letter in her hand, wanting to scream, to weep, to throw the hated piece of paper away, or, most especially, to get up and run after Yael.

She does none of those things.

Instead, she sits beneath the jasmine, knees pulled to her chest as much as her corset will allow, and weeps as the sounds of the party grow louder. Laughter, music, the clinking of crystal glasses together, the hum of elegant voices: It all sounds tawdry and terrible. Perhaps Yael has joined their family in the ballroom already, and is down there now, laughing along with beautiful people, every inch the Clauneck heir.

Or perhaps they've found their own corner of the manor to cry in.

The thought makes Margot sob, but she forces herself to shove the thought aside. She can't afford sympathy for Yael, not with what she must do next. Also, some small part of her still can't believe they've walked away from her.

"It's for the best," she murmurs to herself, the words punctuated with sniffles as she remembers Yael's cruel words.

*"You never wanted me. You wanted a Clauneck."*

Why had they said that? It certainly wasn't true, and she never meant to use Yael or lie to them. She only wanted—- What?

To save her town. To change her own life. To prove that she *did* have as much to offer as Granny Fern. To keep hold of a small measure of happiness of her own with someone she adored.

It was always too much to hope for. And now she must make her way through the world alone again.

With a shaking breath, Margot stands. She brushes petals from her skirt, straightens her hair, and wipes at her eyes. She casts one more glance over the balcony railing at the guests gathered below—Yael isn't among them—and then she flees down endless hallways of the Clauneck manor.

Eventually, she stumbles into the shadowy gardens, ignoring the gasps from startled guests doing secretive things in the shrubbery as she runs across the lawn in her ridiculous heeled shoes. After a few mistaken turns, she makes it to the long row of stables at the back of the Clauneck property.

The stable door is open, and golden lantern light and laughter spill out from the building, illuminating a trio of coach drivers and several stable hands sitting on bales of hay and playing cards. Margot leans against the doorframe, gulping in the warm rich scents of hay, horses and other beasts, and manure. A memory of her and Yael and a few others of their childhood pack sneaking out of the manor and to the stables comes to her unbidden, and she can almost feel Yael's fingers threaded through hers, as they were back then.

A sob breaks out of her, and she quickly holds up a hand to smother it. The coach drivers and stable hands look up, and she removes the hand from her mouth, using it to smooth her hair. She can only imagine what her braids and makeup look like right now.

"Are you quite all right, miss?" a white-haired coach driver in crimson livery asks as they stand to greet her.

Margot starts to speak, instead letting loose another hiccuping sob. She tries to get herself under control. "Perhaps some water?" she manages.

"Only water here is for the horses and other creatures," the driver says. "But we have firewhiskey." They pull a dented metal flask from their hip pocket.

"That will do perfectly." Margot takes the offered flask and tips it back. As its name promises, the firewhiskey burns on its way to her belly, but she doesn't mind. Focusing on that pain is much preferable to thinking about losing Yael and everything the two of them might've had together.

"We can deal you in if you'd like, miss?" the coachperson asks, gesturing to the card game. "Wouldn't be the first time a fine-feathered guest has snuck away from the party for the stables."

Margot isn't sure if they're referring to Yael's flight from the Clauneck Manor all those months ago, or to something else, but it doesn't matter. "Could you please just take me back into the city, to the Glowing Coin Inn by the Golden Court?"

"Sorry, can't do that. I'm driving for the Oreborn family tonight. We can hardly have them wanting to leave the party and their coach not here."

Margot spares a brief thought for how much Yael might enjoy the idea of her stealing the Oreborn coach, then remembers she can't tell them anything now.

"Please," Margot implores the driver. "My hired coach . . . fell through . . . and I have to get back to the inn immediately. I can't stay here a moment longer."

"Are you in some kind of trouble?" the coachperson asks gently.

"Only the kind I've caused myself," she murmurs. "I can pay you."

It's then that she remembers her purse is back at the inn; Yael told her she wouldn't need any money of her own tonight, because she was with them. Another sob claws its way up Margot's throat, but she swallows it down with more firewhiskey.

"I have money in my room," she amends.

The coachperson shakes their head. "Sorry, love. Not worth the risk of losing this job."

Frustrated, her fingers trace the hard studding of the jewels sewn into her dress, sparkling emeralds and shining pearls—Clauneck wealth pressed upon her body.

"What about some of these jewels?" she offers. "Would that make the risk worth your while?" Without a thought for her dress, Margot rips a handful of stones from the fabric, placing them in the driver's hand.

The driver's white eyebrows shoot upward. "Those would do nicely indeed."

# 25

# YAEL

Yael counts each step it takes to reach the ballroom, to pass through the gates, to skirt the waltzing guests on the dance floor. Faces blur around them and they can hardly hear the musicians' instruments over the sound of their own shuddering breath. (Somehow, there seems to be far more of it going out than coming in.) They slip among the crowd, miraculously unseen, then through a pair of ornately carved wooden doors at the far end of the ballroom into a private chamber holding one of the mansion's offering altars. This one's meant for guests looking to find favor with both the family and its patron, but the next nearest altar is two floors down, and Yael isn't sure they can make it that far.

The moment they've closed and barred the doors behind them, they slump to their knees and plant their palms against the stone floor. In front of them is the low table, its top— a thick slab of polished gray stone sliced through by veins of raw, glittering gold—piled high with offerings from guests attending the ball. A fist-sized leather pouch stuffed so full the ties have come loose to show the cut gems inside. A pewter flask stamped with the crest of the Wayanette household. A (presumably ceremonial) dagger with a bone handle exquisitely carved into a faun's naked form. A large violet egg that smells of fireplace ashes. All of it useless to Claudeck except as it increases the wealth of Yael's family (and what's a fire lizard's egg compared with the favor of the most powerful family in Harrow?), which increases the glory of the Claudeck name.

Yael crawls forward and sweeps it all onto the floor to place their palms on the tabletop. Their eyes strain as they stare into one of the dozen flickering purple candles in silver holders that keep the altar room in a state of half light and half shadow.

"Can you help me?" they gasp.

*You would ask me to help you betray your family? Find some loophole in the pact you've already made with yourself?*

"No," they answer, feeling as though they're withering from the inside out. "You were right. I'm thoughtless, and cowardly, and . . . and I don't think I'm strong enough to live like this for a day, or a week, or a season, let alone forever. Not even to save Bloomfield. I will lie awake every night and imagine myself climbing out of bed and making my way back to Margot, until the night I give in to myself. I need you . . . I would ask you to help me stay."

For a second that seems interminable, Claudeck is silent. Then:

*I will make it feel as though it was* your *choice entirely to return to Ashaway—to us—and you will know beyond a speck of doubt that it was the right choice. You will know in your bones that you are where you are supposed to be. And in the knowing, you will be free of this pain, this self-loathing, this loneliness. You will become what your family needs you to be, who you were born to be, and so you will never be alone again.*

"Do it. Please."

Yael closes their eyes and finds that the icy purple candle's flame has seared into their vision—a disquieting light in the dark it may be, but it is the only light they have.

# 26

# MARGOT

argot's journey from the stables to the Glowing Coin is a blur. The coachperson drops her off outside the inn, where Margot strides across the lobby, ignoring the stares of guests up late. Feathers float behind her as she hurries past, like she's some exotic bird, but she ignores them as well. She storms up the grand staircase, tripping on her long skirts and tearing them at the hem, but she couldn't care less.

Once she's outside their suite, she fumbles for her small room key—thank goodness she'd thought to slip that into her dress, at least—and shoves it into the lock. The door swings open, and then as it closes, she is blissfully, entirely alone.

Which is well and good until her eyes fall across Yael's trunk. And their discarded day jacket. And their pillow. And the small flower—a daisy, oh gods—Yael has left for Margot on her own pillow. Where they'd gotten a daisy or when they'd set it out, Margot doesn't know, but it hadn't been there when they'd both been dressing.

She walks to the bed now, picking up the daisy, which is perfectly in bloom and gleaming slightly silver and gold. It's clearly been enchanted to stay fresh. Margot closes her eyes, remembering a moment from earlier that evening.

"I'll be just a second," Yael said as they were walking out the door. Margot had a hand on the knob, and her corset was digging into her ribs, feeling tighter by the second as her anxiety about the ball ratcheted up.

"You can't leave me standing here," she'd said as teasingly as she could manage. "I'm depending on your arm in mine all night, so I don't go tumbling in these heels."

"You'd manage just fine on your own," Yael said, throwing a smirk over their shoulder. "I'm sure of it, but I'll be right back. I just have one thing to do . . ." And then they'd disappeared back into the bedchamber.

A daisy. They'd left her a daisy. Margot slumps heavily onto the bed. Yael's surprise gift is simple, but it speaks volumes. Perhaps it says that they love her.

Perhaps Yael walking away *was* the only real option left to both of them, and underneath it all, it's a noble sacrifice that frees Margot from having to make the terrible choice herself. Which means that Yael might have left in order to protect her. Gods, though, if that's the case, is there any hope for them? Someday? Maybe?

Is that too much to wish for?

Probably, but Margot cannot help holding on to a small ember of hope, even as she weeps.

Not that it matters now, since the Clauneck family has their claws so deep into both Margot and Yael that they can't survive a life of their own together.

Suddenly, the room feels too small. Too gilded. Too much like the Clauneck Manor. Without Yael at her side, Margot feels how very out of place she actually is in this world.

Standing, she goes to the mirror. A line of Yael's golden

kisses still paints her neck and collarbones, the glittering ghosts of their touch. Grabbing a cloth, she scrubs at the lip paint, rubbing hard until her skin is red and painful. But at least the kisses are gone.

"You should go, Margot," she murmurs, repeating Yael's words to herself.

She has to go home. Alone. Now. Perhaps there is some way out of this mess between her and Yael that she's not seeing, but she's been trying and failing to fix her life for years, and she's so tired. She was a fool to think that she could possibly save Bloomfield *and* make a life with Yael Clauneck in Ashaway. Not that she wants a life in Ashaway; she knows that now. If she stayed in the city, even with Yael, she could see herself growing bitter and miserable with missing Bloomfield. Besides, she cannot leave Bloomfield without a solution. Before she finds any sort of happiness herself, she has to make sure the village and the people she loves are safe and secure.

*You will never have a life with Yael Clauneck, thanks to their appalling family.*

The thought levels Margot, and she sinks to her knees as sobs once again rack her chest. When they finally cease, she stands. Reaching behind her, she tugs on her dress. Yael had laced her into it earlier, and the plan had always been for Yael to help her out of it too.

The corset digs more tightly into her ribs, and suddenly she can't breathe. The world spins and her heart races.

She rips at the sleeves, not caring when beads and pearls go skittering across the floor. She tears at the feathers along her neck, shredding the silk and loosening the gems. All her anger at Menorath and Baremon, heartache over Yael, and despair for her own lies that let everything progress this far fuels Margot's hands as she rips the dress from her body. When the gown is finally pooled at her feet and she manages to unlace her corset,

Margot gasps for air. She can almost, nearly breathe again, though her hands still shake.

Stepping away from the pile of silk and feathers, she looks in the mirror once more. Her hair is askew, braids unraveled, but divested of the finery, she almost looks like herself. Stumbling to her trunk, she sifts through the clothing to find her strawberry-print dress, which she packed in a fit of sentimentality. She slips it on. Over that goes a green cardigan that Clementine knitted for her last winter.

Heart heavy, Margot laces up her traveling boots, packs a small bag with her personal effects, and then glances around the room for anything left behind. Her masquerade dress is still piled on the floor, but the Claunecks will pay someone to sort that out. The everblooming daisy Yael left out for her is still on the bed, and Margot picks it up. She can take this at least, to have something to remember Yael by. Though who is she kidding? She'll see them in every flower, in every gleam of a greenhouse window, and every time she walks to Clementine's for a meal.

But she will have to live with that, even if she can't live with Yael.

She tucks the daisy into her pocket.

She really shouldn't leave in this state, but staying another night in this room paid for by the Claunecks isn't an option. If she hires a coach now, she'll be back in Bloomfield before morning. Margot grabs the handle of her trunk and tugs it toward the door, then pauses at the threshold.

There is one last thing to confess before she leaves.

Turning back to the table, she plucks a piece of paper from a sheaf on the desk and quickly scrawls:

*Yael,*
*I'm sorry. For it all.*
*—M*

She wants to say more. She really does, but what else could she say? That she loves them? That she'll always keep a place in the cottage for them, for as long as she can keep the cottage? That more than anything else, she wishes the two of them had never come to Ashaway? That their parents are scheming spiders and both of them got caught up in the web? That maybe, if she figures out the Natural Caster Potion and settles her parents' debts, things can change?

No.

Although she gave the Claunecks their heir back, she's not sure if Menorath will keep her word, or how, and whether she'll ever truly be free of their clutches.

All she knows now is she must live with the hard truths of her own life, and without Yael at her side.

# 27

# YAEL

Yael's first day with the company passes thusly:

They rise with the estate—or rather, with its masters—meeting their parents in the informal dining hall for a quick and silent breakfast of smoked fish, heavy dark bread, and watered wine. Dozens of servants have been busy since before dawn, cleaning and preparing meals and lighting fires in the grates of the many rooms that remain cool even in summertime, thanks to the slick gray stonework of the manor house. They always complete their chores early, then scatter until Baremon leaves for the office, as Yael's father prefers that the staff remain largely unseen. When Yael lived here as a child, some days the sun would rise and set without them passing a single soul within the labyrinthine halls.

After breakfast, the family's gold-crowned ebony carriage ferries them from the estate, up the Queens' Road, and to the Copper Court to begin their workday. The center of industry in Harrow shines as though built from the very coins within the capital's mint. Each office, shopfront, and merchant's club is built of blush-colored stones topped with copper-tiled roofs. One has to shield one's eyes to look up at them. The Clauneck

Company is the tallest of them all, like a lighthouse presiding over an ocean of molten copper.

Yael is put on the fifth of ten levels (ten levels aboveground, that is) in the Hall of Exchange. It is a long, goldenwood-paneled chamber with Uncle Mikhil's office stationed at the far end. His office has tall, narrow shelves of leather-bound tomes—purely for ornament—and tall, narrow windows with scarlet and gold glass panes. Yael occupies a desk in the outer chamber, acting as a sort of river lock in the channel between their uncle and the dozen number crunchers and errand runners pooled together at the front of the hall.

Hour after hour, Yael is brought records documenting the exchange of unminted silver ore and gold dust for the copper, silver, and gold denaris minted within Harrow, as well as the exchange of Harrow's coinage for Perpignan's knygar, or Yang's guarani, and so on. Each record must be cross-checked with the Clauneck Company's statements of account, allowing for fluctuations in the values of the coinage, to ensure that the totals match, that no spellwork has escaped detection, that no fraudulent pieces have slipped through. Compiling these reports is the job of the underlings down the hall, but it's Yael's job to cross-check them. When necessary, they pause long enough to run to the Records Library to grab some relevant file or ledger; only Claunecks and a select few highly ranked employees are trusted to enter, and Yael almost welcomes the task for an excuse to stretch their legs and rest their eyes before it's back to the reports.

When work is done for the day, Yael rides to a nearby merchant's club in the Golden Court with Baremon and Mikhil for a business dinner. Yael is seldom called upon to contribute, but as Baremon explained it in the carriage, their presence paints the picture of a family business—a boon for customers and for potential customers who consider themselves moral, family-loving folk. When Baremon does signal for them to speak, it's to leave their dinner guests charmed and laughing over some recounted escapade from Yael's time abroad in Perpignan or Locronan, or to do some pretty bit of magic for entertainment's sake. They're never asked to offer an opinion on anything important, which makes it easy for Yael not to have any opinions.

At the end of the day, lying in their old bedchambers, Yael can't say that they're happy on this estate, or in this city, or in this life. But they know it's where they ought to be, and that this is the life they should be living. When they wonder *why,* and where that knowledge comes from, a deep pain flares up inside of them—as though the truth is lodged beneath their bones or buried in the meat of their heart, unreachable without sharper knives and stronger magic than they can wield, even having visited Clauneck's altar this very morning.

So the next morning, they do it all again, and the morning after that.

Time passes. Bloomfield begins to feel like a memory from childhood—pleasant but faint, and ultimately lost to them forever now that they've finally grown up.

# 28

# MARGOT

Everything about the cottage is the same as Margot left it. Except, of course, that Yael is gone. Margot stands in the doorway, early-morning light streaming in, and considers the small room in front of her.

While they lived in Bloomfield, Yael had slept at the inn up until the last few nights, but they were frequently in Margot's cottage before that for a cup of tea, which Margot always made, or to bring a treat from the bakery, or to borrow one of Margot's books. Their scarf—a green one Margot had knitted in preparation for fall, even as the weather warmed by the day—is still draped over the back of a chair, awaiting cooler nights. The small strawberry plant they'd proudly grown from a runner sat on the windowsill above the kitchen sink. The last teacup they'd drunk from that morning before leaving for Ashaway was still on the kitchen table beside Margot's.

Her eyes linger on the butter-gold teacup painted with bumblebee designs. Yael had loved that particular cup for some reason. They would sit at Margot's table, hands wrapped around it, eyes sparkling as they told Margot a story or teased her gently about the lumpy pancakes she could never quite get right, though they claimed they preferred her pancakes to Clementine's.

Margot swallows thickly.

"You are not going to get sentimental over a teacup," Margot commands herself as she marches into the cottage, closing the door behind her. "Or Yael gods-be-warned Clauneck."

She grabs the cup, fighting the urge to throw it against the wall. Or to rest her lips against the edge where Yael's lips had been not that many days ago.

Making a disgusted noise at both herself and the ring of mold growing inside the cup, she sets it into the sink and drops down in the closest chair. A poof of dust rises up. Really? Dust? After just a week of being gone? Ridiculous. Margot's bones ache from the all-night coach ride from Ashaway, and though she managed not to weep as she climbed into the nearly full carriage headed for Olde Post, she never did get to sleep, and had to walk the last two miles from the Queens' Road through the outpost walls and to the doorstep of the cottage. Now a deep weariness sets upon her.

Did Yael sleep last night? she wonders. What are they doing now? Have they effortlessly slipped back into life with the Claunecks? Do they think of her as much as she thinks of them?

Will she ever see them again?

Margot plucks the everlasting daisy from her pocket, resting it on the table and swallowing against the lump in her throat.

It doesn't matter. Margot simply can't afford to let her thoughts linger on Yael Clauneck when she has so much work to do.

Another sob rises up to choke Margot, and she lets this one out as she stands to fetch a clean spoon from the cupboard and the last jar of heartbreak-healing jam. Perhaps a spoonful will make her feel better. Anything to take away this pain.

The jam is sweet on her tongue, coating her teeth with sugar and sliding in a lump down her throat.

It does nothing to ease the ache in Margot's heart, though, which just makes her feel worse. How is she ever supposed to make the Natural Caster Potion when she can't even get a simple thing like heartbreak-healing jam right?

Though perhaps there are aches worse than a simple jam can cure.

Letting the spoon drop to the table, she buries her head in her hands in the shadowy cottage where she and Yael might have had a life together and finally lets herself weep all the tears she's held back since leaving Ashaway.

Much later, she wakes, her neck stiff and her back hurting even worse. She'd fallen asleep at the table after crying herself dry.

"Right," she says, standing. "No more Greenwillow tears for the Claunecks." She drops the everlasting daisy into a small vase on the table and walks away.

After changing out of her travel clothes and having a quick wash, Margot leaves the cottage, heading toward her greenhouses. It's late afternoon and her stomach rumbles as she walks, but she wants to check in on things before grabbing something to eat at Clementine's Tavern; she isn't eager for company, but there's no food left in the cottage.

Poppy sits behind the counter of the greenhouse shop, tinkering with a pile of gears spread out on the wood planks. She startles when Margot taps her lightly on the arm.

"Margot?" she asks, blinking like a surprised owl.

"Hi, Pop," Margot says. She picks up Harvey, who's curling himself around her ankles and purring happily.

"What in the world are you doing back so soon? We had bets going that you and Yael would be staying in Ashaway for at least a month . . . if not longer." Here, Poppy peers at Margot and raises an eyebrow teasingly.

Margot flinches at Yael's name. She's going to have to stop doing that. Because of course everyone whom Yael won over in Bloomfield—which is everyone in Bloomfield—will ask about them. What is she supposed to say? That Yael has perhaps tried to do something noble but shattered her heart in the process? Or that the town is in more danger than they can possibly imagine and she has no real way to help them? Guilt claws through Margot, and she avoids Poppy's gaze, burying her face in Harvey's fur instead, which he allows for a moment before hopping out of her arms. "Yael had . . . business to attend to in Ashaway," she says after a long moment.

"Will they be coming back?"

Tears rise in Margot's eyes, and she turns from Poppy to brush them away. "I don't think so."

Poppy remains silent, clearly unsure what to say. "I'm sorry," she murmurs at last.

"So am I. Now, why don't we take a quick walk around the greenhouse, and you can catch me up on everything I missed?"

Hours later, after Poppy showed her the new, impressive watering systems she'd rigged up, and she walked alone among the plants—all of which are growing beautifully—Margot is feeling a bit better. Maybe it's the two bracing cups of tea she drank, or maybe it's just being back with her plants and with people who know her for who she really is.

She's closing up for the night when the silver compact in her pocket chimes. She hasn't heard from Sage since Rastanaya's show, when her friend had been soon to depart for the Serpentine Sea with a new adventuring party. Expecting to find a hastily scrawled message, Margot flips open the compact . . . and nearly drops it as Sage's face beams back at her from the mirror.

"Hi, Margot!" she calls, her voice muffled by a bracing wind that tousles her short blond hair. Behind her on a pale beach, the sea crashes and foams.

"Sage, how—"

"Neat, isn't it? I did a favor for a wizard we met in a tavern in Ironspine, and he gave me a scroll to turn a sending spell into a seeing spell. Temporarily—it'll only work this once—but I wanted to show you the Serpentine Sea at sunset." Sage steps beyond the frame of the mirror and angles her own compact so that Margot has a full view of the sky striped pink and lavender and orange, and the sea painted golden bright.

Almost the color of Yael's lips at the masquerade. Almost.

Margot swallows back a sob. "It's lovely," she says over the whistling wind.

Sage returns, grinning. "Thought you'd like it! Been a bit of hard travel these last few days, but worth it for a view like this."

Eager to speak about anything other than her own problems, Margot asks, "How's the expedition going? Making any friends?"

Sage opens her mouth to reply but is drowned out by a loud growling and the far-off sound of a horn. Her eyes dart to the side, and she grabs her knife from the sheath at her hip. The noises quiet after a moment, and Sage shrugs, returning the knife to its place.

"Things are going well enough."

"What was that noise?"

Sage shrugs again. "Something that wants to eat us? Not sure. It's been a rough one, honestly. Our party leader is . . . well, let's just say I'm glad I never sign on with the same party twice. But I'll survive. How are you? How's your garden assistant and their cousin?"

Margot is surprised when a choked sob leaves her mouth

rather than the calm, collected *fine* she had prepared. Her face crumples, and suddenly she's weeping all over again.

"Margot?" Sage's brow furrows in concern. "What's happening over there?"

"Nothing, it's nothing."

"Certainly looks a lot like something."

"Perhaps I'll tell you the story when you're not standing on a windswept beach surrounded by things that want to eat you," Margot says, swiping at her tears. "I really am concerned about you."

Sage glances over her shoulder and then turns back. "Thought I heard someone being eaten, but nope. It's just the wind. And nice try, but we're talking about you. What happened?"

Margot can't help herself. Although she told Sage about her own feelings for Yael as the months with them passed, she had kept her true indebtedness to the Claunecks a secret. Now she lets the whole story spill out, from the letter she's carried around for years and the Natural Caster Potion she's tried and failed to make, to the first morning after the show when she woke up beside Yael, to Yael ending things on the balcony and her subsequent flight from Ashaway. To the fact that she's not sure whether the plan to repossess Bloomfield still stands.

"Oh, Margot," Sage murmurs. "I'm so sorry."

"I'm sorry too," she admits. "I really messed up and I . . . well, I miss them already, and I'm miserable."

Sage nods. "Love will do that." Her words are heavy, like someone who's known too much suffering at the hands of love.

"Love is nonsense," Margot mutters.

"Complete nonsense," Sage agrees. "But that doesn't make it any easier to lose."

Margot has never heard Sage speak of heartache before— honestly, Sage has never spoken much about any aspect of her life before the two of them met at college—but it sounds as though she knows what she's talking about.

"I wish I were there so I could buy you a drink at Clementine's," her friend continues. "Or better yet, I wish you were here. Want to join us? I could meet you along the road and we could have our own adventures. Like I've said, an adventuring party can always use a plant witch. Think about it!"

For a moment, Margot's very, very tempted. But then there's a loud crashing sound from Sage's side of the compact, and a scream rends the night.

Before Margot can say anything else, Sage swears loudly and draws her knife again.

"What's happening? Are you okay?"

"Just a little trouble with bandits, who may or may not want to eat us. I'll be fine. Go get that drink at Clementine's, and Margot? Talk to the people who care about you in Bloomfield, okay? This isn't something you should carry alone!"

Then Sage's compact slams closed and Margot's mirror goes dark. The silence of the greenhouses descends again—well, not really silence, since the willow sprigs are whispering to one another and the bluebells are singing softly. But still, after the excitement of Sage's call, it all feels so lonely. So empty. So entirely without Yael.

It feels exactly like it did months ago, before Yael walked into her life. Well. That's fine. At least Margot knows tonight that she can go to Clementine's and drink in peace without bumping into any Claunecks.

Clementine greets her with an exclamation of happiness and a warm hug. "Wasn't sure when you'd be back, especially when someone came for all of Yael's things earlier today."

"Who came for Yael's things?" Margot asks quickly. Was it too much to hope that they were back already?

"A representative from the Claunecks," Clementine says, going behind the bar. "Surprised me a bit too, but she told me Yael would no longer be staying here." She pours Margot a frothy glass of ale.

Margot sits down on a barstool, pulling the ale toward her.

This is the worst thing about Yael having made a home in Bloomfield over the past months. Everyone here knows them and loves them, and that means they'll all want to know where Yael has gone. Why they've stayed in Ashaway. Why Margot is alone again in the greenhouses. "What did this representative look like?"

Perhaps it had been Araphi with a message from Yael that this was all a misunderstanding.

"Handsome young woman, blond, had on a fancy suit and showed a business card. Nicest carriage I've ever seen—even nicer than the ones that arrived for the fashion show. We figured the two of you were staying in Ashaway awhile longer, but . . ."

"Things . . . changed," Margot says, taking a long pull of her ale. Her voice catches on the last word, and she swallows the drink.

"Do you want to talk about it?" Clementine asks, leaning over the counter to pull Margot into a half hug.

"Not yet . . ." Guilt sits heavy in Margot's stomach as she looks at Clementine's open, friendly face. How in the world is Margot supposed to tell her that she could lose the tavern? Her home? The whole village? That's not for tonight, and besides, maybe Yael's staying—their likely sacrifice for Margot—will change things. "Some other time, I'll tell you everything. I'm just glad to be home."

"We're glad to see you too. And don't worry, people might come and go, but Bloomfield will always be here for you." Clementine gives Margot's arm one more squeeze and then moves down the bar to help another customer.

Panic overtakes the guilt in Margot's belly, making her heart race as she runs a hand along the smooth, stained oak of the bar. It's been here since Granny Fern drank at the tavern—and Fern's name is carved into the wood two seats down from where Margot sits. Across the room, beside the welcoming, familiar hearth, Mike and Dara sit in a corner booth, arguing over the books they're both reading. Tulip is at a table near the back of the room, chatting with several other women from the village. A low hum of conversation, music, and laughter fills the room. None of them has any idea how close they all are to losing everything.

Margot's eyes fill with tears. Bloomfield might be here for her in spirit always, but it certainly won't be here for her if she doesn't figure out the Natural Caster Potion, whether Menorath follows through on the promised extension or not; either way, it's only a matter of time.

# 29

# YAEL

*Middle of summer*

"Your productivity levels have been impressively steady these past six weeks."

Yael startles, glancing up from their desk to find their father standing over them. Baremon rarely makes appearances in the Hall of Currency Exchange. Through the open door to their outer chamber office, Yael can see the number crunchers and errand runners with their collective heads buried in their work in an effort to escape Baremon's notice, their noses in danger of smudging the ink.

"I— Thank you?"

Their father lifts one salt-and-pepper eyebrow by the smallest degree. "Do you accept the compliment or debate it?"

"Thank you," Yael tries again.

Baremon nods his approval. "The correct response. Remember to take yourself as seriously as you take your work."

Yael looks down at said work. Piles of reports meriting hours of bleary-eyed reading. It's now nearing noon, when Yael will stop long enough to visit the office altar for the magic to perform a clear-thought spell on themself. The air around them will crackle with the smoky, metallic tang of Clauneck magic.

Then they'll return to their desk to forge on, refreshed and re-focused, until the offices close.

"Thank you," they say again. "It is . . . good to be useful."

"Quite. Speaking of, I've a meeting with a client this afternoon who speculates in adventuring parties: funding voyages and profiting from the bulk of their findings. He's got a hand in trades across kingdoms—spices, precious metals, rare beasts. He'd like to expand, hiring underlings instead of agents to forge contracts on his behalf, cutting out the middlemen as it were. It'd require greater guarantees from us, but with the potential for exponentially higher returns. Your mother is on her way to the office to sit in. You'll sit in as well." Of course; much like Yael, Menorath is commonly called upon to present a unified, family-oriented face for the company, while much of what she does to shore up their power takes place beyond the office. "And pay close attention to his proposal. As a representative of the exchange department, your input will be valuable."

This is *not* common. Baremon's never been interested in their opinion before. "All right, I will."

"It's rewarding to watch you finally embrace your potential here, Yael."

This is high praise indeed. And it should feel good, shouldn't it? Their family's acceptance is what matters most in this world. So why is there some poisonous pearl of discontent buried deep inside of Yael?

"Sir, may I ask . . ." They hesitate until Baremon nods his permission, then lower their eyes to the reports on their desk before confessing, "When I left, I . . . I never thought I was important to . . . to the company." Though Yael can't bring themself to look up, they watch their father's shadow across their desk in the brazier light (the Hall of Exchange lacks windows, aside from those in their uncle's office) as he stands immobile, considering them at length.

At last, Baremon asks, "Do you remember when you were a child, and your mother took you along to the mint to watch the currency being made?"

"Yes." Yael does not.

"You recall that the mint holds a dozen screw presses that cut and stamp the coins?"

"Yes." Yael does not.

"A great many moving parts, those machines. The apparatus that feeds in the blanks. The die housing on the spindle. The beam that pushes the spindle down into the housing to stamp the blanks. The weights that contribute the required force to press a picture into metal. The retrieval apparatus for the struck coin. In kingdoms without our resources, they use laborers to do the stamping, six per press, hauling on ropes as violently as they can. But of course in Harrow, the spellcasters of the mint keep the presses running; it's an astonishing achievement of magic and mechanics, paced to strike a coin per second. A marvel of a machine. Until some morning when a caster poorly weights one arm of the beam, which puts uneven pressure on the spindle, which strikes crookedly against the housing, which unevenly stamps the metal, which catches in the retrieval apparatus . . . You understand my meaning?"

"Yes." Yael does not.

Nor does their father seem fooled. "I mean, Yael, that one tiny, *unimportant,* ill-fitting part of a mighty machine can mean the difference between success and disaster. If that little part fails, the entire mint fails in its purpose: to create coinage for us."

"For the kingdom," Yael corrects their father, then winces, unable to stop themself from looking up now.

But their father offers them a rare smile. Baremon's smiles are handsome and always unpleasant in the aftermath, like taking a bite of cake to discover the baker's forgotten to add sugar. "Is it not the same thing?"

The noontime sun is high and hot when Yael leaves the Clauneck Company offices on an errand to the inksmith. It's a chore
that should've gone to one of the department's many subordi-
nates, but instead of passing the job along, Yael kept it for
themself. They wanted to be outdoors after their father's visit.
Devils know why, because now they're sweating. They could've
at least taken a company carriage; the inksmith isn't located in
the Copper Court, with its shining rooftops and polished store-
fronts, but among the shabbier streets to the east, just south of
the Willowthorn River. As they turn down the correct lane at
last and trudge across the cracked cobblestones, Yael can smell
the slip where the ferry leaves for the Rookery. The district on
the far bank where barkeeps and street sweepers and coachmen-
for-hire live—all of those in the serving class who aren't attached to the households of the rich—is an entire world away
from the Clauneck estate.

Yael's taken that ferry a time or three themself. It's something of an Auximia tradition. Occasionally, students would
abandon the fine taverns around the Ivory Court on a whim,
seek out a tavern in the Rookery, and claim it as their own. For
a week, perhaps two at most, they'd shower denaris on the barkeeps before convenience and luxury lured them away again.

How frivolous they were, Yael realizes now, treating the
Rookery like a daring side quest. Disrupting the lives of folk
who had no choice but to be there, then leaving them on the
other side of the river once more and never looking back.

At last they reach the inksmith—a squat brick building
stained with soot, the stink of turpentine wafting out its propped-
open windows. Beside it is a merchant's shop in moderate disre-
pair, the peeling sign advertising ensorcelled items for cheap:

hats of vermin, bags of holding, and the like. Whatever spell-work has been pressed upon the wares will probably wash off in the rain. These are largely the shops that serve the people who serve the students and merchants and nobility, as well as a number of factories. The lane is stuffed with unremarkable brick and cinder structures, but one building catches Yael's eye.

A greenhouse.

Neatly cylindrical and well kept, its glass panes are clear and polished as a cut diamond in the light that falls between its neighbors. Of course, Yael's seen greenhouses in Ashaway before, but they've never gone inside. The Claunecks have grounds-keepers and party planners to handle such tasks whenever necessary.

Now they find themself drifting toward its glass doors.

As soon as they push inside, they're struck by the warm, wet air overripe with commingling floral scents, like stepping into an excessively perfumed bath. It knocks them back a step from the closely packed troughs of plants.

"Can I help you?" a young woman in an apron with a cloud of dark curls calls from the back of the greenhouse. She has to turn and scoot sideways down the narrow aisles. When she reaches the front of the greenhouse, she stops, her lips pursing into a surprised *oh*. "Can I help you, sir'ram?" she amends breathlessly. She might not know who they are, but their jeweled rings, their gleaming gold watch chain, and their fine plum-colored coat and vest give them away as *somebody*.

Little does she know that she's looking at one tiny, unimportant, ill-fitting part.

Yael looks away to examine the buds polka-dotting the greenery: teeny delicate jasmine in one trough, fanned pink and yellow plumeria in another, and in another, broad purple roses the exact color of—

"Sir'ram?" the shopkeeper asks again, twisting her apron between hands with soil stamped into every crease.

"Apologies, I— Are you the owner of this greenhouse?"

Swiftly, she shakes her head. "No, sir'ram, I only work for him."

"I see. What do you grow all this for? And why here?"

"Well, there's a factory next door to us."

"This is for a factory?"

"Aye, where they make the perfume. I pick the buds at dawn before the heat of the day gets to them, and bring them over."

"It's very . . ." Without meaning to, Yael wrinkles their nose.

"There's magic that makes the smell more powerful, so you get more perfume from each batch of pickings. Greater profits from a smaller growing space and all that. They press the petals into oil next door and send it off to the perfumery from there. But that's down by the markets at the Copper Court, where the fancy folk . . . I mean . . . I'm sorry, sir'ram. It's just, customers don't come in here. I thought you were the factory boss coming to complain about the morning's batch," she admits, swiping a curl off the glistening bronze skin of her forehead.

It doesn't look like the kind of greenhouse that welcomes visitors off the lane, now that Yael thinks on it. It's overcrowded and overpowering. The Greenwillow Greenhouses smelled of nature—the very best of it. Like mossy forest floors and buttery sunshine and cool spring rain and . . .

And strawberries.

Yael clears their throat. "Do you like it here?"

The greenhouse assistant furrows her brow. "You mean, do I like the work?" She looks as though she's never been asked the question before. "There are much harder jobs, to be sure. My brother and his husband, you know, they're fishermen out in the Serpentine Sea off the Upper Islands. Perilous labor, and they don't step foot on land for months. Working here, I bring money home to my mother every night. And I do like growing things. The owner lets me keep a little plot for my own garden out back, as there's not much land to be had in the Rookery."

"May I see it?" Yael asks.

She hesitates.

They suppose they are acting a *bit* alarming. Holding their hands up, palms out, they explain, "I, um, worked in a green-house, you see."

"You did, sir'ram?"

"For a little while. And I guess I like growing things too, and I miss . . . the work. Though I was never very good at it."

The assistant looks thoughtful. "Every year, I've got crops that don't take. It's the putting-things-into-the-ground part I love, more than what I pull out of it—though it certainly helps to feed us. Do you really want to see?"

Yael nods around the dam building up in the back of their throat.

She leads them through the cramped aisles (Yael slips more easily between the troughs than she does) and out the back of the greenhouse, where a patchy square of grass has been almost entirely taken up by weather-worn garden beds.

"You see those pole beans are just starting to flower." She points to the delicate, vibrant green vines that curl their way up the wooden stakes. "The bush beans have been giving for months, but you can see the yellow in the leaves. The heat's been vicious, and they're getting tired. But they help the squash grow; they put something back in the soil, couldn't tell you what. I never went to school for it. But my mother told me so when I was young, and I've found it's true."

"The marigolds are lovely," Yael says, proud of themself for identifying the golden-orange flowers, which have grown about half the size of those in Bloomfield. Margot (oh gods, Margot) grew them nearly as tall as Yael.

"They keep the bees coming and keep away the bugs that spoil the tomatoes, right there beside them. I haven't pruned those like I should this year. Mother was sick for a time this summer, and with Momma hired at one of the estates for the season, she couldn't spare me. But see, the marigolds are propping them up—a happy mistake."

"What's that one?" Yael asks, pointing to a plant with egg-shaped leaves and clusters of yellow buds growing in a patch away from the rest of the beds.

"Sicklepod. You can use the roots for medicine, but mostly it's a trap crop. Keeps some nasty bugs from eating my soybeans, since they go after the sicklepod instead. See the holes in the leaves? That means it's working." She walks Yael through the rest of her small garden, pointing to the squash with brown-spotted leaves. "I'll give them a go in another bed next year, see what works for them if I can. I know it all looks a lot rougher than the greenhouse flowers, but I've hardly got a drop of magic in me, and they've got spells on them from the time they sprout; the owner hires a plant witch to do the job. You can see my melons are doing well, though, with the lavender there. It brings the bees right to them."

Yael recalls Margot talking about all of this—companion planting and trap crops and such—but with her prodigious talent as a plant witch, they wondered why she bothered. Perhaps Yael wasn't listening closely enough. Perhaps they were too caught up in trying to prove themself to her. If only Yael could talk to Margot now, they would—

What? What could Yael possibly say after leaving her at the ball? Would they apologize? It was right, their leaving. They made the right choice. A choice so right, they can't even remember making it, but simply knowing it through and through. And yet . . .

If they could talk to Margot, they'd ask questions that truly mattered, and maybe they'd learn how to grow a garden like a living body: with strengths and weaknesses, with unplanned disasters and unexpected support systems, with the grace to try and try again.

"Thank you," Yael says, "for showing me this. What's your name?"

"Miriam." She looks as though she might ask theirs but stops herself, keenly aware of the difference in their stations.

"You know, Miriam, there *is* some land to be found. North of the palace and to the west of the Rookery, same side of the river. It, er, came across my desk, at work." Occasionally, profitability analysis reports to do with land speculation and development will pass through Yael's department, comparing a plot's favorability to potential investors with current rates of exchange and equivalents in valuable trade goods or spellwork. "There's a bank that's keen to snatch it up and sell it off in parts."

"Not to us, though." Miriam smiles ruefully. "It's happened before. The Rookery used to run farther east, nearly to the walls. Now we're more jumbled together than we ever were. Folk in the Copper Court buy it up for a palmful of coins more than we can afford, then sell it for twice or three times the price. Mother says they've even done it without buying the land to begin with, just claiming it and selling it off quick, before we could put up a fuss. Meanwhile, we're not allowed to grow where we don't own, even before the banks get there. And who in the Rookery can afford even undesirable land?"

Yael ponders this for a moment, then scrapes the half-dozen

jeweled rings from their fingers—family heirlooms their mother insists they wear—and plucks the watch and chain from their coat pocket. They hold out the glittering fistful to Miriam. When she only stares in confusion, they stoop down and set it all gently upon the soil. "Now you can afford it."

"Sir'ram, I can't possibly . . . I can't take . . ."

But Yael is already backing away, toward the rear exit of the greenhouse. "Go right to the Copper Court once you're let off work for the day, and you can buy a decent patch before the bank has the chance to bully down the price. Only, promise that you'll share it with your neighbors? It's a good deal of earth."

Then they turn and disappear into the ripe-smelling troughs of factory-bound flowers.

# 30

# MARGOT

*Middle of summer*

On a Saturday morning with little more than a month before summer's end, Margot stands under the oak tree behind her cottage, her feet rooted in the soil, her heart as fragile as it has been since Yael left her on the balcony of their manor six weeks ago. In that time, much to her surprise and despair, she's had no letters or messages from them. It's a resounding silence, which has clipped any tendrils of hope Margot had that things between them might work out. The silence said, loudly, that perhaps Yael was telling the truth and couldn't forgive her. That they didn't need her or want a life together. That she was foolish to hope for anything at all from them.

At least there's been an official extension notice from the Clauneck Company, which arrived a few days after she got home. Menorath has kept to her word and granted Margot another year's postponement, which should be a relief, but it feels like a weight. Especially since Margot is no closer to finishing the Natural Caster Potion despite all these long nights she's spent in her workshop poring over Fern's remedy book.

And so this morning, with the greenhouses closed for the day, Margot decided to talk to Fern herself to see if that might help.

An absurd wish, of course, to believe that Granny Fern will give her a sign or a clue, but desperation haunts Margot's waking hours after years of failure, and she has to try something.

"Hi, Granny Fern," Margot says, kneeling at the base of a large tree root and running her hands over it. The sun beats down on her neck, and a small bead of sweat trickles over her temple. "It's been too long, I know, but I've been busy." She smooths her hand along the root, letting the rough edges bite into her skin, remembering how Fern would tuck Margot's wild hair behind her ears when she was a child.

Fern's ashes are scattered among these roots. At her insistence, there's no marker, but over the years, Margot has hung things from the tree to remember her by. Small wind chimes, interesting feathers, wreaths woven with dried flowers, stones and shells tied with ribbons, metal spoons, some colored glass pieces, a few jam jars. All little trinkets to mark the resting place of a woman who was so much more than she seemed. A woman who was everything to Margot, and who was everything Margot can never be.

"I don't know how to do it," Margot confesses to the tree, putting her forehead against its rough trunk like Granny Fern taught her to do as a small child, so she could listen for the heart of a living thing. "I've tried everything I can think of—everything in the book too! But nothing works."

For the last six weeks, Margot has been desperately working on the Natural Caster Potion to keep her mind off her own heartbreak and to be rid of any obligation to the Claunecks once and for all, extension or no. She's gone through all the recipes in the book, making each remedy to the best of her abilities. Staying up into the early hours of the morning—often sleeping in the workshop or greenhouse—as pots of green or purple potions bubble away. All to no avail. Every spoonful of the Natural Caster Potion she's cautiously tasted has given her unsettling rashes, made her lose her voice, or knocked her out for the better part of the day. Granted, she's not even sure what the potion should taste like when it's done, but she suspects it would feel a certain way, even as a natural caster herself. Like her reservoir of magic was refilled in an instant.

"What am I missing, Granny Fern?" Margot implores the tree. "Is there more to the recipe that you figured out? Something else I can try? I need your help, please! I . . . I can't let everyone down. I can't let you down."

The only answer is the wind through the oak leaves, the tinkling of the chimes, and the bees buzzing in the wildflowers. Harvey slinks up to Margot's side and nudges her hand. Margot strokes his back, and he purrs happily.

After a few long moments of waiting for an answer from Granny Fern that won't come, Margot hauls herself to her feet and picks up Harvey.

"Right, let's get back to the workshop, then," she says. She blows the tree and Granny Fern's resting place a kiss and then turns away, resigned to another day of failure.

※

Hours later and long after sunset, Harvey leaps off the worktable, taking a stack of papers with him. Margot swears as her empty teacup—Yael's favorite one, the one Margot has taken to drinking from almost exclusively—which was sitting on the papers, goes cascading toward the edge. She just misses it as it falls, and the ceramic cup shatters on the stone floor under the table.

"Harvey!" she cries out, her voice breaking on the last syllable. "That was a special cup!"

Tears of exhaustion and bitter frustration fill her eyes as she gets out of her chair and crouches beneath the table, reaching to pick up the scattered teacup shards. It's a porcelain map of her shattered relationship with Yael, the buttery-yellow bee-painted pieces starkly laid out in front of her.

Harvey curls around her ankles, meowing, as if in apology.

"Shoo, get out of here," she says as hot tears roll down her face. "You're going to cut your paws."

Harvey insistently nudges her leg, and Margot gently shoves him away. Undeterred, he leaps onto the chair Margot's just vacated and from there into her arms.

He lands with a thunk against her chest, making her drop the teacup shards again.

"Impossible creature," Margot says, leaning forward to put him back on the chair. Right as she's fumbling directly under the center drawer of the worktable, Harvey lets out a yowl and sinks his claws into Margot's shoulder.

Pain sears through her, and she lurches upward, the top of her head smashing into the bottom of the drawer.

"Ow, Harvey!" she calls out, flinging the cat onto the chair. "What was—?"

The question dies on her lips as she looks at the underside of the drawer. A small piece of wood has sprung open on its bottom, revealing a shallow hidden compartment.

"What in the world?" she murmurs as she reaches into the gap in the wood and pulls out a handful of tightly rolled papers.

Granny Fern's handwriting fills the pages, and the left edges are torn, as if they've been ripped out of a book. The parchment is thick and well worn, exactly like that of Fern's remedy book.

Margot's heart flits in her chest like a butterfly near a flowering bush. These have to be the missing pages from Fern's incomplete Natural Caster Potion notes. Have they really been here all along, just inches from her fingertips as she desperately tried to figure out this potion?

Leaving the broken teacup pieces, Margot clambers out from under the worktable, clutching the pages. She puts them on top of the spellbook and pulls the lantern closer to glance through the diagrams, drawings, and fragments of notes. On the last page is what looks like a journal entry. It's dated two days before Fern died, and Margot can almost hear Granny Fern's whiskey-and-tea-toned voice as she begins to read.

*On the Natural Caster Potion, some thoughts, from Fern Greenwillow:*

*I am near my end. Even as I write this, I can feel the sickness eating away at me, as I've seen it do to many others. Tired as I am, I cannot leave the world without at least putting down the sum of my greatest project to paper. Even if no one else reads it, I need to feel I've finished my work.*

*For many years now, I've been thinking about natural casters in Harrow, and what it means to be born with a reservoir of magic. Is it fair? Is it random? Does it show the favor of a god or some such being from another plane?*

*I don't know and, of course, these are questions best left to the scholars and philosophers who have spent centuries debating them. From my time in school, I do know the theories behind how magic operates in our world, but that's not what got me started. What I wanted to know when I first dug into this potion was this: Is it possible to create something that makes the world a more fair place?*

*Could something like this Natural Caster Potion give those born in the Rookery for whom magical studies are out of reach a better chance? Could it help to balance the gulf in Harrow between those with resources and those without? Could it help to build stronger communities, where both magical access and the money to compensate without magic are lacking?*

*It seemed to me that, yes, it might be possible.*

*Of course, the minute I thought about such things, I also knew that granting a tremendous amount of natural casting ability to those already in power would be reckless, dangerous, deadly. But it seemed something I could control if I could in fact create it.*

*And so I decided to try.*

*My experiments took me years, from the first few notes in the spell-book through all of the formulas, failures, and results I've recorded in the following pages. They tell the story of a journey—one full of frustration, half starts, and many wonderful remedies and potions discovered and concocted along the way. In fact, those potions helped me build my empire as my curiosity took me down one avenue and then the next. And for that, I'm truly grateful. Through it all, however, I kept looking for some miscalculation or missing ingredient that would help me achieve this dream of equalizing magic in Harrow.*

*Then one day, without meaning to, I found it.*

Here, Margot inhales sharply. This is it! The key to crafting the potion that will save Bloomfield from the Claunecks' clutches!

Even as excitement swells within her, another fear rises. Wasn't Fern right that those with power but without stores of magic would do terrible things with such a potion? Margot had seen as much in the dress shop when Menorath's eyes gleamed at the thought of becoming a powerful natural caster, ungoverned by her family's patron.

But releasing Yael from their patron's clutches wouldn't be the worst thing either—no, Margot doesn't let herself linger in that thought. She keeps reading.

*I won't go into how I discovered the secret, though I will admit it originated from a clue in a book I found in a library on one of my rare visits to Ashaway. (A book that is no longer in that library, nor anything but ashes in a faraway hearth.) From that clue, however, a new trail emerged. One that only recently led me to an awful, grim truth:*

*The only way that I have found to make the Natural Caster Potion is to grind up the bones of a natural caster—all of them are nec-*

*essary for a permanent effect—then mix the resulting material
into a three-part potion. Drinking it will forever fill the well of magic
in a person, and give them the ability the other natural caster possessed.*

Margot stops reading, clapping a hand over her mouth. Has she read that right? To make the potion, she must *grind up the bones of a natural caster?*

Her small supper of bread and cheese threatens to come back up. Suddenly, the workshop is too small. Her head is pounding. She rises, stepping backward and nearly tripping over Harvey.

"I just—" she says to the cat before pushing open the workshop door and stumbling into the greenhouse. The smell of plants, earth, and growing things fills her nose, offering instant comfort.

"The bones of a natural caster," she murmurs to herself as she clenches the bottom of her cardigan with shaking fingers.

What an absolutely terrible truth. And yet, if that's the only way to make the potion—and the only way to save Bloomfield . . .

No. She cannot possibly create a potion that requires the bones of another person.

Can she?

Of course not. Perhaps there *is* some other way. There must be another way!

Margot takes a few more deep breaths and then returns to her workshop table to keep reading.

*It's a terrible thing, this knowledge. To know I could change the lives of so many people for the better. Perhaps in some hypothetical world, aged natural casters would donate their bodies after death to give others their magic. But I also know all too well the measure of my fellow man. They are impatient and hungry for power. If they knew how this potion worked, it wouldn't be long before natural casters were murdered for the magical potential in their bones.*

*I cannot let that happen. I will not, and so I'm tearing these pages from my spellbook. I know I should burn them, but I haven't the strength right now to light a candle, let alone a fire. I need to rest, and so I'll hide them until I've regained enough strength to properly dispose of them—*

Here, Fern's handwriting trails off, and her words stop. Margot can almost see her beloved grandmother, stumbling upon this terrible secret even while her own body crumpled.

But now the secret isn't just hers. It's Margot's too. And she can never reveal it. As Granny Fern wrote, the only thing this potion would bring—no matter the good intentions it might carry—is suffering and misery.

Slowly, Margot feeds the page with Fern's written confession to the candle flame. The fire eats the ink, not knowing it's devouring her only hope for saving Bloomfield.

Granny Fern was right: This potion isn't the way. It's never been the way. Margot isn't sure what she's going to do or how she can save Bloomfield, but she'll find another path. Sage's words echo in Margot's ears: *Talk to the people who care about you in Bloomfield, okay? This isn't something you should carry alone!*

Yes, talking to the town—after a good night's sleep—is exactly what she must do. Granny Fern would've wanted her to.

"Thank you, Granny Fern," she whispers, touching the small painted portrait of her and her grandmother on the workshop table. "For guiding me still."

Margot can almost hear the gentle voice of Granny Fern, as if from the next room, as she blows out the candle and heads for home.

# 31

# YAEL

*L*eaving *Bloomfield behind was the right thing to do, even if it meant leaving Margot.*
*Joining the company and rejoining the family was the right thing to do.*

On their walk back to the office from the perfumery greenhouse, Yael sifts through these notions like the gemstone specialist on the fifth floor inspecting twinkling piles of jewels for flaws or curses.

Or for fakes.

Because they're thinking of Margot again. The smell of her: earthy, like rain on good warm soil, and the clean scent of the herbs she adds to her tea, and the lightly sweet sage she grows for cooking and for spellwork. Her habit of tucking berries into her dress pockets to toss to the chickens that wander the lanes of Bloomfield. The titles of her favorite books, and the tunes she'd hum while potting plants at the workbench. How it felt to fall asleep with Margot wrapped around their body, her long legs braided with theirs, and how it felt to wake up to Margot blinking sleepily down at them, her clear gray eyes soft in the morning. Each of these memories feel so much more *true* than a palmful of hollow ideas about Yael's place in the family, or in the company, or in the world.

Yael may be their parents' heir, but they're still just a cog jammed into the machinery the Claunecks built to benefit themselves. The fact that Yael never fit—a failure of the part, according to their family, rather than a failure of the machinery— was why Yael left Ashaway in the first place. They're sure of that much, at least.

Yael's family doesn't care that Miriam's family goes hungry while farmable land lies within walking distance, yet far beyond reach. No more than the Claunecks care about Bloom- field, itself a living thing, like a garden that constantly reshapes itself to support what's fragile and discover its strengths. Yael's family would rip the whole town and everyone in it out by the roots to make space for foul-smelling factories and ornamental lawns, and never let it trouble their sleep.

So how can Yael's obedience to them possibly be *good*?

Nothing about any of this feels good. The Claunecks are locusts, consuming beyond their own appetites whether they have the right to it or not. Yael knows this now. And per- haps . . .

Perhaps there is some way to prove it.

🌿

The belowground levels of the Clauneck Company offices re- place polished wood with cold, impenetrable stone and iron doors. There are guard warlocks posted at every entrance and wards carved into every corridor and door. The safeguards re- quire powerful spellwork far beyond Yael's capability to breach, even with patronage.

Or they would, if Yael weren't a Clauneck.

Their blood is the key that opens every arcane lock, and they needn't even spill it to use it. All they need is their face, known by everyone in the offices, and a purposeful stride to bypass the guards. Each nods deferentially to Yael as they pass. It might not be enough to get them into the vault on the very lowest level—a dragon hoard's worth of coins and valuable goods in trade—but that's not a problem.

The Records Library is their objective.

There are wards branded heavily up and down and across the frame of the library door, and a pair of warlocks standing sentry to either side, with orders to halt anyone coming to claim entry. But here too the blood in Yael's veins is all they need. A cog they may be, but Yael's parents have done everything possible to keep their brokenness a secret. They lift the portfolio they've carried down to suggest a project under way—no further explanation owed—and press their palm to the iron. The door gives way for them, and in a moment they're alone, the door shut and the wards raised again by the warlocks behind them.

Yael turns their attention to the shelves that stretch far down into the frigid air of the Records Library's long aisles. Here are centuries' worth of records detailing every purchase, sale, exchange, and secret of the Clauneck Company, all contained inside thousands of ledgers and files and portfolios such as the one they brought with them for cover.

They had better get to work.

Skimming their fingers along the shelves as they pass, they head for the account files from the past few years. Among them should be a file for the Greenwillows, including ledger entries tallying Margot's parents' many debts from when they went belly-up against the sums of assets seized. If Yael can find it, then . . .

What?

They aren't sure what they hope to accomplish. Even if there is some miraculous difference between the amount of the Greenwillows' debt and the total value of their seized assets (gods help them, they're thinking like a banker), it can't be a village's worth of difference. And knowing the full sum of the debt won't change anything. Margot doesn't have the money to pay it off, and Yael doesn't really have anything but the clothes on their back, absent their jewelry now. But there has to be *something* they can do. Find some loophole in the initial four-year extension. Get word to Margot with as much information as they can gather, at least. They might have left her, but that doesn't change the fact that they love—

*Love who? The woman who would've kept you from claiming your place in this world?*

Yael stumbles in the aisle. "That isn't true," they say aloud in the cold, echoing hush of the library.

*Is it not?*

They linger for another moment, then push on down the aisle. This is what Clauneck *wants:* to distract them from their mission.

*What I want, Yael, is your obedience to the family that made you, in every way possible. The family that honored their contract with you despite your years of unproductive floundering.*

"You flatter me, great-great-great-great-grandfather. But I signed no such contract."

*Your contract was entered upon birth, signed with Clauneck blood. Would you break it to live with a failed plant witch in a ramshackle cottage in the woods, forever in fear of the day you'll inevitably lose it all?*

"Better to love a plant witch in a cottage than worship a petty devil in a manor house," they mutter back, and how could they ever have believed otherwise?

They shouldn't be here. This isn't where they belong. It *isn't* right.

None of this is right.

And there it is at last: the Greenwillow file, miraculously at eye level instead of on some higher shelf, out of sight and out of reach.

*Stop this NOW, Yael.*

They move all the quicker for Clauneck's demands, opening the expected ledger and flipping through to the entries made just under four years ago; success! They find the list of assets seized to settle the Greenwillows' debt: the mansion in Ashaway, their remaining stocks of potions and remedies in the city, the scant profits from one of their few mildly successful ventures . . .

Not the manor house in Bloomfield, though, or the greenhouses. Of course, if they never formalized the seizure or started the procedure before offering the extension, that makes sense. Damn.

*For years now, you've failed in your duty to this family. Fail us now, disobey me now, and I will abjure you as your patron. Your family will abjure you as an heir at my command. And you will be alone in this world without a scrap of magic or a single copper to your name.*

Clauneck's words are daggers; they ought to draw blood.

But it's Margot's words, spoken in their shared bed at the Abyssal Chicken, that float back to them:

*Your deviation from your parents' expectations of you is not a failure on your part. It's a failure of imagination on theirs, if they can't see you for who you are.*

Could that really be true?

Yael thinks once more of a spindle press inside Harrow's mint. Really, how can a mighty machine be such a marvel if one little, apparently unimportant piece might spell its doom? That seems a lot less like a failure of the part than a failure in the machine's design.

"It's been a pleasure doing business these past twenty-three years," they tell their once-patron, tucking the Greenwillow ledger against their chest, "but I think I shall be withdrawing my account from the Clauneck Company."

Yael has spent those twenty-three years listening to their patron berate and bully them, whispering poisonous thoughts into being. But they've never heard Clauneck howl, sounding very like the devil he is. Their eardrums ring with it, and their bones vibrate like violin strings, boiling their blood inside their body. They drop to their knees, afraid that they're shattering apart.

Then the violent clamor is gone.

Clauneck is gone.

Yael is more completely alone than they've ever been, and suddenly, the thing they've always feared feels like the greatest possible gift.

It won't last. Having abandoned Yael for good (and Yael knows with every part of their being that it's for good), Clauneck will muster Baremon and Menorath, who must have arrived for the scheduled meeting by now. Their parents will come running to stop them. Which means that Yael will need to get moving and then keep running until they're well out of reach of the Claunecks.

They set the ledger aside and dip back into the file, pulling out what they recognize immediately as a profitability analysis, same as the one on the fields neighboring the Rookery that came across Yael's desk last week. They loosen the leather thong and pull back the portfolio flap to take a look at the contents, flipping through the opening pages until a map drawn into quadrants and annotated with measurements and proposed sums catches their eye. They recognize it by its shape, encircled by a thick, inked stone wall, and by its coordinates.

This is Bloomfield. Or Bloomfield as it was four years ago, judging by the written dates. This report was compiled while the Claunecks were weighing their options, deciding whether Margot might become an asset of greater value than the land itself, worth granting an extension. The map is followed by sheets of some anonymous number cruncher's notes on the past appreciation of property values, and at the very back of the folder . . .

Yael finds the last thing they expect, but exactly what they need.

It's funny, really. The Claunecks were so afraid that Yael, ill fitting as they've always been in the family apparatus, might bring the whole thing down.

Which means that, just maybe, Yael *can* bring the whole thing down.

They tuck all of their findings into their coat, then rush toward the door that opens for them at their touch. The wards can't tell the difference between blood and family, after all.

On the Queens' Road dead center of the three courts, there is a public stable that lets out mounts, bridles, and carriages to renters according to their wealth and needs. To Auximia students wanting to impress one another during the courting season; to merchants, couriers, and cabmen who can't afford to purchase and keep a mount or cart; to poorer folk with a rare patch of land that needs plowing in spring. The Claunecks have no need for an account there with a stable of their own, and Yael has nothing to pay nor barter with, having given away whatever jewelry they had on them hours before. All they have now are the papers and plans stolen from the office.

That, and a very fine suit.

Not quite as fine as the suit they traded to Arnav the tailor for a rough wardrobe and work boots, but then, they knew at the time that they were far underselling it. This one—a plum-colored frock coat, vest, and trousers—has buttons of pure gold, and luck spellwork stitched into the lining.

Which is how they came to be galloping through the southern gates of Ashaway on a mechanical steed-for-hire named Gloom Stalker, wearing only their undershorts and linen bindings, their socked feet in the iron stirrups, and the ledger and two portfolios strapped to the saddle.

# 32

# MARGOT

A clattering noise wakes Margot in the early hours of the morning. She sits bolt-upright, nearly bashing her head on the low loft ceiling. Was that outside? Maybe hooves on the flagstones? Is someone from the Clauneck Company here to evict her?

Of course not. Not yet, at least. Despite Menorath's year-long extension, Margot knows she'll have to tell the Claunecks that the Natural Caster Potion is never happening, can never happen. Her anxiety over the consequences of doing so has slipped into her dreams and she's slept fitfully, tossing and turning as visions of someone coming in the night to force her from her home fill her sleep.

There's another noise, clearer this time, like a spoon against a teacup. So, not a horse. Adrenaline lights her veins. Looking around her loft, Margot grabs the first thing at hand, a fluffy down pillow. Nerves tingling, she scoots to the edge of the loft.

There's a thump and the murmur of an almost familiar voice. Another rattle—ceramic against metal—brings a whispered string of swear words.

Yes, that was definitely coming from her kitchen.

Margot's fairly certain she won't need her pillow—and a pillow won't do much good against someone here to evict her, anyway—but she won't go down without a fight. Even if it's a pillow fight.

Ridiculous. She isn't thinking properly. She needs a good cup of tea to clear her head and wake her up.

There's another soft thump and then, almost as if reading her mind, the smell of hibiscus and ginger tea floats upward to the loft. Margot inhales deeply, letting the delicious, familiar scent wrap around her.

Did someone break into her house to . . . make her tea?

There is only one person who would do that. But they wouldn't be here after six weeks of heartbreaking absence. Would they? Still clutching the pillow, Margot steps down the loft ladder and lands softly on the living room floor. There's a fire dancing in her hearth, and not a log is out of place. A small bundle of freshly picked daisies sit in an empty jam jar in the middle of the kitchen table next to the vase holding the everlasting daisy.

"Yael?" she calls, her voice wobbly with hope.

There's a long silence.

Then Yael Clauneck walks into the living room from the kitchen, holding a pair of steaming teacups, their jaw-length hair pulled up into a messy half knot. They're the most beautiful thing Margot has ever seen. She digs her fingers into the pillow, just to keep from running to Yael and embracing them.

"You're supposed to be asleep still," they say, frowning. "I got here as early as I could."

Margot wants to weep at hearing them again.

Instead, she says, "Hard to sleep with you clattering around down here."

The side of Yael's mouth kicks up just the smallest bit. "Much easier to make you tea if you didn't insist on keeping the cups up so high."

At that, Margot's smile breaks through any reserve she has. Yes, there is so very much they need to discuss, but at this moment, she's just so damn delighted to see them here, in her cottage. She releases her grip on the pillow, setting it onto the couch. "Did you break into my house just to make me tea?"

"And bring you strawberry scones." Yael nods toward the oven. "They're not terribly fresh after the ride here, since they were in my bag, but they're from one of my favorite bakeries in Ashaway. I didn't get a chance to take you, uhm . . . before we parted. It's just lucky I had some saved in my bag from teatime this morning. Well, yesterday morning. And I thought they might go so well with tea."

Yael sets the cups down gently on the table. It's then that Margot realizes they're wearing nothing but their underwear and chest bindings. And she's in even less than that, since she's naked under her thin shift. As her cheeks heat, she can feel Yael's gaze on her, which is not unwelcome but also not helping her make sense of their presence in her kitchen.

She snatches up a cardigan from a chair and slips it on, wrapping herself in the soft comfort of it.

"Why aren't you wearing any clothing?" she manages as Yael straightens one of the daisies in the bunch in the middle of the table.

"Well, I sold my clothes for a horse."

At least four questions come to mind all at once, but they somehow spill out as a laugh.

"Don't make fun." Yael beams at her. "It was a very fast horse. A mechanical one. I could've gotten here from Ashaway before midnight, but when the sun began to set, I stopped at a crossroads inn; you should've seen the face of the innkeeper. I think she let me sleep in the stables just to keep me out of view of her customers."

Now that Margot can look Yael up and down without blushing (almost), she sees the bits of hay clinging in their dark hair.

"I'm sure I have something I can wear at Clementine's," Yael continues, "but I wanted—no, I needed—to see you first."

Margot pulls her cardigan tighter, as if that will protect her heart from Yael's smile. Their words. The way she's desperate just to hold them again. "There's nothing at Clementine's," she says instead of reaching for them. "All of your things were picked up by someone from the Clauneck Company ages ago."

Yael swears. "Well then, I'll have to work something out, I suppose."

"I still have some of your things. From when you . . . last slept here."

Yael meets her eye, and the words hang between them, whispering of the handful of nights they spent in the cottage together, after the show and before the Clauneck carriage came to drag them off to Ashaway. Their laughter, muffled beneath Margot's quilts, and the strawberry wine that coated their lips as they kissed. The night Yael suggested that they go back to her mother's private gardens, now emptied of guests and expectations, for a memory of Bloomfield to keep them company on their journey, and Margot happily agreed. Small mushrooms had sprung up under her feet with each step toward the house, the plants enchanted ever so slightly by Margot's magic, and the many feelings inside of her . . .

She clears her throat, looking away. "I'll just get the clothes."

Turning, she hurries up the ladder and rummages through the bundle of Yael's clothing that's neatly folded and placed on their side of the bed. Tucked under their pillow to be more accurate. A pile of clothing that she has most certainly not been snuggling when the nights get too lonely.

Yael can never know about that.

"Here you go," she calls out roughly, tossing the bundle down the ladder. "I'll be right there."

Slipping out of the cardigan, Margot pulls on undergarments and a dress. By the time she's back down the ladder, Yael's dressed in their simple greenhouse clothing—a goldenrod-yellow shirt and brown cotton trousers—and there's a plate of warmed scones on the table. Steam rises from the tea. Margot sits at the table, wrapping her hands around her cup. She inhales, letting the familiar scent of lemon, ginger, and hibiscus fill her nose. Yael sits opposite her, biting their bottom lip, as if they're not quite sure what to say.

"When did you learn how to do all this?" Margot says to break the ice—and out of genuine curiosity.

"I spent a little time in the manor house kitchens while I was . . . away." They stare into the steam rising from their teacup. "I don't know why I went down. I never had growing up. But I'd watch Zoy—that's the spit-boy's name—turn a boar for the evening's supper. And I'd ask Ilke questions as he cooked. How much kindling to use to light a fire, how much wood it took to keep it going without a continual flame spell. How the scullery maid cleaned the dishes without a scrap of magic. I think they thought I was addled or something, and I couldn't explain *why* I wanted to know, but . . . but I did. And I learned. A bit, anyway."

"Ah. Well . . . I'm glad to see you," Margot admits.

"Me too. You've no idea how glad I am to see you."

Margot has longed to hear from them for weeks, but suddenly, it's all too much. She stands, going over to the windowsill and picking up the strawberry root Yael had planted in late spring. It's grown since—Margot carefully tended to it since Yael wasn't here to do so—and blossomed with little white flowers that subtly perfume her kitchen.

"My strawberries!" Yael gasps, recognizing the pot. "It bloomed, after all."

"It was well planted," Margot concedes.

"Honestly, it's a wonder you didn't throw them into the pond, after the way I left things. *You're* a wonder, Margot."

Returning to the table, Margot picks up a scone and begins to crumble it over her plate, letting silence stretch between them—the product of too many weeks apart and too many words spoken and unspoken. At last, she manages, "What are you doing in Bloomfield, Yael? I'm grateful for the tea and scones, but I thought . . ."

Yael sets down their tea. "About what happened at the ball, what I said . . ."

"I'm not sure any of that matters now."

"Of course it matters." Yael's eyes blaze into hers. "It's all that matters, Margot. It always has!"

She blows out a breath. "Maybe so, but it *isn't* all that matters." She gets up and starts to pace the room. "Yael, I can't make the Natural Caster Potion. Meaning I can't release Bloomfield from your family's clutches."

"You—"

"No, please just listen. Your family is going to destroy Bloomfield, Yael! Everything Granny Fern and her friends and I and even you have worked for—they're going to destroy it." With every word, Margot's temper grows hotter. "I care about the people in this town and everything they've built here. This is their home. It's my home. And your parents want to take it all and make it into a shopping center or spa for rich people or some such thing! And I'm not going to let them. Somehow, I don't know how, I have to stop them, because Bloomfield deserves better, and you may not care about Bloomfield or me anymore, but you once believed so too!" She heaves in a great breath and swipes at the surprising tears of rage that run down her cheeks.

"Margot?" Yael's voice is painfully gentle. "Daisy?"

"Yes?" she snaps.

"Please, Margot, sit. I know all of this, and I care very much."

"You do?" Margot falls into a chair.

"I do. Why do you think I rode all the way to Bloomfield in my underwear?"

She picks up her teacup again with a trembling hand. "That's a comfort, I suppose, though it doesn't solve the problem."

"No, but . . . I believe I may have found our solution, if we play things just right."

Margot sits bolt-upright. "Really?"

Yael reaches over and twines their fingers with hers. "Really."

Without thinking, Margot squeezes their hand. "Tell me everything, then."

Over tea and scones slathered with heartbreak-healing jam, they do.

# 33

# YAEL

It's well past sunrise by the time Margot and Yael ride out for Clementine's Tavern, fortified by a fresh pot of breakfast tea and a scant amount of sleep. After catching Margot up, Yael had washed themself as best they could with her bowl and pitcher, then curled up in a heap in the tattered but beloved armchair, shoving Harvey off the cushion to claim it. They woke only a few hours later with stiff muscles, their hair in absolute chaos, and not particularly sweet smelling, but they were anxious to get going.

There are plans to be made before the Claunecks come to reclaim what they've taken.

Yael switches Sweet Wind to a halt by the tavern gate and slips down the steed's cold clockwork neck while Margot dismounts from Gloom Stalker. A pleasantly cool breeze ruffles their clothing as they stretch out their back. Gone is the blazing heat that beat down upon them in Ashaway just yesterday, even though autumn is weeks away, and while the breeze brings relief, it also reminds them of the ticking clock hanging over Bloomfield. Fighting a flare of panic, Yael makes themself pause for a moment to tilt their face to the cloudless, cornflower sky and breathe in Bloomfield as it exists: ripe wild berries from the bushes in full bloom, and dew-damp oakmoss that clings to old tree trunks, and breaking bread . . . well, and still a bit of manure, thanks to the fields and the rambling beasts, but that can't be helped.

"Are you ready for this?" Margot prompts, stirring them back to the moment.

Yael sighs. "Ready enough. I don't expect a warm welcome." Deservedly so, after their weeks-long absence and their silence. They'd bargained away their loyalty to Bloomfield along with their loyalty to Margot. That Yael spent six weeks unaware of this decision, only convinced of its correctness, doesn't absolve them of making the choice in the first place.

But they aren't going to lie down and wallow in self-loathing and self-pity or drink themself into forgetting again.

They came here to make things right.

Margot nods with her chin toward the propped-open tavern door and the sounds of townsfolk within. "Some may be angry," she concedes, "or hurt when I tell them the truth I've been keeping from them."

"They'll understand. You've been carrying so much for so long, all alone, and I . . . I wish I'd been stronger sooner. I'm so sorry, Margot."

"Yael, I—"

"No, I shouldn't have . . . I owe you so much more than an apology. I owe you an explanation," they say, swiping wind-blown strands of still-dusty hair out of their eyes with a shirt-sleeve. In their haste to recount their findings in the Records Library, Yael has yet to describe the bargain they made with their patron. They've no idea how to untangle the events that have only just become clear to them in such a way that Margot might understand. That Margot might forgive . . . but that's too much to hope for. "I *will* explain everything," they promise, "but the town comes first."

Margot murmurs her agreement. "Right. The town comes first."

Yael clutches the satchel they borrowed from Margot, with the stolen file inside. Gathering their breath and their courage, they lead the way into the tavern to face the folk of Bloomfield.

Upon their entrance, a hush falls. Conversations cut short, spoons clattering back into bowls of perpetual summer stew. The faces of the folk Yael saw nearly every day for a season are inscrutable as they peer up at Yael and Margot together. Clementine stands behind the bar counter, of course, and there's Dara the chicken witch with her sister, Poppy, and Mike with his reading glasses hooked in the neck of his vest, and Tulip from the Care Cottage. Arnav, who was kind and eager enough to trade with them on their first morning in Bloomfield. Beryl from the brewery, and Yvonne from the butchery, and old Estelle, her cheeks as plump as the bread dough she deals in. Rosiee, who welcomed them to every community dinner.

Nobody speaks to welcome them now.

When the stillness grows unbearable, Yael asks, "Have you got a good wine here? I bet you've got a good wine."

Paused with a plate of cinnamon buns balanced on one palm, Clementine nods. "We do. But if you're accustomed to the stuff they stock in Ashaway, we might not be to your tastes, Yael Clauneck."

"Just Yael now." They summon the pale ghost of a smile.

"Well, Yael." Clementine sets her tray down on the bar. "Pull up a stool, if you've come to spend your coins."

"No coins to spend, I'm afraid." They lift the book and portfolios they've carried in. "But if you've got a scone to spare, I believe I've brought you something better."

Though Yael had intended to make their pitch from atop the bar, Clementine's saner mind prevailed, and she found a spot for them halfway up the staircase that leads to their old room, in full view of the tavern alongside Margot.

"I'll go first," Margot says, voice tight with nerves before she clears her throat. "I have something I need to tell you all," she announces to the gathered crowd, which has grown as word has been spread throughout Bloomfield that a matter of great import was unfolding in the tavern.

"Is it that you and Yael are back together?" Poppy calls out hopefully.

Margot's fingers twitch, and Yael reaches out to take her hand. Only to comfort her, of course.

For a brief moment, her fingers are slack in theirs before she tightens her grip. "What I have to say is about Bloomfield. And about Granny Fern. When my grandmother passed, you'll remember there was uncertainty and fear that my parents might meddle in Bloomfield's business, as they were the inheritors. Or presumed inheritors, since Granny never left a will. We all knew she wasn't great with paperwork—"

"That's an understatement," Estelle the baker shouts. "I couldn't get her to fill out a single order form." This brings a round of laughter from the tavern.

"Exactly. But my parents assured us all that they had no intention of changing things, and we believed them. *I* believed them. And I don't think they meant harm upon the town, truly, but . . . The truth is murkier than that, to say the least. You already know that they lost our fortune, which led to our home being seized by their creditors . . ."

"The Claunecks," Yael chimes in, just so Margot doesn't have to say it.

In the room below, Mike is scowling, and Poppy no longer smiles hopefully. She shares a worried look with Dara while Estelle twists her napkin through her gnarled fingers.

"Right." Margot presses forward. "I knew they'd been in a good deal of debt. But I didn't know the extent of it until after they'd landed in the Care Cottage, when I found a letter from the Clauneck Company. That's when I learned that their debt extended beyond the manor house and the bits of Greenwillow Remedies that remained profitable. The sum they owed . . . Well, it put Bloomfield itself in danger of seizure."

Panicked chatter erupts from the crowd as neighbor turns to neighbor, voices tumbling over one another.

"They can't do that! Can they do that?"

"What's to become of us all?"

"Where are we to go?"

"Is the company on its way right now?"

"Will the Queens' Guard come to drive us from our homes?"

"Surely something can be done . . ."

Yael opens their mouth, but Margot raises her voice over the crowd's, determined to be heard. "I believed there *was* something to be done, a deal the Clauneck Company would accept in place of the land. But as I discovered only yesterday, it's not something I can do. Or rather, I *won't* do it, because the harm it will cause is too great to be worth the cost."

Yael can see the muscles in her throat move as she works to swallow her nerves, along with the tears pooling in the corners of her eyes. They squeeze her hand again.

"I know . . . I shouldn't have left it so long without telling you all," she continues. "But I didn't want the knowledge to burden you. I was so set on fixing things myself, on living up to Fern's legacy. But Bloomfield *is* Granny Fern's legacy, and she intended it as a place where nobody would have to make their way in the world alone. I should have remembered that and trusted in it. I should have trusted you all."

"And what about you, Yael?" Mike calls. "Are you here to speak for the Claunecks?"

The crowd murmurs at this, waiting on an answer.

Yael grips the stairway railing, white-knuckled, with the hand that isn't holding Margot's. It would've been easier to let her explain everything, but they've come this far, and they owe the people of Bloomfield this much and more. "Listen, please! I'll tell you what I've found out, but . . . first, I must apologize as well. To all of you. When I left, I—I didn't mean to stay away for so long. I may not be a pillar of this community, but Bloomfield has felt like home, perhaps my first home, and I hope you can forgive me for it someday."

There's a second stretch of silence just before a plate-sized cinnamon bun slaps them in the chest. It leaves behind a swirl of icing as it thumps to the ground. Yael turns to find the source, eyes wide, and sees Clementine behind the bar counter looking as shocked as they.

"I . . . I thought you'd catch it!" she stammers, clapping her hands to her pinkening cheeks. "I thought we were doing a whole bit, and you'd catch it, and we'd all have a laugh. And then we could move on to the part where you help us save Bloomfield."

"Ah yes, that part." Yael rubs absently at the icing streak only to wipe their now sticky fingers on their trousers, making more of a mess of themself. "Well. As Margot says, she believed that everything that Granny Fern built—the estate in the woods, the greenhouses, the land upon which Bloomfield itself sits—went to her direct heirs in absence of a recorded will, as you all know. And when the Greenwillows let that fortune pour through their fingers, and my family swooped in to recoup the money that, frankly, they could've afforded to lose, the company would have been abiding by the laws of Harrow to seize it all. But when I went down to the company Records Library to confirm—"

"*You* were working for the Clauneck Company?" Mike cries out from the crowd.

Yael can hardly blame him. "I was. It was a very big mistake. The biggest I've made in my life—if one of many. But listen. There was no official record of the company claiming Bloomfield. Because it was never the company's land to claim." Now Yael slips the file out of their satchel, holding the key piece of parchment they found inside it up in view of the townsfolk. "*This* is Granny Fern's will. A will that supposedly didn't exist, but very much does. Its signing was witnessed by a clerk in Olde Post weeks before Margot came here to care for her grandmother. While Fern left a good deal of her wealth to her daughter and son-in-law, the land this town sits on was meant for Margot to inherit and care for, along with the greenhouses and the estate where the manor and cottage sit. Margot lost it all under false pretenses, and the Claunecks knew it. I daresay they're responsible for it."

In the crowd, Yvonne calls to Margot, "Fern never told you about any of this?"

She shakes her head. "By the time I came back to Bloomfield, Granny was gone. And she never liked to dwell on the future, anyhow. I wish that I'd asked, I should have asked, but . . . I suppose I wasn't prepared to consider a world without her."

"What matters is this: Margot never should have been held responsible for her parents' debts. It's against the laws of Harrow. And while we may not be able to prove that the Claunecks had a hand in the will's disappearance from local records—though we might try tracking down this clerk from Olde Post—we *can* prove by their possession of the will that they're wrongfully threatening Bloomfield. And were we to make this known throughout the kingdom, it may just prompt present and former clients to take a closer look at their accounts."

"So we're not going to lose Bloomfield?" Tulip asks.

The crowd erupts with excited chatter.

"Not today," Margot raises her voice to assure them. "And Yael and I have spoken about how to make sure that nothing and no one can threaten our home like this again. The land shouldn't be owned by one person; it should belong to all of us, in equal measure. I know that's what Granny Fern would've wanted and likely would've set up herself, if she'd known how. If she'd had more time."

"Is that possible?"

"It is with a community land trust," Yael says. "It'll take some doing, but I happen to have studied law at Auximia. Granted, it was more of the potatoes-into-gold and gold-into-potatoes type of law, but I know enough to help. And I will. Whenever I'm not working in the greenhouses, of course."

"Did you mean it?" Margot asks as they trot side by side down the forest road, out of the town proper and toward her cottage. "About wanting to work in the greenhouses again?"

They'd lingered at Clementine's for a long while, making furious plans with the townsfolk over a fresh batch of blackberry apple cake—and all right, yes, wine and ale—emerging to the lengthening shadows of late afternoon. Yael's not sure what to do about the night ahead of them. Ride back to the tavern to beg Clementine for their old room, they suppose. Perhaps she'll let them sleep behind the bar counter, if it's been taken since. But it seemed right to see Margot home first. Despite all their plotting in the early hours of the morning, there's so much left to say.

Beginning with this. "Yes, I meant it. I've got some moves to make before we're out of this completely, but without the constant threat of the Claunecks coming to seize the shop, I thought you might be able to spend more time on your remedies—perhaps one that might help your parents—without *my* parents breathing down your neck about that vile potion."

"I see." Margot stares at the road ahead as she contemplates.

"And anyhow, I've come to love growing things. I should warn you, I haven't got a scrap of magic left in me, and no hope of getting it back. But I never had much to begin with. And I'll learn everything I can from you first, if you'll have me. As an assistant, or . . . or an apprentice, if that suits," they assure her. Yael dares not hope for anything but that she accepts their help. Surely, that would be enough.

"Wait, go back a moment," Margot says. "What do you mean, no magic? How does a warlock lose their magic?"

The only explanation is the full explanation, and so they recount their time in Ashaway in full, beginning with their lie. "That night, on the balcony—I never blamed you for any of it, Margot, I swear. I thought that . . . I thought I was saving you. From living under the power of the Claunecks, or living without Bloomfield. I thought that any life we might have together could only cost you everything. I wanted to spare you from that, and from the burden of choosing your own ruin. It was wrong. Margot, I was so wrong."

Margot shakes her head and starts to speak. "I thought this might be the case. Or at least I hoped it might be when I saw the daisy."

They draw in a sharp breath, remembering the flower they'd set on Margot's pillow in the inn just as they left for the masquerade. Spell or no, how could they ever have forgotten?

"But then I never heard from you after, and I really began to doubt . . ."

"Wait," Yael insists. "Please, let me tell you everything." And they do. They recount their desperate, regrettable bargain with Clauneck; the weeks they spent believing that their decision to stay was all their own, and that Ashaway and the Clauneck Company were where they belonged; their visit to the perfumery greenhouse, and the secret garden of the girl from the Rookery; the chain reaction of choices it had set off inside of them, which soon brought down the outpost walls of Clauneck's spell, thrusting Yael back to themself; how Clauneck had withdrawn their patronage for good, leaving Yael as alone as they'd ever been, and more certain of their place and purpose in this world than they'd ever been.

"I see," Margot whispers once again when they've finished, barely audible above the birdsong.

"But I don't want you to think that I'm making excuses," Yael hurries to say. "It was cowardly beyond measure for me to make that bargain."

"Well . . . maybe. But it was brave of you to leave again."

Yael flips the switch to stop Sweet Wind just before the turnoff to the cottage path, and Margot follows suit with Gloom Stalker, watching them curiously. With a deep breath, they confess, "I have *never* been brave, Margot. I have always walked the path carved out by the Claunecks and faulted myself when I stumbled. But denying the life I was born into was no help to anybody, and neither was hating myself for it. So I am here to make things right, as best I can. And . . . and I am here to tell you what I should've told you in Ashaway, had I been brave enough: that I love you, Margot Greenwillow. It needn't change anything between us, because whether you can forgive me or not, I'm going to stay, and I'm going to be of use. But I love you all the same."

# 34

# MARGOT

"You love me?" Margot stammers. She grips Gloom Stalker's neck, her fingers digging into the metal brackets along its pseudo-mane. Her heart is surely pounding louder than the mechanical steed's hoofbeats had been a few seconds ago.

"Yes," Yael says quickly. Their eyes dart to Margot's and then away. "I'm sorry."

She dares to hope they're not sorry for loving her. Or for being there when the town needed them. Or for coming back to her. Or—most important—for saying the words she's been too afraid to let herself think out loud. "You're sorry? Why?"

Yael runs a hand through their hair, sending dust into a cloud around them. "Well, I'm sorry for dropping it on you like this, of course. While we're astride our steeds, and while I'm once again covered in road dust. I should've cleaned up a bit, at least." They shrug—a helplessly adorable gesture that makes Margot's heart kick in her chest.

"I don't have a tub, so that's hardly your fault."

"Even so, I'd imagined telling you somewhere more romantic. Say that was the case . . . What would your reply have been?"

Margot bites her lip, torn for the tiniest of seconds between wanting to keep Yael waiting and wanting to put them out of their misery. At the hopeful, desperate look on their face, she relents. With a thumb on the steering switch, she brings Gloom Stalker closer to Sweet Wind so her leg presses against Yael's.

"I would say . . ." Margot leans over, taking Yael's sleeve in her hand. She runs her fingers over the rough fabric, feeling the bones of their wrist beneath her hand. Suddenly shy, she looks up at them through her eyelashes. Some part of her is absolutely terrified to tell Yael how she feels, though another part knows that trusting Yael with her feelings will be the bravest, most wonderful, most freeing thing she's ever done. But how to say it best?

Should she tell them the seeds of her affection were sown on that first night in Clementine's Tavern, but now, like a plant that's been watered and nurtured, her fondness for them has grown strong until it towers over her, a wild, living, thriving thing? Suddenly, a mere declaration of love feels smaller than whatever has bloomed between them. She's wanted to say the words for weeks now. And if she doesn't say them, this plant will not thrive the way she knows it can.

She circles their wrist with her fingers to gather her courage. "I love you too."

Yael's breath hitches. "You do?"

"Fiercely and entirely."

Yael slumps forward in the saddle in relief. "Oh, that is such good news."

If she weren't in the saddle of a mechanical steed, she'd lean over and kiss them. But doing so would likely land her in a heap on the ground. "Now that we've agreed, can we please get off these damn horses?"

Yael sits up at once, a wicked, hungry smile on their lips. "My thoughts exactly. Shall we go back to the cottage?"

Margot's pulse races at the look on their face. "I have a better spot in mind."

"Better than your mattress?"

"Yes. Follow me."

They ride down the road and into the woods beyond Margot's cottage. The trail snakes back and forth for a bit, and at a towering pine tree, Margot stops her mechanical steed.

"You've brought me to some . . . trees?" Yael surmises.

"So much more. Please, follow me."

"Anywhere," Yael agrees.

Margot slides from her steed and steps off the path, and Yael follows, asking no questions as she leads them through tangled underbrush that tears at Margot's skirts. They don't even complain when Margot accidentally releases a sapling's branch too soon, and it whips backward into their face.

"We're almost there," she promises as the woods begin to thin. The sound of water running over rills fills the air.

She's never brought anyone here before. It's her most secret spot.

She peels back a curtain of moss.

"It's incredible," Yael whispers.

It really is. With satisfaction, Margot surveys the scene in front of her. A waterfall tumbles down a towering boulder, casting a lacy spray over the pool below. All around the pool, tall willows bend their long, waving branches. Oaks hung with moss stand a bit off from the banks, and at the feet of the trees, a dozen varieties of mushrooms cover the ground. There's a thicket of pink and yellow roses on one side of the stream, mingling with a dense raspberry bush. Flowers of all shades—purple wisterias, pink hyacinths, blue and black tulips, yellow dahlias, and white and yellow daisies—grow along the stream.

"Are these strawberries?" Yael asks, bending over to pick the small fruit at their feet.

"Yes," Margot says proudly.

"But how do they grow here with so much shade?"

"Magic." Margot smiles. "I've been working on this spot since I was a little girl. Granny Fern gave it to me to cultivate, and for many years I've been bringing plants from the greenhouses and putting them in the earth, seeing if they would take to it. Nurturing them with spellwork and good care. I couldn't bring myself to suggest that we hold Rastanaya's show here or to tell anyone about it."

"It's wonderful." Yael plucks a tiny red berry and holds it out to Margot.

Her lips encircle the berry as she takes it from Yael's fingertips. She chews and swallows as Yael picks another for themself. It's a quick thing after that to cup Yael's cheek. To lean in closer, pressing the softest of kisses to Yael's berry-stained lips. To take their bottom lip in her teeth and pull on it gently. To deepen their kiss.

"Oh, Daisy," Yael murmurs as their hands twine in Margot's hair.

"Yes, love," she whispers back. It feels so good to finally have the word between them. She loves Yael Clauneck. Somehow, impossibly, entirely, and completely. She loves Yael Clauneck.

Yael doesn't say anything else, just kisses her more fiercely. Their hands fumble for the lacings of Margot's dress even as she slips her own hands under their shirt. Her fingers slide along the dip in their waist, moving lower. Yael's hands grow more insistent, and Margot's dress falls away from her shoulders. Yael's shirt follows, and Margot slides her dress off her shoulders and down her hips, letting it fall to the ground at her feet so she's fully naked.

"You are so lovely, Margot Greenwillow," Yael says, stopping the process of removing their shoes for a moment. Admiration lights their eyes as they look her over.

She basks in their attention, feeling a bit like a plant goddess surrounded by her kingdom. Then a yellow leaf falls from one of the trees above her, breaking the spell.

Flashing a smile at Yael, she steps off the bank and into the pool. It's still warm from the day's heat, though there's a coolness rising from the depths. Yael follows her a second later, plunging into the pool with a splash. They submerge under the water, and Margot's heart soars as she feels hands wrap around her waist.

"Hello," Yael says as they surface. Water droplets sparkle in their long, dark eyelashes. They pull Margot closer.

"This way," she says, wriggling loose and swimming toward the waterfall. She slips behind it, pulling gently on Yael's hand.

They emerge together behind the falls in a hidden pool. There's a small rock seat, and the curtain of falling water makes a cocoon around them.

"This is magical," Yael whispers, looking about.

Behind them, the waterfall catches the afternoon light, casting prisms of color across Yael's skin.

"My favorite spot in my favorite place in the world," Margot says, settling onto the stone seat. "I almost took you here when we were small. I wished you might kiss me," she admits, "though we definitely weren't naked in that daydream."

"I'm glad we made it at last." Yael sits next to Margot, their thighs flush against hers. "Especially as I don't plan to be quiet this time." Yael leans over to trace the line of Margot's clavicle with one finger.

*This time.* For a moment, their stolen intimacy on the Clauneck balcony during the masquerade rises in Margot's mind. The urgency of it, the heat of it, the bitter resolution of the moment as Yael walked away from her . . .

Then all of that's gone as the present comes rushing in. The noise of the waterfall drowns everything out as Yael's lips burn a line along Margot's neck. She arches her head back, letting it rest against a moss-covered rock on the side of the pool. Yael shifts closer, each kiss teasing and devastatingly slow as they move from the swoop of her neck to feather kisses along her jaw. They bury their fingers in her hair, turning her face toward theirs as they kiss the side of her mouth.

Their eyes catch Margot's, dangerous and molten, even as the waterfall's spray haloes them.

"Yael," Margot breathes.

The rest of her words are lost in Yael's mouth as they capture her lower lip. For the first time since they met again in Clementine's Tavern half a year ago, Margot feels truly free. She's not hiding anything from Yael. It's not her responsibility to save Bloomfield. All she has to do in this moment is let herself be loved by Yael Clauneck, and it is the most wonderful feeling in all the world.

She reaches over, pulling Yael into her lap. Their legs slip around her hips, Margot's breasts pressed to Yael's chest. Their kissing becomes more insistent, and Margot is all need, bone melting and desperate.

Yael's hair frames their faces as their kiss deepens. Margot shifts on the rock so her fingers can move along their thighs.

"I can do that too," Yael murmurs against her mouth, breaking the kiss.

"Show me." Even as she says it, Margot slips her hand up their leg, letting one thumb graze Yael's center.

They moan, the noise nearly undoing Margot.

"With pleasure," Yael murmurs. They cup her breasts in their hands as they lean down to take one of her nipples into their mouth. Their tongue traces a circle around it, and heat floods through Margot's whole body.

Then, as Margot's fingers find their way into Yael, they match her move for move. Each touch bringing her closer. Each kiss pushing her toward the edge. Yael's skilled fingers working her with intent and good care.

She falls without warning, and a cry of pleasure. Yael tumbles with her a moment later, their body pressed against her hand, gasping, her name on their lips.

"I love you," Margot says as Yael collapses into her. She wants to say it again and again, to shout the words to the world. Instead, she kisses Yael's earlobe, letting herself relax into the comforting shape of their body against hers.

"I love you, Daisy," Yael manages, stealing another kiss. "And I love this."

Margot looks at Yael as the waterfall pounds the stone all around them. "Shall we do it again, then?"

"Always and forever," Yael says, their voice far more serious than the wicked gleam in their eyes.

⚘

When they leave the hidden grotto several climaxes apiece later, the sun is setting. They dress themselves and make their way back to their mechanical steeds, Margot twining her fingers through Yael's. "Ready to go?"

"To your cottage?" Yael asks hopefully.

"To *our* cottage."

"I'd like nothing better," Yael says, kissing her again before they mount their steeds and ride toward home.

# Epilogue

# YAEL

*Autumn, one year later*

The garden tub was the best idea Yael's ever had.

It's one of the few changes made to their cottage over the past year and a month, though there've been changes aplenty around Bloomfield. In the greenhouses, Margot's private workshop has expanded twofold, and three new houses have been added for medicinal plants so that Margot might bring Greenwillow Remedies back to life—renamed as Greenfern Remedies, to begin something new while honoring the best parts of her past all at once. And the manor house just up the wooded path has been transformed entirely now that Margot's parents have woken thanks to the magical remedy that, without the constant pressure and need to pour all of her time and talents into a Natural Caster Potion for the Claunecks, Margot was finally able to crack. They've taken up residence in the house; Margot's idea, as she preferred to remain in their cottage, the home that she and Yael have made together.

But the tub was all Yael's doing. They alone hooked the cart up to Sweet Wind and hauled in flat slabs of stone from beyond the old outpost walls to support the iron clawfoot tub they purchased as a surprise for Margot. Yael planted daisies and gardenias, spicy-smelling pink dianthus, star-shaped nicotiana for night bathing, and sweet pea to climb the wooden trellis they built for privacy. Not that the Greenwillows leave their house to visit the cottage often; Margot's parents largely keep to themselves, recovered but subdued. Still, Sweet Wind and Gloom Stalker have a habit of standing unblinking at the garden fence for hours at a time now that they've been kept on, allowing birds to perch on their wooden saddles. While a happy sight, it isn't especially romantic.

And that just wouldn't do.

Shielded from view by the sweet pea, Margot reclines in the tub, unfurling like a blossom herself to rest her back against Yael's chest. They kiss the crook of her neck and reach around to slide a palm down the wet silk of her skin.

While Margot's garden blooms nearly year-round as though in perpetual summer, the world beyond their gate is heavily spiced with autumn, the leaves in the forest and in the orchards colored cinnamon and turmeric and saffron. In the community garden, pumpkins and butternut and acorn squash are so ripe on the vine, they nearly glow, like little suns grown from seed. Along with baskets of beets and radishes and lettuce, they'll be picked and ready for the harvest festival this afternoon.

Speaking of which . . .

"There's a lot left to do before the festival." Margot reaches up and back to cup a hand behind Yael's neck. "We should get moving."

"We've a few hours before it starts," Yael protests.

"Yes, and a few hours' worth of work." But she sinks even farther down into them as she says it.

They smile into her damp, floral-smelling hair. "Just rest another moment with me before we need to go."

"*Just* rest, hmm?" She spins and draws her knees up around Yael's hips, sloshing water over the lip of the tub as she settles into their lap. "That's all?"

"For such a clean person, your thoughts are filthy, Margot Greenfern." It's the name she's taken and used for the past year: something new, and something gone, but forever a part of her. They tsk, their hands floating up to touch her. "I've not even had my breakfast tea."

"As though that ever stops you."

Yael murmurs their concession. "Very well. I am yours." They grip her by the waist and pull her closer, to kissing distance. "Do what you will."

Instead, she turns her cheek to lay her head on their chest. "I could do this every day, I think."

"We nearly have."

After racing back to Bloomfield last summer—and after spending their night (and the next day as well, and the night after . . .) properly making up to Margot for their absence—Yael had set out again for Olde Post. According to the town clerk who'd taken the position just over three years prior, the old clerk responsible for filing Granny Fern's will had since moved on from the town, claiming to have fallen into an unexpected inheritance soon after Fern's death. Star student or not, Yael was capable of doing *that* math. They had the new clerk send a prompt letter of notice to the Clauneck Company advising them of their office's "clerical error."

Yael might not have found evidence of the Claunecks' meddling beyond a shadow of a doubt, but evidence of their former family's priorities they had aplenty—twenty-three years of it. And if there was one thing the Claunecks wanted more than a potion as dangerous as it was profitable, it was to preserve their reputation. That was the whole reason they'd wanted their unimportant and ill-functioning heir back in the first place; the reason they spent months spreading rumors about Yael's illness to cover up for their absence, rather than risking exposure by dragging them back.

Slipping a few silver denaris to the clerk bought Yael the chance to add a postscript to the notice of error:

To whom it may concern at the Clauneck Company,

We trust that this oversight, which has wrongfully stripped a young woman of her home, and might have jeopardized the town itself, will be swiftly remedied. Margot and I await your prompt response. Should any doubts linger on the company's end over the correct course of action, I shall be glad to pursue my own course; I have reason to believe that the clerk responsible may be greatly helpful in bringing to light what has remained in the dark until now. Please know that our impatience is nothing personal; it is simply business.

*All best,*

*Yael X*

A prompt response had indeed followed. A letter formally addressed to Margot Greenwillow arrived at the clerk's office on Clauneck Company letterhead, releasing all of her seized property back to her. A separate notice addressed to Yael arrived soon after, formalizing their "termination," also on company letterhead. Termination of employment, and of inheritance, Yael safely assumed. They may not have had any clue where the old clerk *actually* resided, nor whether they'd be at all keen to help, and so an uneasy stalemate was the most they could do without it. But Margot was free. Yael was free. And Bloomfield was free.

The next time they rode to Olde Post, it was with Margot to formalize the land trust.

Now, aside from Yael's trips to neighboring hamlets and communities that have requested Yael's counsel so that they might follow in Bloomfield's footsteps, and Margot's travels to fairs and festivals around the kingdom where her skills as a master plant witch and remedy maker are in constant demand, their days are largely the same: Margot in her workshop and Yael in the greenhouses. Lying in the bed they share at the end of each day and drifting off to sleep, Yael knows in their bones that there could be no happier life than this one.

"I mean," Margot says, sighing contentedly against their shoulder, "that I could do this every day to come—just be with you—and never grow tired of it."

Yael believes her—and what a beautiful gift that is. "Very well. I am yours," they repeat, little louder than a whisper this time.

"That's good to hear. Otherwise, I might've been a bit nervous before proposing."

Where Yael's fingers had been drifting idly up and down Margot's spine, stroking her back, they still completely. "Propose? Marriage, you mean?"

She sits up to look down at them, rain-cloud-colored eyes aglow. "If you like."

"It's . . . it's just so soon, and I've so many options . . ." They try to dissemble, but a grin spreads across their face, unstoppable as sunrise. "Have you gotten me a ring and everything?"

"I have, but I don't exactly have it on me." Margot laughs as they dip their gaze down her body, searching just to be safe. "I'd planned to do this later, perhaps at the festival. You always seem to thwart my plans, Yael Greenfern."

"And who says I'll take *your* name?" But again, they cannot lie without smiling, because it's perfect.

It is who they were born to be.

# MARGOT

"Come with me, this way," Margot says, pulling Yael by the hand. They stand at the edge of town, in a wild-flower meadow between the mammoth fields and the forest that leads to Margot's cottage. Behind them, the sun sinks below the horizon, and above them, the first stars twinkle in the purple-and-orange gloaming sky. In the middle of the field, beyond a copse of oak trees, a fat yellow disk of a moon rises. A warm breeze that smells of autumn leaves and wood-smoke fills the air, bringing with it the sound of fiddle music from somewhere nearby.

"Where are we going, Daisy?" Yael asks wearily. "Let's take a bottle of cider home and celebrate our engagement. I was thinking of revisiting that delicious thing you tried last night . . ."

Margot turns to smile coyly at them. "There'll be time for all that later. I have one more thing to show you."

"What else could there possibly be? I've already seen the best the Bloomfield harvest festival has to offer, and besides, most people have packed up for the night. Nobody but the old-timers were left in the square."

It had been a marvelous afternoon of bobbing for apples, riding mammoths, carving pumpkins into ghoulish and grinning faces, weaving enchanted wildflower crowns for anyone who stopped by Margot's booth, drinking cider and eating apple pastries, browsing the library stall, and watching an outdoor concert, but there's one more stop they still have to make this evening.

Margot adjusts her own wildflower crown, woven with daisies and strawberries from the grotto. "Trust me. You're going to love this."

"Oh, very well," Yael agrees. "Only because I cannot say no to you in that strawberry-print dress."

Margot laughs. "Now you're in trouble, because I shall wear this every day."

"I shan't be able to resist you," Yael says agreeably. "No matter what you're wearing."

Together, they walk along a well-trod path that twists through the field of towering sunflowers. Clusters of purple asters and yellow bunches of goldenrod, such faithful companions in the autumn, grow at the bases of the sunflowers, and small grasshoppers flit along the path, darting away from their feet.

Margot twines her fingers through Yael's, giving them a squeeze. The ring she gave Yael—something simple and lovely that Granny Fern had gifted her—is warm on Yael's finger and fits them perfectly. A quiet contentment fills Margot as they walk. She's found someone whom she adores, and they get to make a life together. Could she be any luckier?

"Daisy, are you quite all right?" Yael asks as the path twists, bringing them closer to the stand of trees.

Margot shoots Yael a watery smile. "Yes, of course. I'm just happy."

Yael untwines their fingers from hers and cups her face in both hands. "Let's aim for happiness without the tears, then, shall we?" Gently, Yael brushes away the tears silvering a path along Margot's cheeks.

"Of course, I just . . . I never saw myself content here. And I certainly never imagined how sweet this life with you could be."

"We're only getting started," Yael murmurs as they stand on tiptoe to kiss Margot. "Believe me, we have much joy ahead of us."

As their kiss deepens and Margot heaves a small, happy sigh, the fiddle song stops and a new one begins. Yael pulls away from Margot the tiniest bit.

"Tell me," they murmur against her lips.

"Yes?"

"What's happening in the woods? Why is there music coming from the oak grove?"

Margot smiles. "Let's go see."

Together, they walk the last few turns of the flower-bordered path, stopping when it opens up in front of the oak grove.

In front of them, amid a circle of ancient oaks, a great feast has been set up. Fairy lights hang among the branches, casting a bobbing golden glow on the party. A merry band of two fiddlers and a drummer—traveling bards who are friends of Clementine's—plays in one corner under the trees. Three enormous pumpkins and heaps of purple and gold mums decorate the area around the band. Smaller gourds and jars full of wildflowers rest on the tables among baskets of bread, pies, and tankards of ale. Everyone in Bloomfield stands around the tables, laughing and talking with one another.

When they see Yael and Margot, a cheer goes up. Clementine raises her tankard, and everyone else in town does the same. Margot's parents sit among the crowds, and tears rise in Margot's eyes as her mother meets her gaze and inclines her head slightly. Margot grins at her and nods back. Her father gives her a small wave. It's so good to have them here.

"What is all this?" Yael asks.

Margot winds her arm around Yael's waist. "It's a party for you, darling. On the anniversary of Bloomfield's salvation . . . or near enough . . . as a thank-you for all you did for the town. We wanted to celebrate *you*."

Yael opens and closes their mouth, clearly too stunned to speak. "Well," they manage at last. "It's the most charming thing I've ever seen, but you've got it all wrong. Let's make it our engagement party, shall we?"

"I'd like nothing better, my love," Margot says as she leans down for one more quick kiss.

Another cheer rises from the crowd as Margot and Yael walk into the oak grove, hand in hand, ready to begin their next adventure.

# ACKNOWLEDGMENTS

*Homegrown Magic* began, as many stories do, around a table with friends.

Specifically, a virtual D&D table with fellow authors. It was Jamie's first official game, while Becca had played for years. During sessions, our characters were strictly pals, but something in the character concepts sparked a story idea, which became our new passion project. This book was a joy to write from beginning to end. We still can't believe how lucky we are to be here, and we're so very grateful for the many folks who helped bring Margot and Yael's story to life.

Thanks to our agents, Kate Testerman and Eric Smith, who saw the potential in this book and these characters from our first pages, and found them the perfect home at Del Rey.

Endless thanks to our delightful editor, Anne Groell, for championing our queer cozy fantasy from the start. We appreciate your keen insights and swoon-strengthening notes. Thanks as well to our UK editor, Sam Bradbury, for helping Yael and Margot find a home overseas.

Thanks to the whole Del Rey team who worked on our dream book, including Ayesha Shibli and Madi Margolis in editorial. Laura Jorstad, the brilliant copy editor who untangled our timeline. In the publisher's office, thanks to Scott Shannon, Keith Clayton, Tricia Narwani, Alex Larned, and Marcelle Iten Busto. In publicity, thanks to David Moench, Jordan Pace, and Ada Maduka. In marketing, thank you to Ashleigh Heaton, Tori Henson, and Sabrina Shen. Thanks to our social media support, Maya Fenter. Thanks also to the amazing art department for such magical designs, including Regina Flath, Rachel Ake, and Aarushi Menon.

Huge thanks as well to our amazing cover artist, Lisa Perrin, for giving us such a dreamy, cozy, perfect cover!

We are also grateful to Kelly Van Sant at KT Literary, and to our film agent, Debbie Deuble Hill.

Thank you, thank you, thank you to the We Are All Bards D&D group—our brilliant DM Rosiee Thor (thanks for the chili cones and iced soup), M. K. England, Linsey Miller, Tess Sharpe, and Tehlor Kay Mejia. Thanks to The Soup for the general nerd support, and the WSBW authors for celebrating along with us. We love you all!

And thank you to all the indie bookstores who have supported our books and careers along the way, including but not limited to Room of One's Own, Riverbend Books, Kismet Books, Powell's, Schuler's Books, Blue Willow, Books of Wonder, and so many more. What would the book world do without you?

*From Jamie*

After so many books, I feel like I'm always thanking the same people, but so it goes when you have a lovely community supporting your dreams, helping you grow, and excitedly cheering the next things. Much like the idyllic community of Bloomfield, my community is a wonderful place to live.

First of all, thank you Becca Podos, for agreeing to co-write *Furious* with me after a random DM and for being such a joyful presence in my life. I love writing books with you; having long calls about kissing and strawberry jam; getting into discussions about the ways rivers work and the mechanics of carriages; and so much more. Cheers to many, many more books together, my friend.

Thank you times a million to my incredible author pals (who aren't in the D&D group) and who have been with me for many years on this journey: Noelle Salazar, Jenny Ferguson, Lizzy Mason, Cindy Baldwin, Autumn Krause, Roselle Lim, Sarah Underwood, Grace Li, Ashley Martin, and so many others.

Thanks to my sisters, Kim and Renee, my brother, Mark, and my dear friends Ashleigh Bunn and Cheryl Clearwater for all the endless support.

Thank you to all the readers, librarians, booktokers, and bookish pals who I've been lucky enough to bump into over the last few years: Mike Lasagna, Gretchen Treu, Chloe Maron, Katy J. Schroeder, Jaria Rambaran, Jamie Butler, Mara Jarvis, Meghan Nigh, Emily Sarah, and Meg Hood, to name a few of the wonderful people out there making the book world lovely.

And, of course and always, thank you to my beloved family: Adam, Marcy, and Liam. You are the starting place of all my stories, and I am so grateful to be a part of yours.

*From Becca*

Thank you first and foremost to Jamie. Writing this book reminded me how to love writing, and I couldn't picture a better partner for it. Whether we're breaking our own hearts, brainstorming euphemisms for balcony escapades, or mutually ranting about capitalism, every step has been a joy.

Thank you to Rosiee, Alex, and Tehlor (and the cards) for supporting this story from the start, and encouraging me to grow my flowers.

Thank you to Eric Smith for absolutely everything.

And thank you always to Tom, for picking up literally every dropped ball while I attempt to juggle writing and life; I couldn't do any of this without you.

Finally, we want to thank you, dear readers. Thanks for coming along with us on this first cozy romantic adventure. Thanks for talking about this book online, sharing it with your friends, and sending us thirsty messages about it. We are so grateful to you for all the support, and we can't wait to take you on the next adventure!

*Yael and Margot's story may be done, but fear not;*
*the adventure is far from over!*
*Sage Wilderstone and Araphi Clauneck now take*
*center stage in Jamie Pacton and Rebecca Podos's*
*next delightful outing:*

# HOMEWARD FOR A SPELL

*A COZY FANTASY ROMANCE WITH PLENTY*
*OF TAVERNS AND ONLY ONE TENT.*

*HERE IS A SPECIAL PREVIEW:*

By the time Sage Wilderstone and her party stumble across the threshold of the Mare's Milk, she's dead on her feet and down to her last copper denari. Their journey from the Upper Islands—an archipelago in the cold and writhing Serpentine Sea off Harrow's east coast—to the western port city of Kingfisher was more perilous than expected. Not that she's complaining. Sage wouldn't be worth her wages if one cave full of giant fire beetles was enough to take her down, or a few dozen coastal raiders.

Still. Running out of money, arrows, and dry underwear along the road *had* been taxing, if she's honest with herself. For that, she blames Gaffa. They'd planned to be back in Kingfisher a month ago, before autumn properly set in. Then their party leader had impulsively signed them up for a side expedition on one of the border islands, and that's where their trouble really began.

Gods, she needs a drink.

But first, she needs her share of the pay.

Sage and the other members of her adventuring party claim a table in the corner of the tavern to wait for The Agent. Sage sits braced against the rough stone wall with her eyes on every exit: a habit after months on the road. The window glass is filmed with salt borne on the ocean breeze, but with her sharp vision, she can see through well enough to the street outside. Surrounding the tavern is a maze of varnished warehouses with sailors coming and going, hauling crates of cargo up from the wharf; one such building holds the spoils of their own journey, locked safely away until their payment is secured. Above the flat steel roofs, the fort overlooking the harbor is just visible in the near distance, its cannons pointed out to sea. There are the customs houses as well, ready to inspect the ships' goods upon docking and, more important, to tax them—for the city, mostly, and some for the queens. Beyond that, the very tops of the tallest ship masts vanish into clouds.

No better place than a port town for Sage to say goodbye before vanishing as well.

"Feels as if we haven't sat on chairs in ages," Raisa complains loudly, reminding Sage that she hasn't parted ways with her traveling companions just yet.

"Only logs and boulders," Reece agrees. "My ass cheeks are hard as stone by now."

Jamile chuckles as they raise one iron finger above their head to summon the barkeep.

Gaffa grabs their wrist, pulling it down to the tabletop. "Got a way to settle that bill, Jam?" she asks. "Shall we pay with the rocks in our boots, since that's all we own between us?"

"Won't need to, once The Agent shows up with our money," Jamile says, smiling dreamily at the thought. "I'm going to order the good stew—the kind with real meat in it instead of leather."

"Hey, our gran' was famous for her leather stew," Reece objects.

Raisa nods. "Aye, Gran' was a brilliant woman. Shrewd, too. Used to rent out our bathtub on Saturday nights for a copper a person. Only tub in our neighborhood, it was. Soon as The Agent pays us, I'm heading to the nearest bathhouse, and I don't plan on leaving it till I'm boiled down to leather myself."

"What about you, Sage?" Jamile turns to her. "What's the first thing you'll do? Stop in at the Bear's Embrace? I'm sure that's where Gaffa's bound." They wink, dodging when Gaffa swipes at them from across the table.

The Bear's Embrace is a cathouse in the harbor, raised up on stilts to withstand waves and storm surges. And so that their bawds will be the first to catch the eyes of docking sailors. Had the party come in by sea instead of by land, Sage might've looked toward its windows and spotted Rosaria, her elbows resting on the sill to frame the perfect pair of breasts overflowing her bodice as she blew Sage a kiss. Or Benyamin, with pansies and calibrachoa and flossflower woven into his dark braids. Or Devyn, tattooed from knuckles to neck with the text from *The Princess and the Pirate*: a classic erotic epic of Harrow's past.

"Not me. I'll find a room in the city and sleep for a week." Sage imagines resting her head on a pillow instead of a pack. Maybe she'll sleep for two weeks, or perhaps she'll just hibernate for the winter. Though a trip to the healing house first wouldn't hurt, she concedes; she twisted her right knee a month back in their brawl with the raiders, exacerbated the injury while dragging the carcass of a giant river rat back to their cooking fire after a hunt, and ever since it's been aching at the end of each day on the road.

Sage flexes her leg to feel the joint's protestation.

If only the cleric Gaffa had lined up hadn't eloped before they set out in late spring. Or if only Gaffa had spared a moment and a few coins to replace him. Now they're all looking worse for wear. Reece and Raisa, a pair of blond, burly twins with a talent for both starting and ending fights, no longer look entirely identical; Reece's nose took a direct hit from a raider's club, and Raisa had shorn her hair with Sage's boot knife after a blast from a fire beetle singed half of it off, anyhow. Their warlock, Jamile, is sporting two iron fingers where once they had a full flesh-and-bone set, though they've taken the loss with good cheer.

As for Sage, while her appearance is the least of her worries, she could do with a visit to a bathhouse after the healer's. And to a barber. She's let her habitual sharp undercut grow out for a bit of extra warmth, while the rest of her blond hair hangs down to her cheekbones, threatening her peripheral vision. And though she's always been on the lean side, now she weighs at least a sack-of-onions less than she did at the start of summer—despite hunting and foraging as much food as the craggy coastal hills could provide in fall: often a handful of small, sour apples and nuts near tasteless from the cold nights, roasted over a low campfire alongside a stringy jackalope or a half-poisonous fish. They simply hadn't been prepared for such a long or late-season journey. If *Sage* were running the party—

"There he is," Gaffa says under her breath.

Nobody but Gaffa has met with The Agent before, and even Gaffa has never met The Client—the unnamed sponsor of their mission. But that's often how adventuring works. Very wealthy noblemen or institutions have the means to reach out to famed adventurers directly, but your average wizard-scholars or un-landed folk don't have the contacts to hire a more, well, *cost-efficient* party, pieced together from lone adventurers in taverns and port cities. Adventurers like Sage. Such clients contract with agents, professional middlemen. It isn't always an anonymous process, but if, for instance, The Client is a wizard-scholar, as Sage suspects from the spell components they were hired to collect in the hostile sea caves of Harrow's eastern shore, and they want to keep the details of their experiments from being leaked to rival wizards, they might choose to remain unnamed.

So The Agent hired Gaffa, who in turn assembled the party. Sage had expected The Agent to look like . . . well, an agent. Some company man with a fine suit and a neat chinstrap beard. But the man who pushes through the doorway in a cold swirl of wind and brown leaf litter is scruffier in appearance, with ash-brown curls just salting to gray under a knit cap, and a spray-crusted peacoat buttoned up to his shaggy jawline. He could be any dockworker or sailor stopping in at the tavern before bringing home what's left of his commission. Scuffing his boots against the sawdust-strewn floorboards, he pulls off his cap to shove back the curls dangling in front of his eyes— a blue so pale, they seem lilac in the firelight.

Sage narrows her own hazel eyes, analyzing his every movement. His easy grin when Gaffa stands to catch his attention, and his silk-smooth voice as he cheers, "The intrepid heroes return!" across the tavern.

Crossing to meet them, The Agent claims a seat on the rough wood bench beside the twins and drops a leather purse onto the table with a *clink*. Reece and Raisa exchange a look, identical eyebrows raised. Honestly, Sage couldn't care less what he looks like, so long as he pays them in spendable denari and not transfigured potatoes.

"Barkeep, a round for the table," The Agent commands, trusting the grizzled ex-mariner behind the bar counter to snap to attention.

Begrudgingly, the barkeep does. "A round of what?"

"Bring us . . . hmm, what's good here?" The Agent turns to the table beside theirs to ask the pair of sailors hunched over steaming bowls and frosty tankards.

"Fuck off," one of the pair mutters around a soup spoon.

"Very well then," The Agent says cheerfully, turning back around.

Sage wouldn't have trusted their answer, anyway. The Mare's

Milk is filled with folk coming in from months at sea; anything that isn't brined meat, dirty water, and tough ship biscuits is bound to seem delicious.

"Bring us the house special, sir'ram," The Agent calls, "and your signature dish as well!"

The barkeep shakes their bristled gray head. "A boil it is," they say, lining up six tankards to fill.

Meanwhile, Gaffa hasn't taken her eyes off the purse in the center of the table. "Hope this round's on you. That bag looks light," she mutters, appraising its shape.

The back of Sage's neck begins to prickle, the way it does whenever the wind shifts in the forest, carrying the scent of trouble across her path in the woods. Only a frayed thread of self-restraint stops her from reaching for the dagger holstered at her hip; this isn't the kind of trouble to be solved at knifepoint. Not yet, anyway.

"Ah, well, yes." The Agent scrubs his knuckles across his beard. "Unfortunately, there's the matter of our agreed-upon timeline. You'll recall, my client's contract required the goods to be delivered by summer's end, before the start of the academic year. But as you can tell from the indecent state of the trees and that frost in the air, that deadline has rather lapsed."

Now Sage isn't sure whether her dagger would find its sheath in The Agent's chest, or in Gaffa's.

Their party leader scrubs a road-dusty hand down her face. "We met with unexpected dangers along the way. Your boss is getting a bargain; we could charge for every lost finger."

Jamile smiles uneasily across the table.

"And I am *very* sympathetic to that. Unfortunately, again, the contract was not." Tugging a legal scroll from his inner coat pocket, he offers it up, and Jamile takes it with their modified hand. "There were no amendments for additional compensation in case of injury, nor extensions."

The warlock frowns, reading, as Reece and Raisa begin to growl in protest.

Sage doesn't bother. Of course Gaffa failed to negotiate a contract with contingencies, then blew their deadline by signing them up for an impulsive and ill-thought-out side quest. If *she'd* been running things . . .

No, she's got to stop thinking that way. Sage isn't like Jamile, the scion of an adventuring legacy family who just happens to prefer following over leading. And she never attended one of the better academies in Harrow, where she might've made connections as Gaffa did (though maybe if she'd stuck around long enough to graduate from the college in Olde Post, she'd have gotten lucky). If Sage was to sign on permanently with a party—or linger for more than one mission, at least—she could have steadier work and higher shares. But with no tide to lift her ship, she must steer herself alone through the narrows and rapids of this world.

Still, that's the way she likes it, isn't it?

Just then, the barkeep approaches, all six tankards miraculously clutched among their knotty fingers. They set them down with a slosh of liquid onto the tabletop, white and foamy and lightly pungent smelling.

"Ah." The Agent tips forward to peer into his tankard. "And this is . . ."

"Mare's milk." The barkeep grunts. "House special."

"The titular drink. I might've guessed. My thanks, sir'ram."

The barkeep retreats, replaced by a young kitchen hand struggling under the weight of a copper pot half her size, with a stack of newspapers tucked beneath one arm. She sets down the pot, fans the papers out in the center of the table with one hand, and then, with a grunt, spills the pot's contents right onto the papers. Whole crab parts tumble out alongside corncobs, nugget-sized potatoes, and some indefinable chopped sausage. The Agent's eyebrows twitch upward in surprise. The man must have two decades on Sage at least, and looks as though he's spent it at sea, but he doesn't know what a boil is?

The party stops grumbling long enough to grab a tankard each of sour, fizzy milk-turned-to-liquor, and to swarm the tavern's "signature dish." Sage's stomach groans so loudly, it's all she can do to crack the meat out of the crab legs rather than sliding them down her throat shell and all.

If she's not to be properly paid, she may as well be full.

🦂

Soon enough, Sage leaves the Mare's Milk with her pack slung over her shoulder, a shallow palmful of gold denari in one pocket, and a boiled corncob wrapped in a spare bit of newspaper in the other. She turns the coins over and over, letting them clink between her fingertips. This will buy her a room and food for a few weeks, at least. More if she sticks to leather stew instead of pheasant or boar.

She blames her rage for the fact that it takes two blocks to realize she's being followed.

Not good.

Cheeks burning, Sage marches steadily forward against the damp autumn wind, chin tucked into her coat collar, moving inland. Beyond the harborside warehouses is a district of large brick factory buildings, scattered through with rickety housing and rented rooms for the city's poor folk. Whoever her tail is, she'll lose them in the skinny streets and alleyways and boltholes. Few guards patrol here, but as a rule, Sage prefers to handle things on her own. Gods forbid she end up in a cell in the courthouse alongside some eleven-year-old pickpocket because the guards were too impatient to untangle the source of the trouble.

When she passes a cluster of sailors carrying casks and

trunks and spools of rope in the direction of the docks, she takes advantage of the cover to duck sideways into a lane of housing built like fishermen's shacks piled precariously atop one another, all weathered gray boards and dented tin roofs. Sage knows places like this one well. While everyone of working age will be away in the surrounding factories, laboring down at the docks, or serving drinks in one of Kingfisher's plentiful taverns, children dart through the streets in laughing packs, watched by grandparents or elder community members from their rickety stoops. Almost the moment she starts down the lane, Sage turns again to slip between two stacks of houses, built so close together that the overhanging metal roofs blot out the sky above completely. From here, she spills out into the alleyway behind a cannery, inaccessible from the main road. She steps soundlessly over broken glass littering broken cobblestones to melt into shadow behind a dumping bin, dropping her pack to tuck herself nearly flat to the ground and peer through the narrow gap between the bin and the factory's brick wall.

Only a moment later, The Agent appears in the gap between the houses. He never looks her way, but leans against the side of the shack to dig a pipe out of his pocket and light it. "You're very good at disappearing," he calls out. "It's just that *I'm* very good at finding people. Sort of my job, isn't it?"

Godsdamn.

She steps clear of the bin—which must be filled with discarded fish bits, judging by the smell—with as much dignity as she can muster. "Unless you've come with the rest of my pay, go find someone else."

"Alas, my employer's purse is empty. Maybe you'll accept an opportunity?"

Sage leans against the alley wall across from The Agent, crossing her arms. "What kind of opportunity?"

"A job."

"In town?"

The Agent shakes his head. "Decidedly out of town."

"Another party, then? I'll pass, but good luck to you. Gaffa will have a hard time finding a ranger willing to travel through winter—at least, one who hasn't been contracted and well paid already."

The Agent laughs and puffs his pipe, lips full and bright under a peach-fuzz mustache. "It won't be Gaffa's problem to solve. I've been hired by a new client, one whose purse is much, much heavier, and I'm looking for a change in leadership. I need someone I can trust to get the job done. I'd bet it was you who located the goods on this last journey, am I right?"

She blinks in surprise. Sage never mentioned as much at the Mare's Milk. Nobody had. But of course, as the ranger hired to guide them to the caves and keep them fed and sheltered along the way, it *was* Sage who'd charted a path by the stars to Gaffa's best guess of a location. And it was Sage who'd found the caves where frost violets grew at the threshold, promising rarer plants within that thrived in freezing cold . . . and, as it turned out, attracted fire beetles. The Client might be bothered by their late return—and fairly so—but they'd have no reason to complain about the spell components the party brought back.

The Agent takes her startled silence as confirmation. "I thought so," he says. "In addition to finding people, I'm particularly talented at reading people. I'm looking for someone reliable, someone capable, someone hungry. Someone with the skills and grit and ambition to venture out when lesser adventurers are ready to hide under their quilts for the season. Not just a ranger—a leader."

To buy herself time to think, Sage plucks The Agent's pipe from his hand, wipes the stem on her jacket sleeve, and takes a long pull that's sweet, salty, and bitter all at once.

She tests out the thought, tastes it with the tobacco: Sage Wilderstone, party leader.

She ought to say no.

She's just come back from one disastrous trip, with little to show for it. Her knee could do with a rest, loathe as she is to admit it. (She certainly won't be admitting it aloud.) And the weather will only worsen as the days shorten. No, she should stick to the plan she had when she left the tavern: Find local work until the ice melts in spring, then hire herself out for another expedition as soon as possible. Another Client, another Agent, another party leader; hopefully a competent one this time, gods willing.

And yet . . .

"Where exactly would I be leading this party?"

He fixes Sage in his pale gaze. "The Northlands."

"You aren't serious!" The Northlands are largely made up of a vast pine forest awash in perpetual fog, where little grows between the trees but fungi, and the beasts that creep and stalk are white as snow and bone. Sage scoffs, handing back his pipe. "You expect me to find adventurers of quality willing to travel this time of year," she asks, "and to the Northlands, at that?"

"If you're willing, others will be. What about those two fighters you left in the tavern? They seemed sturdy."

"No," she says at once, then more quietly, "No. I don't work with party members twice. People get . . . The job changes when things start to feel personal."

The Agent shrugs. "Regardless, I don't expect you'd have a problem finding takers; I've been spreading word, and made sure to mention the prize pot, which I should say is substantial. The Client isn't short on coins, and is willing to spend more of them than you've seen in your life in exchange for discretion and expedience. Besides, I've already found you a fixer—one of the best in the business. You're welcome!" With a flourish of his self-satisfied grin, he gestures to his puffed-up chest.

"*You?*" Sage grimaces. "If you're coming along anyway, why not lead the party yourself?"

"Leadership isn't my area of expertise, alas. No, I'm going along to serve a different purpose, and to make sure our findings are delivered safely and swiftly. I'm an asset, I assure you. You'll need to find yourself a spellcaster . . . unless you can cast?"

She can't. At least not in the way of natural casters, like her friend Margot, or warlocks, or wizards who spend the bulk of their lives in libraries, studying the mathematical formulas for drawing upon and replenishing the magic of devils and divinities. What Sage *can* do is her job, and preternaturally well; her mother had theorized that she was blessed by some divinity of the woods or another. She can smell the ghostly embers of a campfire hours after it's been extinguished. She can tell the direction of a cracked branch in the night by the difference in time it takes the sound to arrive in each ear. And she swears she can sense danger like a physical thing, even in pitch dark and perfect quiet, the moment before it arrives.

But all of that is difficult to explain. And since she can't, for instance, mutter a charm and set The Agent on fire, she shakes her head. "I'm not a caster."

"Well then, get one; we'll need them for the job."

"Casters are rarer than ever these days, natural or not, or haven't you heard?"

"And yet I have faith in you. You'll need a healer as well, maybe a brute or two—I'll leave the rest to your discretion. Then it's nothing but clear skies and smooth seas ahead. Figuratively speaking. It's a week's journey to Briarwall, where we'll stable our mounts," he says, naming the northernmost village on the Queens' Road: little more than a final military outpost before the crown cedes its hold on the kingdom to the wilds of the Northlands. "Just a few days' journey on foot after that, and then the return trip. We'll be home before winter really gets going, and you'll be rich enough to spend the season in fine style. What do you say?"

Sage doesn't like The Agent much, but he's right.

She *is* reliable, she *is* skilled, and she *is* hungry.

And how long will it be before she gets another chance like this?

Besides, Sage never meant to be stuck in Kingfisher for months. When she thinks of resting in one place all winter long, she starts to feel the old panic that's never born of danger, but only silence and stillness, when there's nothing in front of her to chase. Luckily for her, there's always another job to be had . . . and this one could be the break Sage needs to finally make a name for herself.

"One week till we leave?" she asks.

The Agent's soft lips curl into a triumphant grin. "Shall I buy you another mare's milk to celebrate and share the details? Or elsewhere. I've a room above the Pearl and the Grit; that's where we'll hold party auditions, when the time comes."

Sage shakes her head and hoists her pack again. "I'll find you there tomorrow."

Tomorrow she'll begin to plan, to gather supplies with the small advance portion of her pay, to pore over maps as she waits to meet with prospective party members. Tonight she's going to find a room to rent, fall asleep on a real mattress instead of a pile of pine needles, and hope to feel like a brand-new ranger when she wakes.

Especially since a trip to the healing house is currently out of her budget.

Jamie Pacton is an award-winning young adult and middle grade author who lives in Wisconsin with her family. Her YA contemporary books include *Furious, Lucky Girl,* and *The Life and (Medieval) Times of Kit Sweetly.* Her YA fantasy novels include *The Absinthe Underground* and *The Vermilion Emporium.*

jamiepacton.com
X: @jamiepacton
Instagram: @jamiepacton
TikTok: @jamiepacton

Rebecca Podos is the Lambda Literary Award–winning author of YA novels, including *From Dust, a Flame* (Balzer + Bray) and *Furious,* co-written with Jamie Pacton (Page Street YA). By day, she's an agent at the Rees Literary Agency in Boston.

rebeccapodos.com
X: @beccapodos
Instagram: @beccapodos

## ABOUT THE TYPE

This book was set in Garamond, a typeface originally designed by the Parisian type cutter Claude Garamond (c. 1500–61). This version of Garamond was modeled on a 1592 specimen sheet from the Egenolff-Berner foundry, which was produced from types assumed to have been brought to Frankfurt by the punch cutter Jacques Sabon (c. 1520–80).

Claude Garamond's distinguished romans and italics first appeared in *Opera Ciceronis* in 1543–44. The Garamond types are clear, open, and elegant.

# DISCOVER MORE FROM
# DEL REY &
# RANDOM HOUSE
# WORLDS!

**READ EXCERPTS**
from hot new titles.

**STAY UP-TO-DATE**
on your favorite authors.

**FIND OUT** about exclusive
giveaways and sweepstakes.

**CONNECT WITH US ONLINE!**
◎ ⨍ 𝕏 @DelReyBooks

DelReyBooks.com
RandomHouseWorlds.com

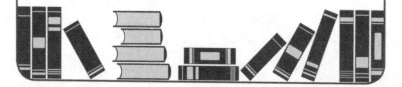